PRAISE FOR *COUNTRY OF ORIGIN*

"Evocative and moving, *Country of Origin* shows the struggles
of two families caught up in the tumult of recent history. Love,
loss, betrayal, migration, all of these are deftly explored in this
fine first novel. Dalia Azim has given us a true and powerful
story of the ties that bind and the ties that break, and our endless
negotiation between the two."
—BEN FOUNTAIN, author of *Billy Lynn's Long Halftime Walk*

"I picked this book up, not expecting the mystery, courage, and
riveting adventure I would find in its pages. I put it down three
days later, changed as the best books change you: stronger, and of
wider, wilder vision. Among the best novels I've read in years."
—DEB OLIN UNFERTH, author of *Barn 8*

"With its devastating and dizzying turns, *Country of Origin*
reminds us that acts of revolution, both public and private, leave
a profound legacy. Dalia Azim is a fearless excavator of what we
leave behind. She writes with curiosity and compassion."
—SIMON HAN, author of *Nights When Nothing Happened*

"Breathtaking and memorable, *Country of Origin* is the kind of
brilliant novel that breaks you open and puts you back together
by the last page."
—S. KIRK WALSH, author of *The Elephant of Belfast*

"*Country of Origin* is a glorious, glowing debut."
—AMANDA EYRE WARD, author of *The Jetsetters,*
    a Reese's Book Club Pick

"A luminous debut, epic in scope yet profoundly intimate."
—FRANCES DE PONTES PEEBLES, author of *The Air You Breathe*

"Lyrical, piercing, and powerful, *Country of Origin* left this reader
wanting to immediately read the next
debut writer."
—LARA PRESCOTT, author of *The Sec*

"A deeply moving and beautiful portrait of a family and its places. Poignant, intimate, heartbreaking, and full of love. Loaded with passion, with a superbly portrayed cast, spanning decades of upheavals, *Country of Origin* is a brilliantly ambitious novel and no doubt the first of many wonders from Azim."
—EDWARD CAREY, author of *The Swallowed Man*

"*Country of Origin* brilliantly depicts the way the political systems we live in and the families we are born to indelibly shape us, even while we can never fully know them. But perhaps, with luck and with strength, we do have the ability to become known to ourselves. Azim's debut is unflinching and ambitious, creating a beautiful marvel that unfolds with its own hidden mysteries."
—STACEY SWANN, author of *Olympus, Texas*

"Elegant, gripping, and deeply felt, Dalia Azim's *Country of Origin* is an unforgettable saga about family, fate, and the different selves we find—and create—at their intersection."
—JENNIFER DUBOIS, author of *The Spectators*

"With lush, unimpeachably precise prose, Dalia Azim unspools a generational, continent-spanning narrative that testifies to an irrefutable, set-in-stone truth: we are all the products of the lives our parents led before we were born, and our first country of origin is our literal motherland, the womb."
—JILL ALEXANDER ESSBAUM, author of *Hausfrau*

"A buoyant debut that leaps in brilliant arcs, Dalia Azim's *Country of Origin* carries the reader across history, over vast geographies, and always lands solidly in character. It is a narrative that runs on compassion, inviting us to care not just about the words, but about the world."
—KIRK LYNN, author of *Rules for Werewolves*

"*Country of Origin* is an unforgettable story of an Egyptian family living through waves of separation and connection. In this dangerous landscape of historical trauma, incarceration, and migration, Dalia Azim portrays a hunger for freedom—political and personal, mental and physical—with tenderness, humor, and hope. This is a beautiful book."
—CHAITALI SEN, author of *The Pathless Sky*

"*Country of Origin* opens with Cairo in flames and never stops burning with the crackling heat that only those rarest of novels that grab at both the heart and mind with equal ferocity can generate."
—SARAH BIRD, author of *Last Dance at the Starlite Pier*

"Dalia Azim's debut novel introduces a masterful and original talent to the world. *Country of Origin* is a story of art, love, loss, history, and how we carry the weight of the past with us. It gripped me from the first page and did not let go."
—MARGO RABB, author of *Lucy Clark Will Not Apologize*

"Dalia Azim's *Country of Origin* is a deeply felt story of family, love, and loss, as well as a revelatory meditation on how we form and reform our selves, carrying on one way or another, pushed forward by fate, grief, devotion, and hope. I loved these characters so much that I've found myself returning to them in my imagination, wondering how they're doing now, wishing them well."
—CARRIE FOUNTAIN, author of *The Life*

"A novel of immense power, *Country of Origin* is an intergenerational epic that explores how one family's secrets and traumas interweave with political and social upheavals in transformative ways. In any year, Dalia Azim's gripping, lyrical debut would be an event. In this moment, it is essential. This book is a revelation."
—MARY HELEN SPECHT, author of *Migratory Animals*

COUNTRY OF ORIGIN

COUNTRY
OF ORIGIN

A Novel

DALIA AZIM

DEEP
VELLUM

Dallas, Texas

A
STRANGE
OBJECT

Austin, Texas

Published by
A Strange Object, an imprint of Deep Vellum

ISBN 978-1-6460-5152-6
ISBN 978-1-6460-5153-3 (ebook)

This is a work of fiction. Any resemblances to actual persons, living or dead,
events, or locales are coincidental.

Cover design by Nayon Cho
Book design by Amber Morena

For my family

PART ONE

\\

HALAH, 1952

REEMA AND I WATCHED from the roof as the city burned. It was not a single inferno but a scattering of fires across the river, downtown—flames devouring buildings, cars burning in the roads, tiny people running around carrying glowing sticks. Smoke painted the sky gray, and the air smelled like how I imagined cigarettes tasted.

I hadn't known that anything was awry when I went down to the kitchen for tea that morning, just a quarter of an hour before. There I found Reema engaged in hushed, excited dialogue with Abu Abdullah about an uprising in the streets. As a courtesy to me, Abu Abdullah ducked out the side door as soon as I entered the room; the majority of our interactions involved me staring at the back of his turbaned head as he silently chauffeured me back and forth to school.

Once Abu Abdullah was gone, I asked Reema if we could go up to the roof. It felt foolish, at fourteen, to seek permission, but the only way to access the roof was a set of rustic stone stairs off the kitchen, which I'd always considered Reema's domain. I led, and she followed behind me at a slower pace, breathing heavily. Besides school, the roof was the closest I came to experiencing the outside world, so it had always been my favorite part of the house. As far as I knew, my parents never ventured up here, saw no reason to. Sometimes my mother would smell the chickens on me after I'd been up to collect their eggs with Reema, and she would make her displeasure clear. *Have you been around those dirty birds again?*

Buildings burned alongside structures that stood untouched by flame. "Do you think this is it?" I asked Reema as I stared at the spectacle across the Nile.

"I don't know what this is," Reema responded in a flat tone, also transfixed by the blazes.

After a few minutes she suggested that we go back downstairs in case my parents were looking for us. We both knew that my mother never emerged from her bedroom before noon, and my father liked to sleep in on days when he didn't have work. My parents had separate bedrooms and kept to their own schedules. The only time we all came together was around the dinner table for the afternoon meal.

When we returned to the kitchen and found it empty, Reema said I should go and tell my parents what was happening. She played up her subservience when it suited her. "They shouldn't hear about this from me," she said.

I knocked on my father's door first. I'd always been closer to him than to my mother, but recently he'd started talking about interviewing suitors on my behalf, and my feelings toward him had soured somewhat. Sounding far away, my father asked, "What is it?" in a raspy voice.

"It's Halah," I told him through the door, as if there could be any confusion about my identity. "Downtown is burning . . . I think this is something you should see." For months he'd been making sly remarks over supper—*The British don't know what's coming. It's time for them to leave Egypt and take their puppet king with them. Soon we will rule ourselves for the first time in 2,500 years, and it will be glorious.*

Inside my father's room I heard drawers opening and closing in quick succession, the rustling of fabric. I stood where I was, fixed to my spot, until he appeared before me dressed in uniform a minute or two later. "What have you heard?" he asked.

I explained what I'd seen as his jaw slowly lowered like a drawbridge. "I have to go," he announced before I was finished, and then he was gone, rushing toward the stairs. I decided to let my mother linger in her slumber a little longer—she always rolled her eyes or guffawed whenever my father mentioned the possibility of Egypt's independence.

Back in the kitchen I convinced Reema that we should go up to the roof again. She was in the midst of shucking corn and acted annoyed to be pulled away from her duty. She'd been with my family since I was three; in other words, she was embedded in my earliest memories. She had five children of her own back in El Faiyûm, whom she visited once a month on her days off.

The fires had multiplied in our absence. Now the glorious Shepheard's Hotel was in flames, burning spectacularly along the banks of the Nile. Flames danced behind the hotel's four stories of windows, leaping above the roofline. Flagless flagpoles stood waving nothing. Egypt's flag, green with a white crescent and three white stars, was only a few years older than me, established in 1923 when Egypt became a kingdom instead of a sultanate, supposedly more independent after having been under varying forms of British occupation since 1882. "We won't be free until they're out of our business and off our land," my father was fond of saying. The British still controlled our foreign relations and communications, and their troops were everywhere.

I watched as a wall collapsed into the blaze and heard a distant crowd of people cheering. It had been years since I'd been inside the Shepheard's, but I fondly remembered its lush terrace and opulent dining room from my childhood visits. This was after the Second World War but before 1948, when it was still socially acceptable for Egyptian military men to laugh and smoke with British and French soldiers the way my father used to when we frequented the Shepheard's, which served as an informal headquarters for foreign officers at the time. I felt strange in my civilian clothes whenever we dined there.

My father's loyalties had since turned vehemently anti-British, and we no longer went to the Shepheard's or to a number of other places where we used to go. King Farouk was known to frequent the Shepheard's, pulling up with an entourage of red Cadillacs, and no one wanted to associate with him. For some reason that wasn't clear to me, my family's British embargo did not extend to the prestigious private school I'd attended since I was five, where all of my classes were taught in English and we were scolded by our white teachers if caught speaking Arabic.

Reema and I were both speechless as we watched the city burn. I don't know how much time passed as we stood there. I'd never been so grateful to live on an island, surrounded by water, a liquid barrier between us and the fires. Most of the time I felt trapped in Zamalek. The only times I left the house were to go to school, a few blocks away, and on rare occasions when we crossed bridges to other parts of Cairo to visit relatives or friends.

Behind one of the windows of the Shepheard's, the outline of a human figure flashed before my eyes. I panicked and reached for Reema's arm. There it was, soft and thick beneath the cotton of her galabeya, ready to receive my grip. For the first time it occurred to me that people could be dying in these blazes, and I felt an overwhelming urge to vomit. Letting go of Reema, I ran toward the chicken coops.

The chirping birds in their cages were there to greet me when I was back on my feet, after emptying the watery contents of my stomach onto a pile of spent bedding from the coops. I'd always loved the fact that we owned chickens, despite my mother's protests. Most things she didn't like she referred to as "country," like the chickens on our roof and Reema's headscarf and the ratty turban Abu Abdullah wore. My father swore that he could taste the difference between a fresh and store-bought egg, insisting that his eggs be freshly laid. I'd learned early on not to develop attachments to particular hens. At least once or twice a month, one would manage to free herself from her cage and disappear, presumably over the edge of the roof. Reema and Abu Abdullah had found dead birds in our yard a few times but always cleared away the bloody wreckage before I could see it. It baffled me how these birds were smart enough to manage escape but not enough to avoid unwitting suicide.

I felt Reema's hand upon my shoulder and turned around to find her standing behind me. "No need to worry, *habib elbi*. No matter what happens after today, your family will be fine." It struck me that she didn't include herself in this equation. "We don't have the kind of revolutions here that they do in France or Russia," she added, making me think of the 1938 American film *Marie Antoinette*, which I'd seen three times in the theater—my only impression of a revolution until now. "Here the rich are always protected," Reema said, looking me coyly in the eye.

It used to trouble me that she was my caretaker at the expense of caring for her own children, but it had been so many years now that the guilt had faded. Her youngest was younger than me, just an infant when Reema came to live with us. Just a few months before then, her fifth and penultimate child, who was especially beloved as one of only two sons, drowned in a terrible accident when Reema took her kids to swim at the lake one hot summer afternoon. She was busy hiding under the shade of a tree and nursing her baby girl when it happened. Blaming her for their son's death, Reema's husband banished her to a life of work in the city, ultimately taking a second wife and moving her into the family home. Reema hated going back to El Faiyûm, she'd confessed to me, and felt humiliated to have to sleep in the living room with her children when she visited. I wondered if she was at least happy to see her kids, but I never asked.

"Let's go back down," Reema suggested now.

"Go ahead," I told her. "I want to stay up here for a while."

"By yourself?" she asked with alarm.

I laughed. "It's not like I'm going to fall off the edge!"

OUR FAMILY "SUPPER" didn't take place until ten o'clock that night, when my father finally got home. It had been the longest Saturday of my life. I'd spent most of the day languishing in my room after my mother smelled smoke on me and forbade my return to the roof. My father announced his return more loudly than usual that night, and my mother and I separately descended to the dining room.

My parents and I occupied one end of a ten-person banquet table, which left us forever dining next to a horseshoe of vacant chairs. Reema delivered the dishes to the table one after another, having undoubtedly reheated them numerous times in anticipation of my father's arrival. He liked to eat within minutes of stepping in the door but came home at a different time every day, sometimes as early as two in the afternoon, and others as late as seven in the evening. I was famished by the time we gathered around the table that night.

Usually my father changed out of his uniform the moment he got home, but tonight he sat at the table in his formal green vestments. He unfastened the top three buttons of his jacket, revealing a thick sprout of black chest hair and a crescent of white undershirt. He exhaled deeply after loosening his garments, as if he'd been holding his breath all day.

"We must look like fools to the rest of the world," he said wearily, "burning our own capital to the ground."

"The criminals who did this should be rounded up and thrown in jail," my mother expressed with uncharacteristic passion.

"I wouldn't call them criminals . . ." my father equivocated. "All the targets were British. We were told to let the fires burn." By "we," I assumed he meant the military. "We want them to feel rattled, to see that we're our own bosses."

"You make me laugh, Mansoor," my mother said without laughing. "Always wrapped up in the latest political trends."

I sat across from my mother and next to my father, who occupied the head of the table. I agreed with my mother but kept this to myself. It wasn't long ago that we used to attend Christmas parties at the British Embassy, given that my father was friends with the ambassador at the time. Everything changed in 1948, when the British Mandate for Palestine expired and Israel declared its independence, thus dissolving the state of Palestine. War broke out immediately, and my father was called off to fight. Since he'd joined the military when I was little, I'd feared that one day he'd have to take up arms. For years my father had laughed it off when I expressed these concerns, but as the clock ticked down on the existence of Palestine and the possibility of war became a strong likelihood, I sensed my father's creeping fears and started keeping mine to myself. He was supposed to teach me how to swim that summer. I'd just turned ten and decided that I was no longer going to be afraid of the waves at the beach, but then my father left with his brigade in June, and I didn't learn to swim for another two years.

My father was different after he came back from the war, not in obvious physical ways but in his underlying temperament. He was edgy now, rarely home, dedicated to the military in a way he'd never been before. Before 1948, he'd talked about getting out, but after coming home, he redoubled his commitment to the army and had since ascended to the rank of general. It was hard to make him laugh now, and he never cracked jokes like he used to. I remembered him as easygoing when I was a child; now he was hard to please, which frequently came out as acid-tongued critiques of Reema's food or housekeeping that irked me deeply to witness. I loved her cooking and thought my father had no right to treat her the way he did, but I assumed he'd had horrible experiences in battle that had made him this way. This idea was reinforced by my mother and by Reema herself, who often said things behind his back like "Bless his poor, wounded soul." During the year when he was gone, I used to sneak into his office and listen to radio reports about what was happening on the war front. Before he left, my father had made it sound as if the war would be over in a matter of days. *We're talking six countries against one*, I recall him bragging. But then one month turned into two turned into half a year. The newscasters on the radio painted a bleak picture. Apparently young men from all over the world were showing up to fight for Israel, ultimately outnumbering the collective force of the Arabs. For months I listened to those reports and imagined my father lying dead on some battlefield, so when he came home alive at the end of March in 1949, I was truly shocked and overwhelmed with relief.

"I have no patience for your egoism today, Nefissa," my father told my mother now, setting his fork down on his plate with a clang. "Your view of the world is dying. You're welcome to join us in the present, or you can stay stuck in the past. *Inte hora.*"

You are free. My father often punctuated his arguments with my mother using this phrase. They'd been married for fifteen years and had always argued, to my memory, but the tenacity of their fighting had increased sharply over the past few months. My father acted as if my mother could leave at any time, but this was her house. We lived in her childhood home, built at the turn of the century by my maternal grandfather with proceeds from his cotton-farming fortune. My mother's brothers had sold their shares of land long ago and moved their money into other industries, the older one into telecommunications, and the other into banking. As the daughter in the family, my mother was entitled to half of what her brothers each stood to inherit. To this day she'd kept hold of the shares of the farmland her father had given her, leaving my father to the daily business of managing the land.

My father had first spotted my mother when she dropped by the bank to bring her brother lunch one day. He liked to say that he knew right away that he wanted to marry her and wasted no time asking my grandfather for her hand. My parents formally met a few days later and were married a few weeks after that. She was sixteen, and he was twenty-seven. They had me a year later. When I was eight and we were at the beach one summer, I asked my mother when she first realized that she was in love with him. We lay side by side on a blanket, and my father was swimming in the surf. "I'm still waiting for that to happen," she told me with a cynical laugh. I lost my romantic illusions about marriage then. And yet the movies I saw were full of love stories, suggesting other possibilities.

My father came from a "good" family but not one as wealthy as my mother's. My parents lived in a rented apartment across the river in Dokki when they were first married, but my grandparents invited my parents to move in once my mother got pregnant with me, worried that the apartment was too cramped, which it was compared with their villa. I can't picture that apartment, which my grandmother described as "dark" and "depressing" when she was still alive. My grandfather passed away first, when I was five, and my grandmother followed two years later. After they died, my uncles tried to get my parents to sell the house so they could get what they claimed they were owed from their parents' estate, each entitled to two fifths of the house's value, leaving my mother with only one fifth. Since we'd already been living in the house for years, my parents claimed legal residency. After the court case, we never saw my uncles again.

Now, almost a decade later, my grandparents' former bedrooms on the second floor remained empty and unoccupied, like shrines, while Reema slept in a tiny, bare-bones closet next to the kitchen and Abu Abdullah lived in an unheated room over the garage. In our household, my uncles were known for their greed and selfishness, but no one ever talked about the injustices taking place under our own roof.

HALAH, 1952

THE FIRES PUT AN END to my education. My school closed for a month after the uprisings, and I heard from a friend, whom we ran into at the country club when my mother and I were having lunch there one day, that half of our British teachers had fled and needed to be replaced. My father decided that it was no longer safe for me to attend when the school reopened, so I never went back.

I spent a lot of time on the roof in the weeks after the fires. It was always a shock for my eyes to adjust from the darkness of the stairwell to the brightness of the roof. When I stepped outside one morning in March, I noticed that the air was clear for the first time since the insurrection, and yet the atmosphere still smelled like an ashtray. Downtown looked like a patchwork of untouched buildings standing next to piles of rubble. From my perch I could see tiny construction workers on the piles, tossing shovels full of rock and glass and metal onto the backs of trucks that drove off once their beds were full, to be replaced by empty trucks.

Armed soldiers now filled the streets, far more than the military presence we were used to seeing. I suppose I was meant to take some comfort from the fact that the soldiers were ours and not British, but I still found their presence unsettling. According to my father's reports at supper, the British powers were enraged by the downtown uprising and threatened to intervene if Egypt couldn't rein in its revolutionaries.

I'd expected to get in another year of schooling, at least, before I had to get married. Female cousins and girls I knew from school always dropped out once they wed. There was dramatic attrition in the upper grades every year, and now I was one of those vanished girls, school over forever. Only, in my case, it wasn't marriage that forced me to quit but the threat of revolution.

I turned fifteen that summer, at the beginning of June. Sixteen used to seem so old—plenty old to get married—but now that I was just a year away from that dreaded age, sixteen felt far too young for a girl to leave her family and enter that foreign adult world of marriage, sex, and children. I'd learned about sex from classmates who'd learned about it from older sisters and cousins; none of our mothers educated us about our bodies and their functions. The idea of letting a man enter me was terrifying and bewildering. The few times I'd pleasured myself under the covers, I felt sick with guilt afterward, certain that *Allah* was judging me for my unseemly urges.

At supper one evening later in the summer, my father reported that the king was on the run. He spoke quickly, his eyes wild with excitement. "We announced a coup this morning, and that coward Farouk abandoned his palace in Cairo and fled for the coast." Reema returned to the room with a plate of rice, her face registering surprise. We made quick eye contact before she set the plate down and left. "Mark my words: that son of a bitch will be gone within days," my father announced when she was out of the room.

I didn't know what was more shocking, what my father was saying or the crude way he spoke. Looking to my mother for her reaction, I found her speechless, her face frozen in surprise. She used to
keep a picture of the king and his first wife, clipped from a newspaper, underneath a sheet of glass that covered her dresser, next to
photographs of herself and family members, but she'd removed the
clipping when Farouk divorced Farida in 1948, supposedly because
she'd produced three daughters but no male heirs. I often wondered
why I was an only child when sons were the primary objective
of childbearing for most couples, which made me think that more
children hadn't been a possibility for my parents. I supposed my
mother sympathized with Farida and maybe even felt some kinship
with her as a mother of a girl, but mostly she thought of divorce as
a disgrace, a great embarrassment for all involved.

"Where will he go?" I asked.

"I don't give a damn!" my father shot back.

I sank into my chair, rattled by his ferocity. It was hard to imagine Egypt without a king, as it was all I had ever known. It struck
me that my father was a hypocrite, invested in upending society on
the one hand, and yet a stickler for the old ways when it came to
me. He was wearing a galabeya, a new sartorial experiment that I
knew annoyed my mother, who found the choice decidedly unso-
phisticated. Halfway through the meal, my father set his fork down
and sat back in his chair, placing his hands behind his head and
winging his arms out to the sides. He smiled with his mouth closed,
looking deeply content. I continued to eat without tasting what I
put into my mouth.

IN THE DAYS THAT FOLLOWED, Reema was more welcoming of
my presence in the kitchen while she cooked. She still wouldn't allow me to do any work, but she seemed to enjoy the fact that I was
there listening to the radio with her. She'd made daily use of the de-

vice since my parents gave it to her for *Eid* last year, which made me proud, though I'd neither conceived of nor given her the gift. Reema laughed as she chopped greens for *molokhia*, in response to a breaking report stating that the king and his family had moved from one of his houses in Alexandria to a refuge directly on the waterfront, speculating they had done so in case they needed to escape by boat. Despite how well I knew her, I had no idea what Reema's political beliefs were; her only true allegiance seemed to be with *Allah*.

"What do you think of the king?" I asked her then.

Reema looked at me and furrowed her brow, considering her answer for a moment. "I think he's a pig," she said quietly but with palpable anger.

I nodded, suddenly coming to the same realization.

I WOKE THE NEXT MORNING to the sound of chainsaws buzzing outside. I ran to look, confronting the obfuscating *mashrabiya* that covered all of my windows. Through the gaps in the intricate wooden latticework, I saw the smoke trails of distant jets receding as the buzzing grew quieter. Watching the tails of the fighter jets, I wondered, as I broke out in a cold sweat, whether we were under attack.

Reema was not in the kitchen, though the raw ingredients on the countertops suggested she'd been there recently. I heard commotion coming from nearby, a tangle of human voices this time, drawing me out the back door that led to the yard behind our house. No one ever used the yard, and it was in disarray by the standards set by the rest of our house, overgrown with weeds, the cushions on the chairs ravaged by animals, stuffing spilling out of their holes. My mother had declared the yard ruined since a number of apartment buildings had sprung up around our house a few years ago, giving our new neighbors a view of our yard. Insisting that she could feel people inside the apartments watching her, she never used the yard anymore, and her paranoia had managed to infect me to some degree as well; I rarely came out here myself, but mostly because it was a breeding ground for mosquitoes, and I was irresistible to mosquitoes.

I was surprised to find my parents in the yard with Reema, all standing together, watching the sky. The jets I'd seen before—or maybe this was a different pair—were approaching from the distance now, coming closer, the hum of their propellers growing louder.

"What's happening?" I asked everyone.

They all turned to look at me. No one had an answer.

"Should we be worried?" I pressed on, past their wall of silence.

My father cracked a smile. "The puppet king is gone. He and his wife and baby set sail in a yacht bound for Italy this morning."

"We're free," Reema elaborated quietly, standing a few feet behind my father, her voice full of shock and her eyes wide and wet.

For a moment I thought that she was talking about herself and Abu Abdullah, as if they hadn't been free before. And then I understood the truth of what was happening: *this* was the revolution.

By afternoon, people had gathered in the streets to celebrate. My father had gone to work, chauffeured by Abu Abdullah, leaving us alone without any men at the house. I wished this didn't make me feel unsafe, but it did. I stuck close to Reema, who went on about her business as if this were an ordinary day, while my mother retreated to her room and pretended the same.

Hearing the jubilation outside, I convinced Reema to come up to the roof with me. There were revelers in the street, cheering and shouting and yelling and hugging one another, mostly men but also some women in the mix, which surprised me. Some were older and dressed as though they came from the country, as my mother would say—sturdy women like you might find selling newspapers or fruit on the street. But I also saw young women dressed in Western clothes with their hair uncovered. Who were they, I wondered, and how had they gained their freedom?

"*Vive l'Égypte libre et indépendante! Vive l'Égypte libre et indé-pendante!*" a group of people chanted below. I understood what they were saying because I'd taken two years of French, but it made no sense to me why the language was being employed in the name of Egypt's freedom. Wasn't France just another Western power? Wasn't today supposed to be about Arab independence?

MY LIFE WASN'T MUCH AFFECTED by Egypt's liberation. My father gloated for weeks afterward, as if he were personally responsible for deposing the king, while my mother picked at her meals and I ate with disinterest, feeling cooped up. There was always so much food left when we were done eating, which Reema and Abu Abdullah feasted on while sitting on a blanket in a corner of the kitchen after my parents and I dispersed. I avoided the kitchen while they were eating, to give them privacy, I told myself, but also because it embarrassed me to come across them in this degraded state. Whatever scraps were left, Reema fed to nearby stray cats.

My father was angling for a position in the new government. He was just outside of the inner circle, according to his own assessment, and needed to get in with the big guys. Muhammad Naguib, whom the Free Officers had just installed as the new president, Gamal Abdel Nasser, Hussein Hamouda, and the like. He went on about these men at supper as if they were people we knew. Outside of these meals, I rarely saw my father anymore and assumed he was at work all the time.

DESPITE ALL OF THE FERVOR and excitement of the nation's rebirth taking place beyond our walls, life inside the house remained boring. There was so much time in the day to account for, and it passed so slowly. I worried that this was what it felt like to be a housewife, always searching for ways to keep busy as the hours stretched on.

Sometimes I pretended I was still in school, taking out my textbooks and studying for exams that I would never have, practicing French vocabulary and math equations for no other reason than to keep my skills sharp. I had no interest in my history textbook now that it was no longer required reading. History had always been my least favorite subject, so many names and dates and events that had no connection to my life, all of them European-centered. If we learned about the history of my own country, I might have had more interest.

Reema was the biggest alleviator of my boredom. I went down to the kitchen often, whether or not I was hungry. Reema didn't like to be "pestered" while she was working, so I always made like I was there to get a snack or something to drink. When I lingered too long to chat and she was in the midst of cooking, she would ask if I had nothing better to do.

"No, not really," I'd taken to answering recently.

This usually got a smirk. "Lucky you."

"You should teach me how to cook," I suggested to her one day.

An assortment of the day's food projects was scattered across the counters: sliced onions on a cutting board, rice soaking in a pot, piles of herbs and vegetables that had yet to be sliced and diced, a bowl of lentils that needed sorting, and another bowl full of raw ground meat. Reema laughed and said, "No need to waste your time. *Insha'Allah*, your husband will be able to afford a housekeeper!"

I used to love to nap when I was little, the chance to disappear into dreams in the middle of the day. Now when I closed my eyes, nightmares took over. Burning houses, me trapped inside trying to escape, searching for Reema through the smoke. My parents' well-being never occurred to me when I was unconscious; it was only Reema I searched for.

My new fear of napping reduced the list of ways to pass the time. I felt trapped in my room, which was expansive but dreary. My windows faced the street and thus were covered with the heavy wooden latticework to obscure the house's inhabitants—me—from passersby. The *mashrabiya* was a holdover from the Middle Ages, the one feature of our house that derived from the East and not the West. My father's room was on the back side of the house and thus unfettered by *mashrabiya* and filled with sunlight. It seemed odd that both my mother and I were in street-facing rooms if we were the ones to be protected from the ogling of lustful men. Once I'd asked my mother if I could move into one of my grandparents' luminous, empty rooms across the hall.

"What's the point in changing rooms when you'll be gone in a few years anyway?" she responded. I was nine at the time. I never asked again.

My father worked more than ever now and was rarely home. He hinted that big change was coming. After a while, this too became tedious and exhausting, because one had to remain on guard against the possibility of another uprising, perhaps one that was more violent. They'd gone after Marie Antoinette for her conspicuous wealth and indifference to the problems engulfing her country. We were conspicuously wealthy, in a fancy house on a large piece of property in a posh area of the city. What if the revolutionaries came after us next?

One day after Reema shooed me away from the kitchen, I ducked into my father's office. I'd recently rediscovered the room as an alternate hideaway. In the three years between my father returning from the war and now, I'd largely avoided the space, associating it with those bleak radio broadcasts I used to listen to. Now I was coming to feel as if his office were my own in some way, knowing there was no danger of him finding me there during the workday. I'd shut the door and quietly lurk around, opening and arranging the backgammon board on his desk and playing against myself; studying old maps of the region taped to his walls; browsing the books on his shelves.

There I discovered that my father had a love of British crime novels, which I found tucked discreetly on a low shelf. I opened one up and immediately found myself transported into its fiction, eventually wandering over to my father's chair. What struck me most was not the male inspectors and their quests but the women in their lives, funny and fierce and bold, like those sophisticated women in American movies who dated men and had modern sensibilities. The movies insinuated sex, but the books were much more direct in a way that was shocking. I found my first sex scene on page fifteen and read it again and again, my face hot; it felt as if there were a clock ticking inside my underwear. This was the closest I had come to a description of the act—the rubbing of breasts, hands sliding down pants, her wetness, his hardness—and it made me nauseated and excited at once.

After a while I began to worry that Reema would wonder where I was. She checked on me periodically throughout the day, showing up at my door with food or simply to see how I was. Tucking the book under my sweater, I took it with me to my room.

I MISSED MY FRIENDS, classmates I'd known for a decade who were suddenly no longer in my life. It made no sense to me that my father could suddenly cut off my education, and with it any connection to people outside my home, though I'd watched for years as older girls dropped out of school to "start their lives." I'd convinced myself that I could persuade my parents to let me finish high school before we started talking about my marriage. We were one of the only families I knew who had a private phone line installed in our house, so there was no way to reach my friends besides writing them letters, which I started to do. There was a delay of a couple of weeks before I heard back from anyone.

It got to the point where my room started to feel like a prison. One night, I went downstairs to get a glass of water, my nightgown damp with sweat. When I walked to the kitchen, I passed Reema's room, with its door that never fully closed. I could tell whether her light was on or off from the gaps around the frame. Now it was off.

Once I was in the kitchen, I usually decided to take a trip to the roof. It always took a few moments for my eyes to adjust when I first came outside. Once the dark, pearlescent surface of the Nile came into view, my internal map of the city fell into place around that. There was something special about coming up to the roof at night, which I'd never done until now, the city particularly beautiful with the light reversed, mostly coming from inside the buildings. Downtown looked like a mouth with a bunch of missing teeth, bright spots interspersed with dark gaps. Cautiously, I moved toward the edge of the roof, remembering our legacy of dead chickens. I'd started to wonder whether their deaths were deliberate, maybe driven by a sense of futility that I was beginning to understand. I had no desire to get married. Marriage seemed like an end rather than a beginning to me. And yet, here I was on that track, with the train coming at me.

When my father was at war, Reema taught me how to pray. On the one hand, she said that everyone's fate was already written but, on the other, that *Allah* responded to our prayers. I worried that if I didn't pray, it would reflect poorly on my father, so as an eleven-year-old, I prayed fervently for his safe return, even waking up before dawn when I heard the early morning call to prayer resonate from the nearby mosque, and then going back to sleep. When my father came home a few months later, not only was I overjoyed and relieved, but I also felt powerful, as if I had swayed his fate through my devotion. In the intervening years, my habits had died off, and now I considered it a success if I prayed once a day. At first I worried that I'd face some kind of divine reproach for slacking off, but nothing obvious had happened so far. Now I had reason to start praying again and decided to pray while I was up on the roof that night, though it was not one of the preordained times. I grabbed a rag from next to the chicken coops to cover my hair, and then I oriented myself east and closed my eyes.

Every word and motion were deeply embedded into the fibers of my muscles and brain after four years of regular practice. Unlike my younger self, I now recognized that prayer wasn't intended as an opportunity to ask *Allah* for favors but rather to pay reverence. It felt good to pray out in the open with the wind blowing against me, tinged with the fragrances of roasted corn and barbecued meat. I'd never prayed outside before, and it felt liberating, making the rote process much more pleasant and invigorating.

MY FATHER FIRST ENLISTED in the military in 1937, the year I was born, when it didn't seem as though the war in Europe was going to expand to encompass Egypt and the Middle East. I have no memory of his long absences in 1940 and 1942, when he was called to fight off first an Italian offensive, alongside British troops, followed by two separate confrontations with a faction of Hitler's army that advanced to within 150 miles of Cairo. He was already a seasoned veteran by the time he was called upon to fight against Israel in 1948, and as a colonel then, he led hundreds of men to battle.

After that, my father joined a faction of the military known as the Free Officers, and it was the leaders of this group who'd taken control of Egypt after the coup. Some of these officers met at our house on occasion—or at least I assumed that the men in uniform who gathered in my father's office were also members of the organization. They were all professionals in the military, and yet they met in secret outside of work. My father had let on that these gatherings weren't totally aboveboard, but the men made so much noise when they got together—laughing and telling loud stories, screaming over one another—that they didn't seem too worried about being discreet. At first I'd found these gatherings annoying, macho and obnoxious, a private boys' club, but once I started paying attention to the words filtering up through the floorboards, I grew quite curious.

The problem is that our people are lazy! We've allowed ourselves to be ruled by imperialists for thousands of years . . .

We need reform. We need justice for the poor and hungry. The problem is that most of our population is deprived.

You young men, I heard my father say. *So idealistic. Let's focus on getting the . . .* he began, and then lowered his voice, losing me.

I was in bed reading the second crime novel I'd pilfered from my father's office when my father's loud friends started to arrive one evening. I decided to go downstairs and see what I could overhear from the kitchen. Noticing the light on behind Reema's door, I moved past quietly. When I turned on the light in the kitchen, I saw spotless counters, the sink empty, all the dishes and glasses put away. It was amazing to me that Reema could pray or listen to the radio or whatever she was doing in her room, the way the laughter and ruckus inside my father's office reverberated down the hall. It also baffled me how these men managed to have such a good time together, when their alliance originated during a war that had gone so horrifically for their side.

I suspected that alcohol fueled their good moods, a theory developed from watching people carouse on film. I'd never actually seen my father consume alcohol, though I'd found several bottles in a cabinet in his office. Drinking was forbidden, according to the Quran, and it upset me that my father would choose to flout this divine decree.

"I think it's time for another round!" I heard someone shout from the boys' club, confirming my suspicions. A few echoed their agreement. Glasses clinked together.

Annoyed, I decided to get some fresh air. For the first time in a long time, when I stepped onto the roof, the stink of the chicken coops was the first scent to greet me. It had been months since the fires, yet the acrid stench of burned matter lingered in the air, though not as perceptibly that night. It was a cloudy evening, the stars hidden behind a veil of gray. I visited the chickens first, answering their anxious squawks. I petted the docile ones and kept my fingers out of the cages of the ones who bit. Despite living in the same conditions, they responded very differently to life, much like people, I reflected, which made me wonder what I would be like as a bird.

The door to the roof creaked open, startling me. I turned around, expecting to see Reema, but instead found a young man in uniform standing there.

"Oh!" he said when he saw me, his eyes opening wide like an owl's. "I'm sorry. I didn't expect to find anyone up here."

"It's my house," I felt inclined to state, though the words sounded silly coming out of my mouth.

"Of course," he said, backing up. "I'll leave."

"No!" I answered with more force than intended. "You don't have to go."

He stood there, looking at me. I couldn't tell in the dark but guessed that his eyes were brown. "I'm a friend of your father's," he offered.

"How do you know I'm his daughter?" I asked, suddenly self-conscious to be standing next to a bunch of chickens. I'd probably looked like I was talking to them when he first walked outside. I wondered how I came across to him. How did he know that I wasn't a servant? People often said that I looked like my father, which made me worry that I was manly and unattractive. I'd inherited my father's broad shoulders, wide hips, olive skin, and thick eyebrows instead of my mother's conventionally pretty features: a slight build and pale complexion and thin eyebrows that she had to augment with paint.

The stranger chuckled quietly. "Good guess?"

"How do you know my father?" I asked.

"We fought together in the war," the young officer said. "I was in his unit." I felt a sharp twinge of sympathy, knowing what this meant. My father's campaigns had gone famously poorly, and very few from his company had survived, making the man standing before me one of the chosen ones. "Anyway, I probably shouldn't be talking to you," he continued. "I don't want to disrespect your father."

"I'm not his property," I answered, an impulse, though technically I was, according to the Quran.

Even in the dark I could see the subtle gesture of the stranger's eyebrows rising skyward. "I wasn't saying . . ." he said.

"If we were in America, I could talk to anyone I wanted," I argued, though I wasn't certain this was right. Was it just female characters in movies who were liberated, or were real women also free to live lives outside of the control of husbands and fathers?

"Are you planning to move to America anytime soon?" asked the soldier, with a twinkle of amusement.

"Why not?" I demanded, knowing I sounded foolish. "You can get there by plane now."

He laughed and told me that his name was Khalil. "I wasn't going to come tonight," he said, followed with, "but I'm so glad that I did."

"Why are you up here, anyway?" I asked, trying to turn the attention away from myself.

Khalil reached into his chest pocket and pulled out a cigarette and pack of matches. "I'd offer you one," he told me, "but then your father would definitely have my head."

RECALLING THOSE MOMENTS on the roof added new excitement to my days. It was amazing how quickly the minutes passed when I thought about Khalil. The details of his physical appearance were hazy in my memory, as they weren't very clear that night to begin with. He had a medium build, neither a very tall nor small man. He hadn't been wearing his cap, and I could see that his hair was thick and had some wave to it. I guessed that he was in his twenties, much closer to my age than most men I encountered. I had a couple of male cousins who were within my age range, and I'd felt pulses of attraction for them too. Maybe this was why society worked so hard to keep women and men apart; I thought about Khalil so much that it almost felt like a sickness.

"You go up there too much," Reema called after me as I headed up the stairs to the roof one afternoon. I paused on the fourth step but didn't answer. It was true that I went up more frequently since I'd met Khalil, as it was the best place to steep in the details of our encounter. Undeterred by Reema's criticism, I continued climbing.

There they were, the charred remains of downtown again. They had made no evident progress on rebuilding, though all the visible debris had been cleared away.

A COUPLE OF WEEKS LATER, my father announced over supper that there was a man he wanted me to meet. "He served in the war and has a house on the Red Sea, in addition to a building in Cairo," he explained as he chewed a mouthful of stewed beef. "His mother lives on the bottom floor, which I think is a good indication of the kind of man he is."

My chin quivered, and I clasped my hands together in my lap. Clearly it wasn't *Allah* guiding my fate but my father who had complete control. It sickened me to think of myself as a prize that he was pawning off to the highest bidder.

"Don't you have anything to say?" my father asked.

I stared through him, into my bleak future, unable to move or answer.

"Come on," my mother said, her voice pinging against the side of my head, "no one's died. Pull yourself together and answer your father."

I clasped my hands tighter, digging my nails into my palms. "Does it even matter what I think?" I managed meekly.

"You're not the first girl in history who's had to get married," my mother answered. "Don't be so dramatic."

My father used this time to get a few more bites down. Even when he wasn't talking, he chewed with his mouth open, exposing his masticated food.

"I'm not being dramatic," I argued, turning to face my mother. I felt blood coursing through my body, reviving me. "I just don't understand the rush."

"Why are you being so dense? We just had this conversation the other day." My mother's voice was high-pitched and grating.

"Calm down, Nefissa," my father told her. "We're just talking. There's no reason for anyone to get emotional."

"Isn't there?" I asked with tears in my eyes. "Aren't we talking about my future here?"

I heard my mother sigh contemptuously, my attention on my father now. "You should know that I only want the best for you," he said; I couldn't tell if the emphasis in this statement was on his intentions or on what I should have known.

"Mmm-hmm," I mumbled.

"I would never allow you to be with someone who I didn't think was good enough," he added. "I have very high standards."

I nodded, my thoughts racing, unfocused.

"How old is he?" I muttered.

My father stilled his jaw in the midst of chewing. I watched the elevator of his throat rise and fall as he swallowed. For some reason this seemed like a difficult question to answer. "Forty-five," he finally said.

Feeling a sickening twinge in my belly, I stood up from the table. My father wanted to marry me off to a man older than himself, someone three times my age. I pushed back my chair as my stomach sent another warning signal, and hurried off, aware of the murmur of my parents' bafflement trailing behind me. I could think of nowhere to go except my room, so I went upstairs.

No one in my life seemed to have loving marriages, so the prospect frankly terrified me. My parents, Reema, aunts and uncles: nobody I knew appeared to truly love their spouses. I wished that living at home indefinitely were an option for me, which had less to do with my parents and everything to do with Reema. Short of that, I fantasized about being one of those modern women in movies who lived in her own apartment, but I knew that my parents would never support such an unconventional choice, mostly because of how it would reflect on them.

"I don't want to be one of those women everyone feels sorry for because her daughter can't find a husband," my mother had remarked more than once, scarring me in my youth.

The next day I appealed to Reema for help. "There's nothing I can do," she answered in a hushed, cautious tone. She'd been married off at fourteen and already had two kids by the time she was my age. She was thirty-one now, which seemed old to me.

I turned to my mother next, though I knew she was unlikely to be an ally. Her door was closed. I knocked softly and waited for an invitation to enter.

I found her seated at her vanity, at the center of a triptych of mirrors. My mother was one of those women who believed in putting on a full face of makeup every day, even if she had no plans to leave the house. My small rebellion was to wear a fresh face all the time, even to my friends' birthday parties, where the rest of the girls showed up with heavily decorated eyes and painted fingernails that they had to strip before the nuns at school checked them on Monday mornings. My mother's makeup struck me as vain armor, and I wanted to be more authentic, look more natural.

Approaching my mother at the vanity, I watched as she leaned toward one of the side mirrors and carefully outlined her right eye in kohl. "Did you want to ask me something?" she queried when our eyes met in the mirror. Hers were dramatically mismatched, one heavily outlined and the other still naked.

Caught off guard by her directness, I forgot why I'd come to her. And then I remembered: "I was thinking that maybe it's not the best time for me to be married," I said, breaking eye contact. "With all of the unrest lately. Maybe it's best we wait until everything settles down before we talk about suitors and all of that . . ." I rattled on. When I tried to find her gaze in the mirror again, she was applying mascara to her eyelashes, making them thick and heavy and cartoonish.

She angled her eyes to catch mine in the reflection. My gaze darted back and forth between her made-up and natural eyes. The one was striking yet intimidating, the other soft and gentle. I didn't know where to focus, which to trust.

Placing her mascara brush back in its box, my mother set it down and turned around to face me. "We'll get a hundred proposals for you now," she answered at last. "Once you reach a certain age, men will assume that something must be wrong with you if you're not already married."

"But what if I'm not ready to get married?" I tried, my voice arching into a plea.

My mother rolled her eyes. "No girl ever feels ready, but what's the alternative? To end up a spinster? No one wants that."

I left her room feeling worse than when I'd entered. After closing the door behind me, I went to my room and shut myself inside, where I climbed facedown onto the bed and cried into the cloud of my pillow.

HALAH, 1952

THE MURMURINGS OF MY MOTHER'S RADIO usually started up around noon, when she finally woke up and took her tea. I was lying in bed next door in my room one day when I heard her shriek and demand, "What?" as if she were talking to the radio. I got up and moved closer to the wall that separated us, picking up the faintest bits of the broadcast: *new leadership . . . land redistribution . . . effective immediately*. And then my mother started crying, which was something she never did, and I went rigid, fearing the worst.

In spite of my concern, I stayed in my room for the rest of the afternoon, too despondent to tackle another crisis. The night before, I'd met the man my father wanted me to marry, and the thought of having to spend my life with him made me want to end it. The only bright spot, in my mind, was the fact that my father was scheduled to host another gathering of his comrades that Friday, and I hoped to see Khalil again.

My father returned home hours after dark, his typical schedule lately. When I heard the front door open, I listened as my mother loudly tromped downstairs in her hard-soled, high-heeled shoes, and then I quietly opened my door.

"Why didn't you tell me this was going to happen?" my mother yelled in the foyer, her voice echoing off the stone floors and rising to the top of the lofted ceiling. "I would have at least tried to sell to the farmers who've been leasing the land. Now they're just going to get it for free!"

My father's loud laugh boomed. "*You* would have tried to sell it? When was the last time you even went to visit those precious acres? Who's the one who visits the farms every month to collect the rent? Who's the one who got you those tenants in the first place? Your father was so rich and complacent that he didn't care that most of the land he owned lay fallow. It was me who drummed up that business after I came into the family, or don't you remember?"

"That land has been in my family for generations. You can't expect me to just let it go," my mother argued.

"It's not *me* asking you to give it up. You have no choice, and neither do I."

"You're a real son of a bitch," my mother shrieked, and then she started to cry again.

I waited for my father to yell back, but his response was calm and measured. "We took control of this country promising to build a more equitable system. The vast majority of Egypt is owned by just two percent of the population. Do you really want to be part of that two percent? We can't kick out the king for his excesses while turning a blind eye to the wealth we'd inherited from our ancestors. The only way to create a fair system is to start fresh."

"Whose side are you on?" my mother demanded, her voice still full of emotion.

"I'm on everyone's side," my father said, in a tone that indicated he was done with the conversation. I heard his footsteps move to-

ward the stairs—so distinct from the patter of my mother's—and
shut my door.

THOUGH I NORMALLY WORE the same house clothes for days on
end, that Friday, excited by the prospect of seeing Khalil again, I
gave a lot of thought to my wardrobe. While my mother was out of
the house visiting a friend, I borrowed a stick of kohl from her vanity and outlined my eyes with the oily pencil. I wasn't sure that I
liked what I saw in the mirror, but at least I looked grown up.

After the first guests arrived, I snuck downstairs to the kitchen
and up the servants' stairs to the roof. Conscious of not wanting to
be caught communing with the chickens again, I stood close to the
edge of the roof, focused on the view of downtown. I didn't want to
sit down and risk getting my dress dirty, so I stood there for a long
time, maybe an hour or more, in a series of poses that I hoped would
look pretty from behind. Finally, I got tired of holding myself so
rigidly and started to worry that Khalil wasn't coming.

As I was walking across the roof to leave, he emerged from behind the door, and our eyes met. He smiled, and we both stopped
in our tracks. "You're here," he said, his expression almost incan-
descent with joy.

"I've been waiting," I said, and then immediately regretted revealing so much.

"Amazing," he said, shaking his head in the dark.

"Don't you think we were meant to meet?" I responded.

He tilted his head. I wanted him to move closer, but we both
stood in our places. "What do you mean?" he asked.

It surprised me that I had to explain it to him: "Do you believe
in fate?"

He laughed nervously and looked down, toeing the rubbery
ground with the tip of his right shoe. "I don't think you really
want to know what I believe." He paused, and I held my breath in

the silence. "If you want to hear my opinion," he followed without prompting, "the world would be much better off without any religion. At least we'd kill each other a lot less."

I was shocked but didn't want to show it. What he said was radical, and yet it made sense. "I never thought of it that way," I muttered.

"Don't listen to me," Khalil said, shoving his hands into his pockets and continuing to kick at the ground. "I'm probably not worth your time."

I hated to hear him degrade himself, when here I'd been thinking he might be the love of my life. "Why would you say that?" I asked him.

He looked alarmed, widening his gaze and suddenly standing up straight like the soldier that he was. "I should go," he said. "Please forgive me." And with that, he turned around and left the way he came. I couldn't move, horrified that I had scared him off.

I TURNED SIXTEEN THAT SUMMER. I'd managed to deflect the first suitor my father proposed, but I knew there would be more and I couldn't reject them all. Around the same time, my father stopped hosting parties with his comrades, much to my disappointment, even though I was too ashamed to confront Khalil again after my embarrassing disclosure. I blamed all of the stupid romantic movies I'd seen for filling my head with nonsense. Rick and Ilsa's thwarted romance in *Casablanca* had shaped my romantic consciousness; if I ever found a love like that, I'd decided at twelve when I first saw the film, I would be true to him forever. But my recent experience with Khalil had caused me to reconsider love.

Then, one Friday in June, a full year since I'd last seen Khalil, my father resumed his parties. It was too hot to stay in my room, and I was excited and jittery at the prospect of seeing Khalil again. On my way to the kitchen in search of lemonade and a cold snack, I ran into him in the hallway outside my father's office. Smoke and laughter poured out around the edges of my father's door. We froze when we saw each other, our faces betraying surprise and recognition.

"Halah," Khalil said, pronouncing my name like it was breath.

My father had introduced me to four possible husbands since I turned sixteen, each of whom I'd raised fierce objections to. The first was too old, and I argued he would leave me widowed and alone at a young age. My father took to heart what I said, and the next candidate was younger but still at least twice my age. The third had been married before, which I didn't like, and neither did my mother, which helped my case. And the last one my mother objected to because she thought he was gay. I knew what it meant to be gay, but I'd never met a gay person in my life and didn't know how to recognize such a disposition.

My mother had become an important ally over the past several months, finding as many reasons to reject these potential husbands as I did. It helped that she was incensed by the agrarian reform bill, which caused her to give up all but a few *feddan* to the government, who supposedly reapportioned it among the poor. Now it was often my mother and I against my father, which felt good for a change.

"Hi," I said to Khalil, feeling my face grow hot.

"I'm so happy to see you," he said.

"You are?" I asked, all my love for him immediately returning. How easy it was to recall the many afternoons I'd spent fantasizing about him and our life together, all of it coming back in a rush. He was just as handsome as I remembered, maybe more so now compared with the four suitors I'd met, all of whom I'd found unattractive. After his rejection on the roof, I told myself I'd meet other men who would make me feel the way he did, but then I met one disappointing potential husband after another and started to think the spark I'd felt with Khalil was truly special.

"Every time I've come back here, I've gone up to look for you," he whispered in a rush. "I keep hoping . . ."

I glanced behind Khalil at the door to my father's office, expecting it to open at any moment. "Follow me," I said, bolstered by his confession, realizing that I was special to him too. I led the way to the kitchen and out the side door to the yard. It had become my new escape over the past year. At first my mother complained that the neighbors would see me when I lounged out in the yard reading books, but I kept doing it, and she stopped saying anything. We both knew that my days in this house were numbered, and she was gentler toward me now than she'd ever been. Sometimes she even invited me with her when she went to get her hair or nails done, when usually Reema was the one who took me to the barber for a haircut. It was funny to me that my mother chose now to grow close, but I supposed it was better than never.

Khalil followed me out to the yard, where I took him to the farthest corner of the overgrown lawn. No other part of our estate was allowed to become so unkempt, and I loved the yard's wildness. Once in the spring and again in the fall, my father hired a gardener to mow down the weeds and trim the trees. It had been a couple of months since the yard had been gardened, and the ground was thick and full again, littered with fallen leaves. There was a lemon tree in the corner that I had decided was my favorite specimen in the yard. I loved to eat the fruit all by itself, biting into the sour flesh, a strange jolt that made me feel alive.

Something had occurred to me in the months since I last saw Khalil, a possible reason to explain his rejection. "Are you married?" I asked him at last.

"No," he answered with a laugh. "Not at all."

"Why is that funny?" I wondered aloud, leaning against the rough trunk of the lemon tree.

"I'll probably be a bachelor forever, at the rate I'm making money," he said. "I'm not exactly husband material at the moment."

I knew that men were expected to bring financial security and property to the marriage, but I'd never considered how this was its own kind of burden. I was used to being around rich people for whom this wasn't a problem, and I felt embarrassed by how limited our circle was.

"I'm sure you'll get married someday," I said, hoping it would be to me.

"From your lips to God's ears," he said, pointing to the sky.

I couldn't help but smile. "I thought you weren't religious."

Khalil shook his head. "The world is full of mystery."

WE AGREED TO MEET AGAIN the next time he came over. Three months felt like a very long time to wait for my destiny, as I had come to think of him. The waiting made me wild with energy. Words built up in my throat like water behind a dam; it was so hard not to tell anyone about Khalil, especially Reema. In lieu of actual conversations, I talked to Khalil in my head, getting to know him, constructing the perfect man. Phantom Khalil wanted to marry me, and in my imagination, I saw no impediments to this. Suddenly I could imagine being someone's wife, as long he was the husband in question.

I often felt like I couldn't breathe inside the house, where the air was warm, damp, and suffocating, so I started spending whole days out in the yard, where it was also very hot but the air moved more freely.

One afternoon Reema came out to find me reading yesterday's newspaper on a lounge chair. "What are you doing out here?" she asked.

"Enjoying life," I said with a big smile that I couldn't hide, though I'd just been reading a rather harrowing article. I'd grabbed the newspaper from my father's desk before Reema had managed to tidy the room and recycle the paper for her own purposes. She couldn't read, but she liked to cover the kitchen counters with old papers while she was preparing food, to make the tidying up easier, ultimately crumpling up the dirtied papers and stuffing them into the trash, the counters still magically clean underneath.

"Since when are you interested in politics?" Reema asked, pointing to the paper lying open across my lap.

"I've always been interested in politics," I answered, though we both knew that this wasn't the case.

"Okay," she said with narrowed eyes and a knowing nod. I bent over the newspaper again and listened as she shuffled back to the house.

Yesterday's cover story was about several members of the ancien régime who'd just been tried by the Revolutionary Tribunal and sentenced to death. I studied the names of these men, wondering if I'd met them, whether they'd been allies of my father's in the not-so-distant past. The names sounded vaguely familiar—*Mohamad Atef Moustafa, Hani Abdelrakim, Lotfy Ahmed Salah*—but they were also common Egyptian names.

There was also a major story about the rising threat of the Muslim Brotherhood. Riots had broken out in the old part of the city, which were immediately suppressed, the perpetrators arrested. Over the past few months, the Brotherhood had become the new public enemy; no one talked about the British anymore. Recently, I'd heard Reema say several things to suggest that she sympathized with the Brotherhood and their platform of instituting a religious government. *What's the point of ruling ourselves if we don't look to our Allah as our guide? I hear that the Christians and Jews are leaving the country in droves—good riddance. Now we can finally live as Allah intended.* It made me uncomfortable when she talked glowingly about the exodus of Egyptians of other religions, but I never questioned her intolerance aloud, instead privately thinking of her as "country," like my mother did.

On the other side, my father's rails against the Brotherhood were now a regular feature of his supper monologues.

"Do you want to be forced to go around wearing a headscarf?" he'd demanded of me just the other day, looking me straight in the eye. "You want to live like they do in the desert, with men collecting harems of wives?"

I shook my head. Of course I didn't want that, and yet it bothered me that this argument was being used to justify the incarceration of thousands of Muslim men, which in many cases led to their deaths. "Those poor men are being murdered for fighting for what we all believe in," Reema had cried to me recently when I came into the kitchen and found her bawling over some story on the radio.

Over the past year I'd noticed subtle differences in her behavior around my parents that suggested a growing resentment on her part. One morning my father complained about his eggs being undercooked, which he often did, and Reema muttered loudly, as she carried his plate away from the table, "I'll leave it to God . . ."

These days when she came home from her monthly visits to El Faiyûm, she was cold and standoffish for a while, in ways that even reached me. She still brought breakfast to my room every morning and delivered snacks in the evening, but she wouldn't linger, instead setting the tray down on the dresser and leaving without a word. Our relationship would eventually thaw back to normal, with her warming up to me and me reciprocating by visiting her more often in the kitchen. By a week or so into her return, we were usually close again.

One afternoon she delivered me a pot of sweetened tea and a sealed cellophane roll of my favorite English cookies out on the veranda. "I have to admit that I'm worried about you," she said as she set the silver tray down beside me. "You're not acting like yourself lately."

I regarded her doubtfully, while deep inside I was terrified that she was on to me.

Luckily, she was scheduled to have the weekend off when my father next hosted his Free Officers comrades. I could pass by her room without fear of being heard, going back and forth between upstairs and downstairs freely. I never worried about being discovered by my mother. It was incredibly rare for her to emerge from her sanctum after sunset, as if she were the opposite of a vampire. My father loved Dracula movies, and I'd seen several with him at the theater, most recently a Turkish film called *Dracula in Istanbul*. "They just keep getting better," my father commented after the film. "Did you notice his sharp teeth? That was a nice touch."

When I went up to the roof, Khalil was already there. He spun around as I stepped onto the soft tar surface. It felt like walking on a cloud, and as I approached him, there was a sense of unreality to it. I could hear the pattern of his breath as I got closer, shallow and nervous. "You came," he said, as if I'd arrived on his property.

"You can always find me here," I said, a line that had stuck with me from one of the women in my father's crime novels. "I have nowhere else to go."

Khalil laughed quietly and pressed his hands into his pockets. "I know what it's like to feel stuck," he said, looking at the ground. "Personally, I'm looking for a big way out—like out of the country."

"What do you mean?" I asked with alarm, my heart starting to race.

"Oh, it's probably bad luck to talk about it," he said, breaking eye contact and scanning the ground between us, "but I've applied for a scholarship to study medicine in New York."

The mention of New York called to mind some of my favorite films—*Miracle on 34th Street*; *All About Eve*; *East Side, West Side*; *Holiday Affair*; *The Naked City*. I'd never thought of leaving Egypt, never realized it was an option.

"Take me with you," I said, uttering the words as soon as they came to me.

"What do you mean?" he asked, repeating the same question I'd asked him moments ago.

I stepped closer, wanting to be kissed. I looked at Khalil with utter seriousness, needing him to understand. "Take me with you,"

I said as I looked up at him, his nose almost touching my forehead. "Take me with you," I whispered a third time.

Khalil tilted his head, and then his hands were pulling my face closer and his mouth was on mine, his lips dry and firm, his breath bitter and warm. I parted my lips but didn't know what to do. As I stood there unmoving, my insides were a carnival of new sensations. My head pounded. My breasts and belly tingled, and I felt a dull thump inside my underwear.

"Oh, Halah," Khalil whispered, pulling away but keeping hold of my head. "Why me? You could have anyone."

"I don't want anyone," I said, my voice unsteady. "I want you."

A single, deep crease formed at the center of his brow. "Let's see if I get this scholarship first, and then we can plan our escape." He looked troubled, but I took this as a sign that he wanted this as much as I did.

A FEW WEEKS LATER my father announced there was another suitor he wanted me to consider. "I think he's the one," he said, with joy in his eyes.

I put on a nice dress for the occasion, at my mother's insistence. As a finishing touch, she smeared a tube of bright red lipstick across my lips. I thought it made me look like a clown, but I didn't wipe it off.

These meetings took place in the room we called the salon. It was the most opulent room in our house and rarely used, typically closed off behind French doors and gathering dust. We entertained there when we wanted to impress people. These days my parents rarely threw parties like they did before the revolution. The only time the salon saw use was for these dreaded meetings with potential husbands.

We spread out among the abundant furniture, my mother and I together on one couch, my father occupying another, and the suitor in one of the Louis XVI–style high-backed chairs directly across from me. Unlike the previous men I'd sat with in this setting, this one was actually handsome, but right away I could tell that I didn't love him. He didn't set off fireworks inside my body the way Khalil did, and besides, I was already promised to Khalil in my heart.

These meetings were generally conducted like interviews between the strangers and my parents, with my father asking most of the questions—questions I got the sense he'd already asked the men before and was doing now solely for my benefit. Where did they work? How long had they been with their employers? Who were their parents? Did they have any siblings? In which neighborhoods did they own property? Did they have any vacation homes or farmland outside the city?

I was struck, once again, by what a hypocrite my father was. Just a year ago he'd argued that it was crucial for my mother to give up her land for the benefit of the larger populace, and here he was, bent on expanding our family's empire through my marriage.

The suitor gave the standard answers, nothing surprising. I drifted away as he spoke, fantasizing about the house Khalil would buy for us in New York.

After the man left, my father asked me what I thought.

My mother answered first: "He's perfect!" she expressed, with great enthusiasm.

Then they both turned to me, and I shrugged. "Can't I have a minute to think about it?" I asked peevishly, and then stalked off to my room, sweeping my arms by my sides.

I'd started packing a suitcase in secret, stowing it beneath my bed, the one place Reema never cleaned. I had so many clothes that it was easy to put away a small wardrobe and still have an abundance in my dresser and closet. I packed a few mementos: a framed family portrait that normally stood on my nightstand next to a photograph of me and my girlfriends from school—the picture was taken when I was seven, and in it I was seated on a tall stool with my parents standing stiffly behind me, like the statuary of ancient kings and queens. My favorite hairbrush also went into the suitcase, which meant I was now relying on a second-rate tool for my everyday needs, and I packed away a thick wool scarf that my father once brought me back from London, which it was rarely cold enough to use in Cairo.

I WAITED ANXIOUSLY for my father to host the officers again. Weeks passed, and in the meantime, my imminent betrothal to the latest suitor advanced, despite my protests. My parents had turned against me and decided I was "too picky," and my father had scheduled a second meeting with the suitor, this time including his parents.

Then one night I heard the familiar rumblings of men gathered in my father's office underfoot. He hadn't mentioned that he was having people over. Getting out of bed, I stripped out of my pajamas and went to my closet to find something to wear. One of the more flamboyant dresses caught my eye, a ready-made piece my mother had bought from a shop in the lobby of the Continental-Savoy hotel and given to me after it turned out to be too big for her. The bodice of the dress was tight, and I could barely manage to fasten the buttons that held it closed, but I loved the long, flowing skirt, which made me feel like Scarlett O'Hara in *Gone with the Wind*. There was another tragic love story that was exquisitely painful to watch. I wanted to be like Scarlett but with a love that lasted.

Down in the kitchen I found Reema elbow deep in the sink, tackling a pile of dirty dishes.

"Why do you look so nice?" she asked when she looked up and saw me there.

"I'm entertaining in my room tonight," I told her. She narrowed her eyes, and when she didn't laugh, I added, "I'm joking!"

I walked over to the refrigerator and opened the door, making like I was looking for a snack. In truth, my appetite had been min-iscule for weeks, food these days an afterthought. Spying a bowl of cut watermelon, I pulled out two cubes and ate them while standing in the cool breeze of the fridge. They dissolved inside the cave of my mouth, liquified sweetness sliding down my throat. I wondered if they had watermelon in America. If Khalil showed up tonight with anything less than a plan for our escape, I would be crushed.

When I couldn't eat anymore, I wandered over to the center is-land and started reading a relatively clean section of the newspa-per that was spread out across its surface. I couldn't focus on the words as I read them; they moved through me like water, leaving no aftertaste, no impression in my mind. Reema finished with the dishes and dried her hands on the lower half of her galabeya. When I looked up, she was smiling in my direction.

"What is it?" I asked, worried that she was on to me.

She shook her head. "I know I can't take credit, but I love you like you were my own. You're such a smart girl. I'm so proud of you. I'll bet that if you were a boy, you'd be headed straight for engi-neering school."

I frowned, unsure how to take this. Whenever she compli-mented my intelligence, Reema made it sound as if it was a handy but extraneous limb I was porting around. "I am yours," I told her. "You raised me."

A film of tears washed over her eyes. We never said "I love you" to each other, and it suddenly seemed absurd that we honored this unspoken code of conduct between the classes. "I love you," I told her. "I love you so much."

Reema really started crying then, and I went over to hug her. She didn't say the words back, but I knew she felt them.

As soon as Reema was gone, I headed for the roof. This time I got there first and waited for Khalil. He didn't keep me waiting long, showing up before a quarter of an hour had passed. He said my name, and I ran toward him. He put his arms around me, and the sensation was everything I remembered and more, like a kind of magic. I needed him to say that he'd gotten the scholarship and we were running away together; at this point, I could imagine no other future for myself.

"I have good news," he whispered into my hair, and I knew before he said it that my dreams were coming true. I couldn't tell whose heartbeat was making my chest thud, mine or his.

"When can we leave?" I asked, pulling away so I could see his face.

"Let's talk a minute," Khalil said, furrowing his brow. "I want to make sure you know what you're getting into. I can't give you the kind of life that you're used to."

"But I don't want this life!" I argued, my voice hitting an embarrassingly high pitch.

"Don't get upset," Khalil said calmly. "We don't want anyone to hear."

"Do you want to be together or not?" I asked.

"Yes," he said, squeezing my shoulders, "but this is a little crazy, isn't it?"

"It's not," I insisted. "It's God's plan."

"You really believe that?" Khalil said, tilting his head as he looked at me.

"Don't you?"

"Okay," he said cautiously, "but I don't think God is up there playing matchmaker. I think it's up to us to decide who we want to be with."

"It's not up to me," I argued, feeling dizzy with confusion and disappointment. "I don't have control over anything!"

Khalil pulled me closer and kissed my cheek. "Don't cry," he said, making me realize I had tears running down my face. "You can have control over me," he said, and then kissed me gently on the lips. "If that's what you want."

I kissed him back, suddenly confident in my abilities. He

wrapped his arms tightly around me, and I lost track of the edges of my body. When Khalil pulled away, my limbs felt like jelly. The steadying force of his hands on my hips kept me upright. "I should go back down before they miss me," he said. "I can't believe this is happening. Are we really going to do this?"

I nodded, still speechless from our kiss.

"I'm supposed to leave in a couple of weeks," Khalil said, and then he looked at me as if he'd asked a question and was waiting on an answer.

"I can go with you now," I said.

"No," he responded with a laugh. "I live with my parents. I have nowhere to hide you."

Embarrassed by my eagerness, I shook my head and said, "Of course, of course."

Khalil named a date later in the month—the day he planned to leave. "I'll come pick you up. I think early in the morning is best, before anyone's awake. Should we say four o'clock?"

I bobbed my head in agreement, though it was suddenly very hard to imagine fleeing and leaving behind everything I'd ever known. "Four," I echoed back mechanically.

"This is crazy," Khalil said, regarding me with a wild smile.

"No, it's not," I protested again.

I CONTINUED TO PREPARE my suitcase in secret while I waited for our departure date. Life proceeded along its course meanwhile, undeterred by my surreptitious planning. The night we were supposed to go to the home of the man my father wanted me to marry, I stuck my fingers down my throat and forced myself to vomit, then told everyone I was sick, so the meeting was called off, Abu Abdullah driving across town to extend our regrets to the family. I was able to prolong that performance into a few days, when Reema finally began to doubt my illness.

"You can't play sick forever to avoid marriage," she teased when she came in to check on me once.

"That's not what I'm doing," I said, but couldn't look her in the eye.

"I'm going to miss you," Reema added, lingering in my room.

My body went rigid under the covers. How much did she know?

"I'm making soup," she continued before I could respond. "I'll bring some up soon."

December 9, 1954—the day my life would change forever. As that date approached, I went back and forth between excitement and terror. Was I making the right decision? What if I regretted it? What if I'd misinterpreted the signs and this wasn't what *Allah* wanted for me? It finally dawned on me that I would never see Reema or my parents again. If I ran away, there was no coming back. And yet the alternative, to stay in Egypt and enter a loveless marriage, remained the less attractive option, a reality I wasn't sure I could survive.

One morning, after my father left for work, I went down to his office and liberated my passport from the drawer in his desk where he kept it, together with his and my mother's. It felt like I was breaking up a set by taking mine, arousing another pang of uncertainty and preemptive regret. Stamps from previous travels to London, Paris, and Naples decorated the back pages of my passport, trips that my mother had planned. My father never seemed happy in those beautiful cities and would stay back in the hotel while I accompanied my mother on daylong shopping trips. To think of these memories now made me sad, already nostalgic for the good parts of the life I had with my parents.

On my last night in Cairo, I kept all the lights burning in my room and, after midnight, pulled out the suitcase from underneath my bed and threw in some last-minute effects—a picture of me and my friends from school, another of my parents on their wedding day, a diamond pendant from my mother, a pair of golden earrings and a matching ring from my father featuring gold Queen Victoria coins from 1873 that he claimed were very valuable.

In the hour between two and three, after I'd sealed up my luggage, I contemplated leaving notes behind. It seemed cruel to say goodbye to Reema in a medium she couldn't decipher, so instead I left a picture of the two of us behind one of my pillows for her to find. The photograph was a few years old—I was still a kid, nine or ten, and Reema looked a bit younger, her cheeks fuller. The picture was taken at one of my parents' parties, the photographer mistaking Reema for an older relative or guest. My mother had kept the rest of the pictures from that night and given this one to me, and though I loved it, I decided to leave it for Reema.

When I sat down at my desk, I couldn't decide what to write to my parents. I tried out dozens of sentences in my head that never made it to the paper, and then finally found a few that seemed true and right:

I need to make my own choices. I am sorry if this hurts you. Thank you for everything you have given me. I will always be grateful. Please do not try to find me. This is meant to be.

Halah

I folded the note in half and left it on my desk. Reema wouldn't come up to check on me before ten in the morning, giving Khalil and me a six-hour head start before its discovery.

Part of me hoped to get caught as I lugged my suitcase down the stairs, losing my grip and banging it against the ground several times. The closer I got to freedom, the more I wanted to escape. I stopped in the foyer to catch my breath and then opened the front door, which yawned loudly on its hinges. Half expecting to be discovered, I walked through the door and shut it softly behind me, and then I hurried across the yard, carrying the suitcase at my side and looking back over my shoulder every few seconds.

On the other side of the gate, I found Khalil waiting for me. He took my suitcase and pointed to an idling taxi waiting for us at the end of the block. In the back seat he took my hand, and we looked at each other in wonder. Neither of us spoke. Perhaps we were both afraid of betraying our transgression to the stranger behind the wheel. Until we were out of Egypt, I would be my father's daughter; only by leaving could I free myself from his possession over me.

HALAH, 1954

MY FEET WERE THROBBING by the time we arrived at the mosque,
a thirty-minute walk from the place we now called home. Every
few blocks Khalil had stopped to consult the map he'd bought from
the newsstand across the street from our new building, until we
finally saw a pair of minarets piercing the sky ahead of us. They
were a welcome, familiar sign after our journey through the dense
urban streets of Queens, which looked nothing like the New York
I knew from the cinema. Half of the buildings were factories or
warehouses, and we didn't pass a single park or green space. The
trees here were scrawny and appeared diseased, hemmed into small
squares of dirt built into the sidewalks.

There was no separation between the mosque and the laundromat beside it. The black-tiled facade of the mosque directly abut-
ted the blue face of the laundromat, as if they shared a single body.

We walked up to the door of the mosque, and Khalil let go of my hand, which he'd been holding since we started our long walk across the city. He opened the door and motioned for me to enter, but I hesitated, unsure whether women were allowed to go in this way. I'd been inside of mosques only a handful of times, twice with my mother when she went to pray after each of her parents died, and a couple of times with Reema, impromptu visits to different mosques we'd happened upon while out together when Reema relented to let me run errands with her. Each experience had been beautiful in its own way, praying in the company of other women, strangers, all facing Mecca and united in verse and movement.

We entered a lobby full of men, a cluster of two on either side of the door and a larger group standing in the middle. I felt them all looking at me and took a step behind Khalil. Scanning the room from my place of safety, I spotted a discreet sign that said "Women" next to one that read "Bathrooms."

"I'll be right back," I whispered to Khalil.

"Where are you going?" he asked, looking back at me.

"To pray," I said, and pointed to the signs.

First I stopped in the bathroom to wash up. It felt good to splash cold water on my face, like being slapped into the present. I focused on performing my ablutions the way that Reema had taught me to do them, beginning with my head and working my way down.

The women's quarters were at the top of a narrow set of stairs. To think of them as quarters seemed grandiose, when really it was just a small, windowless room with a low ceiling, sloppily carpeted with prayer rugs. There were two women inside, both praying when I entered, one of whom flashed me a distracted glance. I'd covered my hair in the bathroom, so all there was left to do was remove my shoes and find a rug.

Praying made me feel briefly at peace, but the sensation was always fleeting. It had been less than twenty-fours hours since we'd arrived in America. Khalil and I had slept in separate sections of our new apartment the night before, without discussion, and in the morning I'd made it clear that we couldn't continue to cohabit unless we were married. He agreed on the spot, turning dopey-eyed and tearful.

After I finished praying, I went downstairs to rejoin Khalil in the lobby, where he looked surprised to see me, as if I might have tried to escape. He'd infiltrated one of the pairs of men by the door and was talking to them in Arabic.

"*Mabrouk*," one of the men told me as I walked up.

I looked to Khalil to explain. "I told them we were getting married," he said.

Sweat broke out on my upper lip; whenever I got nervous, my whole face turned wet.

"The imam should be ready for us," Khalil said, reaching for my hand. "*Ma'a salama*," he said to his new friends, and then led us down a short hallway until we reached a door that was ajar. Khalil knocked and ducked his head inside. "We're here," he announced to someone I couldn't see.

Apparently invited to enter, Khalil waved for me to follow. We walked into the office, which was crowded with furniture and boxes and stacks of books. The imam stood up from behind his desk, a stout, middle-aged man with no hair on top of his head but a long, full beard that covered the lower half of his face. He invited us to sit down, and we took two seats opposite him.

"Did you bring your own witnesses?" he asked, looking only at Khalil, like a devout Muslim man.

"We have no one," Khalil told him, revealing a new truth that I was only then recognizing.

"I guess I will have to find you some," the imam grumbled, sighing like this was an inconvenience. He hobbled out of the room with an uneven gait. While he was gone, I studied the walls of his office: a framed painting of Mecca hung behind his desk, next to a long tapestry embroidered in gold with the ninety-nine names of *Allah*, or at least I presumed, from the sheer quantity of names, that all the variants were accounted for. There were two Qurans on the imam's desk and another leaning on a shelf behind it, next to several books of Hadith, the sayings and teachings of Muhammad collected outside of the Quran. There was something reassuring about being surrounded by all this holiness, but at the same time I felt out of place, as if I didn't belong. The imam returned a few minutes later with a pair of men, making me feel even more like the odd one out.

The men stood behind me and Khalil as the imam returned to his seat behind the desk and opened one of his Qurans to the first verse, the *Fatiha*. He closed his eyes and recited the words aloud while I silently echoed them in my head, creating my own private choir. I didn't hear Khalil repeating any of the verses, though I heard the men behind us whisper the odd phrase. When he was done, the imam closed the Quran with a definitive snap and then opened a drawer beneath him and produced a piece of paper labeled with the Arabic words for *Certificate of Marriage*.

The imam signed first and then handed the pen to me, catching me off guard. I signed and passed it to Khalil next, followed by the two witnesses who leaned in from behind us, one of them exposing me to the cave of his sour armpit. When it was done, all of the men shook hands, while I sat there and quietly contemplated my new existence.

I WANTED TO SLEEP as soon as we got back to the apartment. My body was still disoriented by the time change; though it was only afternoon in New York, it felt like night. When we arrived the day before, Khalil was surprised that the apartment was unfurnished. He'd assumed that a rented apartment would come with all of the basics. He argued with the landlord, the way he'd argued with the taxi driver who brought us the long distance from the airport to our new building, over the value of their services. "That's too much!" he'd admonished the driver. "How can a place this expensive come so bare?" he'd demanded of our new landlord, a fellow Arab immigrant and speaker of our language. I worried that this was not the right way to start our relationship. The landlord loaned us some-thing called an airbed, which Khalil slowly inflated by mouth for more than thirty minutes once we got back to the apartment. Our first night, he'd left the mattress to me and slept on the floor in the next room. There were no walls between the rooms of this new place. It felt like one long hallway sectioned into four pieces, with the kitchen at one end and the room with the airbed at the other. Despite my anxieties about what I had done and my newfound con-cerns about Khalil's solvency, I managed to fall asleep that night, though not before recalling the box of money I'd left behind in my closet in Cairo, filled with cash gifts I'd received for birthdays and holidays over the years. I had been so blasé about money my whole life that I hadn't even thought to bring it.

I took to the airbed again that afternoon. As soon as I curled up on my side, I fell into a deep, dark slumber. I woke sometime later to Khalil's gentle taps on my shoulder and the strong smell of food. My body felt so heavy that it was difficult to sit up. I blinked the barren room into focus, Khalil and a plastic bag full of white car-tons. It was a disappointment to recall where I was.

The food went down warm and soft. I barely chewed, too tired to expend much effort and wanting nothing more than to go back to sleep. We'd subsisted on fruit from the vendor across the street since arriving, and this was our first warm meal. The flavors were nice, but I was too tired to appreciate much.

Thoughts of my family back home swirled through my head as I laid down again. A marriage was supposed to be a cause for cel-ebration, but I knew that not one of them would be happy for me, not even Reema; in fact, they were probably all suffering greatly over my disappearance. This made me feel terrible, so I closed my eyes and willed sleep to come. It arrived before I could worry about where Khalil would sleep that night. When I woke in daylight, I heard him pacing another room of the apartment, close by but in-visible. I still felt exhausted. It seemed no amount of sleep could counteract this weariness, as if I would feel this way forever now.

Khalil was ready with food again when I woke: a boiled egg and a banana. "I know how to boil an egg, but that's about it." He shrugged. It tasted good, the yolk perfectly cooked.

Khalil suggested that we go out to explore the neighborhood and find some furniture. Though the prospect sounded daunting, I agreed and finally changed into some fresh clothes. When we left, Khalil locked the empty apartment behind us.

Khalil took my hand once we were out on the street, and I was grateful for his tenderness. His body next to mine was a comfort in this strange city. As I leaned in closer, he put his arm around me. My body tingled with desire for the first time since our clandestine meetings at my house, what seemed like a lifetime ago, though the last time, when we decided to run away together, was just three months prior. I hoped I could find this feeling again when we were back at the apartment.

We came to a busy corridor called Steinway Street, filled with cars and stores and pedestrians. There was endless commerce in both directions. We turned left, following the route that would allow us to continue down the sidewalk without crossing any streets and passed a grocery store that took up half the block. Pages from circulars advertising sales on their goods tiled the windows, and abandoned shopping carts littered the sidewalk in front of the store, forcing us to zigzag around them. The few times I'd gone shopping with Reema, we'd had to go to three shops to get everything we needed—the butcher, the baker, and a produce stand on a street corner—but here it looked as if you could find it all in one place.

Even though half the people we saw were brown like us, I imagined that we must look foreign to everyone. My mother used to complain whenever my skin darkened during our summers in Alexandria, saying I'd gotten too *sumra*, like this was an unfortunate thing. Despite resenting her judgment, I'd internalized this critical assessment of my own skin color, imagining that I looked best when I was the lightest version of myself. Khalil was several shades darker than me, darker than my father, and darker than all of the suitors my father had brought into our home. And yet I found him incredibly handsome, confounding my inherited biases.

We passed a barbershop advertising pictures of Black men getting haircuts, and I realized how narrow my upbringing had been. Within just a couple of blocks we'd seen Chinese, Indian, Mexican, and Italian restaurants. Italian was the only one of these cuisines I'd tried before. When my family went out to eat in Cairo, we rotated between Turkish, Greek, and Italian options. Italian was my favorite. Thinking about food made me hungry again, but we were on a mission to find a mattress.

Finally we came upon a furniture store. Khalil held the door open for me, and I walked in timidly, immediately catching the attention of a salesman. Khalil conversed with the man, telling him what we were looking for, and the salesman led us to a back corner of the store, where there were a bunch of mattresses set up on bed frames without any bedding. The beds looked naked, the dappled mattress surfaces like the skin of plucked chickens. The salesman invited us to try out the beds, and Khalil proceeded to lay down on the one nearest him, much to my embarrassment. I blushed hot and refused to join him when the salesman urged me to.

In the end, Khalil selected the cheapest mattress on the floor. When he asked if we could have it delivered that day, the salesman said it would cost extra, and Khalil agreed to the charge. We walked home the way we came, my appetite reawakened by the savory clouds emanating from various restaurants. I was desperate to go into one of those establishments, sit down at a nice table, and eat to my heart's content, but I was scared to ask Khalil and hear that we couldn't afford to, so I kept walking. When we got home, I devoured one of the apples we had left, and then I went to the other end of the apartment and fell asleep on the airbed.

WHEN I AWOKE, the apartment was filled with the fragrance of unfamiliar culinary scents. I got up slowly and wandered the short distance to the kitchen, where I found Khalil unpacking food from a white plastic bag. He'd come home with a set of cream-colored plates covered with a pattern of pretty blue flowers and was dishing food from the cartons onto the plates. There were more bags scattered around his feet, presumably filled with other objects he'd procured from the outside.

"What kind of food is that?" I asked as I stood, bleary-eyed, in the doorway.

He looked at me and smiled. "Orange chicken." The answer was surprisingly specific, and yet this told me nothing, as it wasn't a dish I was familiar with. Judging by the red characters on the sides of the cartons, I guessed the food was of Asian origin.

"Smells good," I said.

After he was done serving, Khalil reached into one of the bags at his feet and removed a folded blanket. "Let's take this to the living room," he said. I wasn't aware of having identified a living room yet, but Khalil led us next door into one of the windowless rooms at the center of the apartment. There he unfolded the blanket on the floor, as if we were about to have a picnic, and then he went back to the kitchen and got the plates. There was a sweetness to the simplicity of it all. It wasn't much, but it was enough, and I was so hungry.

The chicken was incredible. I'd never tasted anything like it. I ate until I couldn't imagine swallowing one more bite. From the bags in the kitchen, Khalil also produced a set of sheets, which he expertly put on the mattress that had just arrived. I watched, impressed as he did this, having never made a bed before. As a finishing touch, Khalil retrieved the blanket from the living room, shook off any crumbs, and then spread it over the bed. Then he waved me over.

"Can I kiss you now?" he asked once I was standing in front of him, taking hold of my hips.

I nodded and closed my eyes. His lips were dry and papery, rough against my mouth. His tongue probed mine and felt around behind my teeth, which was easily the strangest sensation I'd ever felt. Then he unbuttoned my dress and reached into my brassiere, and that was even stranger, flooding my whole body with feeling. He led the dance of getting us both out of our clothes and into bed. I cried out when it hurt, and Khalil asked if I wanted him to stop. But we'd already begun. There was no going back now. So I shook my head and gritted my teeth and endured until the pain subsided. My pleasure came when Khalil held me afterward, as we lay under the covers, and he told me that I was wonderful.

I woke in the daylight to find Khalil trying to peel the sheet out from under me like a magician. When I came to full consciousness and realized what he was doing, I noticed a big red stain in the middle of the sheet. The sight of my own blood, there for all to see, made me want to crawl back under the covers or run away. Khalil gathered up the dirty sheets and said he was going to wash them on the corner. I pictured him sitting on the corner of our block with a soapy bucket of water and our bloody sheets, and then I remembered the various laundromats I'd seen in recent days, my first introductions to such places.

Once he was gone, I braved getting out of bed, only to realize that my blood had soaked through the recently pristine mattress. I found a couple of towels in Khalil's leftover bags in the kitchen, and I got to work trying to attack the stain, but water only made it spread, and we had no soap yet. Giving up, I flipped the mattress over to the other side to hide the blemished surface.

THE FIRST TIME KHALIL went to school, I was unprepared for how long he would be gone. Day turned to night, and I began to worry that something had happened to him. Maybe he'd gotten lost or been murdered. I imagined having to carry on without him, figuring out how to survive here on my own, and just as I was really beginning to panic, Khalil came home.

It would be like this most days, Khalil explained, estimating that he would have to be on campus about ten hours a day, six days a week. In addition to requiring Khalil to be a full-time student, his scholarship dictated that he assist a professor in his department for twenty hours a week. I sat in silence as I let this information sink in. What was there to say?

Khalil gave me a weekly allowance to buy groceries. He assumed I would remember how to get to Steinway from our previous excursion to the commercial boulevard, but he was wrong. I got completely turned around the first couple of times I attempted to explore the neighborhood on my own. I gave up and went back to the apartment following my first attempt; though our building was huge and ugly, at least it was easy to spot from a distance. The second time, I persevered and eventually found the giant grocery store. I spent hours there that first afternoon, walking up and down each aisle, studying all the goods on the shelves and in the refrigerated cases. I encountered fruits and vegetables I'd never seen before: pears, which looked like oblong, shapely apples with brownish-green flesh; bundles of green spears called asparagus; perfect purple plums, which were twenty-five cents a pound, but I couldn't resist depositing one into my cart; as well as a whole section of produce, including parsnips, rutabaga, and turnips, that was completely foreign to me. There were aisles and aisles of canned goods. Cans were a rarity in Reema's kitchen; beans were the only food I knew of to come out of cans. In the butcher's section, all of the meat was pre-cut and packaged with Styrofoam and cellophane, unlike the mystery paper-wrapped meats Reema brought home from the butcher. Though tempted to fill my cart with an intriguing collection of discoveries, I put in only the essentials and kept a mental tabulation of the going total so that I wouldn't overspend.

I hated the long walk home, laden with heavy bags of groceries. Not only was it burdensome and difficult, but it also made me feel self-conscious, as if I were out on parade in public. It made me think of Reema and how she did this all the time. It took just the smallest of suggestions to bring my thoughts back to her. I'd taken her for granted, not only all of her labors that I'd consciously benefited from, but also her invisible work.

With the one pot and single pan Khalil had procured, I prepared dishes I'd watched Reema make over the years—grape leaves, stuffed cabbage and peppers, pickled eggplant, stewed lentils— dishes from home that were easy to prepare on a budget. I pictured Reema chopping and stirring and frying and baking as I worked in the kitchen, missing her deeply.

"You're amazing," Khalil remarked each time he tasted anything that I made. "Where did you learn how to cook like this?"

"Reema," I told him again and again, always giving her credit.

EVERY FEW DAYS KHALIL CAME HOME with a random piece of furniture that he'd found on the street. "Can you believe someone was throwing this away?" he remarked one evening, showing off a well-worn, vinyl-covered card table that he'd dragged into the apartment, his face and neck dripping with sweat.

Yes, I wanted to say, but kept quiet.

I'd had no real sense of money before, no idea what my father made or how much my family owned, but now I'd become aware of its value and limitations. I knew the amount Khalil got paid every week and how little it amounted to in the commercial world. We had to save to buy the amenities we needed—a couch and a dresser, a couple of chairs to go in the kitchen around the table Khalil had scavenged. Once we acquired the basics, Khalil surprised me one day with a television. I felt like a child on her birthday, receiving a most-desired gift. I turned through the dial, sitting on my knees in front of the glowing box. The only television in my parents' house had been in my mother's room, so I never got to watch it. Having my own made me feel like an adult.

I began to spend my days in front of the television instead of in bed. Daytime soap operas occupied my attention during the long, lonely hours while Khalil was away. *Guiding Light, Search for Tomorrow, Love of Life*. Around three o'clock, when the programming turned to cartoons and news, I peeled myself off the couch and started cooking. When I knew that Khalil wouldn't be home until late, I took a nap instead.

One day when I was going out for groceries, I discovered a pile of thick books in the lobby of our building. I took one off the stack and flipped through the first few pages. It was a telephone directory. When I got back from the store, the stack was still there, as towering as when I'd left it. After depositing the groceries upstairs, I returned to the lobby to take a copy.

I'd never seen a telephone directory before, and it amazed me what a wealth of information it contained. Could it truly be so easy to find someone's telephone number? And, by extension, was it barbaric that we didn't have a telephone and therefore didn't exist, as far as this book was concerned?

Past the block of yellow pages in the front, I found the personal listings. Scanning the first page of *A*'s, I was surprised to discover a large number of surnames that sounded Arabic in origin: *Abbass, Abdallah, Abdelrahman, Abdel-Azim, Abdi, Abdul-Noor, Aboud*. It occurred to me that this might be a way to find other Egyptians, or at least Arabs—potential friends.

Khalil kept a jar of change on the dresser in the bedroom where he deposited the coins from his pockets at the end of the day. I grabbed a handful of change and the page featuring the treasure trove of Arabic names, which I ripped out of the phone book, and put what I'd collected in my purse and headed to the phone booth on the corner of our block, which I'd passed by but had never used. I began with the number next to the first Arabic-looking name. A man answered, and I hung up. With the next number I tried, the phone rang and rang, and the same with the third. Finally, just as I was about to give up on this foolish initiative, a woman answered.

"Yes, hello," I said, abruptly losing confidence in my mastery of English. "I found your number in the phone book." I coughed to catch my breath. "I just moved here from Egypt, and I was looking for . . . I was looking for . . . friends."

The woman at the other end laughed. "*Ya eini*," she cried, switching to Arabic and using an old, familiar phrase that made me think of Reema. "That's brilliant."

We agreed to meet the next day. She lived in Far Rockaway, and when it became evident that I had no idea where that was, she offered to come to me. I suggested we meet at a diner on Steinway that I'd seen—the only establishment whose name came to me then. I showed up early and secured a small table near the front of the restaurant. When Malek walked in the door, I knew it was her. She looked like an Egyptian movie star, coiffed and made up like my mother. I waved meekly when she looked in my direction, feeling like a child compared to her, realizing that I was, in fact, still a child in many ways.

"Oh, *habibti*," she cooed familiarly as I stood and we embraced.

Malek did most of the talking, telling me an abbreviated version of her life story: born in Jaffa, married off to the son of Palestinian immigrants in New York at seventeen, a mother for the first time at eighteen and then again at twenty. She'd bled so much after her second birth that the doctors had sterilized her on the spot, damming up her fallopian tubes. "No matter," she said, recounting this cheerily. "I would have liked a daughter, but at least my husband got his sons." It amazed me how open she was.

When she asked me questions about myself, I was reluctant to share much, on the contrary. "Yes," I answered when she asked if I was happy here. "Yes" to the question of whether I planned to have children. "Yes" when she asked if I was in touch with my parents, though of course that was a lie, and this made me tear up, which she noticed.

"Are you okay?" she asked.

I nodded, too choked up to speak.

"Forgive me," she said. "My husband always says I'm too nosy."

I shook my head and took a sip of my ice water.

"We should do this again," Malek said when we were done with our coffees. The bill came, and she paid. I knew it would be up to me to reach out to her since we had no phone at the apartment, and I knew, even as I agreed with her suggestion, that I wasn't likely to call her again anytime soon. It seemed that we'd exhausted the possibilities of what to talk about during our brief encounter and were in such different places in our lives. I was a young runaway who didn't want to share anything about herself, and she was a respectable mother of two children who maintained relationships with her family back home.

I kept the folded page of the telephone directory at the bottom of my purse, where the thin paper ripped and smudged, degrading over time.

AFTER THE FIRST FEW TIMES, I found the pleasure in sex and began to crave it. It excited me, the way Khalil caved to my advances whenever I touched him in a certain way. I'd never had so much power over another person, and it felt exhilarating. We made love every night after he got home, often before eating the meals I'd prepared. I'd have to warm them up when we were done, blissful as I stood at the stove, wearing nothing but a robe. I knew he loved me, because he told me so every time he was inside me.

"I love you too," I cried in return, still bewildered by our love story.

I CHECKED OUR MAILBOX DAILY, enjoying the routine of sorting through coupons and circulars and planning my next shopping trip. The landlord put a bill for the rent in an unsealed envelope underneath our door on the first of every month, and each time it came, I worried Khalil couldn't pay it. We never received any personal mail until one day a strange-looking letter arrived for Khalil, addressed in Arabic with an English translation in a different colored pen beside it. A pattern of tiny blue, red, and white boxes bordered the envelope. I wanted to open it but instead tried holding it up to a window to see if I could make out parts of the letter inside, but I managed to only decipher a few innocuous phrases that meant nothing on their own. If I had to guess, I would have said that the author was a woman.

Khalil came home later than usual that night and blamed it on the subway. He looked tired and kissed me chastely, heading immediately for the bathroom. When he walked out, I handed the letter to him. "This came today."

A deep furrow formed at the center of his brow as he tore the letter open.

"It's from Egypt," I said, echoing the information from the thickly inked timestamp on the front of the envelope. "Who there knows where to find us?" I asked. It had never occurred to me that Khalil might be keeping ties with anyone there; I'd assumed he'd cut all of his off the way I had.

"My family," he said, as though this were an obvious fact.

"Do they know about me?" I wondered with alarm.

"I wrote them about you, yes," Khalil said, lowering the letter and focusing his attention on me.

I shook my head, perplexed by this revelation. "What did you say?"

He stalled with a long breath and then said, "I told them that I met someone here. A nice Egyptian girl."

"Lies," I observed angrily. We were lying to everyone.

"What did you want me to say?"

"I don't know!" I shouted. "Nothing!"

I retreated to the bedroom, abandoning Khalil in the kitchen. From the other end of the apartment, I heard him cry out as if he'd been punched in the gut. I froze in place, confused and still mad at him. Then he started cursing quietly, and I knew something was wrong.

"What is it?" I asked, sheepishly returning to the kitchen.

Khalil looked past me as if I wasn't quite there. "My brother," he said, holding the letter at his side. The envelope with the colorful border now lay on the floor. "He's been arrested."

I met Khalil's wild look with one of my own, my eyes widening to the point of pain. I knew that so many men who went to prison in Egypt never got out, like being tossed into the sea with weights tied to your ankles. A number of young men from Reema's village had been arrested over the years, never to return home, and she swore to their innocence, the whole village did, which made me question the legitimacy of the system.

"Why?" I tried after testing a number of questions in my head that sounded wrong: *What did he do? Did he break the law?*

"I wouldn't be surprised if that fool pissed the wrong person off," Khalil mumbled, looking away from me, "but my mother said that he got caught up in some kind of dragnet at the university."

I had managed to forget about Egypt's brutal battle to redefine itself during these months in America, but my memories of all the messy politics came back to me then. "He'll get out," I said, because I thought it was the right thing to say, not necessarily because I believed it.

I STARTED CHECKING THE MAILBOX multiple times a day, hoping for news from Egypt, but weeks passed and nothing came. Fall slammed into winter, and the air turned bitter and cold by early November. I had the warm scarf my father had bought me in London years ago but no appropriate coat or hat for the weather. For the four months of winter I'd endured the previous year following our arrival in New York, I'd worn multiple layers of clothing under my light coat—all I'd needed in Egypt—whenever I had to go out. This year, I refused to get groceries until Khalil supplied the proper clothing, and though I acted like a brat, he went out that night and returned an hour later with a wool coat and a woven set of hat and mittens from Goodwill, a store I'd seen but never entered. I cried when I put them on, partly because I was embarrassed by how I'd acted, and partly because the garments were so warm and cozy.

Sometimes I wore the mittens while watching television; my hands got so cold, and this was like having a personal blanket for each one.

And the shopping wasn't so bad, once I had the proper armor. I even started to find the bracing cold chill of the wind against my face invigorating, and there were few pleasures as nice as slipping into a warm building after being out in freezing temperatures.

Another letter arrived from Egypt just before the end of the year. His brother Hassan hadn't reappeared, and their parents' attempts to find him hadn't been successful. Khalil was sullen for a few days afterward, and neither of us initiated sex for weeks.

One day when I was out getting groceries, a storefront across the boulevard caught my attention, the words *Cheap International Calls* stretched across its awning. The possibilities suggested by these words diverted me across the street. I waited for the signal to cross, despite the flood of jaywalkers who ran out ahead of me, and then I walked.

Entering the call center, I found the small waiting room at the front crowded with people. All the seats were full, and a line formed behind the desk where the attendant sat. Two parallel banks of telephone booths stretched out behind him, presumably all occupied, though I couldn't see inside the booths from where I stood.

Getting in line, I waited for my turn. A clock on the wall tracked the half hour that passed as I slowly advanced to the front; I checked it every couple of minutes, as I didn't have a a timekeeping device of my own. When I finally got up to the desk, the man in glasses seated on the other side asked how he could help me.

"I wish—I wish to call Egypt," I stammered. Though I'd had all this time to consider what to say when my turn came, I had no words prepared. His question caught me off guard, and my heart started beating quickly.

"Just a minute," the man said, and looked over his shoulder at the rows of telephone booths. At that moment, an elderly woman slowly shuffled out of one of the booths at the back. "You can have hers," the man told me, pointing to the woman with his chin. "Do you need change?"

Picturing myself having to change clothes inside one of those glass-faced booths, I was truly perplexed by his question.

My expression must have registered puzzlement, because the man filled the silence with another question: "Do you have coins?"

Then I recalled that "change" was another word for "coins" in American English, and I laughed. "No! Do I need them?"

The man responded with a chirpy, nervous giggle, and his neck turned a bright shade of red. "Yes," he said. "The phones only take coins, not paper money."

From my wallet I produced a crisp five-dollar bill, my allowance for groceries for the week. The man behind the desk gave me four one-dollar bills and a handful of coins in return. I studied the money as I stepped around the desk and moved toward the newly empty booth. It still confused me, which coins were worth how much, especially the strangely diminutive ten-cent piece.

Inside the booth I found a laminated sheet of instructions describing how to place an outgoing call, in pictures and words. The sheet was secured to the base of the phone with a thin chain, though I couldn't imagine anyone wanting to steal it. I organized my coins by value, with the short stack of dimes in the middle, and then deposited five cents to start my call. Following the instructions, I dialed 0 and then 1 and then 1 again, then located the code for Egypt on the alphabetical list of countries that appeared on the bottom half of the instruction sheet, and then, finally, entered the number for my father's office, the part I knew by heart.

When I was nine and we first had a phone line installed at our house, I used to call my father at work semiregularly to try out the new technology. Sometimes he would be in meetings, but most times he would take my calls, and we had brief, sweet conversations about our days.

After I entered the long string of numbers, they repeated back as an indecipherable sequence of blips on the line. The scattershot melted into noisy static, like a fire burning at the other end of the line. I dropped in another coin, afraid that the call might disconnect before it had even started.

Ringing at last. *Ring-ring*-pause-*ring-ring*-pause-*ring-ring*-pause. I unconsciously matched my breathing to the irregular pattern, growing light-headed as I waited.

Finally a woman answered. "Good afternoon."

"Yes, good afternoon," I replied nervously. "I am looking for General Mansoor Ibrahim, please."

The line crackled with static, and just when I thought that she wasn't going to respond, she came back and said, "One moment."

A moment turned into minutes. I continued feeding my nickels into the coin slot until I had only dimes and quarters left. Then the woman returned. "The general is in a meeting at the moment. Can I take a message?"

"Please tell him it's his daughter," I said.

"One moment," the woman repeated like a robot. There was no sense of recognition in her tone, when I'd somewhat expected to be a known quantity around the Ministry of Defense at this point—wouldn't everyone there know about the general's great loss, that I was missing?

I clutched the hard plastic receiver against the side of my face with both hands as I waited. My heart beat quickly, throbbing at the base of my throat. I gritted my teeth, trying to steel myself for whatever my father might have to say, even if he said that I was dead to him, which I imagined he might do.

"Halah?" I heard after what felt like eternity, all of my dimes now depleted too. I had only one quarter and was saving it for last. "Is it really you?"

"Yes!" I yelled into the phone, so loudly that I feared the people in the neighboring booths could hear me. I checked the booths across the way and saw people with their backs turned behind glass doors, absorbed in their own conversations. "Yes, it's me," I said.

"Where are you?" he asked, after a brief, staticky delay.

I hesitated before revealing my whereabouts. "New York."

"New York?" he repeated back.

"Yes. New York. It's a long story, but please know that I'm safe."

The pause felt longer then, as I waited for my father's response. "A long story, I'm sure. But I know more than you think."

My heart hammered. I considered admitting everything, including the many doubts I'd had since running away. A strange, mechanical woman's voice interrupted our conversation and my thoughts to say: *You have thirty seconds remaining. Please insert additional funds if you wish to continue.* For several moments I stood paralyzed with the receiver pressed against my ear, and then I picked up the quarter and dropped it into the slot. The call continued without ceremony.

"I know who you're with. I thought that son of a bitch was someone I could trust. I should have never let that bastard in my house," my father ranted at the other end of the line. He sounded very far away, not just across an ocean but as if he were at the bottom of one. I didn't understand how he could have found out about me and Khalil. Had Reema seen us together, or had someone from Khalil's family betrayed us?

"He's my husband!" I protested, raising my voice again. "Please do not talk about him that way."

"He better not ever come near me again, or I swear to God I'll kill him," my father yelled from across the distance. The mechanized woman interrupted again, telling us we had thirty seconds left. "He will pay for the way he has disrespected me. If he'd come to my door and asked for your hand like a real man, I would have laughed in his face! Who does he think he is? Fucking coward. And of course he takes you to another country, where my powers can't reach. There are ways—" And then the line went dead.

HALAH, 1955

I DIDN'T TELL KHALIL ABOUT THE CALL, though I felt sick from what I'd learned. Alone with this painful knowledge, I replayed my father's words in my head. *He better not ever come near me again. Where my powers can't reach.* On my walk back home, it occurred to me that my father might be responsible for Hassan's arrest. Khalil wasn't in Egypt for my father to punish, so his brother took the hit instead.

I worried that if I told this to Khalil, he would leave me, and then I would have no one and have to fend for myself in New York. A few weeks later, Khalil heard from his parents again. The latest letter was penned and signed by Khalil's father. He reported that Hassan had been located in a prison complex outside Beni Suef and went on to write:

*At least it's not Tora, so we should be able to visit. We've put
in a request and are waiting for permission. Meanwhile, your
poor mother is out of her mind with grief. She cries all the time,
and I always hear her working those prayer beads. I worry she
could lose her job at the factory, the way she's suffering. We are
so grateful to God for the opportunity he has given you, but Egypt
misses you. Honestly, it's probably best to be where you are, with
everything that's going on here. Maybe you had the right approach
after all, joining the military, even though I didn't support it at
the time. You survived, and that's what's important. Look at you
now.* Alhamdulillah.

I read the letters from Khalil's parents over and over while he
was at school, hoping I could somehow heal what was broken. It
bothered me that Khalil didn't seem at all compelled to go back
home and help his brother, and when I asked him about it, he said,
"I promise you that if our roles were reversed, Hassan wouldn't
come home for me." Khalil clearly had no inkling that his brother
might be suffering on account of him.

One morning I woke up feeling so nauseated that I ran to the
bathroom and regurgitated whatever was in my stomach. I thought
it was just my guilt manifesting, but then it started to happen every morning. Khalil usually left before I woke, but he was home
on Sunday to witness the drama and followed me to the bathroom.
"Are you okay?" he asked through the door. I answered with another forceful heave.

When I came out of the bathroom a few minutes later, face damp
from a cold rinse, Khalil asked, "Are you pregnant?"

"No!" I answered reflexively, having never considered the possibility. And then I thought about it and realized that I very well
might be.

My face must have gone ashen, because Khalil told me to sit
down. He asked how long it had been since I last bled, which seemed

like an indecent thing to discuss. No matter that he was studying to become a doctor, no matter that he was my husband. I'd had several periods since we came to New York, which I'd done an impeccable job of hiding from Khalil, laundering my pads and hanging them to dry over the tub while he was at school, and removing them from view before he got home. I tried to think of when I'd last gone through this ritual and realized it had been weeks, maybe months.

"Longer than usual," I confessed, as the realization dawned on me.

"Don't worry," Khalil said, sitting down beside me on the couch and putting a hand on my shoulder. "We were going to have children eventually anyway," he said, though we'd never discussed it. "The timing isn't exactly ideal, but we can make it work."

I felt as if I needed to vomit again, but after I sat with the discomfort for a moment, the urge went away.

"I have a big test today, so I should go," Khalil said, as if our lives hadn't just ruptured. He carried a briefcase back and forth to school, packed with his big biology textbook, assorted snacks and their remnants—pistachio shells, candy bars, handfuls of hard candy, and endless plastic wrappers—as well as a few small books and notepads. "I'll try to get back early," Khalil said as he stood up and kissed my forehead. "Get some rest today."

I lay in bed all day as waves of nausea rolled over me, coupled with the knowledge that these symptoms signaled my imminent motherhood. I lacked the will to even wander one room over to watch my shows on television, though it was Friday, and the best episodes were always on Fridays. The more I thought about it, the more certain I became that Khalil was right and I was pregnant. Though we'd been enjoying a lot of sex, I didn't think I would get pregnant. I thought a woman had to want to make a baby before one could start growing inside her body. I also thought, as it was commonly accepted by my school friends, that a woman had to have her breasts nuzzled during sex if she wanted to get pregnant, and the couple of times Khalil had tried sucking my nipples, I'd pulled his head away immediately.

More weeks passed, and my period didn't come. Feeling sick and sorry for myself, I stopped going out for groceries and cooking. Khalil seemed miffed at first, making his exhaustion evident when he came home and had to turn around and leave again to pick up food for dinner. He left the shopping for Sundays, his one day off, and the choices he made when he went to the grocery store were baffling to me—all meat and cheese, expensive items with no vegetables or fruits or grains to accompany them. The metallic stench of meat cooking turned my stomach. I declined whenever he offered me any. I asked him to pick up bread from the bakery on his way home from school every couple of days, and I subsisted mainly on that and fruit and water.

One day another letter came in the mail from Egypt. I'd also abandoned my mailbox duties in my impregnated dolor, so Khalil was the one to intercept the letter when he got home that night. He'd already read it by the time he arrived at our apartment and walked in to find me lying in bed. He sat down on the edge of the mattress and said, "My mother collapsed and had to be taken to the hospital. They're keeping her there to monitor her heart."

This jolted me upright. The sudden change in equilibrium made me dizzy. I burst into tears, which seemed to surprise Khalil. "Oh, *habibti*," he said, pushing the hair back from my face, "don't let this upset you. My mother's a tough woman. I'm sure she'll be fine. It's just all the stress they're going through."

I couldn't control the tears, thinking about Khalil's mother in the hospital, his brother in prison, the baby inside of me. None of this would have happened if I hadn't been so forward with Khalil all those months ago. All of this was my fault.

THE NEXT DAY I WENT BACK to the call center. Though it was April, a month I normally associated with warmth and spring, an end-of-year snowstorm blanketed the entire East Coast overnight, making conditions icy and precarious as I set out to make my call. Though I'd enjoyed the novelty of the cold when we'd first arrived—and especially those wondrous first snowfalls—I was no longer charmed by the freezing temperatures. It just seemed cruel that winter could persist for so long. I didn't understand how people survived this year after year.

By the time I arrived at the call center, I couldn't feel my face. This time I found no crowd inside and walked directly to the desk. Someone else was on duty today. I asked the man if there was a free booth, and he directed me back. This time I didn't need any change, as I'd brought Khalil's change jar from home. I wondered what he spent money on while he was at school and guessed mostly food and coffee.

My heart started pounding in my throat as I dialed. It took a long time for the call to go through, and my breathing steadied as I waited. A woman picked up—the secretaries were always women—and said, "Good evening," making me realize what time it was there.

I asked for my father and gave her my name. A minute or two later, he was on the line.

"Halah?"

"Baba," I said, so happy to hear his voice and surprised by the rush of joy that I felt.

"I wondered if I'd hear from you again."

"Of course!" I said, though I'd had no plans to call again until the letter from Khalil's father had arrived the day before. On the spot I decided to tell him, "I have some news. I'm pregnant."

"Congratulations," he said coolly after a while—the delay in the transmission coupled with a long pause on his end. "I'll pray for the soul of that poor child."

These words packed a heavy punch, nearly doubling me over. I sat down on the narrow seat inside the phone booth and covered my belly with my free hand as I closed my eyes and bowed my head.

"What do you want me to say?" my father asked into the crackly silence.

"I want your forgiveness," I told him. "I want you to know this baby, and I want you to love me again."

I thought I heard him cackle, but it could have been interference. "That's a lot to ask," he said.

"I know," I told him.

Several seconds passed before his response came through: "You know, it would be easier to have a dead daughter than one who's behaved the way you have."

I lowered the receiver from my ear, unable to take in more attacks. I held it in my lap as I focused on my breath and tried not to cry. When I lifted the receiver back to my face again, my father was saying, "Are you there?"

"I'm still here," I said.

After another long pause, he said, "Your mother is heartbroken, you know. She misses you terribly."

"I miss her too!"

"What you have done is truly unforgivable. We didn't raise you this way."

I wanted to say that Reema was the one who'd raised me, that he didn't deserve much credit. "I know," I said instead.

"Does that son of a dog at least treat you well?" my father demanded to know.

"*My husband*," I corrected.

"Your husband."

"He's a wonderful man. He works so hard," I said in Khalil's defense.

I heard something like a guffaw at the other end. "I'm sure . . ."

"Listen," I said. "It's not Khalil's fault. I promise. It was my idea to go with him. Please don't punish him for this." I took a breath and gathered the courage to ask the question that had impelled me to call him in the first place. "Did you have his brother arrested?"

Another painfully long pause as I waited for his answer.

"Why do you ask?"

"Did you?"

"He's probably a criminal like his brother. If he's in jail, I'm sure he's there for good reason."

"Baba, please. It's not right to torture some poor man because you're mad at me."

"I'm not torturing anyone. I prefer to leave the dirty business to other people."

I knew then that I was right about his guilt. "So you admit it," I said, tearing up.

By the time he came back with a response, I was really crying. "Don't disrespect me, girl," he snapped. "I said nothing of the sort."

THOUGH THE WORST SYMPTOMS of pregnancy let up after the first few months, I carried on as if I were incapacitated, moving back and forth between the bed and couch all day. Khalil brought in nourishing foods from the outside; I was able to eat meat again, and everything tasted good. Every couple of weeks he took me with him to school, where I saw a rotating cast of doctors affiliated with his program. I assumed that we got this medical care for free and that's why we didn't go to someone in the neighborhood. The doctors, including my husband, never discussed my pregnancy in front of me. Khalil sometimes made reference to test results and clinic notes, but I wasn't curious enough to ask for details, assuming that Khalil would tell me anything I needed to know.

I enjoyed these excursions to his campus. It always felt like an adventure, riding the subway to Brooklyn and back. The rides were full of sights and smells and sounds I'd never experienced before—unkempt men and women sleeping in the cars with piles of bags next to them, trumpet players walking through the cars, Black boys singing a capella or doing physical stunts for tips—and with Khalil at my side, I felt safe as I took in this new world.

According to the doctors, my pregnancy was progressing perfectly. I felt like a student getting high marks again, proud of accomplishments that I'd put very little effort toward. I went back and forth about whether I thought I was gestating a girl or a boy, hoping it was the latter but believing, deep down, it was probably the former. To birth a boy was to give life to a person who would have autonomy in the world, while having a girl was just continuing the same cycle that I was caught up in.

My body became foreign to me, my belly growing so round and big that I looked and felt like a wild animal to myself. I stopped fitting into my clothes, and Khalil brought back large, shapeless gowns from the outside world that I wore for days at a time. Khalil spent a couple of hours every Sunday at the laundromat, in addition to grocery shopping and other assorted errands, so that even on his day off I hardly saw him.

The baby inside me began to feel like company the more I felt it moving around. It squirmed and kicked and punched throughout the day, and then would go still for long stretches in the evening and at night, making it hard for Khalil to catch the baby in motion. When it was just the two of us during the day, I talked to the baby, narrating whatever I was doing, whether cooking or looking out the window. I told the baby about Egypt, always speaking to the child inside of me in Arabic, imagining that this was the tongue we'd always communicate most naturally in, like me and Khalil. Whenever I sat down or sprawled out on the couch to watch my shows, I rubbed my bulging belly, and sometimes the baby would respond, and I knew we were connecting.

I looked forward to the baby's arrival and to the company it would bring me following a year of near-isolation. Knowing that I wouldn't have to be alone anymore made me feel a little better about the state of things.

MY WATER BROKE DURING *As the World Turns*, the couch growing wet beneath me. Khalil and I had established a plan in case this happened. I was to take a taxi to the nearest hospital, and if he came home and didn't find me there, he would know where to go. "Leave a note with the time that you left, if you think about it," Khalil had instructed. After gathering my coat and my purse, I scribbled *2:52* on the back of the receipt, which I left on the kitchen table.

As I locked up the apartment behind me, I rested my forehead on the door and cried a little, frightened and heartbroken that I was really having to do this alone.

I caught the attention of an idling taxi driver who was sitting on the hood of his car as I shuffled out of the building in tears, with one hand on my backside and the other on my belly. The driver jumped off his car and ran toward me. He offered me his hand, but I didn't take it, a stickler to religious creed despite the terror I felt. Bowing his head, he ran in front of me to open the back door of the taxi. A contraction seized my belly like a vise as I leaned down to climb into the car. I stood there, my hand gripping the hard metal door frame, until it let up a minute later.

As he put the taxi in gear, the driver offered, "I have three kids at home." He had a thick accent, and there was a distant sadness in the way he said this that made me think that home was somewhere else.

I laughed nervously, anticipating another contraction. I didn't want to be chatting with a stranger; I wanted my husband to be here. I'd never noticed how bad the local roads were until that bumpy and excruciating ride to the hospital, the baby's desire to exit my body making itself known every time the taxi struck a pothole. The driver apologized each time I cried out, but his voice only irritated me further. I didn't want his pity; I just wanted the ride to end.

It wasn't until after the driver dropped me off at the doors of the emergency room and sped away that I realized I had forgotten to pay him.

I looked around, overwhelmed, once inside the buzzing lobby of the hospital. And then I doubled over in pain as another contraction took hold of me. A nurse met me with a wheelchair, and I collapsed into the seat, shutting my eyes against the pain. I felt myself being taken somewhere, and when I opened them again, we were in an elevator. We exited on the fourth floor, and the nurse wheeled me into a room and pulled a clipboard from the wall beside the door and started asking me questions. Did I know how far along I was? Had I received regular prenatal care? When was the last time I felt the baby move? I answered through gritted teeth, feeling as if another boulder was beginning to roll over me: *I can't remember if this is the eighth or ninth month; yes; I don't remember . . .*

Not being able to account for the baby's last movement evoked a look of concern from the nurse. She promptly removed a stethoscope from the wall and asked me to lift up my dress. I stared at the top of her head—a forest of black and gray hairs—as she placed the cold metal disc of the stethoscope against my belly and listened carefully. When she pulled away, she looked satisfied.

Handing me a printed cotton gown to change into, the nurse left me alone in the room. I expected her to return, but the next person to appear was a tall man in a white coat who introduced himself as Dr. Alvarez. He asked me to lie down on the bed so he could check me. I assumed this meant exposing my belly again, but the reality was much worse. He unfolded two foot cradles from the base of the bed and guided my feet into place. He told me to relax and then parted my shaking knees. "You still have your underwear on?" he asked in a tone of surprise, and then he sighed with annoyance as he slipped on a pair of rubber gloves and swiftly removed my panties by pulling down on both sides at the same time. I wanted to throw up. Khalil had been in the room all the previous times I'd been examined. This felt like infidelity, deeply wrong. Turning my head away from the horror of this man seeing me naked without my husband there to protect me, I clenched my eyes shut and gritted my teeth as he thrust his fingers inside me. "You're not ready yet," he announced after a few seconds, and then he stood up and peeled off his gloves and dropped them into the trash on his way out the door.

When the nurse eventually returned, I burst into tears again. "Are you all right, honey?" she asked, rushing to my side.

I shook my head. I wasn't all right. Nothing was right.

"It's normal for first-timers to feel nervous," she told me, placing a gentle hand on my shoulder. "Why don't we get you some medicine to help you calm down?"

She disappeared and returned a few minutes later with another man in a white coat. I was terrified when instructed to lie down again, but the nurse put a mask over my face that was attached to a tube, and after a few breaths, I was no longer a body in that room. I felt the faraway prick of a needle touching flesh, my cloud of thoughts dispersed, and I fell into a deep, confusing slumber. I heard a baby crying and felt the dull weight of an anvil holding me underwater.

When I woke up, I was alone in the room. My wrists hurt and had been rubbed raw, as if they'd been tied to the sides of the bed. My belly felt dull and blubbery, deflated. I panicked, realizing that the baby was no longer inside of me, and screamed for help.

A nurse I'd never seen before rushed in. "Where's my baby?" I cried, terrified that it was dead.

"Lower your voice, my dear. They've got her in the nursery," the older woman said. "They'll bring her back when she's ready."

A mix of relief and sadness washed over me. My baby was alive. My baby was a girl.

THE FIRST TIME I HELD HER, I felt little more than fatigue and a strange and distant curiosity about the bundle in my arms. The nurse instructed me to expose my breast and then positioned the baby so that her mouth suckled my nipple. What ensued was a very targeted and sharp form of torture. I gritted my teeth through the pain as the baby latched and sucked. Resting my head back, I let the tears flow. I was happy to relinquish the baby to the nurse once she was done feeding, so I could go back to sleep.

Khalil woke me when he finally made it to the hospital and found my recovery room. The room had no windows, so I had no idea what time it was, how many hours or days had passed since I'd arrived. "You did it," he said, kissing my forehead. "You amazing woman. I told you that you didn't need me."

Some hazy minutes later, a nurse wheeled in the plastic bassinet containing our baby. Khalil rushed over to see her and then just stood and looked at her for a few minutes, whispering thoughts I couldn't hear as he held on to the side of the bassinet. Finally he reached inside and lifted out our baby, bringing the small bundle to his chest. That image pierced my heart in a way that awoke me from my stupor. We were a family now.

The baby and I stayed at the hospital while Khalil went back and forth to school as usual. The nurses—they were a rotating cast, so many that I lost track of individuals—said we needed to name the baby before we could be discharged. Khalil suggested his mother's name, Zeinab, which I didn't like, but I took his cue and rooted through my family tree for a name that I liked, finally coming up with Amena, after a childless aunt on my father's side whom I'd always adored.

The nurses also said they couldn't release me until I had emptied my bowels, which I'd been afraid to try since giving birth. My whole underside was extremely tender, and each time I sat down on the toilet, I experienced intense pain. Every day the nurses asked whether I had gone yet. It embarrassed me to talk about bodily functions with anyone, let alone near-strangers. "No," I answered sheepishly each time. Finally, on the fourth day, I sat through the pain until the waste passed and was able to give an affirmative answer.

We took a taxi home. This time I wasn't alone. I had the baby in my arms and Khalil by my side in the back seat. I was ravenous by the time we got back to the apartment, but the refrigerator contained little beyond jars of jam and pickles, a stick of butter, and some wilting produce in a drawer. I hobbled into the next room to lie on the couch, while Khalil went after food. It hurt to sit, so I did it only when I had to put the baby to my breasts.

My nipples were raw and cracked by this point and had started to bleed. I worried about Amena consuming traces of blood with my milk, but I was her only source of food, so we had no choice. It annoyed me that Khalil got to continue his normal routine when my life had been so seismically disrupted. This baby was a product of both of us, and yet the responsibility for her care lay fully with me.

One day he came home with a camera that produced instant pictures. We didn't even have a regular camera, so it surprised me that Khalil splurged on such a new model. I'd seen Polaroid ads on television and in magazines and had thought it would be fun to have one of their cameras but assumed we couldn't afford one. When Khalil looked through the viewfinder, he closed his other eye and pointed the lens at Amena, swaddled and sleeping in the crib he had picked up from Goodwill. I startled at the bright burst of the flash and was surprised that it didn't wake Amena. Khalil set down the camera and then stared at the sheet of film the camera had produced, no longer paying attention to the baby. I watched over his shoulder as Amena's image slowly faded into focus, and just like in the ads, my jaw fell open in amazement. Khalil took the picture with him to school the next day, leaving the real baby alone with me again.

I decided to write my parents and inform them of their new kin. I told myself that they didn't have to accept her—us—but secretly hoped she might be the ticket to regaining their love.

I took a picture of Amena with the Polaroid and enclosed it with the letter.

MY FATHER WROTE BACK more than six months later. There had never been a letter in the mail addressed to me before—the mail always bore Khalil's name or that of previous residents. I left the baby napping upstairs when I went down to the lobby to check the mailbox—my one escape each day. On my way back upstairs, I tore the letter open and started reading it.

Habibti Halah,

You cannot imagine how happy this news makes us. Please come home. All is forgiven. I need to hold this baby, flesh of my flesh. Call as soon as you can, and we will make arrangements.

May Allah keep you safe.

Baba

I was afraid to tell Khalil about the letter, and then, when I finally did, right before we went to bed that night, he reacted just how I'd anticipated: "It's a trap. We can't go back home. If we do, your father will have me arrested at the airport or something."

I wanted to tell Khalil he was being ridiculous, but I knew his fears were justified. He still didn't know about the secret phone calls with my father or that my father knew about our relationship, nor did he know that I suspected Hassan might have been arrested because of us.

"How did he find us?" Khalil asked, as if reading my mind.

I told him about the phone calls.

"How could you not tell me this before?"

"You didn't tell me when you were getting in contact with your family."

"That's different."

"Different how?"

"My parents aren't manipulative politicians," Khalil argued loudly, waking the baby in the next room. We'd shifted the living room into the space adjacent to the kitchen and made the room adjoining ours Amena's room. In hindsight, this was a bad idea, as it meant Khalil and I had to pass through her room to get to any other room in the apartment—living room, bathroom, kitchen—and Amena's sleep was easily disturbed.

I shook my head, brushing away Khalil's aspersion. "The fact is that I'm in touch with them now, and they want to meet their granddaughter. We'll go without you if we have to, but I'm taking Amena home to meet her family and to see where she comes from."

"She's an infant!" Khalil argued. "She won't remember any of this!"

At this point Amena was really crying, so I stood to get her because Khalil wasn't going to. It was as if he believed I was the only person in the world who could console her. It was true that I was the only one who could satisfy her hunger, but I still wanted some semblance of a partner in this maddening endeavor.

After a fight there was nowhere to hide from each other except the bathroom, and there was only so long one of us could hole up in there before the other needed to use it. More often than not, I escaped into sleep after we argued.

It seemed like I'd just fallen under when I woke to hear the baby crying again. Khalil was asleep beside me, so some time must have passed, but whatever rest I'd gotten felt negligible. I shuffled next door to the crib in bare feet. It was rare for me to get more than two hours of consecutive sleep these days, which made me want to crawl into a cave and hibernate through the winter. I didn't like being the only lifeline for this helpless, tiny person. One night, after we'd nursed for an hour and she still wasn't sated, popping on and off my wounded breasts and crying like they were dry hoses, I had a vision of filling up the bathtub and holding her under. Another time, when Khalil wasn't there and it was just me and an inconsolable baby for hours, I rocked her violently over my shoulder in front of an open window and thought about dropping her out.

If I'd stayed in Egypt and married whomever my father wanted me to marry, there would have been housekeepers and nursemaids to help with this work. Had it been worth it to follow a flame on a whim to America instead of staying in Egypt and following my pre-scribed course? Probably not, I contemplated sadly. I felt foolish re-calling the naive girl I'd been when I first imagined the future that lay ahead for us in New York. Fate hadn't steered me. I'd brought myself to this fate.

WHEN KHALIL NEXT HAD A DAY OFF, I left Amena with him and went to the call center. It felt strange and decadent to walk around with my arms unencumbered, no baby to hold or nurse. At seven months old, Amena was crawling all around the apart-ment, requiring extra vigilance. Seeing a man exit a bodega across the street with a steaming cup of coffee, I decided that I needed some of that elixir. The coffee was bitter and weak, but I doctored it with milk and sugar and downed the whole cup in the span of two blocks.

By the time I reached the call center, I felt wildly alert. My mind buzzed with possibilities for how to begin the conversation. The prospect of returning to Egypt made me so giddy that I wanted to cry. I marched up to the desk and asked the man behind it for a va-cant booth. I'd brought the jar of change again. My breasts ached as they filled with milk. They'd once turned to bricks in my sleep when Amena skipped a feeding and were so firm and inflated that I had to express some of the milk by hand before Amena could latch on. When I looked down now, I saw a wet spot on my shirt at the latitude of my left nipple and quickly covered my chest with my arms. The man behind the desk acted as if he'd seen nothing and directed me to an empty phone booth. I hurried there.

I stood with my back against the glass door as I dialed, too anx-ious to sit down. When a woman answered on the other end, I asked for my father and announced myself, and then I tapped my foot for the long seconds as I waited.

"Is that you?" he said at last.

"Yes," I said, moved by the tenderness in his voice. "I got your letter. We want to come home."

The wait for his delayed reply felt interminable. Finally: "Good, good. We're waiting for you. Do you need money for a ticket?"

I'd assumed that my father would cover the expense, since I knew Khalil couldn't pay for it. "Yes," I said, though it shamed me to admit it. "Actually," I added, my heart hammering inside my chest, "it would need to be two tickets." My pulse raced for a good while after the words left my mouth. The static in the connection crackled in my ear as the seconds passed.

"I see," my father said at last.

"He's my husband, and my daughter's father," I offered.

"Okay, okay," said my father, his voice so distant and muddled that it almost sounded like he was growling. He gave me the name of a British bank, which I wrote on the back of my hand. He said to check at one of their branches in a few days for the money he would wire.

"We need to know that no harm will come to any of us if we come home, that we'll be free to leave just as we came," I said after he finished delivering his instructions. It terrified me to speak so boldly to my father, and I doubted I would have been able to do it if we were face-to-face.

"Of course," he said, laughing woodenly. "You have my word."

HALAH, 1957

BY THE TIME KHALIL finally managed to take a few days off from school, three months later, another war had broken out between Egypt and Israel, and though that war only lasted six days, Khalil insisted on an indefinite postponement of our visit. It was just after the new year when we finally made the trip. Amena had recently started walking and was exhausting to manage during the long flight. I spent half the time chasing her up and down the narrow aisles, and the other half serving as her bed as she napped, my limbs going numb as I held still for hours-long stretches. Meanwhile, Khalil used the flight as an opportunity to catch up on his sleep, snoozing with his head against the window.

As soon as we started descending into Cairo, Amena transformed into a smiling child, like a metaphor for my heart. I leaned over Khalil to slide up the window shade and look down at the sprawling yellow desert below—a stark contrast from the gray steel-and-stone landscape of New York.

"You look happy," Khalil remarked to my profile as I smiled at the approaching ground.

I ignored him, too distracted by my own thoughts to reply.

Amena clapped as she bounced up and down on my lap.

My father stood waiting on the tarmac when we landed, the only man there in a decorated army uniform and not the uniform of a baggage handler, the only one standing with his arms crossed over his chest while the others ran around working. I saw him out my window as we waited our turn to exit the plane. We were seated toward the back and were among the last to get off. When my eyes met my father's across the distance, he uncrossed his arms and started jogging toward the staircase as we descended. I cradled Amena in one arm and held on to the railing with my free hand, as Khalil clamped onto my shoulder from behind.

When we came face-to-face, my father started crying—big, wet, silent tears. I'd never seen him cry before, and it undid me. Khalil took Amena so I could embrace my father. I wept in his arms as he held me.

As we followed my father into the airport, I noticed that he looked grayer and more hunched in his posture. It was hard to believe that it had been two years since we'd left.

The terminal teemed with military personnel, probably related to the recent war. I noticed Khalil walk stiffly with his eyes on the ground as we moved through the airport. He'd been against Egypt since before the recent conflict began, telling me on several occasions that Nasser should have seen his humiliation coming after his brazen attempt to nationalize the Suez Canal that summer, angering countries around the world when he took control of this major trade pathway. Three months later, Israel invaded with the support of the UK and France, collectively determined to dismantle Nasser's reign over the canal and Egypt. I'd been obsessed with any news

I could find on the conflict. Khalil called Nasser an idiot whenever the topic of the war came up, and when I reminded him that thousands of men had died, he said, "And they will keep dying. This war will never end."

Thanks to my father and his credentials, we bypassed the usual passport control and customs protocols. His status conferred us no advantage in the chaos that was baggage claim, however, a large room filled with people and bags that all looked alike. Baggage handlers rolled in large new carts bursting with luggage and proceeded to deposit the new bags wherever there was space. Khalil handed Amena back to me and left us with my father at the edge of the room, and then entered the fray.

"*Bismillah*, you cannot imagine how happy it makes me to see you," my father said, his tears gone but his eyes now red and puffy. "When you left, I thought I'd lost you forever. God works in mysterious ways . . ."

"I truly am sorry," I told him, "but you have to understand that I felt trapped. Looking back, I can't believe how impulsive I was, honestly. Now I understand why seventeen-year-old girls shouldn't have control over their own destinies," I said as a joke that I didn't really mean.

"Maybe I shouldn't have pushed you so hard," my father offered. "You were young. We had time."

It felt as if we had forged some degree of peace by the time Khalil returned with our luggage ten minutes later, my father catching me up on stories about relatives and others I had known who'd gotten married or died or had children. It was so good to be with him, to be back in Egypt, that it seemed like my heart was going to burst.

Outside the terminal, a crowd of people standing behind a chain-link fence watched all who exited. As I scanned the overwhelming wall of faces, I heard Khalil let out a startled yelp beside me. "Mama!" he yelled in my ear, and then he broke into an awkward jog, carrying our suitcases, one in each hand. When he got to the edge of the fence, he dropped the bags and threw his arms around an older woman who I realized was his mother. Next he hugged the older man standing beside her, Khalil's father. I walked slowly, with my father at my side and Amena in my arms, overwhelmed by the prospect of meeting them.

When we reached them, I watched Khalil's parents recognize us for who we were, their expressions shifting into surprised alertness. Khalil's mother had soft cheeks and a big smile that turned her eyes into little crescents. Khalil's father had a more austere presence. He nodded and smiled only slightly when we were introduced, clasping his hands behind his back and looking at the ground.

I'd assumed that Khalil would come to my parents' house with me and Amena, but he told me in the parking lot that he was going home with his parents instead. We came to my family's car first, parked illegally on the curb with Abu Abdullah behind the wheel, and there we divided up by family of origin, with Khalil and his parents continuing on toward an unknown destination in the depths of the parking lot. My father had replaced his old Bentley with a sleek new Volga. His choice of car always seemed to mimic his political alliance of the moment, the Bentley when Egypt was still occupied by the British, and then briefly an American Ford when it appeared that America was Egypt's ally, and now a Soviet car.

Abu Abdullah climbed out of the car and bowed in my direction five or six times as if I were returning royalty. Blushing, I shook my head and told him, "It's wonderful to see you too," before climbing into the back seat.

When we got to the house, my mother and Reema were waiting there for us, my mother in full makeup and a party dress, and Reema in a purple galabeya and printed headscarf. They both looked festive and happy to see me. Almost immediately and in sync with each other, they turned their attention to Amena. My mother bent down and cooed in her face, while Reema hung a few steps behind and marveled from a distance. I felt a small flash of jealousy, wondering if my mother had ever looked at me with such wonder and admiration. The beam of Reema's love, however, was a force of nature that I recognized from my own childhood.

We settled into the salon, which my grandmother had furnished based on postcards of Versailles. It felt strange to have the salon opened up for my arrival, as if my parents were entertaining outside company, and then realized this was precisely what I'd become—a visitor. Reema disappeared into the kitchen to assemble snacks and drinks, no doubt, and I wished I could follow but knew that my place was with my parents. Wriggling in my lap, Amena started to whine, and I recognized that I was going to have to hide away and feed her soon.

By the time we said our goodnights, I was so tired that I no longer remembered the details of our conversation. Nothing controversial came up. We mostly talked about the baby, and then my parents left Reema to work out the details of my sleeping arrangements. Did I want Amena to stay in my old room with me, or did I prefer her to have her own room, she asked. In the months since she'd been born, I'd never had the option of being fully separated from Amena overnight. The prospect of an uninterrupted night sounded amazing, even if it meant sleeping through Amena's cries. "Let's try to put her in her own room," I said.

Having already prepared for this option, Reema showed us to my grandmother's old room, where Reema and Abu Abdullah had lowered the mattress from the bed to the floor. I imagined what it would be like to live in this house again, with Reema to care for me and help with the baby, and then admonished myself for indulging in such fantasies. I wasn't a kid anymore. I couldn't go following my whims wherever they led me. I was a married woman now. I had obligations.

Reema offered to take Amena from me and put her to bed. The

look of concern on her face made me wonder how exhausted I must look, how overwhelmed. "Get some rest," she urged me. "We'll talk in the morning."

I FELL INTO PERHAPS THE DEEPEST—and what felt like the longest—sleep of my life. When I finally woke up, my breasts were as hard as rocks. There hadn't been a single night since Amena's birth when I hadn't woken with her every few hours. Discounting my engorged breasts, I imagined that this was what a bear must feel like when emerging from hibernation, heavy-limbed and deeply rested, disoriented upon first waking. It took me a few seconds to remember that I was in my childhood room—to recognize the setting. Not in a rush to get out of bed, I lingered there for a while, taking everything in.

The room was enormous compared with our room in Queens. I missed my beautiful old furniture, of a quality I could appreciate only now that all of our furnishings were cheap. Solid carved wooden pieces, a large four-poster bed with a matching dresser, mirror, and nightstand, and plush wool rugs that covered every exposed section of floor and felt much softer beneath my feet than the synthetic ones we had in New York. I even experienced a nostalgic appreciation for the *mashrabiya* that covered my old windows, for they too looked like works of art with their detailed woodwork and the complex, shifting way they let in the light.

I smelled my favorite dish cooking downstairs: fried potatoes. When trying my first French fries in America, I discovered that fried potatoes spanned cultures, but no fries I'd ever tasted were as good as Reema's "chips"—one of the only English words she'd adopted into her vocabulary, along with "commode" (for bathroom) and "Pepsi" (for any sweetened sparkling beverage).

The savory aroma of Reema's chips beckoned me to the kitchen. She stepped back from her squinting inspection of the bubbling oil as I entered the room. "Good morning," she said, with her hands on her hips. There'd been no opportunity to embrace the night before, and I wanted to hug her now, but she looked preoccupied and defensive. There was so much that I wanted to talk to her about, so much I wanted to know. Was she the one who'd discovered me and Khalil together and given us away to my father? What had the mood been like around the house after I ran away? Did anyone still miss me?

"I'm making your favorite dish," Reema announced proudly. To one side of the oven sat a pile of raw potato wedges, and to the other, glistening fried chunks rested on a large plate lined with newsprint. I walked past Reema to the plate of fried potatoes and picked one up. It melted in my mouth, crispy on the outside and still warm and doughy inside. "How are they?" she asked as I chewed. I nodded with my eyebrows raised, affirming their perfection, and then took another one.

"I've missed you," I said when my mouth was nearly empty.

She narrowed her eyes and looked at me skeptically. "Did you?"

"Of course," I said, resisting the urge to take another potato, to fill my mouth again so I wouldn't have to explain myself.

"It was a dark time after you left," she said, shaking her head softly. "We mourned you as if you were dead. I've never seen your father so upset. Your parents lost their only child, and you know that I've always seen you as one of my own. It was incredibly hard for all of us."

"Did you know about Khalil?" I asked. "Did you tell my father about us?"

Reema turned her head. The cheek she offered me flushed a warmer shade of brown. "I was in my room and heard you in the hallway talking to him once," she admitted. She turned to face me again, her eyes wet with tears. "We had no idea what had happened to you. The police were alerted. They dredged a section of the Nile looking for your body! Your father came to me and asked if I had any suspicions. I couldn't lie to him," Reema explained with a wavering voice. "I told him I'd heard you two talking outside the door one night and that the conversation was quite . . . disturbing." Recalling how forward I'd been with Khalil during our courtship, I was now the one to blush. "I'll never forget the look on your father's face when I told him this, a terrible mix of sadness and rage. I worried that I'd said the wrong thing, and honestly I thought he might hit me in that moment, but then he told me that the same young man had just left for America." Reema looked up at the ceiling, tears streaming down her face. "When you finally called and confirmed that you'd run away with him, your father gave me a raise, the first I'd ever gotten from them. Maybe it's just a coincidence," she suggested, shrugging, "but I'm grateful for the money. If it wasn't for your parents, I wouldn't have anything."

I leaned back against the counter, overwhelmed by the flood of information. It wasn't clear if Reema was asking for forgiveness or just explaining what had happened. I felt numb and, for a few moments, couldn't think of anything to say. At last something came to mind: "What you did might have gotten Khalil's brother arrested."

Reema looked stricken. "I know nothing about this. What brother?"

I looked around to make sure no one was coming down the hallway and then said, in a lower voice, "His name is Hassan. He was arrested shortly after I left with Khalil, apparently picked up by the police for no apparent reason. He's spent the past two years in jail, possibly on bogus charges trumped up by my father as a way to get back at me and Khalil."

"*Bismillah al-rahman, al-rahim*," Reema said, which struck me as both appropriate and too general, something she said whenever she was truly impressed or fearful. "I swear on my father's grave that this is the first I'm hearing of this brother. I thought by telling your father we could find you and bring you home."

I bit my lips together and closed my eyes, imagining this scenario. How easily she assumed my autonomy could be overridden. My feelings for her shifted abruptly between love and anger.

"I should go check on the baby," I said. My breasts were starting to leak, well-timed for once, giving me an excuse to exit. Khalil had been trying to encourage me to wean our daughter, but nursing was still the surest way to calm her down when she was upset, and as long as she sought out my milk, I wasn't going to turn her down.

"I just put her down an hour ago," Reema said, turning to drop another handful of potatoes into the sputtering, bubbling oil. "I fed her a bowl of my famous *molokhia*, and she went right to sleep."

MY FATHER OPTED TO STAY HOME instead of going to work for the first few days of my visit. "It's misery around the office lately, everyone so down about how the war effort is going," he explained. "And we're the lucky ones, the old guys with the high blood pressure and bad knees and back problems, the ones who don't have to fight."

"Do you think we'll fight to take back the Sinai?" I asked him.

"We?" he laughed. I didn't know what was funny, the possibility of Egypt going back to war again so soon, or the idea that I still lay claim to Egypt.

We were sitting in my father's office, playing a game of backgammon. When it was my turn, I rolled double twos. "Do you still feel secure in your position?" I asked him with my eyes on the board, moving a pair of my chips two spaces ahead.

He shrugged and rolled the dice around in his cup. "I'm used to the upheaval at this point. I just try to avoid making strong alliances and keep a low profile."

I preferred to use my hands to roll the dice, rather than the cups that came with the backgammon set. There was something deeply satisfying about the feeling of two dice clanking around between my palms. I shook my hands together for a few seconds and rolled a five and a six. This left two of my solitary pieces exposed but put them each closer to home; I hoped that my father wouldn't roll numbers that would allow him to capture my isolated chips.

"Can I ask you a question?" I piped up nervously.

My father looked at me and held his cup in midair. "It depends on what kind of question."

I didn't laugh, knowing he didn't entirely mean this as a joke. "It's about Hassan, Khalil's brother."

"Yes, you've asked me about him before."

"You didn't really give me an answer then."

My father's face turned red. "Do you know how many people get arrested in this country every day? You expect me to keep track of some random person I've never met? The brother of the man who took you away from me, no less?"

I swallowed down a lump of fear. "Did you order his arrest?"

My father darted his eyes to the side, confirming what I already suspected. "It's my job to identify people who might be a threat to the government. You're talking about something that happened two years ago." The specificity of this felt like another gut punch, further affirmation of his participation. "Like I said, it's been a very tumultuous few years."

I returned my attention to the game, in a mild state of shock. It took me a few minutes to recover and think of what to say next, and in that time I lost my lead, my father capturing two of my pieces. "Would you look into his case?" I asked finally. "You hear about a lot of men who are incarcerated unjustly, who sit in prison for years without ever having a trial, men who just disappear into the system."

My father laughed bitterly. "You sound like an American. Don't let them brainwash you. Everything that we do is for the good of the people. If you choose to believe otherwise, then you're a traitor to this country."

I leaned back in my chair, silenced. Looking at the backgammon board, I couldn't remember whose turn it was and lost all interest in the game. After a minute my father got up to go to the bathroom, and I snuck out while he was gone. Overwhelmed by a sudden desire to hold my baby, I found her playing with Reema out on the back patio, Amena's high-pitched laughter drawing me to them. Amena reached for me as I approached, thawing the icy feeling in my chest. She was my family now. Amena and Khalil.

MY MOTHER OFFERED TO TAKE ME to her *coiffeur* to get our hair done together. "It looks like it's been a while since you've had yours cut," she observed. On our way to the salon, sitting in the back seat together as Abu Abdullah drove, my mother reminded me of her stylist's list of celebrity clients, including the actress Hind Rostom. Ahmed was now in his fifties and had gained quite a bit of weight around the middle since the last time I had seen him. He still chain-smoked cigarettes as he cut and styled, one always slowly burning between his lips. He struck me as gay, but the only homosexuals I knew were caricatures in television shows, so I was no great judge.

I had to admit that I liked what I saw in the mirror once Ahmed was done with me.

"Now, that's better," my mother concurred.

I left the salon feeling fresh and attractive, and also unusually close to my mother. Abu Abdullah was waiting for us when we were done, having sat in the parked car outside the salon during the hours we were inside. He got out to open the back door for us, keeping his gaze down and wearing a permanent deferential smile. I felt selfish for never having expressed any curiosity about him; I knew next to nothing about him, though I'd known him for most of my life.

My mother retreated to her room that afternoon to watch television; I heard the operatic murmurings of soap opera fights and passionate declarations bleeding through the wall between our rooms. After changing clothes, I went to look for Amena and Reema, whom I found napping on the mattress on the floor of the room where Amena was staying. They made a funny pair, Reema huge next to

Amena, both lying on their backs with their faces turned in opposite directions. It was lovely to see them together, two of the people I loved most in the world, and it was heartbreaking to think of how this bond would be short-lived, knowing we were going back to New York soon and had no immediate plans to return to Egypt.

ON OUR THIRD DAY IN CAIRO, I planned to take Amena to pay Khalil's parents a visit. Khalil would pick us up at my parents' house, which I knew he was nervous about, fearing an encounter with my father. I was also scared of his parents, though I hadn't shared that with him.

I told Khalil to pick us up at noon, hoping that my father would be out of the house since he usually prayed at the mosque at noon on Fridays. My father left before the call to prayer, just as I'd hoped, and Khalil also arrived on cue, much to my relief.

He looked visibly nervous when I answered the door, darting his gaze around and behind me. "Is he home?" he asked with agitation.

"You're safe," I told him, holding open my arms for him to embrace me. He stepped forward and grabbed my waist, pulling me in close. I'd missed him these last few days.

We left the house expediently, ahead of my father's return. Khalil hailed a taxi, and we all climbed in the back together. Amena crawled back and forth between our laps, clearly excited to see her father but never settling with him for very long.

Khalil's parents lived in Mohandessin, just across the river, though it felt like a different city. Mohandessin was bustling and dense compared to quaint and lush Zamalek. We entered a world of traffic in Mohandessin, a mess of cars and buses and trucks all crowded together on wide, multilane roads. Most of the buildings we passed featured retail on their ground floors, and the sidewalks were full of pedestrians.

"Here," Khalil said, leaning toward the front and directing our driver to pull over on the busy street.

We found ourselves in front of a twelve-story building made of unadorned brick. The vestibule was open to the street, as if the building weren't yet finished. Old newspaper and other trash littered the exposed space, and the floor and walls were dark with grime. I held Amena tightly against me as Khalil led us to a metal stairwell and then up to the third floor.

I stood a few steps behind Khalil as he knocked on the door to his parents' apartment. Between the car and now, Amena had fallen asleep on my shoulder, overdue for her afternoon nap. Khalil's father answered. When he saw us, he nodded demurely and said, "The day is brightened by your arrival, *Alhamdulillah*," and then he bowed his head.

We followed him into the apartment, entering a crowded foyer. Several pairs of shoes and house slippers lined the wall. I wondered if any of them belonged to Hassan. Next to the shoes, a coat rack overflowed with coats and bags. We continued down a narrow hallway, past two shut doors, to a small sitting room. The furniture was dated and worn: a pistachio-green velvet couch that looked as if it had been around since the thirties, an old wooden coffee table, and a pair of mismatched armchairs with sunken seat cushions.

My father-in-law invited us to sit. Wondering where his wife was, I realized that the sounds coming from the kitchen next door were probably her. I sat down at the edge of the couch, setting off a brief symphony of screeches from the springs below. Khalil sat beside me and held his hands out for Amena, whom I gladly handed off, my arm going numb. I felt self-conscious in the nice silk dress I'd chosen to wear, an old favorite I'd rediscovered in my closet. It seemed too fancy, as if I were trying to show off. The soft fabric clung to my damp back.

At last my mother-in-law appeared, carrying a tray piled with snacks and four full cups of water. I jumped to my feet and offered to help, but she clicked her tongue and shuffled past me, setting the tray down on the coffee table on top of an open newspaper. Once her hands were free, she turned around and cradled my face, her palms warm against my cheeks. The sudden gesture brought tears to my eyes.

"You're an angel," she said to me. "Look at you."

I swallowed hard. "God bless you," I responded meekly.

She let go of my face and shook her head in continued disbelief. We sat down in our respective seats. We sat close enough to one another that everyone could lean in and reach the food on the coffee table: a plate of sliced cheese, a plate of blood-red *basturma*, a basket full of quartered pita bread, a jar of homemade pickled eggplant, and a plate of glistening tomato slices. I appreciated the casual nature of it all, compared with the formality of gatherings at my parents' house. We each reached for what we wanted, all of it delicious. Now that my stomach was no longer turning with anxiety about meeting with my in-laws, I was ravenous.

At some point in the conversation, Khalil's father mentioned Hassan. "Poor boy was so jealous when he heard that his younger brother had found someone to marry. He didn't even have a chance to look for a wife before the thugs took him away."

I froze in place, the last few bites of a mini sandwich pinched between my fingers, a concoction of pita and cheese and pickled eggplant. Khalil turned to look at me. "We have approval to visit tomorrow," he explained. For a moment I thought "we" included me, and my heart started beating faster. Then I realized that I wasn't part of the equation, and my nervousness turned to disappointment.

"Where is he?" I asked meekly, my voice barely above a whisper.

"Abu Zaabal prison," Khalil's father answered, flashing me a sidelong glance. I'd heard of the prison, located in an industrial suburb north of Cairo known for its military arsenals and chemical plants in addition to its massive prison complex. It was the prison where a few of my father's old associates—men I used to call "uncle"—were rumored to have gone after disappearing from our lives, their names from my father's vocabulary.

"I'm so sorry," I said, my eyes filling with tears.

"He's lost at least fifteen kilos," Khalil's mother lamented, shaking her head. "Not to mention the bruises," she added, her voice breaking. "There's always guards standing nearby, so he can never tell us anything. I can only imagine . . ." she trailed off, her face creased with worry and sadness.

My chest tightened as I listened, as if in the grip of an invisible vise. By the time she finished speaking, I could hardly breathe. I must have looked a fright, because suddenly Khalil's mother was trying to comfort *me*: "Oh, *habibti*, I didn't mean to upset you. We shouldn't bother you with this terrible family business." I sank back into the couch, my spine growing soft and round. Her apology made me feel even worse—doubly guilty.

Khalil took Amena and me back to my parents' house via taxi around dusk. It was a quiet ride, with Amena asleep in my sore arms in the back seat and Khalil silently watching the city flash by out his window, his arms crossed over his chest. When we arrived at my parents', Khalil asked if it was okay if he didn't come inside. "I'm too tired to put up a good fight if your father goes after me," he joked. I told him it was fine for him to leave.

I COULDN'T STOP THINKING about Hassan. The next time I saw my husband, I plied him with questions about his visit to the prison.

"Why are you so concerned about my brother all of a sudden?" he asked.

"I'm not," I argued, shaking my head. "It's just, you hear about the conditions at these prisons . . ."

Khalil rolled his eyes and sighed with bemusement. "I guess we should be grateful that he's still alive. My parents' neighbors lost their son. He was captured in a raid at Al-Azhar University, and two weeks later his father received a notice to come collect his body from the morgue."

"That's terrible," I muttered, raising a hand to my throat.

"I used to play ball with Mahmoud in the streets," Khalil recalled. "He wasn't any good at running with the ball, but he was a natural goalie. He didn't have to go to war like I did. Went on to university instead and then to Al-Azhar to get a doctorate in medieval Arabic literature. He was less concerned with politics than anyone I've ever known. Apparently they were sweeping the campus to gather up as many Muslim radicals as they could. Poor Mahmoud was just in the wrong place at the wrong time."

The amount of tragedy there was in the world overwhelmed me. I'd done nothing to deserve my good fortune, and yet I'd had the audacity to feel sorry for myself on many an occasion. I felt like a spoiled child in the face of true suffering.

"Don't cry," Khalil said, wiping tears from the corners of my eyes. "Your father will think I've said something to upset you, and it's not like he doesn't already have enough to hold against me."

We were seated in the salon, awaiting my father's return from the office. My mother had apparently decided to wait until my father got home before joining us. Khalil had arrived fifteen minutes ahead of the time we'd set, and now my father was thirty minutes late.

Khalil had waited until his final day in Egypt to call upon my parents. He would be returning to New York the next day. By the time my father finally arrived—nearly an hour later—Khalil and I had moved beyond the topic of state incarcerations and were talking about how cute we thought our daughter was.

My father didn't apologize for being late. He greeted Khalil by name and brusquely shook his hand, and then he leaned in to kiss my cheek, calling me *habibti*. My mother joined us a few minutes later. She hadn't mentioned my husband or my marriage in the week that I'd been home, and it was clear from her avoidance that she wasn't interested in learning more about either.

When we sat back down, I noticed Khalil's knee bouncing in my peripheral vision. The reverberations of this tic shook the couch we shared and, consequently, me. "Well, if it isn't the happy family," my father said with discernable disdain. He leaned back in his chair, on the other side of the inordinately large brass-and-glass coffee table that separated us, his knees spread out like wings.

Khalil looked down at his lap as though he had nothing to say. I wanted to smack him.

"You have the nerve to steal my daughter away from me, and now you don't even have the courage to look me in the eye, boy?" my father asked, leaning forward.

Khalil looked up, his spine going as straight as a lightning rod. I moved my gaze back and forth between my father and my husband, dreading whatever was to come. "I beg your forgiveness, sir," Khalil began, and hearing those words, I softened my shoulders. "I didn't mean to disrespect you. I thought I was saving Halah." He glanced at me. "When I met her, she sounded so desperate to escape, I worried she was going to run away by herself and get hurt or worse." Khalil kept his eyes fixed on my father as he said this. It was haunting to hear his account, a perspective he'd never shared with me before.

My father sucked his bottom lip into his mouth as he considered this. After a few moments, it rolled back out, glistening with saliva. "So you want me to think of you as a hero, then?"

Khalil shook his head. "No, of course not," he protested. "I was just trying to . . . trying to . . ." It pleased me somewhat to watch him flail, searching for the right words. I leaned away from him, resting on the armrest on the opposite side. "Explain myself," he finally spat out.

"Well, don't bother," my father said, waving his hand and looking away. "I don't want to hear your excuses."

It felt like the gathering was over, though Reema hadn't even brought out refreshments yet. Khalil stood, signaling his intention to leave. I got to my feet and followed him out of the room. Both of my parents remained seated.

I had to walk quickly to keep up with Khalil. "Wait," I called after him once we were outside. "I didn't think he would be like that," I whispered when Khalil turned around. "I'm so sorry."

Khalil shrugged, his eyes growing wet and red. "I have to go," he said. I'd been looking forward to having a few weeks in Cairo without him. Now I felt guilty for looking forward to his departure and gave him a dry kiss on the lips.

"Thank you," he said, looking surprised. In New York I wouldn't even hold his hand in public, and I blushed with embarrassment whenever we came across other couples openly displaying affection.

"I love you," I told him, as if saying it could reinforce the feeling in myself.

"I love *you*," he said, even more emphatically.

AFTER KHALIL LEFT THE COUNTRY, I got the idea to visit his brother at the prison. Without a letter of permission, I knew I would have to invoke my father's power somehow. He'd gone back to work, and while he was out, I snuck into his office like the old days. Reema was attending to an overly tired and whiny Amena, whose cries I could hear overhead, and my mother was watching television in her room, so I knew I was safe.

Right away, in the top drawer of my father's desk, I found what I needed, his military identification card. My Egyptian ID listed him as my father, making cross-identification easy.

It would take me at least an hour each way to get to the prison by cab, so I invented an excuse for being gone all day, telling Reema that I was going to visit an old friend from school who lived in the country and asking if she could watch Amena. "She's a nightmare on long car rides," I said, which was a lie (usually they lulled her to sleep).

"Of course," Reema said, wiping her hands on her galabeya and tracing big wet spots across her thighs. "I'd drop anything for that sweet little girl. Even if it means suffering a scolding from your father if his supper is late."

I didn't laugh the way she did, instead grimacing at her reference to my father's authoritarianism. "Thank you," I said, and went to get ready. Upstairs I put on makeup and then wiped off the lipstick,

admonishing myself in the mirror. What was I doing? I changed
clothes three times, finally settling on a high-necked sweater and a
skirt that reached my ankles, topped with a long wool coat that was
too heavy for the weather. Sweat ran down the sides of my body,
underneath my sweater, as I rode in the back seat of the taxi, refus-
ing to take off my coat.

As we exited city limits, I felt a flash of panic. All signs of civilization dropped away, replaced by sandy, rolling hills. Ours was
among the only cars on the road, save for the occasional vehicle
passing in the opposite direction. This suddenly seemed like a very
dangerous idea, and for what? I needed to face what I had done, I
reminded myself, and seek forgiveness.

After a while the driver turned on the radio. The fuzzy sounds
of a man reading the Quran swelled to fill the car. My shoulders relaxed, and I settled into a lull, watching the endless filmstrip of desert out my window.

And then there were suddenly buildings on the horizon. They
looked like big stone blocks in the distance. Even from far away, it
looked like what it was: a prison complex.

"Do you want me to wait here?" the driver asked, idling in front
of a gate guarded by a pair of armed men.

His concern for me was touching. "Would you?" I asked, realizing as I looked around that there were no other taxis in sight, and
without him I might not be able to easily get home. "I'm not sure
how long this will take," I told him truthfully.

He shrugged and gave me a bashful smile. "This is Egypt. Nothing ever moves quickly."

I approached one of the armed guards and showed him my father's identification card. He looked puzzled, so I explained that I
was the general's daughter and was there to visit a prisoner. The
guard looked to his partner across the way, who wasn't paying attention, and then told me to follow him inside.

He unlocked the gate and pulled it open with effort. It was more than three meters high, like the entry to a giant's home. My body felt heavy, weighed down by a sudden resistance, but at this point it felt as if I had no choice but to proceed.

I followed the broad-shouldered guard to a room filled with more uniformed men. Not a woman in sight. This struck me as another one of those wild ideas too impulsively acted upon, like deciding that Khalil and I were destined to be together because our lives collided on a rooftop.

My guide brought me to a desk and explained to the soldier sitting behind it whose daughter I was. I wondered whether they knew my father or if it was simply his title that garnered respect. "She wants to visit one of the prisoners," he elaborated to his peer.

The soldier behind the desk asked the name of the person I was there to visit. "Hassan Seif," I said. His eyes betrayed no glimmer of recognition. He stood up and retrieved a cumbersome ledger from the shelf behind his desk and opened it up to the middle. Rows of names, handwritten in a mix of blue and black ink, filled the visible pages. A few names jumped out at me—the ones that were most legible upside down. They all began with the letter *T*—*Tantawi, Tarhouni, Tawil*. He'd gone too far in the book, past *Seif*. He flipped back a block of pages and into the territory of Hassan's—and my husband's—last name.

It overwhelmed me to think of how many names were recorded in the book, how many men were imprisoned here. At last finding Hassan's name, the soldier wrote down his cell number on a scrap of paper and closed the ledger with a thud.

"What is the reason for your visit?" the soldier asked, writing something down into another book.

I took a step back, caught off guard by his question. I conjured something impulsively: "He's my cousin. I'm here to deliver news of his mother's death."

The soldier considered this for a moment and then asked, "Why didn't the general come himself?"

I didn't know how to respond. If I were a man, he likely wouldn't have felt at liberty to ask this. "The general is not well," I said, attempting cool confidence.

"May God bring him a swift recovery," the soldier said, scribbling something else in his notebook. "Take her to the east wing," he told an associate nearby. "Her prisoner is in 118."

I hugged my chest tightly as I followed my new escort. He led us down a corridor and then out to a partially exposed hallway that was covered with what looked like chicken wire. The same material filled the gap between the top of the wall and the wooden armature of the ceiling. It felt as if I was in a long, narrow cage. At last we came to what I concluded was our destination. We'd reached the end of the corridor, where another civilian, an older man, stood talking to a prisoner through the fencing. There were several stations delineated on the visitors' side, with metal railings separating makeshift spaces.

"Wait here," my escort instructed. "Your man should be here soon."

His words made me uncomfortable, the insinuation that Hassan belonged to me.

Another armed soldier guarded this room from the far corner. He watched me warily, unsettling me further. I waited with my back against the wall, studying the prison through the wire-covered window. It was monolithic, a giant block of concrete surrounded by a big concrete wall, on the other side of which I stood. I could see other portions of the wall in the distance, topped off with rusty, barbed poufs of wire, certain to impale anyone who tried to escape.

I tried not to listen to the conversation between the father and his son as I waited, but it was impossible not to take it in. The father had hired a new lawyer and was feeling very hopeful about his son's case, while it was evident that the son had lost all hope and wasn't doing well. Then I heard footsteps approaching on the gravelly ground, and I approached the wall to see if it was Hassan. Positioning myself between a pair of metal railings, I pressed my forehead against the fence to get a better look at the approaching men. One was a guard, identical to all the rest. It was the other who held my attention, tall with an easy, loping gait, as if he'd trod this path many times before. He looked nothing like Khalil, long where Khalil was stout, angular where Khalil had soft edges. He looked over and caught my gaze, and I stepped back from the fence.

A few moments later, he was standing in front of me. He gave me a quizzical, somewhat amused look and asked, "Do I know you?"

"No," I said, swallowing. My hands were shaking. "You're Hassan, yes?" I waited for him to confirm, with a slow, uncertain nod. "I'm married to your brother. My name is Halah."

With this, Hassan's eyes widened by several degrees, and he peered at me with such keen interest that my heart felt as if it tripled in size and my chest ached from the pressure. He had high cheekbones and thin, triangular lips, which I felt a strong impulse to kiss.

"I've come to apologize," I told him, my heart racing.

"For what?" he said, extending his fingers through the bars as if trying to reach for me.

I moved closer, until the toes of my shoes met the bottom of the wall. "I believe I'm the reason that you're here," I admitted, my voice small and strained. "My father might have had you imprisoned to get back at me and Khalil for running away together."

Hassan's expression moved through a full change of seasons, from warm to icy and then thawing out again. "I don't believe it," he said, curling his fingers around the wiring that separated us. I didn't know whether to press or be taken aback. "My brother finds love, and I'm the one who suffers?"

"I'm so sorry," I said, my voice wavering, feeling a quake in my chest.

"I thought it was because I was cavorting with revolutionaries," he said, looking past me, as if into his own history.

My spirits lifted at this, the suggestion that there might be other reasons he was in jail.

"Maybe you saved my life," Hassan speculated. "If I wasn't here, I'd be serving my time in the military and probably be lying dead in the Sinai somewhere." He leaned toward me until our faces were too close, a double layer of chicken wire narrowly separating us from sin.

"I feel terrible," I admitted. "I've asked my father to intervene, but he's no use."

Hassan's face cycled through more changes as he listened to me. From surprised to confused to admiring. "You did that for me?" he asked when I finished explaining.

"Of course," I said. "I've felt responsible."

He smiled. "God bless you."

Our fingers touched, and it was then that I realized mine were wrapped around the fence next to our faces and our pinkies were threaded through the same hole.

"You're a good woman," Hassan added quietly. "Thank you for trying to help me." He moved his hand down and held on to mine through the fence, his fingertips clasping the back of my hand. My impulse was to pull away, but I couldn't move. I didn't feel like a good woman, quite the opposite. I'd taken one wrong turn after another and ended up here.

"I need to go," I finally managed, my mouth as dry as the desert surrounding us.

Hassan withdrew his hands, bringing them down to his sides. He looked down, a half nod. "Your visit has brought me light," he said, and though these were common parting words, I took them to heart and felt warmed inside.

As I started to step away, I saw the guard on the other side of the wall move forward and grab Hassan roughly. Hassan tried to shake him off, but then in a twitch of muscle, he turned compliant and walked ahead of the guard, looking back twice to see if I was still there.

Outside the prison gate, I found my taxi waiting and was so glad we'd made this arrangement. "*Insha'Allah*, you had a good visit with your relative," the driver said as I slipped into the back seat.

I nodded, suddenly overcome with emotion and trying to hold

back tears. As we started to drive away, the call to prayer crackled from a tower inside the prison complex, amplified and tinny: *"Allahu Akbar, Allahu Akbar,"* the muezzin sang, drawing out each syllable like sticky confection. As a child, I'd believed that the call to prayer was the voice of God and that the sky itself carried his voice down to us. When Reema told me that it was just a mortal man singing the call to prayer—and a different man at every mosque—it made me question everything that I'd believed were signs of the divine, and the world lost a little of its luster.

PART TWO

\\

KHALIL, 1967

"MAMA'S GONE," AMENA CHIRPED at the other end of the line, her voice high-pitched and choppy.

It was the middle of the night in New York, maybe slouching toward morning, but there was no sign of the sun yet. Khalil was on his own for a few weeks while his wife and daughter spent half the summer in Egypt without him again. Every year the two of them traveled there, usually without Khalil. He'd join them every third trip, largely so his parents wouldn't feel neglected. He had little love left for Egypt, and every time he went back, he was reminded of how lucky he was to live in America. Halah and Amena had been in Egypt for two weeks, and it was never a good thing to get a call in the middle of the night.

"Where did she go?" Khalil asked groggily, his heart racing, leagues ahead of his brain in grasping the urgency of the situation.

"I don't know!" Amena said in the whiny tone that always irritated him.

"It's okay," Khalil told her, mostly to calm her down.

"*Sitto* called the police," Amena informed him.

Khalil leaned against the wall in the hallway with the telephone receiver cradled between his shoulder and his ear. He finally pulled back his sleeve and checked the time: *4:45*. Late morning in Cairo, he realized.

"She probably just got carried away with an old friend and spent the night," he told his daughter. "I'm sure she'll be home any minute now." Even as he said this, Khalil doubted the veracity of his words. When had Halah ever gotten carried away with a friend and unexpectedly spent a night away?

"But she always comes home," Amena argued on the other end, her urgent ten-year-old voice pushing through the static.

"Is your grandmother there?" Khalil asked.

"She's right here," Amena said, pulling the receiver away before completing her thought, her voice growing fainter.

Khalil braced himself to talk to his mother-in-law. Twelve years of marriage to Halah, and her parents had never accepted him. Since he and Halah and Amena first visited as a family in 1957, Halah's parents had shown no inclination to forgive Khalil and embrace him as a son-in-law. They'd reflected the same icy disposition when he saw them in 1961 and 1964. Khalil gave up on the idea of ever being invited to dinner at their house and settled into a peaceful coexistence with the general and his wife that depended on Khalil keeping his distance and relinquishing his wife and daughter to them whenever they were in Egypt. The general had passed away earlier that summer, and in her grief Halah had made it clear that she resented Khalil's lack of effort to make peace with her father.

"Hello?" his mother-in-law said now, as if she didn't know who was on the other end, as if she hadn't been the one to help Amena place the call to him.

"Yes, *ya fendim*," Khalil answered politely. "Please tell me what you know about Halah. How long has she been missing?"

His mother-in-law took a while to answer, but it may have just been the delay in the transmission. She explained that Halah had left the afternoon before. "I didn't talk to her before she left. The maid said she was going to see a friend."

This changed the equation for Khalil, knowing she'd been gone a full twenty-four hours. He thought ahead to the shifts he would have to cancel as he distractedly packed a bag. Once it was dawn in New York, he called his mother-in-law again, who reported that there was no change in the situation, then he called the hospital to say he needed to take an emergency leave, and then took a taxi to JFK.

When Khalil arrived at his in-laws' house more than twelve hours later, Halah was still missing. It had now been almost two days since she was last seen.

Khalil was up all night pacing the dark hallways of his wife's old home, which he would always think of as the general's house. He imagined Halah's dead body lying in a ditch. He pictured her getting kidnapped, attacked in an alley, beaten, raped. Interspersed with these terrible imaginings, he remembered his first impressions of the general's house, a welcome distraction from worrying about Halah. He recalled the awe he felt at being a guest here when he was twenty-two and first invited to a gathering at the home. At the beginning they got together under the pretense of remembering their fallen comrades, but as time went on, the focus of their conversations shifted to the need to liberate Egypt from its oppressors. After the revolution, the general swiftly ascended within the ranks of the new military-backed government. As the general became increasingly important, Khalil took greater pride in his relationship with the older man, never missing an invitation to his home. And then one day Khalil met Halah, and that gave whole new meaning to his visits.

By the time he met Halah, Khalil had become deeply disenchanted with politics and the general himself. It started when Khalil and other guards of his station began discussing the higher-ups' unreal salaries and the seemingly endless perks that came with being a part of leadership—shorter hours, private cars, air travel to various destinations, while the underlings like Khalil traveled in miserable caravans over rocky roads. The big turning point for Khalil was Gamal Abdel Nasser's infamous rally in Alexandria in October of 1954. As a new member of Nasser's private security detail, a job arranged through General Ibrahim, Khalil had been working for the prime minister for only a few weeks at that point.

The square filled up early, hours before Nasser was supposed to speak. Soon the crowd spilled beyond the edges of the park and into the streets, diverting traffic. Men and women mixed together at these rallies in a way Khalil rarely saw outside of this context, the sexes segregated in school, at work, and at the mosque. This played out even at social gatherings, where the men generally congregated in the living room and the women collected in the kitchen. Whenever he saw a young woman, Khalil thought of Halah, whom he'd met the year prior but hadn't seen in months. He thought of her constantly, which sometimes felt like an exercise in breaking his own heart. He knew that the general would never accept him as a potential suitor for his daughter, no matter how much he pretended they were peers when they drank together. The general was ultimately a rich man and Khalil a poor one. Khalil lived in fear of getting caught when he went snooping around the general's house looking for Halah, and yet he felt a gravitational pull toward her that he couldn't resist. For several months now, he'd failed to find her when he went up to look for her on the roof, where they'd had their previous encounters. Khalil was tempted to ask the general about her, but he knew that would reveal too much. The general rarely talked about his wife and daughter, to Khalil's disappointment. At the same time, Khalil dreaded the day when the general would announce that his daughter was getting married.

"Gamal! Gamal! Gamal! Gamal!" the crowd in the square started chanting when it was almost time for Nasser to arrive. The first few times Khalil heard this refrain, it had surprised him, the intimate familiarity of calling the great man by his first name. To Khalil, he was Lieutenant Colonel Gamal Abdel Nasser, or Lieutenant Colonel Nasser for short. And yet there was something charming about the casualness of the way the masses embraced him, as if Nasser were a movie star or famous singer. He had that air about him, handsome and clean-cut and charming, forever sporting his trademark dark moustache. There'd been a sharp uptick in the number of men wearing moustaches since Nasser started to capture the attention of the nation. It was hard to walk around Cairo these days without noticing the honeyed scent of moustache wax in the air. Khalil himself hadn't given in to the trend, abhorring the look of stubble on his face, the way it reminded him of his grizzly days on the battlefield.

Khalil picked up on the sound of approaching helicopters before they were visible—the war had trained him to look for threats coming from the sky. Today it wasn't the enemy approaching but the man of the hour, the person they were all waiting for. When the helicopters were almost overhead, people in the crowd began to notice them and cheer. It was a long prelude to the main act. Twenty minutes later, a line of black sedans and police cars approached, sirens blaring. The cars pulled up alongside the park, and the police got out first, using whistles and raised clubs to coax all those in the vicinity to back away. Once they'd created a bubble of protection from the crowd, the party leaders climbed out of the vehicles. A violent hush settled over the crowd as Nasser emerged from the middle car.

And then: "Gamal! Gamal! Gamal!" Louder than ever.

The lieutenant colonel smiled and waved, looking from one side to the other. Allure radiated from him like heat from the sun. A few civilians tried to rush at Nasser and toppled a section of the fence. Snapping to attention, Khalil raised his weapon and pointed it at them. His rifle skills were just as sharp now as they had been on the battlefield six years ago, which he found unsettling, as if he were consigned to be a soldier forever.

"Get back!" he yelled, his voice and body trembling, holding his rifle at the ready until the men obeyed. Lowering his weapon, Khalil took a deep breath and caught a whiff of roasted chickpeas, which had been his favorite treat as a child. He would save up his piastres and milliemes to spend at the local street vendor whenever he had enough money, always making sure to finish his snack before going home, afraid Hassan would force him to share.

Nasser and his entourage finally ascended the stage. Nasser approached the podium with slow, measured steps, waving at the crowd as they cried and screamed and chanted his name.

"You!" he said, leaning into the microphone. His booming voice fell like a wave over the crowd. "Alexandria's noble citizens . . ."

Their screams and cries grew louder still. They were utterly in his thrall.

"As we stand here today and celebrate our liberation," Nasser continued, "we must remember that the struggle is not over." He was always quick to arrive at this point. "I have been a conspirator for so long that I distrust those around me," he said, careful not to defame the current president in public. There were rumors circulating that Naguib was forming alliances with the Muslim Brotherhood and harbored dictatorial aims.

"I don't want you shouting *Gamal*!" Nasser shouted, suddenly turning angry. "We need to be serious if we're going to build a country based on strong principles!"

Khalil was unusually riveted by the day's proceedings. He'd never seen Nasser snap at the audience like this before and felt tension in the crowd behind him, like the buzz of an electrical force field. Khalil's jaw ached, and he realized he was clenching his teeth.

Just then, a shot fired out. Khalil spun around, searching for the source, frantically scanning the massive crowd. *Pop! pop! pop! pop! pop! pop! pop!* Several more bullets fired off in close succession. There was a scramble, and Khalil could see only what was immediately in front of him—bodies flashing by. Screams coming from all directions, people collapsing on the ground near his feet. Then Khalil was the only one in his vicinity standing, everyone else crouched low. He ducked down, afraid of intercepting scattered bullets. He squeezed himself into the small space afforded him in the intimate pileup, cradling his rifle as he listened for more gunshots.

"Everyone stay where you are! Everyone stay where you are! Everyone stay where you are!" Nasser shouted from the podium.

Khalil looked up at the stage. Uniformed men had crowded around Nasser, but he held them off with a raised hand.

"My life is for you! My blood is for you! My life is for you! My blood is for you!" Nasser yelled into the microphone.

Khalil stared at the man behind the podium in disbelief. "Let them kill Nasser!" Nasser cried from the stage, his voice cracking as he shouted his own name. "It doesn't matter, as long as I have instilled honor and pride in you. Stay where you are, my countrymen, stay where you are! Everything I do is for you! Let them kill Gamal Abdel Nasser! If I should die, then you will be Gamal Abdel Nasser, because each of us is Gamal Abdel Nasser who is willing to sacrifice his life for this nation."

Nasser's hysterical words pelted Khalil like a succession of small stones. He wondered, even in that frantic moment, whether this was a hoax—the way everyone on the stage stood still while those on the ground panicked.

The assailant was found to be a member of the Muslim Brotherhood. Nasser pinned the assassination attempt on Naguib, given his connection to the Brotherhood, and had the military put the president under house arrest. With no one in his way, Nasser took the helm, and thus ensued one of the most brutal crackdowns in Egyptian history. Hordes of Muslim Brothers arrested, entire neighborhoods depleted of their men. Several of Khalil's professors were taken, rumored to have affiliations with the Communist Party. Everyone knew someone who'd been rounded up by the military.

As the weeks passed, Khalil discovered more and more people who'd disappeared from his circle, childhood friends, soldiers he'd fought with, students from his cohort. He lived in fear that they might come for him next, especially since he wasn't called back for another job after the rally in Alexandria.

After the new government settled into place, General Ibrahim was named a deputy minister within it. Khalil had grown deeply wary of the general but was scared to shun him. The atmosphere at these gatherings was more subdued than before, as if everyone was in on a secret that no one wanted to talk about. Khalil limited himself to one drink, wanting to keep his inhibitions intact so he didn't say something he would regret. He thought about the people he knew in jail and felt like a coward for not advocating on their behalf to General Ibrahim, but he didn't trust the general not to turn against him. Khalil began to see the wisdom in Hassan's decision to move abroad. He'd thought his brother was foolish and selfish to move to London the year before, like a dog following the British home after the revolution, but now Khalil decided that his brother had been smart to avoid the cesspool of current events. To be inside a nation that was in the process of forming itself was like being in the path of an active volcano.

"DADDY, WHERE ARE YOU?" Khalil heard Amena cry out in panic early the next morning. He was down in the kitchen, dipping stale bites of pita bread into a bowl of soft feta cheese. "I'm downstairs!" he called back to his daughter, his mouth still full of food.

By the time she found him, Amena was in tears. "Why'd you leave me?" she sobbed.

"I didn't," Khalil tried to argue, pushing the bowl of cheese aside. "I'm right here."

"I couldn't find you!" she countered, distress drawing her voice into a whine.

Khalil swallowed down the last bits of food in his mouth. "I was hungry," he said.

"Don't leave again without telling me!" she admonished.

"Okay," he agreed, though he knew this was a promise he couldn't keep.

Amena ran toward him and wrapped her arms around his chest, settling her cheek against his rib cage. Khalil wrapped his arms around her, feeling the weight of her needs and his bundled together. Amena started sobbing, gasping for breath, stirring Khalil's deepest fears about the reality they were facing. He couldn't imagine life without Halah, a family composed of just him and Amena. He regretted all of the stupid fights he'd had with his wife, some of which had been especially bad recently. He hated to think that their discord might have contributed to her disappearance, but it was worse to imagine that something outside of Halah's power might have taken her away.

Halah's mother emerged from her room late that morning. Khalil had exchanged just a few words with her since he'd arrived, nothing of substance. He was eager to talk to her in private now. After setting Amena up with a game of solitaire on her bed—she'd picked up a love of the game from watching him play endless rounds at the kitchen table on his days off—Khalil went downstairs to find his mother-in-law.

She was in the kitchen, standing in front of the stove, boiling water in a pot. Khalil told her good morning, and she pulled her robe closed and gave him a tight smile. "Good morning," she echoed back. Her hair was pulled into a ponytail at the nape of her neck, less glamorous than Khalil had ever seen it, with an inch of white around the crown and the rest a brassy, faded brown. Usually she wore it coiffed, and Khalil had never seen a gray hair on her head before. Her lack of self-consciousness was refreshing, putting him at ease.

"Can we talk when you have a few minutes?" Khalil asked her.

"We can talk now," she said, crossing her arms over her chest. "Shall we sit?"

They went next door to the room everyone referred to as the salon, pronounced in the French way. The room looked French, furnished in the style of Versailles and as large as a tennis court. It felt like the wrong place to have the conversation they were about to have.

"Please tell me what you know," he prompted once they were both settled.

"I don't know anything," she said, shaking her head and widening her eyes. "She seemed happy to be back in Egypt. She kept saying how good it felt to be home. I mean, she was beaming one minute and then crying over her father the next, but that's to be expected. His loss has been very painful for all of us."

"May God be charitable to him," Khalil expressed automatically, looking down into his lap. He and Halah had had one of the worst fights of their marriage right after she learned that her father had died. She was distraught and accused him of having no compassion, of having always harbored ill will toward her father. Khalil didn't try to deny this, and Halah responded by turning icy and distant, erecting an emotional wall between them that was still in place when she left.

"Bless you," Halah's mother thanked him, closing her eyes briefly.

"Did she seem . . ." Khalil began tepidly, "like she might be . . . When you say that she seemed happy to be home . . . did she say anything about leaving New York, about leaving me?"

His mother-in-law raised her eyebrows but said nothing for a few moments. "We didn't talk about that," she answered quietly.

"Never mind," Khalil said, embarrassed to have revealed insecurities about his marriage, and especially to someone who'd always been against it. "I'm just trying to understand what happened."

"We all are," his mother-in-law said with uncharacteristic gentleness. "Did you notice the police car parked out in front of the house? There's a whole team of people out there looking for Halah. I've been assured that they have the best men on the job."

On the one hand, this was reassuring to hear, but on the other, it evoked Khalil's long-standing skepticism of Egyptian officials. If Halah had come from an ordinary family—or God forbid, a poor one—there would be no team on the lookout for her, no police cars assigned to watch the house.

"I'm glad to hear it," Khalil told his mother-in-law. "I'm sure they'll find her soon." The more he said this, the less he believed it, the hollower the words sounded.

"I wasn't always the best mother," Halah's mother confessed then. Her hand shook as she rested her teacup down on the saucer. "I'm afraid that I took my frustrations with the world out on her sometimes. I've never really apologized to her for that."

"You'll get a chance," Khalil reassured her, spouting more vacuous optimism.

"I'm not so sure," she said, shaking her head and gazing at the reflective surface of the table. "I've lost her like this before. It feels like the past coming back to haunt me again."

"This is real," Khalil asserted, unnerved by her hypothesis. "This is now."

"I know," his mother-in-law said. "Welcome to my reality."

THE CHIEF OF POLICE CAME to visit the next afternoon. Khalil responded to the loud rapping on the door, clearly the work of a male hand, while Amena and her grandmother stayed behind in the salon, looking through photo albums featuring Halah as a girl.

A burly man in a uniform and cap stood on the other side of the door. He looked wearily at Khalil and then asked, "Are you the husband?"

It took a moment for Khalil to parse the question, simple as it was. And then he answered, "Yes."

"May I?" the policeman asked, gesturing toward the inside of the house.

"Of course," Khalil said, stepping aside. "Do you have any news?" he asked in a rush as the officer entered.

The man removed his cap and shook his head. He carried a pistol on one side of his belt and a knife on the other. "I wish I had good news," he said remorsefully. At this, Khalil's throat closed up, and he couldn't breathe. "But I'm afraid we haven't really found anything," the officer continued. Khalil exhaled loudly, both with disappointment and relief.

"Then what's the reason for your visit?" Khalil asked bluntly. He didn't see the need to spend any more time with the man if he didn't have anything valuable to share.

The policeman cleared his throat. "We just want the *ustazah* to know," he said nervously, in deference to the woman of the house, "that we are looking for her daughter—your wife."

"We're grateful to you," Khalil answered stiffly, though he ultimately hoped that law enforcement wouldn't be the key to finding his wife, for if it were, it would likely be because she'd been the victim of a crime. "Thank you for stopping by," he told the policeman, and then closed the door behind him.

AFTER MEETING THE UNIMPRESSIVE POLICEMAN, Khalil decided to take the investigation into his own hands, focusing on looking in the places he knew best: hospitals. He called information from his in-laws' house and got the addresses of all the local hospitals, and when Amena asked if she could come with him, Khalil told her frankly that she couldn't. He'd treated many anonymous women with grave injuries in the ICU where he worked in Brooklyn. It made him shudder to think of Halah succumbing to some of the gruesome fates he'd seen. Women raped, beaten so badly their internal organs looked like casualties of war. Khalil saw only

the most extreme cases, the milder ones generally treated and dispatched through the emergency room.

Khalil brought his credentials with him to talk his way into the
hospitals. The first one was the nearest to the Ibrahim residence,
just across the river from Zamalek. It seemed the most likely place
for Halah to end up, assuming she hadn't wandered very far from
home. The lobby of the hospital was full of people, many with obvious medical needs. Khalil knew that if you walked confidently
through the lobby of a hospital, few people were likely to stop you
and ask where you were going. He made a direct line for the elevators and followed the signs to the critical wards.

Khalil had known from the beginning of medical school that he
wanted to work in acute care, shaped by his experiences during
the war. He'd watched men succumb to fatal bullet wounds and be
blown apart by land mines. The ER and ICU were the wards of the
hospital that were most like war zones, but at least in the hospital
Khalil knew how to help, and his intervention often meant the difference between life and death, which was gratifying after failing
so many of his comrades. The part of his job that he hated the most
was having to pronounce someone dead, holding his fingers against
flat carotid arteries for the requisite two minutes while staring into
vacant eyes, knowing that the person was already gone. The best
parts were the victories—and there were many victories, like the
night before Amena's phone call, when he discovered a clot that
had caused a twenty-four-year-old woman to have a stroke during
birth and removed it with the aid of a catheter, bringing her back
to consciousness. Finding the ICU of the present hospital, Khalil
walked up to the nurses' station and asked if they had a patient
with Halah's name on their roster. Both nurses sitting behind the
desk wore *hijab* with their uniforms, which hadn't been a common
sight in Egypt's professional sector before he emigrated. It made
Khalil wonder whether a conservative wave was sweeping through
the country and if, soon, the majority of Egyptian women would

be covering their heads. One of the nurses consulted a handwritten list on her desk, giving Khalil a clear view of the pink silk scarf covering her hair.

"There's no one by that name here," she concluded a few moments later, looking back up.

"What about *el fulana*?" he asked, lowering his voice as he referred to their Jane Does, the term also slang for "prostitute."

Both nurses looked at him with concern bordering on fear. "We only have one of those in the ward at the moment," the second nurse answered. "A sixteen-year-old who was found in an alley a couple of nights ago."

Khalil shook his head and backed away. "That's not the person I'm looking for."

He walked down the hall to the emergency room and went through the same process. According to the nurses at the front desk, there were no women in their care matching Halah's description. This was mostly a relief, but it didn't bring him any closer to finding his wife.

In the taxi on his way to the next hospital, Khalil thought of the *fulana* he'd once partially dissected as part of the first anatomy course he took while still a student in Cairo during his first and only year of medical school in Egypt before moving to New York to complete his studies. There was a severe shortage of cadavers in Egypt due to the country's predominant Muslim population, who believed that their bodies had to be returned to the earth. His entire class of three hundred students had to share a single dissection specimen, the cadaver of an unidentified fifty-three-year-old woman whose body had never been claimed from the morgue. These were the only cadavers available for the purposes of science.

By contrast, the American medical school system was rich in cadavers, and when Khalil repeated gross anatomy in New York, he shared a specimen with only nineteen other students. Both times, Khalil found the process of cutting into dead flesh deeply unnerving. No rush of blood as he pressed the blade of the knife through gray-blue skin. There was a prescribed process for dissecting a body, which purposefully left the head for last so would-be doctors didn't form emotional attachments with the people they were cutting up. With living bodies, Khalil always found the sight of ebbing blood when he cut to be reassuring, a sign of life.

In the back seat of the taxi, Khalil imagined Halah's unidentified corpse destined for a dissection table, and the thought made him sick. He unrolled his window and leaned his head outside, afraid he was going to vomit, but the nausea dissipated, and after a few minutes he pulled his head back inside the car. Back when he was in medical school in Cairo, the woman he'd participated in dissecting had been almost fully disassembled by the time Khalil got his turn at the table. Hundreds of students had gone before him, weeks of waiting for his turn according to a rotating daily roster. When Khalil finally got up to the front, the poor dead woman's body was a collection of cut-up flesh that had been lazily put back together. Once the doctors-in-training opened up a cavity and dissected all of her organs, they put everything back in place. And yet Khalil saw gaps all over the body where edges of skin didn't come together, windows into deeper layers of flesh and bone. The woman on the dissection table was about the age of Khalil's mother at the time, and this made Khalil identify with her in a way that he knew he wasn't supposed to. Now it was time to dissect the head and neck, and Khalil found himself making a long lateral cut all the way from the occipital bone at the base of the woman's skull, over the top of her head, and down the middle of her face, bisecting it into two near-perfect hemispheres. It was unsettling how easily the skin peeled away once you made the necessary cuts. The woman's chemically desiccated hair felt like wiry sponge in his hands as he lifted away her dermal layer.

Over the course of the next few hours, Khalil visited five hospitals, but in none of them did he find a patient who went by the

name "Halah Seif" or "Halah Ibrahim," trying both his and her father's last names in every instance, nor a thirty-year-old Jane Doe.
Khalil returned to his mother-in-law's house exhausted that night,
dejected from his solemn quest, and yet also satisfied that Halah
wasn't languishing in a hospital bed within Cairo's city limits.

AFTER THREE DAYS OF BEING IN EGYPT, Khalil decided that he
needed to visit his parents. It had been three years since he'd last
seen them. He called them on each of their birthdays and for *Eid*
every year—he'd had a telephone line installed at their apartment
during his visit in 1961—but otherwise he was bad about keeping
in contact, rarely getting around to responding to his mother's pe-
riodic letters. In addition to these annual phone calls, Khalil had
sent home steadily larger monetary gifts over the years. His parents called the gifts a godsend and never complained about Khalil's
long absences. Instead they would write with reports of how they'd
spent the money—on a new mattress, for the first time in twenty
years, and then, the next year, on a modern refrigerator to replace
their old icebox. One year they used the money to make a deposit
on a trip to Mecca (the first time for both of them to make the pilgrimage). Knowing that his money helped improve their quality of
life allayed some of Khalil's guilt.

"Do I have to come?" Amena asked when it was time to leave for
his parents' place. Though irritated by her resistance, Khalil tried not
to take it personally, recognizing that it was his fault for neglecting
to cultivate his daughter's relationship with his side of the family.

"Yes, you have to come," Khalil told her with calm insistence.

"Okay," Amena frowned, defeated.

They took a taxi across town. It was less than ten minutes between the Ibrahims' house and Khalil's parents' apartment building, but it felt as if they crossed into another world when they en-

tered Mohandessin. Moving from Zamalek, an island of villas and
lush gardens and country clubs, to Mohandessin, packed with shops
and plain brick apartment buildings. Khalil's old building was in
the middle of a busy street, tucked between an auto mechanic and
an electronics store that had been a fabric shop in Khalil's youth.

Khalil noticed Amena's surprise as they exited the taxi. It was
clear that none of this looked familiar to her, the way she clung to
his side as they crossed the busy sidewalk, moving past a nearly
toothless man in a galabeya loudly hawking guava out of the back of
a donkey-drawn cart and, a few feet away, a blind woman sitting on
the sidewalk, holding out a limp burlap sack. Because Amena was
watching, Khalil dug coins out of his pocket to give to the woman.
He'd become inured to the sight of beggars at a young age, and the
example his parents set was to ignore them. Halah had never seen
people on the street until she moved to New York; her life in Cairo
had been so sheltered, and as a result her heart was much softer toward them. If Khalil passed someone on the street when he was on
his own, he wouldn't give them money, but if he was with Halah,
then he would.

The "lobby" of Khalil's old building wasn't fully enclosed, the
side that faced the street completely open to the outside world. It
had been left deliberately unfinished, along with the top two floors
of the building, which didn't have glass in the windows, so the
owners could avoid paying property taxes for going on sixty years
now. This was something you saw a lot in this neighborhood—old
brick-and-mortar buildings with open lobbies and no siding and
windowless top floors. Khalil took it for granted when he was a kid,
but now he saw its absurdity. The law was so easy to exploit, or else
it wasn't well enforced, or both.

Because of its exposure to the elements, the lobby was filthy,
coated in dust and covered with litter and cigarette butts. One corner seemed to be designated for trash, and there were bags upon

bags piled there, plus whatever detritus had escaped the bags encircling the mess. The air smelled rancid.

"Is this where you grew up, Daddy?" Amena asked with wide-eyed wonder.

"Yes," Khalil said, disappointed that she didn't remember their previous visit, when she was seven, or the one before that, when she was four.

A wrought-iron staircase was the only means of accessing the upper floors. When he and Halah moved to Manhattan from Queens and into a building with an elevator five years before, Khalil had felt he was moving up in the world. Halah always hated their cramped apartment in Queens, and Khalil suspected that she complained to her father about it because after one of Halah and Amena's summer visits to Egypt, her father opened up a large bank account in Halah's name, the contents of which she ultimately used to buy their apartment in Manhattan.

"I want nothing to do with your father's dirty money," Khalil tried to protest when Halah first told him about the gift.

Amena appeared out of nowhere as soon as Khalil said this, having been tucked away in her room playing. "How can money be dirty, Daddy?" she interjected.

Before Khalil could speak, Halah responded, "Don't listen to your father. He doesn't know what he's talking about."

Their argument continued behind closed doors late at night, both of them working to keep their voices down but sometimes lapsing into elevated tones. Halah threatened to leave Khalil behind in Queens if he didn't want to move; she was buying a place in Manhattan. Halah found a real estate agent on her own and looked at places while Khalil was at work and Amena at school, finally settling on a spacious two-bedroom apartment with a balcony in a high-rise at the edge of Kips Bay, on the east side of the city. The large complex occupied the corner of Twenty-Third Street and Second Avenue, a cluster of nearly identical high-rises that shared a plaza dominated by a grand, flowing fountain. Even after they all moved in, Khalil thought of it as Halah's apartment. Now he had a long commute to work that involved three trains, whereas it used to be just one. He made no secret of how much this wore on him, often complaining over dinners that were usually cold by the time he got home.

Spinning over the ways he had failed Halah as a husband, Khalil steeled himself to knock on the door of his parents' apartment, which brought up a whole new host of anxieties.

His mother burst into tears when she opened the door and saw him and Amena standing there. *"Ya Rab, ya Rab!"* she cried, throwing her hands up in the air. "I can't believe my eyes!"

Khalil's father came around the corner, walking with a pronounced stoop. His eyes widened when he saw Khalil, and he pulled his chin back like a turtle. "Son?" he asked, as if he didn't quite believe what he was seeing.

"It's me, Baba," Khalil reassured him. "I've been gone too long, I know," he acknowledged.

"You have!" his mother agreed, wrapping her arms around Khalil and hugging him tightly. "How could you?" she laughed, with her cheek pressed against his neck. Khalil felt her tears wet his skin and trickle down his shirt.

When she let him go, she turned to Amena and leaned over, holding her arms out. Amena approached timidly. Khalil resisted the urge to push her along. She kept her arms tucked across her chest as she received her grandmother's embrace.

"Why didn't you tell us you were coming?" Khalil's father asked once they'd all exchanged greetings.

"This was unexpected," Khalil said carefully, wanting to settle in before launching into an explanation of their state of emergency.

They all moved into the living room, which looked like a time capsule from Khalil's youth. The furniture was unchanged—the well-worn pair of brown armchairs his parents used, the love seat whose upholstery once featured brightly colored flowers that were now faded beyond recognition, and the same small wooden coffee table they'd always had, the surface now heavily scratched and dull. When Khalil sat down on the love seat, he could hear and feel the springs in the cushion beneath him. His parents had never gotten a television, and their dusty old radio still held pride of place on the table against the back wall. They had few adornments on their walls: a framed poster of the Kaaba in Mecca, the thin paper wrinkled beneath the glass, a calendar featuring a different month from the previous year, and a crooked clock. There were no family portraits hanging; they'd never been able to afford such a luxury. Comparatively, Halah's parents' house was filled with professional pictures of their family. They had an entire table in their foyer dedicated to photographs of Halah throughout the years.

"Will she eat chocolate?" Khalil's mother asked, standing to retrieve a bowl of candy from beside the radio.

"She loves chocolate," Khalil confirmed with a smile.

His mother brought the bowl over and held it in front of Amena, who looked to Khalil for approval before taking one of the foil-wrapped balls. Everyone watched as she slowly unwrapped the chocolate and popped it in her mouth, like there was nothing better than watching a kid enjoy a treat. Khalil took one too, but it tasted waxy and too sweet to him.

He then launched into the story of how Amena had called him a few days before to tell him that Halah had disappeared. He told them the scant facts he knew surrounding her departure—how she'd said she was going to see a friend and no one noticed until the next morning that she hadn't returned—and about how the police were involved and hadn't yet found any leads, which Khalil considered a good thing. "I'm just so afraid they're going to come back and tell us they found a body," he said, grateful he could speak in a language with his parents that his daughter barely understood. "I want to believe that she's safe somewhere. Honestly, I'd be relieved to learn that she left me and was hiding out with another man, if that meant she was okay."

"Oh, black day!" his mother cried. "This is a nightmare."

"Calm down," his father scolded his wife, reminding Khalil of his father's tendency to police his mother's emotions, a dynamic that had always bothered Khalil. "Let him finish."

Khalil shook his head, not knowing what else there was to say. The fact was, he didn't know what had happened to his wife.

"Have you heard anything from Hassan lately?" Khalil asked, to change the subject.

His parents looked at each other as if to reach consensus. "It's been a month or two," his father said finally, "but, yes, we hear from him sometimes." Then he turned to Khalil's mother and said, "Show him," gesturing toward the dining room/bedroom next door, the room Khalil used to share with Hassan.

A pair of rickety French doors separated that room from the one they were sitting in. Khalil's mother went next door to retrieve something from underneath his former bed. Khalil experienced a momentary flash of panic, as this was where he used to keep the hand-transcribed pornographic stories that he and his friends would pass around. It made him laugh to think about how innocuous those stories were compared with the magazines he could get his hands on now. He had well-worn copies of *Playboy* and *Hustler* rolled up and tucked behind the water heater in their apartment in New York, where he was sure no one ever looked but him. He must have thrown away the handwritten smut when he moved out, Khalil reasoned, as he'd always been acutely aware of where those papers were when he lived here and wouldn't have just left them under his bed to be discovered.

Sitting on her knees, Khalil's mother pulled out a wooden crate from beneath the bed. There was another twin bed pushed against the wall on the opposite side of the room, where Hassan had slept during the years he and Khalil had shared that room, and possibly where he slept again after Khalil moved out and before he was arrested. The room continued to function as the family's dining room, as it always had, with a round table and four chairs crowded into the center, between the beds. It added to Khalil's sadness that his parents kept his and Hassan's beds intact, as if they might return to use them one day.

His mother made aching noises as she got back to her feet, and then she bent down to pick up the crate, carried it into the living room, and set it by Khalil's feet. Visible at the top of the crate was a stack of letters bundled in twine. Khalil looked to his mother for direction, not eager to begin digging through random ephemera.

"What do you want me to see?" Khalil asked.

His mother leaned over to pick up the bundle of letters, which she handed to him. The stack was at least six inches tall, the envelopes thick and wrinkly, as if they'd been left out in a rainstorm. "The letters we get from him . . . They don't tell us much."

"Take a look," Khalil's father urged from his chair. "It amazes me that they take so much time going through the letters. Why not just burn them all?"

His interest piqued, Khalil untied the twine and opened the top envelope. He removed the letter gingerly, sensing that there was something precious about it. The paper it was written on was as thin as onion skin, and big black swaths of words were redacted with a thick marker that bled through the paper.

██████████

My beloved mother and father—

You cannot imagine how I ██████████. ██████████ ██████████ I would be the first to admit that I have not led a perfect life, but ██████████. The way they ██████ us here. All the other men in my cell ██████████ But you don't want to hear about that. Last week ██████████

█. I pray to God █████████████████. I wish I had some happy news to share. I guess what's most important is that you go on with your lives. Forget about me. If ████████████████ ████████████████████, don't try to do anything. Don't go looking for answers, for that can only lead to ██████.

Your loving son

When he finished reading the letter, Khalil started from the top again to see if he could glean anything more on a second reading, but the content remained just as elusive. Khalil tried to imagine the person making these redactions, carefully reading the prisoners' letters for content deemed unacceptable or damning. There was no such thing as privacy, and who knew whether letters sent from the outside world would ever reached the prisoners? Khalil put away the first letter and set it down on the couch between him and Amena, who sat watching him with silent curiosity. The second letter looked like a variation of the first, like another word puzzle.

Dear Mama and Baba,

Not a day passes when I don't think of your sweet faces. I was such a bad son, never appreciated you enough. Last week ██████ ██████ learned that his mother died. The ██████ won't let him ████████. They don't ██████████████████. If there's a ████████, I hope there's enough space for these ████████ ████████. One guy's family ███████████████████████ ██████. Maybe you could ███████████████████████ ████████████████████████. I'm ████ they're go- ing to ██████████████████. No one would ████████████████. That's the ████████ part. I don't know how much lon- ger I can ███████████████████████. There's a chance

██████████████ ████████████████████████. I know it's far away and hard to get the time off work, but I hope you'll visit again one of these days. I miss you ████████████████.

Hassan

. . .

███████████

You're probably wondering ████████████████████████ ████████████. They give us extra time in the yard during Ramadan. I suppose █████████████ they treat us well. I'm

██
██
██
██

████████ Khalil. His wife's father ██████████████████████.

I know you pray for me and it was wrong to ████████. I believe █████ would be ██████████. Even if there is no ████████ now, one day there will be ██████████████. That's what helps me ██████████████████████████ here.

Keep me in your prayers.

Hassan

. . .

My dear parents,

God is great. I never believed in miracles until now. I can't say ██████████████████████ because there is always ████████████████ ██████████.

██████████████████████████ I beg forgiveness for my sins, for there have been many. Nonetheless, I insist upon my ██████████████. They never had any right to ████████████████

██████████████ will be tried in the next life. I pray I will see
████████████████████████████████. But if it isn't to
be, I won't judge His will.

Your loving son

Khalil stopped reading when he was just past the tipping point where his frustration outgrew his fascination with the mysterious, obliterated missives.

"When was the last time you went to visit him?" Khalil asked his parents, stacking all of the letters on his lap and tying them back together. He set the bundle gently down inside the milk crate.

Again his parents looked at each other to confer, and then his father answered: "It's been a couple of months."

His mother added: "It's very hard for the two of us to get the same day off, and Hussein doesn't want me to go up there without him."

"How does he seem?" Khalil asked with faint dread. His brother wasn't his favorite person, but Khalil didn't wish for him to suffer.

Amena pulled on Khalil's elbow. "Can we go yet?" she whispered when Khalil gave her his attention.

"Have some patience," Khalil whispered back, bringing all of the fingers on his right hand to a point and holding them up, a gesture he'd learned from his mother. Amena slouched back against the couch, obviously disappointed.

"What does she want?" his mother asked.

Khalil shook his head. "Nothing."

"Maybe you can pay a visit to your brother while you're here," Khalil's father suggested.

"I can't think about that now" was Khalil's immediate response.

"Of course, of course," his mother agreed.

Khalil looked down at his shoes, feeling vaguely ashamed. There were numerous reasons he didn't want to visit Hassan, chief among them that Halah was all that mattered to him now. Last time he came to Egypt, Khalil had gone to see Hassan, and they'd had a depressing and awkward encounter, which Khalil wasn't eager to repeat. Hassan had whispered complaints about his terrible living conditions and expressed jealousy over Khalil's life in America. Khalil was happy to talk about his daughter when his brother asked how she was, but when Hassan brought up Halah, Khalil turned private and defensive. Hassan had never met Halah, and it felt invasive for him to ask about her. Khalil and Hassan had always had a contentious relationship, beginning in their youth with stupid fights over their few shared toys, and extending through their adolescence and beyond. Khalil thought Hassan was selfish and inconsiderate, and Hassan treated Khalil as an annoyance. As much as he disrespected Hassan for defecting to the homeland of their longtime colonizers, Khalil considered it a great relief when Hassan moved to London and they didn't have to live together anymore.

And then, less than a year later, Hassan returned. This baffled Khalil after his brother showed so much bravado when he got accepted into school in London. Hassan chose to sleep on the couch in the living room when he moved back in, but often in the middle of the night he would wake Khalil by walking past his bed to get to the fire escape outside what used to be the room they shared. The first few times, Khalil pretended to sleep through the annoyance, but by the fourth or fifth time he heard the window squeak open, he got up and demanded to know what Hassan was doing.

Hassan was already halfway out the window, his backside to Khalil. After fully popping outside, he turned around to acknowledge Khalil's question. "I'm in the mood for a little drink. Care to join me?"

Khalil considered, tired but intrigued. The only time he drank was at General Ibrahim's house, and though he enjoyed the sweet, fleeting joy of alcohol, he didn't have the resources to buy it on his own.

Crawling out onto the fire escape, Khalil was reminded of the first time he witnessed death, when a young goat in their family's care fell between the rails of the fire escape and plummeted to the street below. Khalil brushed aside the vivid memory to be with Hassan in the present.

Hassan pulled out a flask from his back pocket, took a sip, and then handed it to Khalil without ceremony. Khalil tipped some of the mystery drink into his mouth. It burned his throat on the way down. "How long have you been committing this delicious sin?" Khalil asked his brother after taking another swig.

"I guess you could say it's a new habit," Hassan responded, reaching for the flask.

"Drowning your sorrows, or trying to reach a higher plane?" Khalil asked, arching an eyebrow.

"A bit of both, I suppose." With his bare toes Hassan dug at a gap between the slats on the balcony, avoiding eye contact.

"You're not happy to be back?" Khalil speculated. This much was clear to him.

Hassan finally looked up. "No. Not particularly."

They passed the flask back and forth, quickly growing tipsy; this alcohol was of a stronger sort than any he'd tried before. "Why did you come back, then?" Khalil finally got up the courage to ask.

"Bigotry," Hassan answered soundly, with conviction. He looked at Khalil as if he expected a challenge, and when Khalil didn't say anything in return, Hassan added, "It's a racist country."

"Did they make you leave?" Khalil ventured. Hassan looked him in the eye without a word, giving Khalil his answer.

For a few weeks after that, they drank together on the fire escape every night, starting around eleven or twelve, after their parents went to sleep, Hassan continually refilling his flask from an unknown source. One night Khalil told Hassan about Halah, and for once Hassan didn't interrupt while Khalil talked, enraptured as he listened, with a glint of anger in his eyes. Their boozy camaraderie came to an abrupt end when Khalil learned that he'd won an academic scholarship and announced his intentions to move to America. Suddenly, either Hassan quit drinking, or he stopped doing so on the fire escape outside Khalil's room and in Khalil's company. They had a frosty rapport in the weeks leading up to Khalil's departure, prompting Khalil to revert to his negative feelings about Hassan. Khalil was happy to leave his brother behind and even happier to begin cohabiting with a beautiful wife instead. When he learned that his brother had been arrested, Khalil's first thought was that Hassan had probably done something to deserve it, moody and secretive as he was.

"I wish there was something I could do for him," Khalil told his parents now. Together they'd spent money that Khalil should have been putting away for Amena's education on lawyers who never made any headway on Hassan's case, but it had been a couple of years now since there was last talk of lawyers, as if they'd collectively given up.

"Do you pray?" his mother asked him now.

Khalil considered lying. "No," he ultimately admitted.

"You should pray," she said.

"I know," Khalil said.

"Leave the poor boy alone," his father said.

Amena looked over at him with confusion. He often wondered how much Arabic she understood; she frequently surprised him with details she surmised from private conversations he'd had with Halah, repeated back to him when he least expected it.

"I think it's time for us to go," Khalil told his parents, for once happy to indulge Amena's impatience.

"When will we see you again?" his mother asked him at the door.

"Soon," Khalil promised hesitantly.

Amena reached for Khalil's hand on the stairs as they were exiting the building. He took great comfort in this gesture, as if she were parenting him instead of the other way around.

Outside the building, Amena let go of his hand. Khalil looked up toward his parents' apartment and the fire escape where he used to drink with Hassan. He let himself remember the incident with the goat, the way he'd watched in disbelief as the animal flew over the railing and landed with a cracking thud in the street below. Khalil ran inside to enlist Hassan's help. His brother was lying in bed on his stomach, doing his homework. Khalil was in the third grade and Hassan in seventh then. Hassan acted annoyed to be disrupted and took a painfully long time lacing up his shoes after Khalil made his tearful declaration. The goat had been Khalil's sort-of pet for the past three weeks, acquired by their father at the beginning of the month of Ramadan for fear that if he didn't get one early, supply would run out and the family wouldn't have one for the feast. By the time the goat went to the butcher to be slaughtered every year, Khalil had formed a bond with the animal. It made him sick to eat the fragrant meat, but his father made sure that everyone in the family partook of the special meal—and without fail, Khalil spent the last night of Ramadan puking in the bathroom.

Once Hassan had his shoes on, he started moving quickly, grabbing his pocketknife from the dresser and jogging out of their room and out the front door of the apartment. Their parents weren't home; they usually didn't get back until Hassan and Khalil had been home from school for hours. Hassan was fleet-footed when he wanted to be, racing down the stairs and across the dusty lobby. Khalil lagged a good distance behind him, and when Khalil got out to the street, Hassan already had the goat upright and pinned against him. Khalil ran up next to them just in time to see his brother drag the blade of the knife across the goat's neck, releasing a gurgling strip of blood.

"He was only half dead," Hassan turned to Khalil and explained. "I'm putting him out of his misery."

AS KHALIL WAS SCRATCHING Amena's head to put her to bed that night, he noticed a small leather-bound Quran peeking out of the drawer of Halah's old nightstand. After Amena's breaths turned deep and even, Khalil slipped off the bed and took the Quran from the drawer, returning to his room next door. There, he turned on the lamp on the nightstand and sat at the edge of the bed and then gently opened the palm-sized book to the first page. He expected to find something different from his previous encounters with the holy book, because it had belonged to Halah, but at first glance it looked like every other Quran he'd seen.

Flipping through the pages, Khalil came across a passage that was underlined. His heart started racing, as if he'd found a secret message from Halah: *It is not possible for the sun to reach the moon, nor for the night to overtake the day, for neither can swim outside of its orbit.*

Khalil had to read the statement twice to make any sense of it. Like the poetry he used to study in school, the language was beautiful but slippery, hard to grasp. His mother used to read him passages of the Quran when he was a child, and he'd had the same experience then. Dog-earing the page with Halah's markings, Khalil continued to carefully flip through, page by page, looking for more evidence of his wife's journey through this book. Each time he found an underscored passage, he read it twice and turned down the corner of the page, until he had a slew of poetic/prophetic lines swimming through his head.

If you are grateful, I will give you more.

God does not burden a soul beyond what it can bear.

The sun runs on a course toward its stopping point.

Do what is beautiful. God loves those who do what is beautiful.

No one knows what he will learn from tomorrow.

The life of this world is only the enjoyment of deception.

No foundation that has been built in Islam is more beloved to Allah *than marriage.*

He has made spouses for yourselves from your own selves so that you may take comfort in them.

Have you seen him who takes lust as his God? Allah *has knowingly let him go astray and sealed his hearing and his heart and put a cover on his sight. Who shall guide him after* Allah?

Closing the Quran, Khalil ran his finger over the gold filigree lettering on the cover. His fingertip came away flecked with gold. He touched his finger to his lips and closed his eyes, pleading to the unknown for Halah's safe return.

AFTER ABOUT A WEEK IN CAIRO, Khalil began to wonder if it was time to think about going home. He couldn't absent himself from the hospital forever if he wanted to keep his job, and Amena's school was starting up again soon. The police chief dropped by again on Sunday. This time, Halah's mother was the one to answer the door, and she invited him in for tea. Khalil refrained from asking for an update on the case the moment he entered the room, waiting instead until Halah's mother went to make the tea before launching into his inquiries.

"I'm so sorry, *ya docteur*," the policeman respectfully apologized. "We've telegrammed alerts to precincts all around the country, but no one has responded with any news."

Disappointment and relief welled up at the same time. "Have you checked with the morgues?" Khalil asked with dread, grateful that his mother-in-law was out of earshot.

The policeman tilted his head from side to side, half nodding, half shaking his head. "We're in contact with the facilities where the unclaimed bodies go. Sometimes it takes a while for them to get there, but so far no one fitting the description of your wife has turned up."

Khalil nodded gravely, vaguely reassured.

Halah's mother appeared in the doorway then, carrying a silver tray populated with a tea service. "I hope I didn't ruin it," she said, as she set down the tray. "I'm still learning my way around the kitchen since I had to let go of my girl."

Khalil bristled at the diminutive reference to Reema, whom he knew his wife had loved and respected dearly. *She's the one who really raised me*, she'd told Khalil. It had taken Khalil a day to notice Reema's absence from the house after he arrived in Cairo, preoccupied as he was with Halah's disappearance, and when he finally asked his mother-in-law about Reema's whereabouts, she shrugged and said, "I couldn't afford to keep her now that there's no more money coming in." Khalil wondered whether Reema's dismissal had anything to do with Halah's mysterious departure.

"Has anybody reached out to Reema since Halah disappeared?" Khalil asked suddenly as his mother-in-law was pouring the tea, causing her to jump and trickle some hot liquid outside one of the mugs.

"Not me," she said, setting down her ornately decorated pot.

"Who's Reema?" the policeman asked.

Khalil sighed impatiently, intent on taking matters into his own hands. "I'm going to go and see her, then," he said, addressing his mother-in-law. "Do you want to come?"

She shook her head very subtly, almost like a tremor. "It wasn't pretty when she left. She begged and cried, and in the end, I had to threaten to call the police to make her go."

Khalil puckered his mouth, trying not to betray his disgust. Even without her husband's income, the woman probably had more money than 99 percent of Egyptians; Khalil didn't believe that she couldn't afford to keep Reema on. "She worked for you for thirty years," he told his mother-in-law. "I trust you know where to find her?"

"Let me go find my address book," she said quietly, and left the room.

While she was gone, the policeman picked up the saucer and mug closest to him and downed the steaming beverage in three big gulps, as if the tea were his true reason for being there and he didn't want to let it go to waste. Khalil felt as if he was among fools and didn't want to waste any more time with them. His mother-in-law returned a few minutes later and handed him a folded piece of stationery inscribed with an address in El Faiyûm. Khalil went upstairs to check on Amena and see if she wanted to come with him.

"How far is it?" she asked.

"An hour or two," he speculated, trying to remember how long the trip there had taken when he was part of Nasser's guard.

Amena bookmarked her Nancy Drew mystery and put it down. "I'm coming," she announced, sliding off the bed.

The policeman had already left by the time they returned to the first floor, and Halah's mother was sitting alone in the salon, sipping her tea. "We're leaving," Khalil announced from the doorway. She nodded and took another sip, pursing her lips around the rim of the thin porcelain cup.

"In the old days I would have had my driver take you," she said as they were walking away, "but of course I had to let go of him too."

Khalil kept walking, holding his arm around Amena. The heavy front door put up a fight when he tried to pull it open, jammed against the frame at the top right corner. After a sharp jerk, it finally gave, and Khalil exerted a similar amount of force into closing it behind them. Standing at the curb, Khalil let a few run-down taxis pass before flagging down one that looked newer and cleaner. He inspected the back seat before ushering his daughter inside and climbing in beside her.

As they drove, Amena stared at the passing scenes out her window. They traveled from the dense bustle of Cairo to the place where the tall buildings ended, followed by a long stretch of desert. Witnessing his daughter's fascination with the changing landscape, Khalil felt a renewed appreciation for the vernacular beauty of his homeland.

They arrived at El Faiyûm quicker than he expected. The village first appeared as a collection of houses on the horizon—an expansive smattering of one-story, earth-colored structures that resembled architecture from an earlier century. From a distance, it looked like Beni Suef, the village where his grandparents were from, which he used to visit when he was younger. Most of Khalil's old friends from school and the neighborhood were only a generation or two removed from village life. Halah was the only Egyptian he knew who claimed no lineage outside of Cairo, insisting that her parents' families had lived in the city dating back to the days of the Ottoman Empire.

When they reached the edge of the village, Khalil retrieved the address from his pocket and recited it to the driver. He nodded and stopped the car to ask a passerby how to get to the street in question. Khalil hadn't noticed where the paved roads ended, but all the roads here were made of dirt, rough and stuttering beneath the taxi's tires. Roads dead-ended, and they'd have to reverse to the nearest intersection and try another direction. It was like driving through a maze, except there was competing traffic that forced the taxi up against walls to let other vehicles pass. There were no signs to indicate the names of streets, and after a while their driver stopped and rolled down his window to ask for directions again.

Finally they arrived at what a local told them was the right location. The taxi's meter was broken, so the driver named some random sum that sounded high to Khalil by Egyptian standards but cheap compared with New York rates. "Here," Khalil said, handing over crisp Egyptian bills he'd gotten from an exchange window at the airport for his American money. "But you and I both know that's twice what another man would have charged me," he added on principle.

Amena held tightly to Khalil's hand as they approached the door of the house. It was squat, with a thatched roof and frayed linens hanging in the otherwise exposed windows, like almost every other dwelling they'd passed on the way here. The door rattled on its hinges when Khalil knocked. He heard a small commotion on the other side, and a few moments later, a veiled woman answered, holding a baby on her hip.

"Excuse me," Khalil said in greeting, looking away from her face out of respect and instead making eye contact with her alert and chubby baby. "I'm looking for *Sit* Reema," he said to the infant, who tried to swat at his face. "I'm afraid I don't know her surname."

"She doesn't live here," the woman replied with obvious annoyance. Khalil returned his attention to her face, surprised by the edge in her tone. "If you need to find her, go check with her son Rafik," she said, pointing up the block, adding, "21 Al Samkari," and then she shut the door.

"She didn't seem very nice," Amena observed as they walked away from the house.

"You're right about that," Khalil conceded, putting his arm around her shoulders.

He had to ask several people for guidance before he found 21 Al Samkari. A veiled woman carrying a baby answered the door there too. Khalil repeated his introduction, hoping for a better outcome this time.

"May I ask what your business is with the old lady?" the woman answered.

"She was my wife's nursemaid. She worked for my wife's parents for years," Khalil explained.

"Oh!" the woman answered, as if piqued by this news. "Your wife must be that beautiful woman who came to visit us a few weeks ago."

Khalil's heart started to pound. "When?" he demanded breathlessly.

The woman wrinkled her brow and rocked the fussing baby in her arms. "Was that a month ago?" she ventured loosely.

"What is she saying?" Amena whispered beside him.

Khalil ignored his daughter, overwhelmed by the stranger's revelation. "My God!" he exclaimed, hope expanding in his chest like a balloon. "So you saw her? Was she okay? Why did she come here? How long did she stay?"

Clearly overwhelmed by the litany of questions, the woman stepped back and said, "Come inside. You should talk to the old lady." She opened the door to reveal a room full of people behind her. Several mattresses were pushed against the walls of the living space. A group of kids were wrestling on one of the mattresses and didn't look up when Khalil and Amena entered. On another mattress across the room sat a pair of older women clad from head to toe in black. One of them looked at Khalil with familiarity, and at the same moment recognition sparked in him. It had been years since he'd seen Reema, and the oval of her face—the only part of that remained unconcealed—appeared significantly more craggy than the last time, and she'd also gained a lot of weight.

Reema rocked forward onto her hands and knees and came to her feet with effort. Once she was upright, she limped toward Khalil and Amena with her arms out as if they were revered guests. "*Ya docteur!*" she said, which was how she had always addressed him, though he'd told her several times over the years that she should call him by his name. "What on earth brings you here?"

Khalil hated to break the terrible news, hated to say the words aloud: "Halah's missing," he explained. "She's been gone for a week now." He paused for a moment to allow this information to be absorbed. Reema dropped her hands to her sides, and her expression also fell. "I heard she came to visit you," Khalil continued. "Please tell me what you know."

"Missing?" Reema echoed back. "What happened to her?"

"That's what we're trying to figure out," Khalil said impatiently. "When exactly was she here?"

Reema looked up at the ceiling, as if the bare bulb hanging from its center might contain the answer. The walls of the house were plastered in old newspaper, presumably for insulation. The articles and pictures on the pages had mostly faded, leaving behind columns of black smudges and ghostly rectangles. There was no other furniture in the room/house aside from the mattresses and a few cushions on the floor. A corner of the room had been designated for cooking, judging by how a small propane stove occupied the space next to a pair of blackened pots. A shelf above the improvised kitchen held a stack of mismatched dishes and empty jelly jars.

"It was right after the full-moon fast in late July," Reema responded assuredly after a moment. "I'm sure of it. I cooked her favorite dish, and I was still so hungry from the fast that I devoured it with her."

Khalil looked down at the ground, doing some calculations of his own. Halah had disappeared on the tenth of August, likely weeks after this encounter. She hadn't mentioned taking a trip to El Faiyûm when she and Khalil had talked on the phone a few days before she disappeared, but the call then was brief and the connection garbled.

"Did your mother come here a few weeks ago?" Khalil turned to his daughter and asked.

Amena shook her head. "I don't know. She went out to see a lot of friends."

Khalil considered this. He was ashamed to realize that he couldn't think of a single friend his wife had in Egypt. Halah often complained that he didn't listen to her, and maybe this was evidence of that. Switching back to Arabic and returning his attention to Reema, he asked, "How did she seem when you saw her?"

Reema furrowed her mouth and brow, answering with her face

before saying anything aloud. "She seemed very upset," she finally shared. "I told her she didn't have to worry about me, but she was so angry with her mother. I had to take her out of the house for a while, afraid she would upset the children with all of the tears and yelling."

Khalil pictured Halah hysterical in these streets, Reema trying to comfort her. "How long did she stay?" he asked, working to piece together Halah's last traceable days.

Reema looked down and sighed with defeat. "I wanted her to stay the night, but she insisted on going back in the dark." A look of violent worry clouded over her face. "When's the last time she was seen?"

"Five days ago," Khalil answered precisely.

Reema closed her eyes and mumbled what Khalil assumed were a few lines of prayer. When she opened her eyes again, they stood in silence for a moment, and then she said, "She didn't seem like herself when she was here, *ya docteur*. So agitated, her thoughts everywhere at once—it reminded me of my husband when he would drink too much, the way he would stop making sense after a while."

"What do you mean?" Khalil pressed, though he immediately recognized what she was saying. He'd seen his wife worked up into a fervor on multiple occasions, typically on the heels of trips to Egypt. Two summers before, she came back and couldn't stop talking about how Egypt was a police state and no one there was safe. Khalil didn't understand why his wife was only then coming to this realization, when this was a big part of the reason why he'd wanted to leave the country in the first place. More than once, when she'd been in the midst of particularly volatile emotional stretches, Halah brought up her a wild theory about Hassan being in jail on account of their relationship.

Khalil laughed darkly in response the first time she did this. "You think our love is that powerful?"

"My father," she said tersely. "I think he targeted your brother to get back at us."

"You can't think that way," Khalil told his wife. "The Egyptian prison system is a monster with an insatiable appetite. Innocent people get arrested all the time. We can't blame ourselves for that."

Halah was not appeased, and for the next couple of days she barely spoke to him. Several times during that strange period of weeks, Khalil woke up in the middle of the night to find Halah's side of the bed empty. He located her out on the balcony once and, another night, sitting in front of the television watching the staticky, distorted preachings of a Christian evangelist. Another time, he couldn't find her anywhere in the apartment and paced around for an hour, growing increasingly anxious and terrified. He was just about to call the police when Halah walked in through the door with two full sacks of groceries she'd procured from the all-hours bodega down the street. It was four in the morning. She said she couldn't sleep. That was the last of Halah's nocturnal adventures, at least the last one Khalil woke to. After that, she slipped into a long period of lethargy, and Khalil would often come home from work to find her napping in their bedroom while Amena played alone in her room.

Reema lowered her voice and dropped her gaze as she continued, "It was like she was another person . . . altered."

Khalil let this sink in. What she said confirmed some deep-down suspicion that Halah hadn't been in her right mind before she vanished. He thought back to when they'd met, the way he'd been seduced by her breathless, astounding proclamations. For a long time he'd believed that it was passion that brought them together, but later he started to wonder whether Halah's forwardness was fueled by something else. During his psychiatry course in medical school, Khalil came across a clinical description of his wife's behavior in a diagnostic manual. *Mania*, a condition often coupled with depression. There was plenty of evidence of that throughout their years together as well, long, somber stretches when Halah slept a lot and struggled to engage. Khalil never shared his secret diagnosis with

Halah, but it occurred to him again now as a plausible explanation for her disappearance.

"Honestly," Reema offered after a few tense moments of silence, "the Halah I saw a few weeks ago made me think of the girl she was when she ran away with you. We were all so shocked," she added, shaking her head, tears falling now. Khalil looked away, embarrassed. "I raised her as my own child," Reema continued. "I thought it was normal for a girl to complain about being promised to a stranger as a wife. I felt the same way when I was her age. But I never imagined that she would consider leaving behind everything she knew and everyone who loved her—" Her voice caught, and she broke off.

Reema's words left Khalil nearly speechless. "We should be going," he managed, though they'd arrived only a few minutes before. Everyone around the room was looking at them now, intent on their conversation—the woman who'd answered the door, who was standing against the far wall, still rocking her baby, the other older woman and Reema's twin in black, and even the children who'd been wrestling. Ready to leave, Khalil reached for Amena's hand and said goodbye.

AMENA, 1974

AMENA PULLED ON THE LIGHT in the closet, illuminating her mother's old dresses. She needed one to go with the shoes she'd picked out: a pair of open-toed pink sandals she remembered her mother wearing to the playground when Amena was a kid. Amena pictured the shoes speckled with sand, her mother's red toenails peeking out at the front. It was now the summer after her junior year of high school, and while she had time on her hands, Amena was determined to get rid of the clutter from her mother's left-behind life. There were still reminders of her everywhere—Amena's father hadn't given away a single item of clothing or pair of shoes to charity, leaving everything untouched.

So far he hadn't seemed to notice her paring-down efforts. She'd cleaned out inches of his closet and emptied an entire drawer in the dresser he used to share with her mother and continued to use only half of. At the beginning of the summer, when Amena started giving away her mother's clothes, she offered a couple of bags of garments to a homeless woman who often roamed their block. The first time Amena saw the woman wearing one of her mother's old blouses, it took her breath away. She'd never had a true experience of doing something that came back to haunt her, but now Amena saw a ghost every time she encountered the woman, always wearing something that had belonged to her mother. After that, Amena decided to take her mother's abandoned wardrobe further afield.

These days Amena kept a few articles of clothing in her backpack to deposit at random places across the city in private ceremonies that she invented on the spot. Like the time she tied a bunch of her mother's scarves over the heads of statues in Union Square. Or when she hung one of her mother's nightgowns from the horizontal arms of a lamppost and watched it billow in the wind. Or when she left empty purses on benches in the galleries of the Frick Collection. Or the previous Monday night, while her father was on call, when Amena had filled a trash bag with her mother's shoes and taken the subway uptown to Seventy-Second Street. From there she walked to Central Park and directly to the ballroom-like tunnel leading to Bethesda Terrace. Once it was empty of everyone but her, she made a parade of empty shoes down the middle of the tunnel. Though curious about how long her ephemeral gestures stayed intact, Amena didn't stick around to see and never checked back on the sites of her interventions.

Only one of her friends knew that she was doing this. Zakaria. He was someone she knew from school and also the first person she'd slept with. They'd had classes together since they were freshmen but only started to get close over the past year in chemistry, when he sat down beside her on the first day and effectively made himself her lab partner. Zakaria was also the child of a single parent and darker complected like Amena, which bonded her to him. Zakaria lived with his mother, who was white, leaving Amena to imagine that his father was dark-skinned. He never talked about his father, an impulse Amena understood. Beyond telling him about her strange ways of dealing with her mother's clothing, Amena had shared almost nothing about her absent parent. She rarely talked about her mother to anyone, not even her father, though she thought about her all the time. Amena remembered her as beautiful and moody, sometimes playful and full of laughter, and other times completely withdrawn. Her mother had been gone for seven years now, almost half Amena's life. At one point it had felt like there could be no future without her mother, but here they still were.

Zakaria was a bad boyfriend, and Amena doubted that he even considered himself her boyfriend. They'd never talked about it. Instead they'd slipped into sex while hanging out and listening to records in his room after school one afternoon. This became their ritual, and they never discussed the sex or its implications. Their relationship had felt stronger when they were in school and saw each other regularly, but now it was summer, and he called her infrequently and Amena was afraid of scaring him off by calling him. They always met up at his place. Amena never invited him to hers for fear her father would finish a shift early and come home to find her with a boy, which wasn't explicitly forbidden but Amena assumed wasn't allowed. It clearly embarrassed her father to talk about things like boys and dating, so he avoided these and all adjacent topics and left it up to Amena to make good choices.

Zakaria had called her that morning to see if she wanted to come over, and Amena said she was free. She wore her favorite pair of jeans, fitted through her waist and thighs and widening into dramatic bells around her calves, paired with a Led Zeppelin T-shirt that she knew Zakaria admired. Clear lip gloss was the only makeup she used. Everything left behind by her mother had either dried up or become too tacky, and Amena didn't have the kind of girlfriends who discussed things like makeup, making her a minimalist in this area. She didn't think of herself as pretty by conventional standards, mostly because her high school boasted an abundance of blond, athletic beauties, stereotypically pretty girls. Amena had been surprised when Zakaria started paying attention to her, because no boy had ever paid attention to her before. He was smart but not particularly ambitious, unlike Amena, who was both. At a time when so many of their classmates dreamed of going to universities across the country, he wanted to apply only to SUNY schools, Amena suspected for financial reasons.

Zakaria lived next to Gramercy Park. It was the only private park in the city that Amena knew of, and Zakaria and his mother didn't pay the fee to get a key. Zakaria had convinced her to jump the fence after dark once, and they'd made out on a secluded bench for a while. Whenever he smoked pot, a daily habit, he blew his cloudy exhalations out of his second-story window and over the park. There were a number of impressive historic buildings surrounding the park, but Zakaria's wasn't one of them.

Unlike Amena's building, where a doorman greeted residents and visitors alike, an electronic buzzer served as the gatekeeper in Zakaria's building. Amena pressed the button next to Zakaria's apartment number and, after a short delay, heard the buzz signaling she could enter. She had to move quickly, as there were two doors she needed to pass through, one on the outside, and another past the lobby/mailroom. It embarrassed her to have to buzz a second time, next to the inside door, if she didn't make it through before the doors locked again.

As soon as she reached the second floor, Amena heard the Beatles' *White Album* roaring from Zakaria's apartment. He insisted on listening to his music at full volume, often annoying the neighbors. As a compromise, he now blasted it only during the day, when most people were at work.

The door to Zakaria's apartment was slightly ajar, which was her invitation to enter. She followed the loud music to Zakaria's room at the back of the apartment, where she found him sitting on the edge of his bed with his head out the window, smoking a joint. He'd introduced her to pot earlier that year, when they first started hanging out at his place. The first time she smoked, she couldn't stop laughing, to the point where Zakaria was almost ready to take her to the hospital. Her reactions were less extreme after that, as she'd learned how much to smoke to get into the perfect zone of happy and light-headed but shy of loopy, usually just a couple of hits. Zakaria waved her over to sit next to him and then offered her the burning joint.

They started making out as they were smoking, Zakaria blowing smoke from his mouth into hers. If Amena wasn't careful, she'd soon be on another planet. As he kissed her, Zakaria put his hand up Amena's shirt and reached inside her bra to fondle her breasts. The combination of pot and foreplay was almost too much sensation, and yet she felt too disembodied to stop it. The music added another prickly layer of stimulation, the record now spinning out Ringo's clangy "Don't Pass Me By." "Why Don't We Do It in the Road?" came on next, and Amena and Zakaria both laughed. Zakaria didn't like to have sex in his bed, always on the floor. Amena suspected that she might be allergic to the coarse, synthetic fibers of his orange shag rug, the way her back burned red for days after they fucked.

"What are you doing later?" Zakaria asked when they were lying on their backs on the ground afterward. Whenever he said this, Amena took it as a signal that he was ready for her to leave.

"Finally going to Roosevelt Island," she told him.

"You're going to love it. It's wild," Zakaria expressed with uncharacteristic enthusiasm. He was the one who'd told her that it used to be known as Welfare Island and about its past function as a space to corral criminals and people with smallpox and tuberculosis and severe mental illness. Amena had noticed the abandoned-looking island before, a narrow slip of land between midtown Manhattan and Queens, but until Zakaria told her its story, she hadn't known who went there or what it was for.

"You should come with me," Amena suggested, anticipating that Zakaria would say no.

"Nah, not in the mood to leave the house today," he responded, predictably.

Amena shrugged, feigning indifference, when really she would have loved his company. They did little together outside of listening to music and messing around in his room, which was beginning to feel repetitive and claustrophobic.

"What offerings are you going to make to the gods today?" Zakaria asked her.

Amena didn't understand what he meant at first, a little too stoned to make the connection, but then all of a sudden it was obvious.

"That sounds like a beautiful ritual," Zakaria had observed when Amena first told him about what she was doing, elevating the activity to a higher plane.

"Less depressing than dumping everything at Goodwill," Amena had joked in return.

It was Zakaria who first hypothesized that her mother might have had a mental breakdown. His mother was a social worker, so he believed himself to be an amateur authority on psychology. "My mother says people snap all the time," he'd shared before. Amena was not reassured to hear that this was a common occurrence. "Sometimes people vanish and then reappear years later," he'd added, which Amena also did not find helpful. Zakaria asked whether her father ever took her to a therapist to "process" what had happened with her mother, and Amena admitted to him that neither she nor her father had ever considered it. Zakaria frowned in response, suggesting that his mother wouldn't approve. His mother had a crushing caseload and worked long hours, which meant she was almost never home when Amena visited. This was

a relief to Amena, who was afraid of having her life and mind ana-
lyzed by a real expert.

AMENA HADN'T BEEN BACK to Egypt since the summer of 1967,
when her mother disappeared. Her mind often took her there, to
that awful summer, and to prior fun and memorable visits. Though
she understood her father was in pain, Amena thought it was wrong
of him to avoid his parents, a consequence of his avoiding Egypt,
but she didn't have the kind of relationship with him where she felt
comfortable criticizing him. He rarely lost his temper with her, but
she'd seen him unleash it on waiters and bad drivers. It was easy
for her to stay on his good side. He often told her he was proud of
her and that he loved her, and Amena felt his pride and love. There
was perpetually a sadness about him, as if he regretted being all
that she had. It was hard to remember what he was like before 1967
while riding on the continuum of their relationship. He was around
less then, her mother the primary caretaker, while he was in the
throes of his residency. For the first few years without her mother,
they'd relied on an older German woman in their building whom
Amena called Oma, who babysat Amena after school until her father got home. When she turned fourteen, Amena convinced him
to let her stay home alone, but she continued to visit Oma on occasion, less frequently recently, and every time, Oma served homemade apple cake.

It was Amena who first realized that her mother was missing.
She was up before her grandmother that morning, and when she
went to check on her mother, she found the door to her room open
and the bed neatly made. Amena expected her mother would be in
the kitchen or out in the back garden, but she was neither of those
places. Next to the kitchen there was a dark spiral staircase that led
up to the roof, but the staircase spooked her, so Amena avoided it,

and she couldn't imagine her mother having any reason to go up on the roof of the house. Amena checked her grandfather's office, then the dining room, then the salon, but all the rooms were empty and looked like sets in a Victorian period piece. There was only one room on the first floor left to check, the small space that used to belong to Reema, who'd been recently let go. Amena had never looked into that room before, and its paucity surprised her, so austere and minimal compared with the other bedrooms in the house. Amena quickly shut the door, feeling like she wasn't supposed to be there.

Finally she knocked on her grandmother's door. "Come in," her grandmother called from inside, remaining in bed.

Amena entered cautiously, taking small steps into the darkness. Heavy drapes covered the windows, blocking out the morning light. "Mama's not here," Amena said when she reached the edge of the bed.

There was always a delay with her grandmother's response, Amena presumed because she had to translate in her head. Her grandmother spoke stilted English, good enough for Amena to understand, but awkward in the ways of a nonnative speaker. "Your parents fail you by letting English in your home," she'd told Amena on a previous visit. "Such a shame that you have no Arabic."

Though she spoke Arabic like a toddler to her own ears and therefore refused to practice, Amena understood the language better than people thought. Her parents consistently underestimated her degree of comprehension and spoke freely in front of her in Arabic, saying things that caught her by surprise in both awful and amusing ways. *You're selfish and heartless* (her mother). *Don't you look sexy tonight?* (her father). *You don't appreciate how hard I work* (her mother). *Stop acting like a spoiled little rich girl* (her father).

"No need for panic," her grandmother finally said in thickly accented English. "She probably goes shopping or finding you some sweets."

But hours passed, and no mother or sweets appeared, at last triggering her grandmother's worry.

For once Amena wished that her father were with them in Egypt. She tended to prefer visits when it was just her and her mother, as her father's presence tended to add an uncomfortable tension that Amena felt but couldn't identify the source of. She asked her grandmother if they could call her father in New York, and her grandmother looked at the clock on the wall and said, "He will be sleeping. We wait a few hours and try then."

In the meantime her grandmother turned on the television in her bedroom to watch her shows. Amena loved hanging out in her grandmother's bedroom, where she always felt welcome. The room was the size of a large studio apartment by New York standards, with a sturdy mahogany bed at the center, surrounded by a love seat, a pair of chairs, and a chaise longue framing the edge of the room. The television stood atop the tall cabinet that faced the bed. Her grandmother sat in bed when watching television, while Amena opted for the chaise, her favorite spot to sit in her grandmother's room. The chaise reminded her of the movie *Cleopatra*, starring Elizabeth Taylor, which Amena watched with her mother whenever it came on television at home, entranced by the notion that she was culturally connected to the world of the film. Amena focused her eyes on the television, where spirited melodramas played out, her mind spinning with worry about her mother. Even with her limited understanding of the characters' conversations, Amena gathered the emotional gist of the stories from their body language and sing-song tones. Amena also recognized the tropes from her mother's American shows, which played in the background of their afternoons when Amena got home from school. If they were running late, Amena's mother would make them jog the ten blocks home from PS 226 so she could catch the beginning of *Guiding Light*. When they were good on time, Amena could persuade her mother to stop at one of the many fresh fruit stands they passed to let her choose a snack.

Amena eventually fell into an accidental nap and woke up sometime later in a panic. Her grandmother was still there, still watching television. "What time is it?" Amena cried out, rubbing her eyes into focus.

"Almost noon," her grandmother said

"Can we call my daddy now?" Amena asked.

"Okay," her grandmother said with a sigh, suggesting reluctance. She got out of bed and walked over to the television and turned it off.

Amena followed her out of the bedroom and down the hall. The telephone had its own niche, set into a concave cutout in the wall, which made it look to Amena like an object on display in a museum. The phone was fancier than the plastic one they had at home, with a brass receiver and cradle and a heavy ceramic dial. Amena's grandmother lifted the receiver, hooked her finger inside the hole for the 0, and turned the dial all the way until it stopped. It sounded like a spray of tiny bullets as the dial twisted back to reset. She asked Amena if she knew her number at home, and Amena was proud to answer that she did, an artifact of her mother's training. Amena told her grandmother the number, one digit at a time, waiting for the dial to complete its machinations before she fed her the next one. When her grandmother was done dialing, she pushed the receiver toward Amena as if it were something she was eager to hand off.

Amena pressed the bulky apparatus against the side of her face as the line started to ring. *Ring, ring,* and then a pause, *ring, ring,* and then another pause. And then something clicked, and there was her father's groggy voice: "Hello?"

He said he would come right away, but it would be another day before he made it.

In the meantime, a pair of policemen came to the house. Amena's grandmother invited them inside and led them into the fancy room that reminded Amena of period movies set in France. Every time Amena and her mother visited Cairo, her grandparents would host a party and invite a bunch of relatives and friends to celebrate their homecoming—until this trip, which from the start had been uncharacteristically somber and gloomy. Amena's grandfather had died earlier in the summer, just a week after Egypt fought and lost a brief war with Israel—the Six-Day War, Walter Cronkite called it on the evening news. Amena and her mother weren't scheduled to go to Egypt for another month, but after her father died, Amena's mother tried to move up the tickets, to no avail, the airspace over Egypt indefinitely closed. When flights resumed to Cairo a few weeks later, Amena's mother packed hastily, and when they arrived in Cairo, they discovered that she'd forgotten underwear and socks for Amena and toiletries for both of them. When they arrived, Amena was surprised to find her grandmother dressed in a somber black dress, when she normally wore bright colors. Her face was also unusually bare, free of makeup, and when Amena asked her about this in private later, her mother said it was because her grandmother was in mourning.

Two weeks later, her grandmother was still dressed in black. Amena sat beside her in the salon as she conversed with the police in rapid-fire Arabic. They kept addressing her as "*ya ustazah*," a term Amena didn't recognize but gathered from the context was deferential. The men glanced around the room as if impressed, but when they looked at Amena, there was sadness in their eyes. She felt like a mute pet at her grandmother's side, understanding little of the conversation taking place and unable to contribute.

At one point, in response to one of the officers' questions, her grandmother stood, leaving Amena alone on the couch. She had an impulse to jump up and follow her guardian but instead did so only with her eyes as her fingers dug into the silky cushion beneath her. Her grandmother returned with a framed portrait of her mother, though the young woman in the picture looked little like the person she was today, hair ironed flat and swooping upward dramatically at the ends, skin as smooth and flawless as a doll's.

"This is her," her grandmother said, thrusting the picture into the hands of one of the officers, uttering a few words Amena finally understood.

"That's not really how she looks now," Amena added in English. Her grandmother and both policemen turned and stared at her blankly. She knew her grandmother would understand, but it wasn't clear whether the officers did.

One of the policemen pulled out a sketchpad and pencil and began to transfer his interpretation of the photo onto a piece of paper. His hurried sketch resembled her mother even less than the photograph did, causing Amena's hope to deflate.

Every few hours, Amena's grandmother led a trip to the kitchen to find something to eat, usually some combination of bread, cheese, pickles, and preserves. Her grandmother ate very little herself. She was a skinny woman, with a long, gaunt face and a bony physique. Amena ate at least twice as much as she did each time they visited the kitchen. From what Amena had managed to glean from sparsely understood arguments in Arabic between her mother and grandmother right after they first arrived, her grandmother had let go of Reema, the longtime housekeeper, and Amena's mother was devastated and enraged by this.

"How could you?" she'd demanded. Amena's grandmother shouted something back that Amena didn't understand. "What will she do?" her mother shrieked at a high pitch, followed by a few unfamiliar words.

"I'm a . . ." her grandmother said. "You can't expect me to . . ."

"Where is your heart?" Amena's mother asked, through tears. This was a phrase Amena often heard her mother use when arguing with her father.

Her grandmother turned away with tears in her eyes and disappeared into her room, leaving Amena and her mother to fend for themselves.

After eating, Amena and her grandmother returned upstairs to her grandmother's bedroom, where her grandmother resumed watching her shows. Time seemed to move very slowly, the hours attenuating around her mother's absence. Every once in a while, the call to prayer interrupted the programming, whatever drama was on-screen switching abruptly to a slide inscribed with Arabic words Amena couldn't read, overlaid with the sound of a man chanting, *"Allahu Akbar. Allahu Akbar . . ."* Farther out and always at a slight delay, the call to prayer resounded from what sounded like a set of speakers perched on top of a building in the distance. Her mother liked to laugh and tell the tale of Amena breaking into sobs whenever the call to prayer echoed during her first visit to Cairo as an infant. "It terrified you so!" her mother teased.

With a heavy sigh, Amena's grandmother climbed off her bed and left Amena alone in the room, with the sonorous prayer echoing from the television. When her grandmother returned a few minutes later, her hands and face were damp and her cheeks ruddy. She kept her prayer rug and shawl draped over the back of a chair close to the bed. She put on the shawl first, covering her head and shoulders with the silky white fabric, and then unfolded the prayer rug onto the floor. Amena had seen her mother pray a few times, but as far as Amena knew, it wasn't an activity she engaged in regularly.

Watching her grandmother from the sidelines, Amena was mesmerized. When her mother prayed, she prayed in secret, behind semiclosed doors that Amena had peeked around a few times while her mother was in the act. Amena was surprised the first few times her grandmother prayed in her presence over the past few days. Her grandmother's apparent lack of discomfort eventually put Amena at ease. She rather enjoyed these regimented interruptions, calmed by the elegant flow of the older woman's body moving through the poses. A few times on her own, when she was sure that no one was watching, Amena had tried out this dance herself, beginning in a tall standing pose with her hands cupped over her belly and her eyes closed, then bending at the waist with her eyes on the ground, and finally getting down onto her knees and pressing her face to the floor, repeating the whole sequence a couple of times. No words accompanied Amena's prayer beyond the opening phrases—*Allahu Akbar*. She always felt at peace after performing this secret ritual and imagined that the experience must be even more powerful for those who knew what they were doing.

"Will you teach me how to do that?" Amena asked when her grandmother was done.

Her grandmother gave her a perplexed look, and then her face disappeared momentarily as she lifted the shawl off her head. "Your mother never teaches you?" she asked, laying the shawl over the back of the chair where she kept it.

Amena shook her head, embarrassed on behalf of both her mother and herself for this failure in her education. When Amena had asked her mother directly whether she believed in God, "it depends on the day," her mother had mused, with the mysterious diction of a fortune-teller.

"Later," her grandmother responded with a heavy sigh, waving her hand dismissively. "We wait for your mother first. She comes home, and then we worry about other things."

Amena intermittently fell asleep on the chaise in her grandmother's room. Her parents flashed in and out of her quick, discordant dreams, so it wasn't a surprise to hear her father's voice vibrating at the edge of her consciousness at some point. He murmured something about the police, triggering Amena's awareness that he might be anchored in reality. Focusing on his voice, she accelerated toward consciousness. He was speaking in Arabic. *Was she angry? Was she acting strange?*

Opening her eyes, Amena took woozy stock of her surroundings. For a moment she didn't understand where she was, and then all at once she did.

Amena tumbled out of the chaise and hurried toward the sound of her father's voice, bare feet padding over an alternating landscape of textured rug and stone floor tile. Halfway down the stairs, she missed a step and lost her footing. She fell and slid down the rest of the way, head bumping on the last few steps. Landing in the foyer, Amena spotted her father and grandmother rushing toward her. Her father called her name, and at the same time her grandmother shouted some endearment. They were both upon her, hands gripping her body, asking if she was okay in overlapping Arabic and English. And then she was rising up into the air, her father's breath warm and sour on her face. "Oh, *habibti*, what happened?"

Amena twisted in his arms, eager to be on her feet. Every part of her cried out in pain, from her head to her belly to her legs. Even the backs of her eyes hurt. But mostly she was embarrassed that she'd fallen and was being treated like a baby. Nothing made Amena feel prouder than being told by adults that she seemed mature for her age. She thrived on demonstrating to others how smart and strong-willed she was. *I'm fine*, a voice in her head yelled as she untangled herself from her father. *I'm fine. I'm fine. I'm fine.*

FROM ZAKARIA'S PLACE, Amena caught a bus to midtown and then transferred to another one headed east, ultimately destined for Forest Hills, Queens. "Where do I get off for Roosevelt Island?" Amena asked the driver as she boarded.

"There's a stop halfway across the bridge," the driver answered without skipping a beat. "From there you can take an elevator or stairs down to the island."

Amena thanked him and sat near the front of the bus. The Queensboro Bridge rose over the eastern edge of Manhattan, shrinking the swath of the city beneath them. The island was such a short distance away that if it were okay to swim in the East River, Amena would have been able to get there from Manhattan. In the middle of the bridge, the driver pulled to the side of the road and waved at Amena. "This is you."

She was the only passenger to exit. Standing at the edge of the bridge once the bus rolled off, Amena felt as if she'd been dumped in the middle of a highway, with multiple lanes of traffic rushing by in both directions. She walked over the rails of a defunct trolley line and found the stairs leading down to the island.

As she descended the desolate staircase, Amena wondered whether this was the kind of place where teenage girls got murdered. She did a lot of things that her mother would have considered risky, from riding the subway to wandering around Central Park at night, but Amena normally felt safe in the city and avoided places that were known to be dangerous. She felt protected by the presence of strangers almost everywhere she went, but this was certainly the oddest place she'd ever been to in the city, the northern half of the island populated with modern buildings and the southern half covered with weeds and architectural ruins. The island's dark history as a dumping ground for society's outcasts had captured Amena's imagination. Her mother had grown up on a different urban island, on the Nile in the middle of Cairo. Amena identified an affinity that she couldn't quite put into words, compelling her to visit Roosevelt Island with some of her mother's things.

As Amena walked toward the southern end of the skinny landmass, she didn't see anyone else around. She didn't think of New York as a city that harbored ruins from past eras, but straight ahead lay evidence to the contrary. It was strange to discover such an empty expanse of land so close to the city, traffic racing by on the FDR just across the dark strip of the East River.

Approaching the crumbled edifices, Amena thought about her mother. She considered the possibility of her mother having wound up in an asylum, banished from civilization like the onetime inhabitants of this island. Without any real knowledge, Amena assumed that ending up in a public mental hospital in Egypt would be a very grim fate. Her father had raised her to be critical of Egypt and its systems, and after her mother disappeared there, this was an easy sell.

The hospital had been out of commission since 1957, when the Charity Hospital and the Smallpox Hospital that were last housed there moved their operations to Elmhurst. Judging from the one facade that remained standing and intact, the hospital had three floors, three rows of windows that were identical on the bottom two floors and topped with triangular flourishes on the top row of windows. Vines grew up the walls like vertical rugs, covering the face of the building. Amena stepped closer and peeked through the first-floor windows and saw that the interior shell of the building was also overcome by nature, carpeted with weeds and vines. She'd never found such a perfect place to leave behind traces of her mother. Amena walked around the building until she found a wall that was half collapsed and easy to climb. Then she was inside what used to be the old hospital. She looked up at the open sky, imagining a time when there would have been a ceiling, when these rooms were full. Wandering around the ruined labyrinth, Amena climbed over broken walls from one semi-enclosed space to the next. She thought of mothers separated from their children, of children separated from their mothers, and she cried thinking of her mother. "I don't really know what I'm doing," her father had said a lot in the beginning, when it was just the two of them, when it came to packing her lunch for school or doing laundry or trying to learn how to braid Amena's hair. He figured most things out (except the braiding, which he never mastered, instead compelling Amena to keep her hair short until she could braid it herself).

Opening her backpack, Amena took out her "offerings," as Zakaria had called them, the outfit Amena remembered her mother wearing to the playground, and she laid the dress on the ground, spreading out the skirt and arranging the sleeves as if they were inhabited. It was remarkably easy to imagine her mother lying there. Amena wiped her wet face with the back of her hand as she fished out her mother's sandals from the bag and arranged them where the feet would go, pointed outward in opposite directions. Her father had asked her recently if she thought about her mother often. Caught off guard and always wanting to seem strong for him, Amena lied and told him, "No, not that much."

"I think about her all the time," her father said in return, stabbing Amena with his honesty.

For a finishing touch, Amena found the last few items at the bottom of her bag: a pair of gold earrings and a matching ring made from old British coins. Amena couldn't recall her mother ever wearing this jewelry, which looked gaudy to her. The only earrings she remembered her mother wearing were the small diamond studs she'd had since getting her ears pierced as a baby, and the only ring she wore was her slim gold wedding band. Amena discovered the set inlaid with coins while going through her mother's things, in a satin-covered jewelry box tucked behind her mother's underwear. Amena asked her father about them, and he said he had no idea what they were or where they came from. Her mother's diamond earrings and wedding band disappeared with her, but she left behind a wooden box on her dresser filled with necklaces that she used to rotate between, the only type of jewelry she collected and wore besides her staples. Amena treasured that wooden box, with its delicate little drawers holding small, pretty things, and would never give it or any of its contents away. But she had no trouble parting with the coin earrings and ring, foreign as they were to her, setting them at the approximate positions where ears and a finger would be. On her way home, Amena felt lighter, both in cargo and spirit.

AMENA, 1976

AT THE BEGINNING of the winter term of her freshman year at
Stanford, Amena took a field trip with her art history class to San
Francisco to attend a gallery opening. There were only thirteen people in the class, including a few graduate students, and Amena felt
conspicuously young and naive in their company. She'd taken a
survey of modern art with the same professor the term before and
became so enamored with both the woman and the subject that she
decided to sign up for whatever the professor was teaching in the
winter, no matter that it was an advanced seminar. Amena tried to
disguise her insecure grasp of the material by taking furious notes.

They squeezed into three cars, their professor driving the lead
vehicle. After almost an hour, their caravan exited the highway
and entered an industrial part of San Francisco. The neighborhood
reminded Amena of the western edge of Manhattan, full of ware-

houses and idle delivery trucks and homeless people sleeping in front of shuttered businesses. There were no charming hills in this part of town, no view of the ocean. Their caravan turned onto a dead-end street, revealing a bustling scene where the road culminated, people spilling out of the one storefront on the block that was lit up. Their professor parked in front of a fire hydrant, and the other two cars pulled in side-by-side on a short driveway heavily labeled with "No Parking" signs.

Climbing out of the car, Amena felt as if she were stepping into a secret world. Sweat broke out on her forehead and upper lip as she scanned the sophisticated crowd in the distance. Their haircuts and clothes made statements, unlike the drab jeans and sweatshirt she was wearing and her schoolgirl, shoulder-length bob with bangs. She felt like a kid and probably was a kid compared with everyone else here. Even her classmates had an age advantage over her and looked cooler and more mature. She'd never felt so desperate to overhaul her personal style than at that moment. If Amena had known that she would end the day in San Francisco at an art opening, she would have borrowed something from her roommate, Angela, who had much better clothes.

The crowd outside the gallery formed a circle around what Amena came to recognize as a performance taking place in the middle of the street. A naked woman stood at the center, painting her skin with a large paintbrush that she dipped into buckets of paint at her feet. Her legs, already coated, dripped with blue and green pigment, and she'd painted her crotch a bright red; the dark wiry hairs there were beginning to reemerge as the paint slithered off. The audience stood transfixed. When Amena finally brought herself to look away from the performer, she noticed that the vast majority of people here were women. This put Amena at ease in a way that made her recognize she'd been scared for the woman before. Now she realized no one here was going to hurt her, and if someone tried, there was an army of other women here to protect her.

When Amena glanced back over her shoulder, she noticed that

everyone she'd come with was gone, leaving her in the company of a bunch of strangers. Hugging her arms tightly across her chest, she zigzagged through the crowd toward the door of the gallery, afraid that her classmates would leave without her and she'd have to find a way to get back to campus on her own. But then she spotted two people she knew standing in line for the bar near the door. The setup was like at a house party, with a folding plastic table serving as the bar and a couple of people pouring drinks on the other side. A sparkling gold tablecloth covered the table, making this decidedly fancier than any party Amena had ever been to. Not normally one to shy away from free drinks, Amena felt nervous about imbibing in front of legal adults, so she didn't join her peers in the bar line. Instead she walked deeper into the gallery, coming around the corner into an expansive space filled with even more guests and a string of framed photographs hanging on the walls. The pictures looked small within the high-ceilinged, cavernous space, though they were much larger than any photographs Amena had ever seen, each around twenty-by-twenty-four inches. She was used to photographs being something you pasted into albums or carried around in your wallet, and these were enormous by comparison.

Their content was also like nothing Amena had ever seen. A plastic woman leaning over the railing of a dollhouse balcony past the tipping point, frozen in that moment of certain disaster. Another female doll pinned beneath the body of a male doll on the floor of a windowless dark space next to a green couch. Another doll hiding in a closet that was just slightly ajar, the room beyond the closet in a violent state of disarray, dresser overturned, mattress flipped off the bed, clothes and small objects littering the ground. One photograph showed a figure whose head and torso were submerged in an open oven. Another, a woman wielding a knife over small plastic vegetables. Each image was disturbing in its own way, perhaps more so because they cast childhood objects in such a dark light.

While slowly circling the perimeter of the room, stopping to look closely at each photograph, Amena ran into one of her classmates. By then she'd forgotten that finding company had been her goal. "What do you think?" Rita asked, and Amena was startled to be called upon to give an opinion. She shrugged as if to say she hadn't formed one yet and turned the question back on Rita: "You?"

"I probably shouldn't say what I think in case the artist is right behind me," Rita answered in a quiet voice.

They both turned to look at the crowd behind them, groups of various sizes clustered together, talking and laughing among themselves. There was a particularly large group at the center of the gallery around which all of the surrounding planets seemed to orbit. A tall brunette was clearly the energetic center of that cluster, the focus of all her neighbors' attention. She had short, spiky hair and wore a patterned vest over a men's dress shirt, and she gesticulated theatrically as she spoke, too far away for Amena to hear what she was saying.

Rita leaned in and shared her thoughts at last, speaking just above a whisper: "I think it's a little too obvious, frankly. I don't like art that tells me how to feel."

Amena looked back at the photograph hanging in front of them: a plastic doll standing over a dollhouse sink with her hand inside a headless chicken. It reminded Amena of her mother, the only person she'd ever seen clean and prepare a raw chicken. This made Amena's heart ache a little. Suddenly, thanks to Rita, Amena felt suspicious of the photograph's capacity to evoke her emotions and glared back at its mirrored surface.

Upset by the intrusion of her mother into her thoughts, Amena decided to get a drink after all. She got in line behind an older man with scruffy hair that covered his neck, wearing a T-shirt and wide-legged jeans. He turned around to greet her, and Amena felt her face go hot and red. Her embarrassment was twofold: he was handsome, and she was afraid of getting caught. He turned back around without another word. Amena pulled the cuffs of her sweatshirt down over her hands and covered the logo on her chest with her arms. Her father had bought it for her from the university gift shop the day he dropped her off at school. Usually he didn't buy her clothes, instead taking her to Macy's twice a year to let her shop for what she needed while he went to the café on the seventh floor and read the newspaper. Amena liked the sweatshirt because it was from her father, but she felt like an idiot wearing it, the way it marked her both as a college kid and as an overachiever. When it came his turn at the bar, the man in front of Amena swiveled around and asked her what she wanted.

"Beer!" she answered in a panic.

He smiled and turned back to the bartender. "Two beers," he said, and the bartender cracked two cans of Rheingold and handed them across the table. The man passed one to Amena and toasted her by raising his can in the air, and then he walked away to join a group of friends in the distance. Amena stood for a moment with the beer in her hand, not knowing what to do, flustered by the man's sudden departure.

She and her professor and classmates stayed until the gallery emptied out and somebody working there turned off the lights around ten o'clock. Standing outside the gallery, their professor hugged and kissed the brunette with the vest and spiky hair, now confirmed as the artist, and Amena felt starstruck by the intimacy of their friendship—that her professor was close with an artist who showed her work in galleries. It felt as if this world were in Amena's grasp suddenly, and she wanted to be a part of it. They rode back to campus in the same cars as on the way up. Amena was happy to let everyone else do the talking while she let the magic of the night soak in.

AMENA DIDN'T LOOK FORWARD to going back to New York for the summer. By moving to California, she'd accomplished exactly what she'd set out to do: escape New York and her past. Surprisingly few people at college had pressed for details when it came up that her mother was absent, which was liberating after years of feeling like someone who couldn't escape being known as the girl whose mother had disappeared when she was in the fourth grade. Even her roommate, who'd become a good friend, knew only the contours of the story, the wispy details Amena offered. *We're not really sure what happened to her. She's been gone for so long now. I almost forget what it was like when she was around.*

Her father had made it clear that if she chose to go to school across the country when there were so many good options in or near New York City, where she could have free room and board, then she would have to pay for her own rent and food. So Amena worked in the central library on campus for twenty-four hours a week to earn her keep, and as soon as she got back to New York, she found a job at a local bakery. She was assigned the early shift, responsible for arriving at five in the morning and taking the trays of raw, formed bagels out of the refrigerator, letting them rise, and baking them. With the batches that required toppings, she had to work quickly after taking them out of the oven, shaking on the seeds or salt or sprinkling on dried bits of onion or garlic. At the end of every shift, she got to bring home bags of bagels and pastries, which were her mainstay outside of the takeout dinners her father brought home, causing her to gain fifteen pounds in the first three weeks.

She would come home from her job and nap for hours, getting up to eat dinner and watch TV with her father, and then going to sleep again. As always, her father's favorite genres were detective shows and police procedurals, which meant that Amena had passively absorbed hundreds of hours *Kojak*, *Hawaii Five-O*, and *Cannon*. She didn't understand why these shows appealed to her father, especially given the preponderance of missing women they featured, when they made her feel numb inside, sending her back to bed.

She'd had lackluster reunions with old friends from high school over the holidays and wasn't eager to reconnect with them while she was home for the summer. Amena felt somewhat embarrassed to be back in New York, as if she were regressing in life and none of the past year had happened. And yet, she found the energy to send postcards to all her friends from college at their respective summer locations. Amena bought stacks of generic postcards from newsstands, picturing the Empire State and Chrysler Buildings, the Statue of Liberty, the iconic Island of Manhattan seen from another shore. Usually she wrote just a few words on the cards—*Have you ever wished you could scale a building like King Kong?* or, *I heard once that the mob likes to dump bodies in the East River,* or, *I grew up here and have never been to the Statue of Liberty. Can you believe that?* Friends wrote back letters to say how much they loved her post-cards, which Amena found ironic, that they wouldn't reply with postcards.

"I hate to let you go again," her father said at the end of the summer.

Amena nodded in response, hiding her joy that summer was coming to an end. The sense of heaviness that used to weigh her down when she was growing up had returned over the past few months, and she was eager to get back to school and resume what she thought of as her real life.

"How did I let you talk me into letting you go to school all the way across the country?" her father asked.

Amena didn't answer, looking up from her packing only to shake her head and smile with patient frustration.

"I suppose I left my parents behind and went even further away," her father mused. He had a knack for making Amena feel guilty and sorry for him in the same instant, setting his expectations for her in the context of his own failures.

"You did what you had to do," Amena offered, in defense of both their actions.

RESOLVED NOT TO SPEND another depressing summer in New York, Amena searched for opportunities to avoid that fate. Early on during the fall term of her sophomore year, she applied for an internship at a biology lab on campus, and after a couple of interviews she secured the position. "It's rare to get female applicants and especially unusual to see students of your background applying for these jobs," the lab's principal investigator told Amena during her second interview, marginalizing her in a way that she recognized was supposed to be positive but made her feel small and inferior.

There were five other people in the lab besides Amena and the PI. The last couple of weeks of her sophomore year, Amena trained at the lab under one of the graduate students who worked there. The lab bred fruit flies—*Drosophila melanogaster*—to study the transference of genetic material from one generation to the next. A fruit fly's life cycle lasted only ten days, the grad student explained, which allowed scientists to trace many generations over a short period of time. Amena's job was to organize data and put dead fruit flies inside small glassine envelopes, which she labeled with the dates of the insect's life cycle and stored in neat trays inside the freezer. After just a few weeks on the job, Amena grew bored of the tasks and the tedium.

The past year had confirmed her love of art. She'd dedicated all of her electives to taking classes in the department, including a photography course that was the highlight of her year. Her professor carried around a point-and-shoot camera everywhere he went and was famous for black-and-white pictures he'd taken at parties in the sixties. At Amena's request, her father bought her a compact camera for her birthday, but it mostly sat like a weight at the bottom of her backpack. She felt self-conscious taking it out in public and didn't have the nerve to photograph people without their permission. She didn't understand how all of those street photographers were so bold and courageous, and then it occurred to her that all of the ones she'd studied were white men. Amena's photographs tended to gravitate toward the private sphere, on the other hand: surreal collages of inanimate objects or abstract self-portraits. Her professor commended her work for its originality, cementing her desire to be an artist.

But the jobs all seemed to be in science, which was what had led Amena to the lab. It felt like an insurance plan to keep a foot planted in science while she pursued her love of art. With her meager earnings from the lab, she rented a room in an apartment off campus that she shared with a junior who was spending her summer interning in a lab that studied butterflies. Shannon was unequivocal about what she wanted to do once she graduated: she planned to begin straight away on her PhD, and she had a long list of programs that she planned to apply to the following year. Though she found the prospect of such a future grim, Amena could fully imagine herself following the same path.

Her father made a visit to California for a long weekend in the middle of July. "Since you never come home to visit me anymore," he claimed. Amena felt the stab of this criticism but laughed it off.

Her father rented a car and a room in a motel near her apartment. Amena took him on a tour of the lab, which he walked through with the joyous expression of a kid at an amusement park. "I could understand if you wanted to do this instead of being a doctor," he offered at the end of the tour. "There's something to be said for not having to deal with death—human death," he qualified.

Amena took a couple of days off to spend time sightseeing with her father. They drove to the beach in Santa Cruz and across the Golden Gate Bridge to Muir Woods, where they stood beneath a canopy of two-hundred-foot-tall redwood trees. They spent a day in San Francisco, where they explored the city's famous hills by car, stopping in North Beach for ice cream. Later, they ate clam chowder out of bread bowls at Fisherman's Wharf and afterward went for a walk down the blustery pier near the wharf. Alcatraz loomed in the middle of the bay, a defunct prison and lighthouse sitting on an island, imposing even from a distance. It made Amena think of Roosevelt Island and of its past lives.

Her father said, "Reminds me of going to see my brother in prison."

Amena was too surprised to answer. The few times she'd tried to ask her father about him, he'd brushed her off.

"Do you think he's still in jail?" Amena wondered nervously once she'd recovered her voice.

Her father paused to look into another cell, peeking into the small, dark space beyond the bars. "There's no knowing, now that my parents are gone. They would have been the ones to tell me that before." He shrugged. "They were the only thing connecting me to Hassan."

"You've never tried to find him?" Amena inquired, feeling bold.

Her father frowned and shook his head. "No good could come from that."

"What do you mean?" Amena asked. They were now standing face-to-face at the end of the pier, the wind whipping around them and turning Amena's long, loose hair into a nuisance.

"He's not a good person," her father answered matter-of-factly. He regarded her seriously for a moment, as if weighing whether or not to share what was on his mind. "Did you know that he was one of the last people to see your mother alive?" he finally said.

"Is she dead?" Amena asked with alarm, afraid that her father knew something crucial that he was keeping from her.

"I meant, one of the last people to see her, period," her father corrected.

"How?" Amena asked, none of this quite making sense.

"She visited him at the prison," her father revealed. Amena saw tears form in his eyes, and he looked away. "He told that to my parents in a letter later, confessed that she'd been visiting him there for years."

Amena stumbled backward. Her impulse was to run away from this unwelcome information, which added a new layer of mystery to an already inscrutable enigma. "Does he know what happened to her?" Amena asked in a high, desperate voice, catching the attention of several passersby.

Her father turned to look at the prison again. "Nothing he had to say was of any use," he answered spitefully, after a pause. "My father was the one to visit and get the story. If it had been me, I would have killed him . . ."

Reading into his subtext, Amena considered for the first time that a love affair might have sparked her mother's disappearance. Of all of the disasters she'd considered, this was not one of them. She pictured her mother on the night she disappeared, dressed nicely and heavily made up. Amena had wondered aloud whether her mother was going somewhere fancy, which her mother denied and dismissed.

"Are you saying . . . ?" Amena began but couldn't finish.

Her father ignored her half-question and started walking back to where the pier began. "I'm not saying anything," Amena heard him mumble as she scrambled to catch up. "I never should have opened my mouth."

For the rest of the weekend, he acted closed off and quiet. They stuck close to campus and ate at overpriced Italian restaurants. Both alone and with him, Amena ruminated over what he'd told her. She remembered her mother as a woman of faith, pictured her with covered hair kneeling with deference on a prayer mat. It felt like her father had tossed a bomb into their home and blown the roof off their heads.

Instead of discussing the wreckage, they talked about what classes Amena was going to take in the fall. Her father was enamored with the fact that she was going to take a course from a celebrated biologist who'd helped solve the nucleotide sequence for transfer RNA in the fifties. "You're so lucky. I'm so jealous," he told her repeatedly, which made her feel guilty for her own lack of enthusiasm.

It was a relief once her father left, Amena shamefully recognized. She went to bed early that night and slept in the next morning, exhausted from the past few days.

IN THE FALL, THE UNIVERSITY'S art department hosted a series of lectures by visiting Land artists. Not previously familiar with the genre, Amena spent hours at the art library reading through articles in magazines from the past decade. The first invited artist was a soft-spoken British man in his late forties who walked long distances across remote landscapes, efforts he recorded with photographs, maps, and drawings. The second artist in the series had built a cave in West Texas that thousands of people a year made a pilgrimage to visit. After his visit, Amena committed to attending every lecture in the series. To her surprise, she found that she recognized the third visiting artist, Adam Locke. As she sat in the second row of the auditorium listening to the chair of the department introduce the guest seated at the center of the stage, it dawned on Amena where she'd seen him before: he was the guy who got her a beer at the opening of the show of pictures of dollhouse tableaux. Amena's breath caught in her throat. The audience clapped—she joined in belatedly—and the artist approached the podium.

Afterward, at a reception for the artist in the lobby of the art building, Amena found ways to loiter near whatever groups he was a part of. The professors and graduate students mainly vied for his attention. When Amena saw her photography professor take her turn talking to the artist, she saw an opportunity to infiltrate.

"Oh!" Amena's professor announced as Amena sidled up to them. "This is Amena Seif, one of the most promising young artists in our department."

Amena's face reddened as the artist looked at her and smiled. His hair was considerably shorter than it had been a couple of years ago, chopped to within an inch of his head now, and no longer wavy. "What kind of work do you make?" he asked her.

"Um," she said, her heart pounding. "I'm still figuring that out, but I like to take pictures, I guess."

"Fair enough," Adam said. "The best artists are the ones who can't be pigeonholed."

In the brief slideshow retrospective of his work he'd just taken them through, he'd shown a wide variety of pieces, from drawings to sculpture to video, and finally, of course, large-scale works that involved the landscape. Amena had been attracted to him in a dull, girlish way before, but now she was fully enamored.

"When will your crater be done?" she blurted.

He smiled again. "The eternal question. I guess when I decide that I'm done with it."

The last piece he'd shown was a work in progress, his most monumental project to date. It was on the site of the property where he'd grown up in Arizona. He'd razed the house, and his initial idea had been to dig a hole in the ground as deep as the house, like a negative house, but now the crater extended almost to the edges of the property line, and he wanted to make it "as deep as one of those craters caused by a meteor hitting the Earth." During his lecture he'd laughed that the neighbors weren't happy and there were lawsuits pending—Amena couldn't tell if that last part was a joke.

Soon a new swarm of sycophants swooped in, and just like that, Amena's conversation with the artist was over. For the rest of the evening, she kept an eye on him while sipping ginger ale, and a few times she caught him looking back at her.

A few weeks later Amena came up with an idea for an artwork she wanted to make. She would record her mother's story onto an eight-track cassette tape, in the first person, which people would be able to listen to on headphones in a small, dark gallery. She told the idea to Liz, her photography professor—Amena's only professor who insisted on being called by her first name—who said it sounded brilliant. "You *need* to make this," she advised Amena, and then helped Amena secure $500 in departmental funding to spend the following summer producing the work—enough to live on without having to take another job.

Amena sailed through the rest of junior year on a high, knowing she'd achieved some success as an artist. This made her feel sexy and alluring in a new way. She attracted the attention of two boys at once, after having had no romantic prospects for years. The first one was a graduate student in the English department who lived in the building where Amena shared an apartment with Angela, roommates now for the third year in a row. The other was a boy her age who had a painting studio in the art department, where Amena frequently ran into him. She hooked up with both of them and ended up with two lovers.

Neither of them talked about commitment or demanded exclusivity, so Amena found no need to mention her polygamy. Paul, the grad student who lived on the eighth floor of their building, came down to see Amena once or twice a week, and they always ended up in her bedroom fucking. Still stunted from the rejections she'd faced in her freshman year, Amena never went up to his apartment to initiate contact. Then there was Ben, the painter, who invited Amena to parties on the weekends. Their first few nights together had ended chastely, much to Amena's disappointment, leading Amena to accept that he just liked her as a friend. And then, a month into their friendship, he surprised her by inviting her back to his place instead of dropping her off at her apartment complex. He offered her another drink, though they were already both drunk, and then they promptly abandoned those drinks once they were behind the closed door of Ben's bedroom, Ben turning suddenly serious and taking Amena's face in his hands to kiss her.

Both relationships faded by the end of the year. Apropos of nothing and following a night of sex that had been full of tenderness, Paul abruptly ceased to visit. Too cowardly to go upstairs and see him, Amena stewed in the shame of feeling rejected. A few weeks later, she ran into him in the lobby with his arm around a pretty,

green-eyed redhead. Amena made brief eye contact with him before Paul and his date hurried off toward the elevators, leaving
Amena standing by the mailboxes, forgetting what she was there
for. Around the same time, at the end of the semester Amena went
to find Ben in his studio, only to discover that he'd packed up and
moved out. She didn't have his phone number, and he hadn't asked
for hers. He'd mentioned that he was going home to Chicago for the
summer, but she'd assumed he would tell her before he left.

Angela moved to Boston for an internship at a publishing house
that summer, leaving Amena with the apartment to herself. Since
she could cover the full rent with money from her stipend, she decided not to take on another roommate. She spent the first few days
of summer arranging the apartment to allow for maximum pro-
ductivity: she moved her desk from her bedroom out to the living
room and stacked up the books she'd checked out from the library
on the floor next to the couch. For months she'd been collecting
blank notebooks, with the idea that she would need many once she
started writing. So far, she hadn't started writing.

After arranging the apartment, Amena started digging into the
books she'd checked out for research. A large book of photographs
featuring Cairo in the forties and fifties, to put her into the mind-
set of her mother's childhood; a voluminous twentieth-century history of the Middle East; Nelson Mandela's *Conversations with Myself*; and several books each by Maya Angelou, Jacques Lacan, and
Michel Foucault.

A month into the summer, and Amena still hadn't started writing. Each time she sat down at the typewriter and tried to write as
her mother, she couldn't conjure a single word that sounded true
and right. She'd type out a few sentences only to rebel against them
minutes later, ripping the sheet out of the typewriter and tossing it.
These efforts left her feeling depleted and weak, crying in bed. She
doubted the whole enterprise of what she was doing and started to
think that she'd duped those who thought she could be an artist.

In her isolation she ruminated on her concurrent abandonment by Ben and Paul. Amena feared there was something fundamentally unsound about her, something broken. She'd been careful not to mention her mother with either of them, always afraid of coming off as desperate and vulnerable, believing that boys didn't like girls who were needy. Maybe it was obvious even if she didn't mention it, a deep sadness that she couldn't hide.

Her father called her to check in every Sunday evening. One night he told her, "I don't like the sound of your voice," which Amena recognized as a direct translation of a common Arabic phrase but which struck her as unkind nonetheless.

"Gee, thanks," she told him, on the verge of tears.

"Did I wake you up?" her father asked. "Are you feeling well?"

Amena sat up in bed, cradling the phone against the side of her face. It was five in the evening. She'd laid down to rest at two. "I didn't sleep well," she lied, when in fact she'd slept for ten hours straight the night before.

Amena could hear him thinking through the phone during the long silence that followed. "Have you thought more about coming home for a visit?" he asked finally. "It might be good for you."

At that moment Amena could think of nothing more soothing than lying in her childhood bed, and yet something held her back from agreeing to his proposal. "I'll call a travel agent tomorrow and get you a ticket," her father persisted, in spite of Amena's lack of response. She started crying at the thought of going home—at the thought of giving up. "It's decided," her father said firmly. "Get a good night's sleep, and I'll call you in the morning."

IN HER ENERVATED STATE, Amena found it arduous to pack, almost as difficult as studying for her final exam in organic chemistry a few weeks before. Every step felt like labor: unearthing her suitcase from underneath her bed, finding clothes (she hadn't done laundry in weeks, so she resorted to packing dirty garments), recalling what toiletries one needed when practicing normal hygiene. None of her friends had stuck around for the summer, and she hadn't bothered to make any new ones, so she had to rely on a taxi service to get to the airport. She planned this too late and arrived with less than an hour to spare before her flight. They'd closed the gate to her plane by the time she arrived, and Amena burst into tears in front of the airline workers. One of them ran out from behind the desk to comfort her and, in concert with her coworkers, reopened the gate to let Amena onto the plane.

She slept for the entire flight, from takeoff through touchdown. A flight attendant woke her up to tell her they had landed. It was dark in New York, nine o'clock at night. Amena was the last person off the plane, and when she stepped into the terminal, one of the first things she saw was her father regarding the people exiting ahead of her with a cross expression. When he caught her eye, his face lit up, entirely transforming. He ran to her, and she fell into his warm and sturdy embrace.

"Why are you crying?" he asked her, pulling away and lifting her chin.

Amena barely recognized that tears were falling from her eyes. "I think something's wrong with me," she sobbed.

Her father felt for a fever and said, "You're not too warm."

"Can we go home?" Amena quietly pleaded, sensing the unwanted attention of strangers watching them.

Traffic clotted up the freeway between JFK and Manhattan, coming to a complete standstill near the mouth of the Williamsburg Bridge. Amena closed her eyes to keep from crying, overwhelmed by the sensation of being home and shame over the failure that had brought her here. Her father periodically reached over to touch her shoulder, but that was their only communication for the entire ride.

At last, the taxi pulled up in front of the colossal gray blocks of their apartment complex. The first thing Amena did once they were inside the apartment was go and take a nap in her room.

The scent of fried garlic pulled her back to consciousness sometime later. This wasn't the smell of takeout but home cooking warming on a stove. She stumbled to the kitchen to find her father stirring something in a pot. "What are you making?" Amena asked incredulously.

He turned back and smiled when he saw her. "*Molokhia*," he answered, with a pronounced guttural inflection. There was no equivalent for the *kh* sound in English; it was soothing to hear even just a little bit of Arabic. "You used to love this when you were a kid," he told her as he returned to stirring. "Your mother used to make it."

Though it had been over ten years since she last ate the viscous green soup, Amena conjured a vivid memory of the way it tasted. She leaned over to look inside the pot, smiling into the fragrant steam that wafted up to heat her face. She couldn't recall a single instance of her father cooking a meal besides scrambled eggs or *ful maddamas* before. It struck her that he was rising to meet the gravity of the occasion of her breakdown, which made her want to cry anew, but she backed away from the pot and swiped the back of her wrist across her eyes.

After they'd eaten and pushed away their bowls, Amena's father told her, "I always worried something like this might happen."

The warmth in Amena's stomach turned into a sharp ache. "Like what?" she mumbled, afraid.

Her father took a deep breath and crossed his arms in front of him along the edge of the table. "Your mother went through ups and downs," he admitted slowly. "At the time I thought it was just moods, but later I came to understand that it was something different, more serious."

Amena tried to grasp what he was saying, coming to a hazy conclusion: "You mean you think she was ill?"

He gave a few small nods and added, "Mentally ill," recalling Zakaria and the possibility that had lived in Amena's head since he
first introduced it.

Amena's head grew light, and she wanted to lie down again. She
stood to leave, unsteady and dizzy. "I don't mean to scare you," her
father said, coming abruptly to his feet. Amena shook her head, too
stunned to speak, and retreated to her bedroom. As if by some unspoken rule, her father unerringly recognized her privacy whenever her door was closed, and he didn't knock now, though part
of her wished that he would. Amena curled up into a ball and burrowed under the quilt that had kept her warm in this bed since
childhood. Tremors took over her body, but her eyes remained dry.
What she felt wasn't shock so much as the agony of assimilating a
painful secret she'd always known.

AMENA, 1982

AMENA WAS IN THE FIELD catching butterflies when her father called her apartment in San Francisco and left four messages, four days in a row, on her answering machine. His words and tone were almost identical in each one: "Hi, *ya asphora*. It's your dad. Please call me back." Amena had neglected to tell him that she would be off the grid for the week, on her lab's annual excursion to the Sierra Valley, along the eastern crest of the Sierra Nevada mountain range. She'd joined up with the lab just two months earlier, after a series of rotations through various labs during the first few months of her graduate program. Amena couldn't imagine devoting a career to the study of fruit flies, nor was she interested in doing experiments on other mammals. This left her with two choices from among the labs she'd tried: an intimidating research factory led by a famous, well-published entomologist who was also the chair of the department, or the smaller-scale, calmer *Colias* lab run by Valerie Ruckoff, who was one of the department's few female faculty members.

Amena's job in the field was to keep a ledger of all the butterflies they caught. A more experienced member of the team, a postdoc named Erik, was in charge of tagging their wings with tiny stickers imprinted with the numbers that Amena wrote down. Those who had been with the lab for a while complained about how all of the stickers from last year had fallen off the specimens, littering the ground of the lab's butterfly pavilion with little white numbered flecks and rendering months of study useless. This year they'd chosen stickers that had tackier backings and were meant to firmly adhere to the silky, delicate surface of the butterflies' wings.

Following her failed art project and her father's revelations about her mother, Amena fell into a long depression that she rode out at home under her father's care, taking two terms off from school. All of her friends graduated on time, leaving Amena behind to finish up her degree. She tackled her final requirements at once and hunkered down for a busy final term. She had more than enough credits to qualify for a degree in art but was still a few courses shy of finishing in biology. Haunted by thoughts of her recent breakdown and seeing her collegiate career coming to an end, Amena applied to graduate programs in biology across the country, plotting her future on the solid foundation of science. She received several offers and was surprised by every one. Though her grades were good and she was coming from a top school, she felt like an impostor—not only because, until now, she hadn't thought she'd commit to science, but also because of what that professor had implied when she applied for her first internship in science several years ago: that he was hiring her only because she was different.

From among her choices, Amena opted for the university in San Francisco, just a short distance away. She found a cheap one-bedroom apartment in the ironically named Sunset District, eighteen blocks from the ocean, where it was always cloudy and gray.

School was a short bike ride away, perched on a hill at the edge of the Sunset. She'd finally learned to bike during her second year of college, tired of being the only one of her friends who relied solely on her feet to traverse the large campus. Two friends had taken Amena to an empty field to teach her on one of their bikes, running alongside her, each holding on to one of the handlebars until she got enough momentum and outpaced them. She fell several times that afternoon and for weeks afterward had scabs on her knees and elbows to prove it. For her birthday that year, Amena asked her father for a bicycle.

When she wasn't going to lab, Amena relied on buses and trains to get around the city, though she rarely ventured beyond her neighborhood aside from walks in the park and to Haight Street for takeout. Her all-consuming new life as a graduate student left time for little else. She missed studying art and struggling to make it. All of that felt like a lifetime ago. On weekends she thought about heading downtown or to the warehouse district where her professor had brought them for that art opening once upon a time, but a wincing sense of failure kept Amena from taking any action. By some accounts she was doing well, even prospering, but she felt as if she were letting herself down.

Valerie's lab endeavored to make sense of the hereditary pattern of the *Colias* butterfly, a species whose gene transmission didn't follow standard biological rules. Not only did its DNA shift almost entirely from one generation to the next, but also two butterflies could have completely different DNA and look exactly the same. Cryptic speciation, this was called. Science was full of poetry.

Amena returned from the lab's annual trip to catch butterflies to find her father's four messages. In the shower—her first in days— her mind spun with possibilities regarding what her father might have to tell her. He usually gave her a few days to return his calls, so despite his staid tone, Amena could tell from the frequency of the messages that something was urgent. Was he sick? Or was there news about her mother after all these years?

With her wet hair toweled into a turban on top of her head, Amena picked up the phone, pulse accelerating, as she dialed her old number.

"Hello?" her father answered in his sharpest English, which still had an unmistakable Arabic lilt.

"It's me," Amena told him, bracing for whatever he had to say.

"*Habibti*," he said, almost like a sigh, followed by a long pause. "It turns out I'm very sick."

He said this as if it were a continuation of a conversation they'd already begun. "What do you mean?" Amena demanded, gripping the phone against the side of her face.

"Leukemia," he answered quietly. "Late stage." He cleared his throat and made a sound like a sob or hiccup. "The cancer's in my blood."

"No!" Amena cried. In resistance. As a command.

"I'm so sorry," he said, comforting her, when he was the one who was sick.

"No," Amena said again, her mind temporarily vacant of all other words.

"You might want to come home soon," her father suggested gently. "I'm not sure how long I have."

"Of course," Amena responded automatically, remembering how he'd nursed her back to health during her depression. They'd spent so much time in front of the television together that the glowing box practically felt like another warm body in the room. For months Amena watched essentially without affect, and then one day she started laughing during an episode of *Mork & Mindy*, and her father turned to her weeping and said, "Oh, thank God, you're back."

The next morning, Amena went to the lab one last time to let Valerie know that she had to leave and hand over the ledger she'd been keeping in the field. "You're welcome back here whenever you're ready," Valerie told her, hugging the ledger to her chest. On her way out, Amena visited the butterfly pavilion to take it in once more before she left. The pavilion was a two-story-tall glass box down the hall from the lab's office space. Amena unlocked the door to the pavilion and quickly stepped inside before any of the butterflies could escape. She was happy to find no one else there, all of her lab mates working at their benches down the hall. The light-infused room was like a mini forest, filled with wispy aspens and a sprawling cottonwood tree, riots of colorful flowers covering the ground for the butterflies to drink from, and a field of alfalfa at the center of the pavilion upon which the caterpillars fed. Walking slowly along the path, Amena looked for chrysalides hanging from branches or other horizontal surfaces; sometimes she found them attached to the netting that enclosed the garden to keep the butterflies from striking the glass walls and ceiling. Amena had spent enough hours studying chrysalides to know which ones were freshly sown and which were about to hatch; the former were an opaque, milky shade of green, while the latter grew so dark and translucent that you could see the patterns of folded wings through the thin membranes of their self-made wombs. Amena locked the door to the pavilion on her way out, not knowing when she would be back.

AMENA WAS SHOCKED by her father's appearance when he answered the door to the apartment. He'd always had a round face and been a little chubby around the middle, but now he looked gaunt, like he'd lost at least fifty pounds. Amena hadn't visited home since the summer, and her father hadn't come to see her in California either. He answered the door wearing a galabeya, what he always wore to bed, though it was the middle of the day. Amena found it charming, this sartorial ode to his heritage, when he wasn't a particularly proud Egyptian otherwise. As they stood in the doorway now, facing each other, Amena could see her father's ribs pushing through the thin white cotton of his gown.

Suppressing an urge to comment on his shocking state, Amena hugged her father and kissed the air by his ear as their cheeks touched. She felt his lungs rise and collapse against her chest, slowly and steadily. Her own breaths were jagged as she fought the impulse to cry.

After talking for a few minutes in the living room, her father said he needed to lie down. He slept all the time these days, he warned her. "My body's shutting down. I can feel it," he elaborated. A little sob escaped Amena's mouth. She swallowed hard and looked away.

While her father napped, Amena unpacked her duffel bag in her old bedroom. The room was exactly the same as when she'd left for college: at the center, a four-poster bed from which she'd deinstalled the canopy her first summer home, embarrassed by the frilly, old-fashioned style she'd once found so appealing; the rug her mother had purchased from a small shop in Khan el-Khalili during one of Amena's early visits to Egypt, as a waist-high five-year-old watching her mother haggle in a strange language; and the same old posters on the wall, one of John Travolta in a white tank top, and another featuring a painting of ballerinas by Edgar Degas, something Amena had begged her father to buy from the gift shop during one of their rare outings to the Metropolitan Museum of Art, always made at Amena's prompting.

Hearing her father stir, Amena went next door to check on him. He was sitting up at the edge of the bed with his back to her, facing the curtained window on the opposite wall. Amena watched from the doorway quietly, not wanting to startle him. He sat there for full minutes, shoulders slouching, back hunched. The balance of his hair tipped toward white, with black strands now in the minority. He'd started to go bald on top, and it surprised Amena how pale his scalp was there.

"Daddy?" Amena finally whispered from the doorway.

He turned his head thirty degrees to the left and met the obvious limit of his neck's mobility. Amena took this as an invitation to walk toward him. "Are you okay?" she asked timidly as she sat beside him on the bed.

"I'm dying," he said frankly, with a heavy look of concern.

Amena bit a callus inside her bottom lip. She couldn't bear to say goodbye or let him go. "I know," she managed.

After he got out of bed, her father wanted to talk about assets. He spoke slowly, laboring for breath, showing her a binder he'd put together including the title to the apartment and various documents relating to his retirement and bank accounts. Amena was grateful for his foresight and organization, but the conversation made her desperately gloomy. As soon as he handed her the binder, she put it aside and changed the subject.

After he fell asleep again, Amena cleaned. The apartment had a fetid odor, which she'd noticed the moment she stepped inside. She took out the overflowing trash in the kitchen and bathroom, and then she washed the pile of dishes stacked in the sink and wiped down the counters with bleach drizzled straight out of the bottle. Though she knew her father preferred the manufactured environment of an air conditioner, Amena opened the windows in the living and dining rooms. "I might not have been such a grumpy child if we'd had a way to keep cool in the summers," he'd joked with Amena before. "Science is just too slow sometimes."

"What's that smell?" her father asked when he shuffled out from his nap later. Amena no longer smelled anything—not the stench from before nor the sharp ammonia tang of the bleach.

"What smell?" Amena answered, rushing to close the windows.

HER FATHER ENCOURAGED HER to get out and do something fun whenever he got tired of Amena doting on him, but the whole idea of trying to have fun while he was dying seemed ridiculous to her. She had no interest in reconnecting with old friends, with all that was going on, and found it depressing to go to the movies by herself. In her mind this left only museums, so she decided to spend a couple of hours at MoMA one afternoon. Along with her ticket, she picked up a brochure for upcoming programs at the front desk and saw that Adam Locke, the artist who dug up a crater in suburban Arizona, whom she'd originally met at the opening for the dark dollhouse photographs, would be speaking at the museum later that evening.

Amena went home to shower and change and check on her father. She'd had plans to cook dinner but then, for expediency, picked up a large container of pho from their longtime favorite Vietnamese restaurant around the corner. Her father ate a few bites and then clutched his stomach to signal he was done. Amena felt guilty telling him that she was going out again, but he encouraged her to leave.

"This must be awful for you," he said, waving at the air in front of him. "I wish I hadn't told you to come."

Amena knew that he meant this for her sake, but she absorbed it like an insult. "Well, I'm here," she said meekly, on the verge of tears, and then went to the bathroom to make sure her mascara wasn't running.

The auditorium at the museum was almost empty when Amena arrived. She claimed a seat in the second row and studied the old exhibition posters hanging on the walls while she waited. The room was more than half full by the time the program began, the seats filling up around her. A curator of contemporary art introduced the artist, and Adam stepped up to the podium. Amena's face went hot with recognition, and she felt desire pressing against her crotch. Barely able to concentrate as he spoke, Amena imagined kissing him, darting her tongue into his wide, beautiful mouth. Then they were in bed together, Adam propping himself up on his long, sinewy arms as they made love.

Adam signed books about his work for a long line of fans after the talk. The museum had published a thin paperback monograph featuring photographs of the Arizona crater. Feeling conspicuous standing there without one, Amena went up to the cashier to buy a book. She held it against her chest as she waited in line, its pliable form curving to conform to her body.

When she got to the front of the line, a girlish nervousness took over. Her heart started beating quickly, and she fumbled what she meant to say. "You remember we keep meeting," she accidentally announced instead.

He looked at her and smiled. "Yes, you look familiar," he said. "Let's catch up after I'm done here, okay?"

Dumbfounded, Amena stepped aside to make way for the person behind her in line. She stood at the edge of the room, watching as Adam signed books and conversed with his fans. His hair had grown long again and fell almost to his shoulders in a casual, moppy style. A couple of times he looked over and smiled, making Amena's head swim. He wore a denim polo shirt over jeans a few shades darker. During his talk he'd seemed very relaxed and matter-of-fact, giving off a nonchalant, confident air, along with a sense of mystery and appeal. Amena worried that she'd given him the wrong impression and he'd asked her to hang around out of a confused sense of obligation. When he finished with the last person in line, he capped his marker, slid it into his back pocket, and walked over to Amena.

"San Francisco, right?" he asked, arching his eyebrows with uncertainty.

Amena inhaled sharply with surprise. "Yes!" she told him, heart pounding.

"We met at that opening," he continued. "And then again somewhere else . . ."

Amena nodded, blushing hotly. She didn't want to remind him that the latter encounter was at her university when she was a student, not wanting to call attention to her relative youth. She guessed that he was in his midthirties, at least a decade older than she was.

"You're an artist, right?" he remembered next.

"No, not really," Amena said, looking away with embarrassment. "I was interested in doing that once, but I couldn't make it work."

"Story of my life," Adam offered lightly. "I start every day thinking I'm a failure and have to build myself back up again."

Amena felt like laughing and crying at once, which came out as a nervous giggle. "I was never serious about it . . . not like you," she said.

"We'll see about that," Adam remarked with a teasing smile. "Do you want to grab a bite to eat?"

They went to an old Greek diner five blocks away from the museum. "They used to have this all-you-can-eat lunch buffet when I lived in New York as a student," Adam explained. "I was so poor that I lived for that buffet once a week. First I'd spend all morning at MoMA, working up a hunger, and then I came here and filled up on grape leaves and grilled meat." Adam was modestly sized, relatively short for a man, and lean. He didn't look like someone who had an insatiable appetite.

"When was that?" Amena asked as they paged through their laminated menus. Amena couldn't concentrate on any of the words in front of her, confounded by her circumstances.

"Late sixties, early seventies," Adam responded. "I came here for grad school but then dropped out because no one there understood the kind of work I wanted to make. I stayed in the city for a few more years after that, just because I didn't know what else to do. It was a great time for looking at art but a bad time in terms of me making any."

"I grew up here," Amena offered. "I know a lot of people who say they can't live anywhere else, but I get sad whenever I'm back here, honestly. Maybe it's just the bad memories. I don't know," she considered aloud.

"I can understand that," Adam said, putting his menu down. Panicked that he'd already decided what to order, Amena forced herself to focus on what the restaurant had to offer. "Going back to where I grew up is hard for me, too," Adam continued. "That's what the crater in Arizona is all about."

Amena struggled to understand what he meant by this, and then all at once it was clear, almost too obvious. A crater as a giant cavity. As a site of former impact. "I'd love to see it sometime," Amena said, realizing that it was the kind of work that had to be experienced.

"Well, I don't usually take girls there on the second date, but for you I might make an exception," he said, beaming.

All the calm that Amena had managed to cultivate vanished at once. Her heart started racing, and she felt her cheeks burning. Again she worried that he had her confused with someone else. "Is this a date?" she wondered with a nervous laugh.

"Not if you don't want it to be," Adam said, turning serious. "I didn't want to come off like a creep."

"You didn't," Amena tried to reassure him, horrified by how out of practice she was with flirting.

The waitress came and took their orders. Amena hadn't gotten past the appetizer section of the menu and ordered a bowl of lemon chicken soup. Adam asked for the moussaka. When it was just the two of them again, Amena made another attempt at normal conversation: "So, how long are you staying in New York?"

"Through the summer," he said, and started scratching at a mark on the table, adding quietly, "I have a residency downtown. Supposed to be coming up with my next big idea."

"Nothing great so far?" Amena gathered.

"Not even anything good," Adam responded with a frown.

"I'm sure you'll come up with something," Amena told him, assuming that his past success was a strong indicator of future potential.

"Can I call you up whenever I need to hear that?" Adam asked, his clownish frown melting into a smile.

The waitress returned with their food and placed the steaming dishes in front of them. They unfolded their napkins over their laps at the same time, and then Adam dug into his dish without further delay.

"Do you really remember me?" Amena asked, watching his face as he chewed. He had thick, full lips that she wanted to kiss, and dark, unruly eyebrows.

He finished chewing before he spoke. "You have a very distinctive face," he said, "and I'm good at remembering faces."

Amena unconsciously touched her jaw, considering the aesthetics of her face. Was he saying she was attractive or just different?

When Adam turned the questions to her, Amena was reluctant to share much about her life. "You're a scientist *and* an artist?" he exclaimed after she divulged bits of her recent trajectory. "That's brilliant."

Amena couldn't understand his admiration. She felt like a failure by his standards. "I don't know about that," she said, finally dipping into her soup.

"How about I give you my number, and you decide if you want to call me?" Adam said when they were standing outside the diner about to part ways later. He wrote the number down on the back of a grocery store receipt that he pulled out of his pocket and unfolded. He wrote it twice, the first time faint, before the ink fully traveled to the tip of his pen, and the second attempt dark and legible.

THE DAYS WITH HER FATHER felt long and slow and sad. He slept in his bedroom for hours at a time while, down the hall, Amena watched whatever was on TV, periodically getting up to check on him, perpetually terrified of finding an unmoving body in his bed. Sometimes she lingered at his bedside, listening to his deep, intermittent breaths, wondering why it had taken so long to discover the cancer, especially when he was a medical expert. How could his declining condition have evaded his own notice until now, or had the cancer appeared suddenly and spread through his body like a forest fire?

Sometimes Amena came upon her father when he was obviously in the middle of dreaming, his eyes closed as he spoke out loud to imaginary characters.

"How long have you been here?"

"You can't imagine how much I've missed you."

"Don't leave. Take me with you."

"Whatever you want. *Inte hora.*"

He must dream in Arabic, Amena realized during his final days.

She understood most of what he said, except that last phrase, which she asked the Lebanese grocer down the street to translate.

"You are free," he said, and then repeated the Arabic back to her: "*Inte hora.*"

AMENA PICKED UP THE PHONE several times with the intention of calling Adam, and then hung up. It felt wrong to be contemplating a romance while her father lay dying. By the time she finally gathered the resolve to dial his number, five days had passed.

"Oh, hi!" she chirped after he said hello. "This is Amena. From the other night."

"Hi!" he replied with obvious enthusiasm, which set Amena's heart pounding. "I'm so glad you called."

He suggested that they meet at a coffee shop that afternoon. Amena told her father she was going out to see a friend.

"Good," her father answered. "Friends are important. They'll be all you have when . . ." He let the thought trail off.

In the elevator alone as she was leaving the building, Amena allowed herself to cry. When someone got on at the third floor, she quickly pulled herself back together.

The coffee shop Adam suggested was near Chinatown. Amena caught the 6 train down to Bleecker Street and then walked south and east a few blocks to the intersection where Adam had directed her. The coffee shop was right there on the corner, just as he had said it would be. Amena was there five minutes early, but Adam was already inside. He stood and waved as she walked in the door.

"It's good to see you," Adam said when she arrived at the table.

"It's good to see you too," Amena told him, acknowledging the tingles she felt all over her body.

When he asked how she was, Amena shrugged.

"What's wrong?" Adam prompted, wrinkling his brow with concern.

"My father has cancer. He's dying," she said, too weary to lie or evade the subject.

Adam impulsively reached both of his arms across the table, gesturing for her hands. Amena produced them, laying her hands on top of his. He squeezed them hard in a way that communicated both tenderness and assurance. She looked into his soft green eyes, and her internal walls crumbled. "I'm so sorry you're going through that," he said. "I've been there too."

Amena took a deep, staggered breath, fighting for control of her emotions. "My mother's already gone," she found the courage to say. "My dad's been my only parent for a long time. I don't know what I'm going to do without him."

Adam squeezed her hands again. "I know it seems like you can't get through this, but I'm living proof that you can."

He told her that he lost both of his parents at once, in a car accident, the fault of the other driver. "I drank way too much for a couple of years after that," he explained, finally letting go of her hands. "And then I got my shit together, as they say, and decided it was time to do something with my life." They were briefly interrupted when the waiter came to take their orders, and then Adam added, "But you seem like you already have your shit together. So you have a head start."

Amena laughed at this. It felt good to laugh. "You seem to have a very high opinion of me," she remarked.

"I do," he confirmed with conviction, retracting his chin.

After coffee Adam walked Amena back to the subway station. She was disappointed that he didn't try to kiss her but also appreciated that he wasn't looking to take advantage of someone in a vulnerable position. He asked her to call him again the next day and then departed on foot for his studio. "Moving helps me think," he said, shrugging, as he set off.

The next day Adam came to Amena's neighborhood, and they walked twenty blocks up First Avenue to the United Nations; after admiring the glimmering tower on the water for a few minutes, they turned around and headed back downtown. Two days later, Adam invited Amena over to his studio, and just when Amena had convinced herself that he was interested in her only platonically, he greeted her with a kiss.

She melted against him, surrendering to the sweet, delirious sensation. It had been years since she'd been involved with anyone romantically, and never before had she felt so attracted to another person. His hands ran over her back and buttocks, the tops of her thighs. She anchored her hands on his shoulders, arms wrapped around his back. His studio had a bed and couch in one corner, the rest of the space dedicated to his work—a large wooden table and several easels covered with sketches and maps. They kept kissing by the door for a while and eventually migrated to the couch. Adam lifted off her shirt, and Amena reached back to unfasten her bra. The sensation of his mouth on her nipples was so intense that she almost came on the spot. Amena wasn't on birth control, so she asked Adam to use a condom. He disappeared into the bathroom for a long time to look for one. At last he emerged and strolled toward her triumphantly, his erection sheathed.

"Come over anytime you want to do that again," Adam called out as Amena was getting ready to walk out the door an hour later.

Amena stepped softly into the apartment when she got home, afraid of waking her father. Inside she slipped off her shoes and set her bag down on the floor, and then she padded quietly toward her father's room. The door was open, the bed empty. Amena panicked, imagining momentarily that he'd vanished. No longer concerned about the volume of her footsteps, she jogged around the apartment, first to the living room, then the kitchen, then the dining room, all vacant, and then back to the other end of the apartment, past her father's room, then hers, finally finding herself facing a closed bathroom door. Amena knocked gently and addressed him through the door. "Dad?"

He didn't answer immediately, and then he mumbled, "Don't come in."

"I'm just seeing if you're okay," Amena said.

He cleared his throat with audible effort. Amena heard the sound of movement. She waited a few seconds and tried again. "Are you okay?"

"No!" he barked back. "I fell off the toilet, and now I can't get up."

"Let me help you," Amena pleaded, unconsciously bringing her hands into prayer position in front of her face.

"I don't want you to see me like this," he said with quiet exasperation.

"It doesn't matter," Amena told him. "Let me in."

She waited for an answer and then tried the handle, which she found to be unlocked. "I'm coming in," Amena warned him before opening the door.

He was sprawled on the floor with one leg twisted behind him at an awkward angle, his galabeya bunched around his waist, and his underwear around his thighs. Amena avoided looking directly at his exposed parts, feeling his shame. He was up on one elbow, his face resting against the base of the toilet, his eyes closed and weeping. Amena knelt down beside him and lifted him up by his armpits. She pulled him against her to raise him up further, and then shakily got to her feet, bringing him with her. He exerted little strength beyond grasping onto her in return. Amena leaned him against the sink, pulled up his underwear, and then reached over to flush the toilet and lower the lid, finally sitting him down. His breaths were shallow, labored, and he hunched over to the point where his head and back and thighs formed a perfect *C*.

"I'm done," he said, lifting his head to look at her.

Amena regarded him with confusion. There were so many things this could mean. "Do you want me to take you back to your room?" she asked.

"I'm so tired," he said, shaking his head and gripping the sides of the toilet. "I just want to go home."

"You're here. You're home," Amena said, alarmed by his lack of recognition.

"No," her father said, nodding toward the ceiling. Amena looked up and noticed a dark cluster of dead bugs gathered at the center of the plastic fixture covering the light and heard her father say, "I'm ready to go now."

Amena looked back up at the dead bugs, mostly to keep tears from falling down her face. A few days prior, her father had told her that he'd promised his body to science. *What use can I be to anyone buried in the ground? Let those medical students cut me open and see what they can learn from me.* Amena didn't appreciate the graphic image, having to picture her father's body as a bloodless specimen on a slab. *Whatever you want,* she told him, though she struggled with the idea of having no gravesite to visit after he was gone, especially with having no closure regarding her mother.

IT WAS ALWAYS AMENA who called Adam. She didn't want the phone ringing in her apartment and disturbing her father while he slept. He usually woke irritable and in pain, past due for his medication. Whenever Amena went out to see Adam, she made sure to do it right after she gave her father his pills and after he fell asleep, so she could be gone for at least a couple of hours. Her father's appetite had vanished. Now he ate no more than a couple of bites of anything Amena offered and took just a sip or two whenever Amena held a glass of water to his mouth. He was disappearing before her eyes, which was devastating to witness. She didn't know which was worse: losing someone without warning or watching a loved one go over a period of time.

Adam was always available when Amena wanted to see him, making her think there weren't other girlfriends in the picture. She posed the question to him directly while they were fucking one afternoon. He laughed and threw his head back. "Not at this moment, no."

"How about back in New Mexico?" Amena persisted, maintaining her rhythm as she moved on top of him.

He shook his head. "Not there either," he answered breathlessly.

HER FATHER'S CONDITION steeply declined at the beginning of her third week home. He could no longer get out of bed and go to the bathroom without her help, and sleep became his default mode, his moments of wakefulness fewer and further between. She called Adam as her father slept and told him that she couldn't see him for a while, silently recognizing that her father would probably be dead the next time she saw Adam, as this was surely the end.

Whenever she heard her father stirring in his room, Amena went to check on him. Often she would find him unconscious, sometimes having moved in the bed but usually in a prone position with his neck twisted and head turned to one side.

One time she came into his room to find him unexpectedly alert and sitting up in bed. He looked at her for a moment as she entered the room, almost as if he didn't recognize her, and then said, "I'm so sorry."

"Sorry for what?" Amena asked, rushing to his side.

"Sorry to leave you here," he said, brushing her cheek with dry, bony fingers.

Amena shook her head, too choked up to speak. She wondered what he meant by *here*. Their home? This country? Among the living?

Within a few minutes he was tired again, and Amena helped ease him back down so he was lying on the bed. She kissed his forehead over and over and over again before leaving him to rest.

AMENA WOKE UP FEELING heavy-headed and groggy one morning and realized that it was almost noon. She sat up and got out of bed, panicked that her father was in pain and needed his medication. There was no answer when she knocked on his door. Slowly, she turned the handle and peeked inside the room. Her father was lying on his back, which was unusual, his arms splayed out to his sides and his feet falling in opposite directions. His eyes were slightly open, fixed on the ceiling.

Amena rushed to his side, fearing the worst. "Daddy!" she cried out, feeling around the loose skin of his neck for a pulse. She pawed at his cheeks, sinking her fingers into the rough beard he'd started growing when he gave up shaving a few weeks ago. Finding no inkling of life, she laid her head down on his chest and listened for a heartbeat. Nothing, just his ribs pressing against the side of her face. Not wanting to be convinced, she got up and went to find his medical bag. She'd loved to play with it as a child, finding her father's heartbeat with a stethoscope, pretending to measure his blood pressure. He stored the bag in the same place at the end of each day, at the bottom of his closet. Finding it there, Amena pulled out the stethoscope. On her way back to the bed, she plugged the headset into her ears. With her left hand she pulled up his galabeya, exposing his underwear and belly, and with her right she positioned the chest piece over his left breast. Holding her breath, she listened for his heartbeat. Anything.

Amena adjusted his galabeya and pulled a cover over him before leaving the room and shutting the door. She went to the living room and sat in silent shock, unable to move, unable to cry. Her father had given her instructions for when he passed. She was to call a number at the hospital in Brooklyn where he'd done his training, and someone would come and collect the body. She couldn't bring herself to make the call, instead lifting the telephone receiver from the cradle and leaving it off the hook, waiting through the drone until it went silent. She didn't want to talk to anyone. Besides the hospital, her father had given her a list of people to call and inform of his passing, mostly colleagues whose names she recognized, a few names she didn't know. *Don't bother with a funeral*, he'd said.

I never understood the tradition of throwing a party after someone dies. Go on a vacation. Take care of yourself. Save the money.

She couldn't bring herself to go back into her father's room. Hours passed as Amena hid out in the living room, getting up only to use the bathroom. Her room shared a wall with his, so even being in there felt too close.

Her mind flashed through discordant memories, like a tangle of filmstrips, some as recent as conversations they'd had during this visit, and others from long ago. She remembered his care during her depression in college, cooking for her, bringing home pints of ice cream, and encouraging her to watch TV with him instead of hiding out in her room at night. The way he helped with math and science homework but demurred whenever she asked him to read her essays. *Your English is much better than mine.*

Her mind was so busy that there was no immediate space for grief, her father reanimated at a thousand different moments as she suppressed the thought of his dead body down the hall. And then Amena recalled the steps of human decomposition from her advanced biology class in college, beginning with large-scale cell rupture and the release of enzymes that consumed the cells from the inside out. Gathering her courage, she replaced the phone in its cradle and then waited a few seconds before picking it up again. Her hand shook as she keyed in the number her father gave her. A pair of men arrived an hour later, and Amena stayed in the living room while they collected her father on a stretcher.

"Ma'am?" one of them called when they were at the front door.

"Yes?" she answered from the couch.

"We're leaving now," he said.

"Okay," she said, and then clenched her teeth until she heard the door close behind them.

AMENA COULDN'T SLEEP THAT NIGHT, her mind still buzzing with the past. She lay in bed, flattened by her memories. And then, in the middle of the night, an idea came to her: she should go to

Egypt and find her uncle. Her last blood relative, it dawned on her, the only connection to her family she had left. He'd always been a dark, shadowy figure in Amena's life, someone her father didn't like to talk about and who she remembered her mother sobbing about once. When she was a child, Amena used to fear the kids at school discovering that she had an uncle in prison and ostracizing her for it, but now she was ashamed of that old shame. Her poor uncle. Maybe he deserved her sympathy.

Amena sprang out of bed, not even bothering to turn on the lights, as she padded through the dark to her father's room. She got down on her knees and pulled out the box from underneath his bed that she knew contained her father's important and sentimental papers. Amena needed light to see its contents, so she got up to flip on the switch by the door.

She pulled out the pictures and papers one by one and scattered them around her outstretched legs. So many photographs of Halah. It always devastated and delighted Amena to see her mother's face again. The pictures made Amena smile and also buckle with grief. Her father had taken all of the photos of her mother down and put them away at some point, apparently into the box beneath his bed. Digging deeper, Amena found a stack of letters bundled together with a rubber band. The envelopes were flecked with red, white, and blue around the edges and were addressed to her father here at 316 E. 23rd Street. Beyond the writing on the front of the envelopes, the correspondence contained no traces of English. Even the return address was written in Arabic, and each letter was full of beautiful, inscrutable Arabic script. Amena suddenly regretted the way she'd cried and screamed, demanding that her mother let her quit Sunday morning Arabic classes at the mosque on Riverside Drive because other kids in the class made fun of the fact that her father didn't pray there. In the end, Amena took only a handful of the classes and had learned nothing.

Now she studied the unreadable letters, trying to determine from the shape of the words whether they were written in a man's or woman's hand. The script looked heavy and hurried, perhaps slanted towards the masculine. This was enough to convince her that the letters were from her uncle, so she took the stack, rubber band and all, and decided to bring them with her. To Egypt.

THAT NIGHT SHE WAS ON A FLIGHT, ticket purchased at the airport with cash. She'd packed light, unable to focus on the practicalities of what one needed for travel, ultimately throwing a few random clothes into a bag and almost forgetting her passport. A new host of memories bombarded Amena during the twelve-hour transatlantic flight. Of other flights. Other times she'd been to Egypt. The summer they lost her mother there, and that terrible flight home without her.

As the airplane descended into Cairo's brown expanses, Amena's chest swelled with recognition. So joyful to be back, even the tedious airport bureaucracies didn't faze her—passport control followed by another long line to buy a visa, the chaos of baggage claim, and then having her bag thoroughly inspected by two men with machine guns.

Outside, a cluster of taxi drivers clamored for the business of travelers leaving the airport. Overwhelmed by their attention, Amena locked eyes with an older man in a galabeya who had a dark prayer bump at the center of his forehead and nodded to indicate she would go with him. He took her bag and motioned for her to follow. His taxi was a long distance away, across a sea of irregularly parked cars scattered across a succession of dirt lots. The driver asked where she was going, and Amena conjured enough Arabic to tell him to take her to the center of the city: "*Wasat el balad.*"

"To a hotel?" the driver asked.

"Yes," Amena told him, figuring that she would know a good one when she saw it.

The landscape transformed from open desert to dense city as they drove. There were only a few other cars on the road by the airport, but the city streets were full of traffic. "Which neighborhood, *ya madam?*" the driver asked as they approached downtown.

"Garden City," Amena said, randomly recalling a nice neighborhood she'd visited on the east bank of the Nile once.

The driver nodded and continued driving. Once the river was in view, Amena started looking out the window for hotels. There were several obvious ones—imposing buildings with stacked rows of identical windows or balconies. "Here," Amena called out as they approached one whose architecture she particularly liked, distinguished by a grid of modern-looking art deco balconies hanging off the facade.

The hotel's elegant design scheme continued inside. Amena admired the lobby's tiled surfaces and grand columns as she crossed the impressive space, not noticing until she was at the desk that she was the only woman in the room. A couple of men in business suits stood against one of the columns smoking, and the hotel clerks and bellhops were all male. Amena told the man across the desk that she needed a room, and he asked how long she planned to stay.

The question puzzled her. She'd bought a one-way ticket to Cairo, planning to do the same on the way back. How long would it take her to find her uncle? And even if she found him soon, why would she leave before taking some time to explore this beautiful city from her youth?

"Two, three weeks," Amena told the hotel clerk, speaking quickly, off the cuff. "Maybe a month?"

The clerk raised his eyebrows, obviously surprised by her response. He worked out a math equation on the pad beneath him and quoted Amena a weekly rate that sounded very reasonable by American standards. Plus, her father had just left her a large sum of money, so the expense was hardly a concern.

"That's for a room with a view?" Amena wondered.

"I will be happy to upgrade you. No extra charge," the clerk responded with a small conspiratorial nod. "We want you to be happy here."

"Great," Amena said. "Listen, I need to ask you a favor. I need you to translate something for me." The clerk nodded, and Amena kneeled down to remove the letters from her bag, pleased with how easily her Arabic was flowing. While she was rooting through her stuff, she also retrieved a notepad and pen.

Standing back up, Amena handed the bundle of letters over with gravity. The clerk held them in both hands and looked down with curiosity. "Who does it say they're from?" Amena prompted, feeling impatient.

The clerk read aloud the information in the top left-hand corner of the envelope: "Seif, 36 Salah Salem Street, Mohandessin, Cairo."

Amena scribbled this down in a flurry, heart racing with excitement at how easily everything was falling into place. Just to be sure that this "Seif" was her uncle, Amena took one of the letters out of its envelope and asked the clerk to read the signature on the last page. He squinted at the words and then said, "Your loving mother."

Amena froze in the process of recapping her pen. "Mother?" she repeated incredulously.

The clerk nodded slowly, obviously wary of her response. "Look at another one," Amena demanded, her hands shaking as she removed another letter from its envelope. She shoved it toward the clerk. He reluctantly took it. Turning to the last page of the letter, he shook his head.

"It's the same," he said.

FROM HER HOTEL ROOM nine floors aboveground, Amena took in her new view. Traffic and pedestrians and street vendors whose carts sent up plumes of fragrant smoke; the dark ribbon of the Nile curving by below, and another bright swath of the city on the other side. She was at a loss for what to do now that her plans had failed based on faulty assumptions. It even occurred to her to throw herself out the window of her hotel room, not a physical impulse so much as a very vivid mental image.

Sitting on top of the bronze duvet covering her bed, Amena picked up the phone and dialed 0. *"Hadritic?"* a man with a low voice answered.

"I need to call America," she said, her Arabic faltering.

"That will be one pound per minute, charged to your hotel bill," the low voice said. "Would you like to proceed?"

Though it was an easy calculation, Amena struggled to translate this amount to dollars. She wasn't worried about money, so she authorized the purchase and gave him Adam's New York number, which she'd memorized over the course of their three-week affair.

After a long series of clicks and across a sea of static, Adam answered. He sounded far away, as if he were underwater.

"It's me," Amena called across the distance, speaking in a rush. "I'm in Egypt. My father died. I'm sorry I didn't call you before."

"Amena?" he asked, as if he didn't trust that it was her. "I've been worried about you, and also a little bit hurt, to be honest."

Amena apologized again, without an excuse.

"How'd you get to *Egypt*?" he asked, pronouncing the country's name at a higher pitch.

"I flew," Amena answered without inflection.

"Of course," Adam said, laughing quietly. And then, after a moment, "Are you all right?"

"I'm not sure," Amena said, feeling like she was on unsteady ground. "I decided to come here, and then I just did."

"About your father," Adam said, shifting the direction of Amena's thoughts. "I'm so sorry."

Sadness lurched up through her chest and throat, racking her body. "I went to check on him"—she stopped to think about how long ago this was—"in the morning a day or two ago, and he was dead," she related with a shaking voice.

"I wish you'd called me. I could have come over," Adam said through the static.

"It felt"—Amena paused again to consider her words—"wrong."

Silence except for the crackly noise of the line. "I understand,"

Adam said finally. "But you shouldn't feel guilty about what happened between us. It's possible to experience joy and grief at the same time."

His capacity to read her mind, especially when he couldn't see her face, amazed her. She wished there weren't 6,000 miles between them so she could curl up in his arms. "When are you planning on coming back?" he asked after a few moments.

"I'm not sure," Amena answered honestly.

THE NEXT DAY AMENA TRIED to visit the building where her father's parents used to live, but instead she found a bank in its place. She tried to confirm with the people nearby that she was at the right address, asking a woman sitting outside the bank begging for money, and then a boy selling guavas off the back of an idle donkey-drawn cart. They both shrugged as if they didn't understand what she was asking. So Amena went into the bank and joined the line of waiting customers. There appeared to be several tellers seated at desks up at the front, but only one of them was tending to the line. It took thirty minutes to get to the front—to ask her question.

"I'm trying to find out if this is where my grandparents used to live," she told the clerk. "36 Salah Salem Street."

"That's where you are," the teller said, and then repeated the address back to her.

"How long has this bank been here?" Amena asked with annoyance.

The teller shook his head and wrinkled his brow. "This is only my second day . . . I have no idea."

"Can you find out?" Amena persisted.

The teller muttered something under his breath and then stepped over to speak with his colleague at the neighboring register. When he returned, he had an answer: "We've been open for about three months," he said.

Realizing that her father's parents' place was no longer, Amena wondered whether her mother's parents' house was still around, that wild old mansion that had fueled so many years of imaginative play for her, the endless hallways she'd raced down in her mind, even when she was across the ocean in New York. Amena pictured her grandparents' property—something from another age—demolished, a pile of rubble. Gone.

Amena walked back to her hotel, having more or less memorized the route on the taxi ride over. Her hotel was a beacon across the river, taller than most other buildings in the vicinity. She attracted hard, sometimes openly lascivious stares from many of the men she passed on the street. Folding her arms over her breasts, Amena pointed her eyes straight ahead and kept walking. It amazed and frightened her to find herself in Cairo, the mesmerizing metropolis she remembered from her youth. Street vendors on every corner and on the blocks in between, every few seconds shouting what they had on offer over the noise of the traffic. The tantalizing smells of roasting *shawarma* and charred ears of corn, mixed with the noxious fumes of burning diesel gas.

Once Amena found her way to the Nile on the Mohandessin side, all there was left to do was cross it. Finding a break in the traffic, she darted across the busy thoroughfare that ran alongside the corniche, making her way to the sidewalk by the water. From there she walked a few blocks north to a bridge that spanned the river. She followed the narrow walkway, moving slowly compared with the rushing cars to her left. Back in her hotel room, Amena fell into bed, experiencing the first wave of exhaustion she'd experienced in days.

Feeling guilty for the way she'd treated Adam, Amena called him again that night. He picked up on the second ring and answered with her name stated as a question: "Amena?"

"How did you know?" Amena asked, stupefied by his telepathy.

"From the way the phone rang. It sounded like an international call," Adam told her, bursting the illusion. "Are you okay?"

"I don't think I am," Amena admitted with sadness. "I'm not sure. It's hard to know."

"Come home," Adam said in a way that suggested that home was where he was.

"Okay," Amena agreed, a sob catching in her throat. It made her dizzy to think about all the steps she'd have to take to get from here to there.

"How about I get you a ticket?" he said.

"I'll pay you back," Amena told him gratefully, which made him laugh.

"I don't care about that," he said. "Let's get you home first, and then we can negotiate."

HASSAN, 1981

HASSAN WAS STUDYING in the library at his university when the troops stormed in and took into custody everyone who didn't manage to escape. Twenty-six years had passed since then, and he was still in captivity. At first he'd fought his incarceration, and his jailers fought back, subjecting him to endless, brutal investigations that cost him fingernails and toenails, once a tooth, his dignity, and for a while his will to live. In those rooms he was accused of being connected to the Muslim Brotherhood, though it wasn't until much later that he actually joined the organization. He hadn't been a member, or even religious, before he was arrested, but his years behind bars, living among Brothers, who, as public enemy number one, made up a large concentration of the prison population, had changed him.

More than half of Hassan's cellmates were Brotherhood, and one belonged to another Muslim group, El Gama'at El Islamiyya. The rest of the inmates were a motley crew that included Communists, criminals, gays, and others whom their society didn't look kindly upon. For a long time, Hassan had obsessed over every possible association he'd had that might have looked problematic to law enforcement. He used to sympathize with Communist ideals and had gone to a few party meetings at his university. Likewise, he'd been close to an economics professor who was also arrested, a few months prior to Hassan, accused of being a spy for the British. He and Hassan had bonded over having both lived in London briefly and how much they missed the vast alcohol selections available in pubs there. Hassan and that professor had gone out to drink at a hotel bar after class a few times, among the only places one could find alcohol in Cairo, and Hassan wondered whether that had put a target on his back.

Each cell contained at least three bunks and usually a few scattered bedrolls on the ground, the prison always beyond capacity. There were big spikes in the population whenever the government ordered waves of arrests, piling new inmates into already overcrowded cells. Sadat did this when he came into power following Nasser's death, in 1971, calling for the arrest of thousands of dissenters, including many Nasser loyalists. A couple of Hassan's cellmates were prisoners from that era, so when they learned that Sadat had been assassinated, there were muted celebrations in their cells. President Sadat had been shot during a parade commemorating Egypt's invasion of the Sinai in 1973; that war against Israel had ultimately gone very badly for Egypt, like the rest, but Egypt did manage to get back the Sinai Peninsula, recovering a limb of the country that had been taken over during a previous conflict. Now the sixth of October was not only a day to celebrate but also the day when their leader was killed.

Now there was a new president, Hosni Mubarak. No one on the inside seemed to have any hope for him. He looked just like every other military thug who'd come before him, promoted from within their own ranks. But every man liked to make a show of his independence, as Sadat had by filling the prisons with Nasser's men, and it was announced that a large wave of pardons was coming down from the top, ordered by Mubarak himself. Perennially suspicious of the government, the prison population saw this as a naked attempt by Mubarak to curry favor with legions alienated by Sadat.

After the guards finished their rounds that evening, Hassan's bunkmate, Marwan, pulled his pocket-sized Quran out from the stuffing inside his pillow. He was their de facto leader when it came to these nightly study sessions, always the one to initiate and guide the discussion. Even those among them who claimed not to be religious listened in on these sessions, captive audience members inside their cramped cells. Everyone respected Marwan.

In his years behind bars, Hassan had been in much worse situations than the one he lived in now. The eight men in his cell got along well enough, or at least no one fought. Once he'd seen a cellmate have his head bashed in by another and never return from the infirmary. That was in one of his previous prisons. He'd moved around a lot at the beginning, as if he were a piece in a shell game, so no one who came looking could find him. His parents received a letter from the state eventually and came to see him in the prison he was at then, where the conditions were considerably less atrocious than the previous two. After he was transferred to his latest, and now long-standing, prison, Hassan didn't see his parents for a year; they'd lost track of him despite the letters he sent them.

"What sura are we reading tonight?" Hani, one of Hassan's cellmates, asked in a low but commanding voice. He had been a journalist in his former life and, like Hassan, hadn't actively been Muslim then. He'd been reporting on the incarceration of his peers under Nasser's regime when he was arrested more than two decades before. Hani had his own copy of the Quran, twice the size of Marwan's, procured from the prison's bustling underground market. To this day, Hassan had resisted acquiring his own copy, afraid of the repercussions if it were to be discovered by prison officials. Whenever he imagined this scenario, the particular torture memory that came to mind was having his balls taped with electrodes and zapped with excruciating electric sparks—the worst pain he'd ever suffered.

Hassan listened along as Marwan read the passage he wanted to go over that day, his voice slow and sonorous, as if he were reading poetry. There was no longer a passage in the Quran that Hassan hadn't heard or read numerous times over years of participating in these clandestine meetings. He'd always been a clever student, and he viewed these lessons as opportunities to engage and exercise his mind, activities from the outside that he sorely missed.

As the conversation around tonight's chosen sura died down, Mohamed, one of their younger cellmates, whose affiliation with a radical Islamic group landed him in prison, forcefully interjected, "Don't you get tired of all this genteel conversation? It makes me feel like a fucking kid in school. We could spend our time doing this, or we could look at the Quran as a road to action for once we get out of here."

"Exactly what kind of action are you looking for?" Hani asked. A few men snickered.

Mohamed looked at Hani squarely without smiling. He had the dark complexion and eyes of a person from Upper Egypt, not like Hassan's solidly brown stock. "I think if we want the world to pay attention, we have to think beyond our own borders, beyond Israel. We have to strike at America or Western Europe. Otherwise, no one will listen."

Of all of Hassan's cellmates, Mohamed was the biggest rabble-rouser in the mix, the one most likely to get them in trouble. Since Sadat's assassination, he'd become even more politicized, as if the killing of the president opened the door to an even wider battlefront.

"Let it be known that if I ever get out of here, I will be involved in no such thing," Hassan responded for levity but also honestly, raising his index finger.

"I'm with you, God willing," Marwan said.

Mohamed murmured something under his breath, and they all moved on.

HASSAN'S CONVERSION BEGAN after he learned that Halah had gone missing. He'd been behind bars for thirteen years at that point. A few months before, Halah had visited him in prison, as she had the past several years. She was distraught over her father's death, distraught that Hassan was still in prison, and started ranting about corruption and the system, worrying Hassan on behalf of each of them. After years of leading at the backgammon tables, which doubled as a means of gambling for the inmates, Hassan had accumulated a small fortune for someone who didn't smoke or drink or look at pornography, the hottest items at the commissary, so he'd saved most of his winnings and could, at that moment, afford to bribe the guard to let him out for the night to be with Halah. He didn't expect them to consummate their relationship when he made that deal, but once there was no longer a wall between them, all roads seemed to lead in that direction.

In the fall, his parents came to visit and reported she was missing. Hassan anxiously interrogated them about this news, to the point where his father asked, "Why are *you* so upset? You didn't even know her."

"Yes, I did," Hassan objected, feeling compelled to announce the truth. "She came to see me this summer."

His parents both looked taken aback, literally retreating from the window as they regarded Hassan with disappointment and confusion.

"I don't understand," his mother said.

"I fell in love with her," Hassan tried to explain.

"*Shhtt*," his father hissed, like a teacher scolding a student.

"I know it was wrong," Hassan continued, "but she was the one who came to me, and . . . No. There's no excuse."

"Why would she come to you?" his mother whispered loudly with her brow furrowed. "I don't understand."

Both men looked at her, Hassan and his father, as did a couple of others nearby. "*Haraam*," his father scolded under his breath. And then, to his son, "I think we've heard enough."

Hassan's parents never visited him again after that. He continued to write them letters, but they didn't respond. He knew that he'd offended their religious and moral sensibilities, and in his letters, he told them that he'd started praying and was trying to become a better man. It was true that he'd taken up prayer, but it was less for his own sake and more for Halah's. He felt responsible for triggering her disappearance and helpless that he couldn't help bring her back.

If a person wanted to study Islam in prison in Egypt, there were countless men inside who were willing to teach him. Hassan didn't have to look far to find a mentor. He'd always admired the kind and steady temperament of a neighbor on his cell block named Lotfy el Husseini. They began their conversations over meals in the mess hall, Hassan opening up about needing to be saved. "I'm so lost," he said. "To tell you the truth, I can't stop thinking about ways to die."

"It would be *haraam* to take your own life," Lotfy reminded him gently.

"I've done a lot of things that are *haraam*," Hassan admitted, laughing at himself.

"What's been done cannot be undone," said Lotfy. "The only thing we have control over is what we do in the present moment."

Lotfy was probably just a few years older than Hassan, but to Hassan he seemed like a father figure. Their relationship expanded beyond the mess hall, and soon they were spending all their free time in the yard conversing in the scant slivers of shade that lined the perimeters of the buildings. The yard was a large rectangle of dirt at the center of the prison, fully enclosed by the four identical concrete wings of the structure, each one four stories tall. The main part of the yard was fully exposed to the sun at all hours of the day, turning even the faint-complected among them a coarse-skinned reddish-brown. The back of Hassan's neck was smoky brown from so many hours of hunching over backgammon tables while in the yard during breaks. This was how he'd spent most of his time in the yard before the catastrophe with Halah. It had cost Hassan almost a thousand pounds to buy the cooperation of the guards that night. Afterward, he swore off gambling and money, striking at the corrupting forces that had enabled him to sin so grievously and possibly destroy someone he loved.

Lotfy was in prison as a political dissident and predicted to Hassan that he wouldn't make it out alive. He turned out to be right and, a few years later, died in his sleep from a heart attack two cells down. Hassan had been in prison for so long that there were eras to his incarceration. The Lotfy era was long gone, but Hassan still thought of his old friend often.

Hassan had now spent half his life in prison. He'd entered as a spry, young student and was now firmly middle-aged. For the past year he'd been experiencing excruciating back pain, which he suspected was related to an untreated injury he'd incurred twenty years before, when he was strung up by his ankles during an interrogation and suddenly cut free, landing on his shoulder and the back of his head. For weeks he couldn't turn his neck, and to this day he had a permanent knot—about the size of a grapefruit—at the base of his right scapula.

THOUGH THE ACCUSATIONS leveled against him were bogus, it was true that Hassan wanted to bring down the government at the time of his arrest. Once the authorities had him in custody, they asked with violent relentlessness about people and meetings and plans Hassan knew nothing about. Later he came to understand the incredible ineptitude of the prison system—of course they wouldn't have it straight which prisoners belonged to which rogue organizations.

Hassan was at the university in Cairo, enrolled in the first year of a doctorate program in economics for the second time. He'd begun his studies in London, working as a grocery stocker to put himself through school, and had every intention of graduating from there and even possibly staying beyond. Instead, when he applied for a renewal of his student visa, he was denied. At the bottom of the one-page rejection letter, in the box listing reasons supporting the school's ruling, it read: COUNTRY OF ORIGIN.

As he absorbed the implications of this, Hassan rubbed his face until his eyelids hurt. Then he started pacing around the square of empty floor space in his tiny room. He lived in a tower of apartments filled with other graduate students, in a quad with three other first-years all randomly assigned together. Almost everyone in the building was from somewhere else—France, Germany, Switzerland, Italy, the United States, Canada, South Africa, Lebanon, India, Pakistan, China, Japan—which made Hassan feel less strange as a foreigner. London was such an international city; he couldn't understand on what grounds he was being denied permission to stay and finish his education. Was this some kind of minor retaliation because Egypt had ousted the British in 1952? He hadn't even engaged in any of that business at the time, instead practically living in the library while his peers burned things down and protested in the streets. And if that weren't proof enough of his admiration for British society, he chose to move to London for his education two years after Egypt's revolution.

From Hassan's perspective, the majority of Egypt's advanced curriculum was based on an educational system introduced by the

British, so why study a diluted version of his subject when he could go to the source? Studying mathematics as an undergraduate, he'd had to essentially relearn everything. In public school he'd been taught to use Arabic-Indic numbers and read and write equations from right to left, and then in university he had to get used to Latin and Greek numbers and move from left to right. And then in his third year, all of the textbooks abruptly shifted to English because there were no Arabic textbooks on advanced math. So when Hassan decided that he wanted to keep studying toward a graduate degree, he didn't even consider the local option, applying only to school in London.

According to the letter from the British government, Hassan had to "vacate" England by the time his current visa expired at the end of the term. He lied to his roommates and told them that one of his parents was sick, too ashamed to admit the truth. He couldn't afford to fly home, so he patched together passage by train and bus and boat, trusting that at each juncture he would be able to buy a ticket for the next leg. The train was full all the way to Paris, where two thirds of the car let out, allowing Hassan to sprawl across a row of vacated seats. He awoke in Dijon and continued on to Lyon. There he transferred to an eastbound train bound for Turin. At the Italian border, an immigration agent came onto the train and canvassed the aisles, asking for papers. Hassan produced his Egyptian documents as well as his newly expired English visa from the front pocket of his valise.

Arriving in Venice, Hassan felt like he was entering a scene from a movie. He carried his suitcase across town from the train station to the port, walking alongside picturesque waterways dotted with people floating by in gondolas. And yet the beauty didn't penetrate, dejected as he was about having to return home. There were three massive ships at port. Hassan walked until he saw one with *ITALY EGYPT LEBANON* emblazoned on its side. He bought the cheapest ticket listed on the menu of options next to descriptions in Italian that he couldn't read. This turned out to be a ticket to ride on the open deck at the top of the ship. The deck was already crowded by the time he got to the top of the scissoring ramp. Hassan found some empty space and set down his bags. The deck looked filthy, stained and covered with indeterminate muck, so Hassan used his suitcase as a seat. It was falling apart and would probably have to be thrown away at the end of this journey anyway.

When he got back to Cairo, Hassan moved back in with his parents and brother, opting to sleep on the couch instead of sharing a room with Khalil again. And then, just a few months after Hassan's return, Khalil announced that he'd gotten a scholarship to study in America, which felt like a slap in the face to Hassan, who'd just been robbed of his own chance at a future beyond Egypt. He behaved distantly toward Khalil in the weeks leading up to his brother's departure and didn't wake up to see Khalil off the morning he left. They didn't hear from Khalil for months, and then when he reemerged, he was suddenly married, having found some young Egyptian woman to wed.

He sent a photograph of him and his bride tucked inside the letter. She was lovely, with a narrow jaw and dimpled chin and a warm smile that lit up her face. From that point on, Halah became a keen object of desire for Hassan. Arrested only a few weeks later, he took Halah with him to prison, holding a fantasy of her inside his mind; she was his constant companion, not only someone he fantasized about but also someone with whom he imagined having long, thoughtful conversations.

So when Halah came to visit him for the first time in 1957, Hassan recognized her immediately on the other side of the bars. She was upset, insisting that she was responsible for his incarceration, fearful that her father had retaliated against her and Khalil by having Hassan arrested. Hassan was in a mild state of shock at seeing her and struggled with how to respond and say the right thing. He'd long suspected that his various controversial involvements on campus were what marked him, and he also wondered whether his temporary residence in England had been viewed by Egyptian officials as some kind of failed defection. But he'd never considered *this*.

Halah's visit only fueled Hassan's fantasies, so that when she came to see him the next time, two years later, it felt like the love of his life had returned. This time she was more relaxed, conversing with him as if he were a cousin or an old friend she'd come to check on. She asked how he was being treated and whether there was anything she could bring him and showed him pictures of her little girl, his niece Amena, who had a round face like her father and a shy, toothless smile. These gestures amplified Hassan's crush on her, and by the end of that visit, he made her promise that she would come and see him again.

It would be another two years, but she held true to this promise, returning on her next visit to Egypt. This time she brought him a small pile of homemade handkerchiefs that she'd sewn for him in New York. "I thought these might be useful," she said, shrugging as she pushed the cloth stack through the bars. Hassan cherished those delicate, soft white squares of fabric, admiring the imperfections in the seams along the edges—evidence of her hands at work. He knew he couldn't use them as they were intended, as he would have no way to launder them and didn't want to sully Halah's beautiful work. These precious objects were still with him, the complete set of four, in almost perfect condition, except for the deep creases of folds held for years. The way Marwan kept his Quran inside the quilting of his pillow, Hassan kept Halah's handkerchiefs inside his.

HALAH CAME TO SEE HIM for the last time in the summer of 1967. It had been an incredibly hot and devastating summer, beginning with what immediately became known as the Six-Day War for its extreme brevity. The prison population melted into a collective depression in the humid stink of their sweltering cells. It was humiliating to think that their country had lost another war to Israel—Egypt's third attempt and failure now. No matter that they happened to be prisoners of the state, they still wanted their country to be vindicated.

There was also a terrible bout of food poisoning that went around that summer, sickening more than half the population and leading to fierce competition over the grotesque toilets in their cells, men urging others to hurry up with their business and, as usual, no one having any privacy when he took a shit.

Hassan felt filthy as he went to greet the visitor he'd been told was waiting to see him. He hadn't had a visitor in months. He hoped it was Halah and wished there were an opportunity to take a quick shower. She was standing on the other side of the fence-topped wall when Hassan came to the visitors' corridor.

"There you are," she said when he came up to her, grabbing hold of the bars between them.

"I hoped it was you," Hassan said, lining up his hands adjacent to hers along the bars.

"My God, just once I wish I would show up here and they would tell me you'd been released," she said. "All the men who put you in prison are dead now, including my father. Have you ever even been charged for your alleged crimes? What is it they say you did, anyway? Do you know what the American press writes about the prison system here?" She kept asking questions, without leaving time for him to answer. "They call it medieval," she continued. The visitors and prisoners to either side of them were all watching Halah now.

Worried about the implications of having such a conversation in public, Hassan asked Halah to wait while he ran over to talk to one of the guards. The man in question was well known for being easy to bribe and must have earned a fortune through his lucrative side business. Over the years Hassan had heard of prisoners who bought their way out of prison for a matter of hours, either to visit family or to have sex with a loved one or prostitute. For years Hassan had dreamt of buying time to have a rendezvous with Halah. Hassan's thoughts at the moment, however, were not focused on sex so much as on getting Halah out to a place where others couldn't hear her rant.

After Hassan struck up an agreement with the guard, Hassan went with him while Halah was led by someone else to a meeting point just outside the prison. There, Halah rushed over to embrace Hassan, and Hassan went soft and hard at once, wrapping his arms around his love for the first time.

They were escorted into the back seat of a military van, where their driver, another guard, said, "Enjoy, lovebirds," as he whisked them off.

Hassan tentatively put his arm around Halah in the back of the van. She rested her head against his shoulder, seemingly giving him permission. They didn't talk for a few minutes, and then Halah sat up and asked, "What's happening?"

"I just bought us a little time together," Hassan told her quietly, "without a wall between us."

When the driver asked if Hassan had a destination in mind or if he needed a suggestion and Hassan answered the latter, the driver laughed knowingly, looking straight ahead. The hotel was on the seedy side and looked as if it hadn't been updated since the forties. When they got up to the room, which was filled with dingy furniture, Hassan asked Halah if it was okay if he took a quick shower. "You don't know how long I've fantasized about the dignity of a private bathroom," he told her.

"Of course," she said. She'd been quiet since they'd left the prison. Hassan didn't want to presume that they were going to make love tonight, but just in case.

Mold crisscrossed the shower walls, and the faucet and handle were covered with rust spots, but it was still remarkably nicer than the communal basins he'd been subjected to for decades. The water in the prison showers came down red from the rusty pipes, but here it was clear and hot and amazing. If there hadn't been a beautiful woman waiting for him outside, he would have stayed in there for hours.

After drying off, Hassan put his uniform back on. It smelled, but he had no choice. He came out of the bathroom to find Halah still sitting on the edge of the bed. She looked up as if surprised to see him there. Hassan walked quickly toward her, overcome with desire at the sight of her. "You're so lovely," he said, sitting next to her. "I can't believe we're together."

Halah closed her eyes and parted her lips very slightly, in a way that suggested that she wanted to be kissed. Hassan took her face in his hands and brought it up to his, tasting her actual skin this time, not just dreaming. It was overwhelming to be touching her at last. It had been so many years since he'd touched anyone. Halah raised her arms overhead as Hassan lifted off her dress. She removed her own bra and underwear, and then Hassan peeled off his dirty clothes again, kicking them to the corner.

When he was finally inside her, Hassan grasped the concept of ecstasy for the first time. He'd never experienced such rapture. He'd had one other lover, in London, but that had felt nothing like this.

"I've wanted you for so long," Hassan confessed in Halah's ear, fully smothering her with his own body. She moaned in response, which brought Hassan to the brink.

Immediately afterward, she started crying. When Hassan asked her what was wrong, she only shook her head and sobbed louder, turning away from him. "Now I've done it. Now I've really done it," he thought he heard her mumble behind her hands. "It's over now."

"Please," Hassan said, lightly touching her back. His erection started to rebound at the mere sight of her naked body from a different angle.

Halah shuddered at his touch. Hassan withdrew his hand. All at once, she bolted upright and covered her chest with her arms as she shuffled toward her pile of clothes and put everything quickly back on. As soon as she was dressed, she grabbed her purse and made a dash for the door. Hassan was slow to follow, spent and bewildered after sex. By the time he got down to the street, she was already gone, and the security guard was waiting to take him back to prison.

AFTER HIS AFFAIR WITH HALAH, Hassan believed that he deserved to rot in prison, but in order to survive the years, he'd had to find ways to forgive himself and move on. Committing to Islam had been his main salve. The only true peace he found was during prayer. He usually prayed while seated on the edge of his bunk (thankfully a lower one, given his seniority and respective age), mostly to avoid pressing his face into the filthy prison floor, but also because he didn't like to give off the appearance of being overtly religious in front of the guards. It was an ironic evasion, as most of the guards were Muslim and likely prayed at home, but being devout on the inside was far more dangerous, a cause for worry among those watching.

One afternoon a few months into Mubarak's presidency, Hassan was summoned from his cell. "The general wants to see you," the guard told him.

Hassan's mind spun as he followed the guard down the dank corridor past an active fight going on in one of the cells, which the guard ignored. "The general" could have applied to any number of officials whose power extended over these halls. The Egyptian military was incredibly rich in generals. Halah's father had been a general and was possibly the person who'd originally pointed his finger at Hassan, so Hassan had cause to fear men of this rank.

The guard led Hassan down into a bunker beneath the prison, revealing an underbelly to the infrastructure that Hassan had thought existed only in rumor, where the authorities could flee to safety in case of a prison riot. Sure enough, Hassan found himself in a windowless underground complex separated from the prison by concrete and a bolted door.

The bunker was lined with offices behind more closed doors. Plaques on the doors announced the occupants' names, many labeled with the title of "General." The guard stopped in front of one of the doors, and Hassan held his ground at a distance. A booming voice from inside announced, *"Tafadal!"* inviting them to enter.

The man behind the desk looked up from his work, as if he'd been caught unawares despite having just invited them in. "This is Hassan Seif," the guard announced, pointing to Hassan, who was standing by the door. Hassan had never seen this man before and had no idea where he fell in the chain of command.

"Ah," the wide-chested man behind the desk answered, nodding. "These are the visits I like best." He pushed a few papers aside to reveal a notepad, which he consulted. "This is your lucky day," he said, looking back up at Hassan as he slouched over his papers.

Hassan took a few steps forward, coming up to the latitude of the guard. "How do you mean, sir?" he asked nervously.

The general motioned for Hassan to take a seat. Hassan's knees were shaking. He lost sight of where the guard was in the room, somewhere behind his back. "Your name is on a list of pardons that just came down from the top," the general explained with an emotionless smile. He paused for a moment, and then added, "You're free."

Once that was said, Hassan was dismissed and led out of the office, and then up and out of the bunker, and then down an unfamiliar hall, led by the guard who'd become his guide along the tenuous new path unfolding before him. The guard took Hassan into a room where there were a number of other prisoners waiting and told Hassan to have a nice life.

"Am I really getting out?" Hassan asked him, still disbelieving his sudden turn of fate. The guard laughed and nodded. "But will

I get a chance to say goodbye to the men in my cell? To collect my things?"

"What things?" the guard asked incredulously, skipping over Hassan's first question entirely.

"My pillow," Hassan blurted out. Halah's handkerchiefs were all that mattered to him among his scant personal effects.

The guard looked at Hassan like he thought he was crazy, and then said, with evident condescension, "Don't worry; we'll get you your pillow."

In the end they brought him the wrong pillow, one that didn't have a telltale hole cut into its stuffing, and nothing hidden inside. Knowing better than to press his luck, Hassan abandoned the drab pillow substitution behind the curtain when he went to change into the civilian clothes he'd just been issued. And yet, when Hassan went to a window to collect objects that had supposedly been on his person when he was arrested all those years before, he was amazed to find his old billfold and house key inside a small burlap sack imprinted with his handwritten name and date of birth. He found it incredible that a system possessed of such mismanagement and carelessness could manage to pair a man up with his belongings twenty-five years later. Hassan peeked through the cracked billfold and found his old student ID but no cash inside; he didn't remember if he'd had any money on him at the time of his arrest. His house key was still on the Eye of Horus amulet that his mother had given him for his sixteenth birthday to ward off the evil eye. He knew nowhere else to go but home, though he hadn't seen his parents in years and suspected, deep down, that they might not be alive any longer.

Outside of the prison, Hassan was loaded into the back of a van with a bunch of other dispatched prisoners. Each was given a handful of change for bus fare. The bus station was a short drive away, in what looked like the middle of an industrial center, the landscape populated with factories that produced muffled clattering sounds within. There were a few men already waiting at the bus stop when the freed men were released from the van. The waiting men eyed the new men warily, stepping aside to make room for the new arrivals.

There was no schedule posted for the bus and no clear indication that they were waiting in the right place except for the two men who'd preceded them, which gave Hassan confidence that a bus must be coming. Finally, after nearly an hour, a large vehicle announced itself in the distance, kicking up a large dust cloud. All the men who'd taken a seat in the road, including Hassan, rose to their feet. Hassan didn't feel particularly impatient for the bus to arrive. All he felt was bewilderment at his newly free condition.

The ride back to Cairo was long and bouncy, the road unpaved for much of the way. Hassan sat by the window, mesmerized by the moving vistas flying by. At the end of the dirt road, a few shantytowns popped up along the edges, and then the road turned smooth beneath them and there were buildings everywhere. Suddenly they were in the city. Still, nothing felt familiar for a while. There was a bunch of new construction at the perimeter of the metropolis, neighborhoods at the edges that he'd never seen before. When the bus got closer to downtown, Hassan finally found his bearings. The impressive Cairo Tower, which was under construction when he went to prison, was no longer under scaffolding. It gleamed like a beacon from its island on the Nile.

Hassan got off the bus at a stop between the zoo and Cairo University, confident that he could navigate the rest of the way to his old building on foot. On his way there, he got turned around a couple of times but eventually found himself on his old street, a few blocks down from where he used to live. He walked the rest of the way slowly, with his hands shoved into the pockets of his oversized pants. He remembered the facade of the building being olive in color, but when he arrived, he saw it was more of a dirty gray now, layered with dust and pollution. He felt a mix of fear and joy as he entered the lobby, a space that was deeply familiar to him and yet felt like part of another life.

After climbing three flights of stairs, Hassan was winded. The way to his old apartment was ingrained in his muscles, and his body brought him there without thought. He knocked on the door and then took several steps backward as he waited for an answer.

After a few moments, he heard shuffling on the other side, and then a strange woman opened the door, confirming his worst fears. He let out a brief, high-pitched cry and was immediately embarrassed.

"May I help you?" the woman asked with alarm.

Hassan's heart was racing. "Do you live here?"

"Yes, yes," she stammered. "Why?"

"Oh," Hassan responded, letting this sink in. All at once he realized how mad he must look to her and tried to explain. "I used to live here. A long time ago. And then my parents were here for a long time after I left . . . And I didn't know that they weren't here anymore."

The woman opened the door a crack further. "May *Allah* have mercy on them and see to it that they live in the vastest paradise," the woman offered kindly.

It struck Hassan that this meant she knew they were dead. "Did you know them?" he asked anxiously.

The woman looked down at the ground and shook her head, still grasping the door frame with one hand and the door with the other. "I moved in after they were both . . . gone. The landlord offered us free rent for the first month if we cleared out the apartment ourselves."

Hassan was a little slow to grasp what this meant, that she'd trashed all the furnishings and belongings that had once filled his family's home. This brought tears to his eyes, and the woman reacted with concern.

"I'm so sorry," she said. "Would you like to come in?"

Hassan nodded. Even if this wasn't his home anymore, he wanted to step inside and see it one last time. "How long have you lived here?" he asked, the pressure of his suppressed emotions making his throat feel sore.

"Ten years," she mumbled, essentially telling him how long it had been since he'd had a living parent. Hassan wondered who'd died first and how life had been for the widowed one. He wouldn't have been surprised to learn that they passed one after the other, the way he'd heard of long-term couples dying weeks or months apart, as if one were unable to live without the other.

The woman stepped aside to allow Hassan to enter through the door. He took in the familiar surroundings as a physical sensation across time, transported back to the years when this was home, without even having to look around. When he did, he saw that everything was different, from the coatrack standing beside the door and the coats hanging from it to the shoes and slippers crowded underneath it, to the pictures hanging on the walls. He had a vivid image of this woman and her faceless husband putting all their old furniture and clothes and shoes out on the street as trash. Much of it had probably been scavenged, he rationalized, and it comforted him to think that his family's effects were at least being used by people who needed them.

"Can I offer you some tea?" the woman offered timidly.

"I don't want to trouble you," Hassan said, though he wanted more than anything to sit down in his old living room and drink tea.

"It's no trouble," the woman said, to Hassan's relief.

She indicated for him to lead the way, and he knew where to go. The walls looked like they hadn't been repainted since he'd lived there, still a creamy gray-brown with large chunks of plaster missing, leaving gauges in the wall that showed old layers of paint below like a palimpsest. Otherwise, nothing in the living room looked the same. The new tenants had installed a thick orange shag rug over the original stone floors, and the room now centered around a large box television. An assortment of mismatched chairs formed a semicircle in front of the television, as if when they weren't watching TV, the new tenants hosted religious discussions.

Hassan randomly chose a seat somewhere in the middle of the arc.

"I'll be back in a minute," the woman said, and then left him alone in the room.

Hassan noticed a newspaper unfolded across the coffee table in the middle of the room, its bold-faced headline clearly visible from where he sat: *Islamic Militants Connected to Sadat's Killer Apprehended in Midnight Raid*. Reading this made Hassan sick to his stomach, even if the men were guilty.

The new tenants looked like your average Muslims, with an embroidered verse from the Quran hanging on the wall and a pair of prayer rugs carefully rolled up next to the base of the television stand. It was unclear to Hassan whether they had children. The door to the room where he and Khalil once slept was fully closed off, so he couldn't see whether it was being used as a second bedroom or for some other purpose.

The woman returned with a tray full of food and a single cup of steaming tea. She apologized as she set the tray down on the coffee table, on top of the newspaper. "I just threw together a few things we had in the fridge. A modest offering, I'm afraid."

The word "offering" struck Hassan as odd, as if she were saying that she owed him something. "It's very kind of you," Hassan said, salivating at the cornucopia of fresh food, hardly modest in his eyes. For the sake of civility, he waited a minute before reaching for the bounty.

"I recognize you from the pictures that were left behind," the woman offered as she sat down across from Hassan, not partaking in the food. "You had a brother, right? There were a number of pictures of two boys, one with a long face, like yours, and a smaller one whose was round."

Hassan nodded, touched by her recognition. He'd just eaten two slices of salted fresh tomato in a row, and he wanted to cry, it was so tasty.

"If I may ask," the woman started, "did you lose touch with your parents?"

"I did," Hassan agreed morosely.

"A falling-out? Or something of that sort?"

Hassan was taken aback by her forwardness. Had women become so much bolder over the past quarter century, while he was behind bars? It was possible, he reasoned, and yet still surprising to witness. "Something like that," Hassan said, reluctant to share more.

"I shouldn't have asked," the woman observed aloud, and Hassan didn't say anything in return.

Hassan reached for another bite of bread and cheese. He couldn't help himself. After a minute, the woman had a new question: "Were you just here to pay them a visit, or . . . ?"

"The latter," Hassan answered, his delight in the food bringing out his honesty.

"Oh," the woman said, and that seemed to quiet her down, for they sat for the next few minutes in silence while Hassan enjoyed a few more bites, and then he stood and said that he'd already taken too much of her time. She didn't disagree, instead leading him to the door. On his way out, she offered a few parting words that nearly brought Hassan to tears: "I heard from the neighbors that your parents were wonderful people. May *Allah* make this the last of your sorrows." Hassan took her words as prophetic. Maybe he had suffered enough.

NOT KNOWING WHERE TO GO NEXT, Hassan followed the sound of the call to prayer, tracing the voice back to its source, to a mosque a few blocks away. He didn't remember a mosque being here when he used to live in the neighborhood, but then again, it looked as if much had changed. So many landmarks from his childhood were gone—the convenience store on the corner where he used to spend his change on candy, the field where he used to play soccer with his friends now the site of a ten-story office building, a number of properties where his buddies used to live that had been razed and replaced by newer structures. And then there were the stalwart establishments that had withstood the test of time, bringing up memories from the past: the well-lit and expansive Carrefour supermarket where Hassan's mother loved to spend hours on her days off, buying only a few token items in the end, all she could afford, and around the corner, the gleaming window displays of Seoudi's department store, another shop where she liked to browse aspirationally, most of the merchandise out of their family's price range.

Hassan noticed that there were a lot more beggars on the street than before. Men and women with various disabilities sat outside buildings holding donation buckets, while other boys and men scrambled to wipe down windshields with dirty rags whenever traffic stalled, and others tried to sell boxes of tissue or wreaths of fragrant jasmine flowers by knocking on car windows. Seeing so many poor people made Hassan acutely aware that this could be him soon. As a teenager, he used to be ashamed that his family couldn't afford things like vacations or a television, but now he understood just how lucky he'd been.

The muezzin was still singing the final, drawn-out bars of the call to prayer as Hassan stepped into the mosque, bathing him in an ethereal sense of welcome. A few men were loitering in the lobby, a large, open space furnished with only a sizable wooden shelf for shoes and a billboard cluttered with posts that Hassan couldn't make out from across the room. No one paid attention as he walked inside and leaned against the shelf to take off his shoes. The feeling was unnatural to him after being under surveillance for so long.

He had holes in his socks—the pair dispensed to him by the prison damaged upon receipt. He looked around—still no one was watching him—and decided to pull off his socks and stuff them inside his shoes.

Hassan ducked into the bathroom, not only to perform the necessary ablutions before he prayed but also to relieve his desperately full bowels and bladder. He felt almost giddy with impatience as he pulled the door closed and sealed himself in the private, clean stall. The moment he sat down, everything started to stream out at once, his body voiding itself of all of its waste. He sat there for a long time, enjoying the afterglow of this relief, experiencing one of the most primal joys of freedom.

Finally leaving the stall, Hassan went over to the blue-tiled row of stools and faucets that lined the wall across from the toilets. There were no regular sinks, only these stations for washing oneself before prayer. Hassan chose a stool at one end of the room, next to the corner, sat down, and started rolling up his oversized pants legs, followed by the billowing sleeves of his roomy shirt. Another man came into the bathroom while Hassan was adjusting his clothes. He looked at Hassan for a second and then away, moving into the stall Hassan had just used.

Turning on the faucet, Hassan let the cold water run over his fingers, relishing the baptismal glory of the clean, cool water. His fingernails were filthy, he was ashamed to notice. He never spent time looking at his hands and had rarely gotten the chance to wash them in prison. He dug out the nails on his opposite hands with the long nails of his index fingers, using them as little tools. When the other man came out of the stall, he selected the stool as far away from Hassan as he could get. Sensing that this was meant as an affront, Hassan took it personally. He suspected that he smelled, given how long it had been since he'd had a proper cleaning, but he had no nose for his own scent. Hassan didn't see any soap, but the water felt cleansing in itself.

He bent toward the water, starting at the top of his body and working his way down. Opening his eyes, he watched brown water circle around the drain, so he splashed water over his face until the water ran clean and his eyes burned from all the dousing. Protocol required washing each area of the body three times, but now that he had the chance and no one was there to stop him, Hassan cleaned around and inside his ears at least six times, until he felt no more dead skin or wax accumulate under his fingertips. By this point the other man had performed his speedy ablutions and left. Hassan's hands were already clean, so he moved on to his arms, washing them both up past his elbows and wetting the rolled-up cuffs of his shirt. He always left his feet for last. They were hard to wash in the conventional prison sinks, so he usually cheated by wiping them with a damp, dingy towel. The showers in prison were usually backed up, forcing the prisoners to shower in inches of filthy standing water, so Hassan's feet needed particular attention.

Hardened calluses fell away like chipped-off barnacles as Hassan rubbed his feet under the force of the spray. So did small sheets of skin at the sites of former blisters. He watched the dead flesh accumulate below, clogging the drain, and felt a grotesque sense of renewal. Before anyone else came in to witness his transformation, he scooped up the debris from the drain and flushed it down a toilet, and then he came back and sat in front of the running faucet for a while longer.

When he finally emerged from the bathroom, he felt deeply refreshed. He'd unrolled his pants and shirtsleeves and now sported dark wet stripes across his knees and elbows from where his clothes had gotten wet. This time he did attract the attention of a couple of men in the lobby, who both looked at him with furrowed brows. Hassan wondered if there was something in his posture or face that communicated that he'd spent the last half of his life in prison, that he was a neophyte in the free world.

Trying to ignore the attention of the strangers, Hassan walked toward the prayer hall and then entered the large room filled with light. Sunlight filtered in through the stained-glass dome that covered the hall, refracting against the walls and filling the room with an unearthly glow. For a moment Hassan thought that he'd never experienced such beauty, and then he remembered Halah, who'd struck him just as profoundly. He thought of her as he closed his eyes and turned his face toward the light.

There were other men scattered throughout the prayer hall praying, all facing Mecca by orienting themselves toward the *qibla* carved into the eastern wall. Hassan hadn't prayed this openly since he was a teenager and was dragged to the mosque during Ramadan to pray with his father and Khalil on Fridays. To see men fully prostrated now, with their torsos folded over their knees, foreheads pressed against their prayer rugs, arms extended, was strange and exhilarating, like he'd reached a promised land. Hesitant to join in at first, Hassan found a large swath of empty space toward the back of the prayer hall. The floor was covered with a grid of prayer mats held together at their edges with a variety of tape, silver and black lines crisscrossing the floor. An elaborate light pendant hung overhead, composed of three concentric iron rings spanning almost the entire room. Each ring was spiked with round glass globes, which were illuminated even now, in the broad light of day.

Hassan lined his feet up with the back of the prayer mat, folded his hands over his belly, and looked down. The rug he'd chosen was nearly threadbare, the illustrations once woven into its design now just ghostly impressions. It was the same with the other rugs around, some worn down fully to their plastic backings, a sign of robust pedestrian traffic through the space. It wasn't obvious from the main prayer hall where the women's quarters were. There was no visible cordoned-off section within the men's area, nor a balcony overhead.

Turning his focus to *Allah*, Hassan put women out of his mind. One had to be fully committed in the moment of prayer. Hassan always began by focusing on his breath, inhaling and exhaling deeply several times to center himself. Then he brought the outside edges of his index fingers to his temples and whispered, *"Allahu akbar, Allahu akbar . . ."*

Getting down onto his knees was no longer an easy affair. Hassan moved slowly, his joints arguing every step of the way. He kept his toes curled beneath him, the muscles that ran along the top of his feet too tight to go flat. This also raised up his heels and made it easier for his butt to rest on them. Folding himself over and pressing his forehead to the ground, Hassan felt incredible relief. He discovered that this wasn't just a pose to show subservience, but also one that felt glorious. Hassan had the sensation of melting into the ground. When it was time to sit back on his heels, he didn't want to get up.

After praying, Hassan lingered in the prayer hall, taking a seat against the back wall. He had no desire to leave and didn't know where to go. Before he realized it, hours had passed and it was time for the sunset prayer, the call resounding from the minarets that rose above the dome of the mosque, visible to Hassan through the glass ceiling. The voice that had drawn him here, singing again.

There was a brief rush at the mosque in the hour that followed, with men streaming in and out to pray. Hassan waited them out against the back wall. Aside from the man in the bathroom and a few glances from others, no one had acknowledged Hassan in the time that he'd been here. This seeming invisibility made him feel safe in a way that he wasn't used to. The globes of light seated on the rings of the chandelier overhead were even more glorious now that the sky was getting dark. Once the rush was over and there were only a couple of men left in the prayer hall, Hassan prayed again.

When he went to use the bathroom, Hassan saw a man sleeping in the lobby, and when he returned to the prayer hall, there was another man sleeping there. Feeling utterly fatigued, Hassan saw the other men's actions as license to take a quick nap in the house of God. He returned to his spot against the back wall and laid down on his side with his back to the wall, his eyes losing focus as they lazily traced the tape lines connecting the prayer mats. Soon he was unconscious, the sweet anesthesia of sleep taking over.

HASSAN WOKE TO FIND sunlight streaming in through the glass dome overheard. Disoriented and frantic, he sat up quickly and got his bearings. He was still at the edge of the room, where he'd fallen asleep, but somehow the night had come and gone in the interim. There were a few men praying, two as a pair and the others independently. Hassan's heart raced as if he'd done something wrong, but still no one seemed to be paying him any mind.

Slowly, he got up and went to the bathroom again. This time he found a man spraying down the stools in front of the faucets with something out of a bottle that had a chemical smell. He looked up and said, "God bless you," as Hassan entered, catching Hassan off guard.

"God bless you too!" Hassan chirped back nervously. He went into a stall and peed standing up, listening to the sound of spray misting out of the bottle and the squeaky motions of the man wiping down the wet surfaces with a rag.

When Hassan came out, the man was still cleaning. Because he'd been spotted, Hassan felt obligated to wash his hands (the prison had long ago broken him of such habits). While he was there, Hassan decided to wash everything and pray, wondering when someone was going to notice him and ask him to leave.

Back in the prayer hall, Hassan belatedly prayed for the *Isha'a* he'd accidentally skipped the night before, and also for the *Fajr* he'd missed that morning, incredulous that he'd managed to sleep through not just one but two calls to prayer, and faintly remembering the call weaving through his dreams.

Hassan resumed his position against the back wall as morning visitors filtered in and out. Then it was time to pray the *Dhuhr*, and this time Hassan took notice of the sheikh leading the prayer at the front of the room, no bodies between them this time. The imam was the man Hassan had seen cleaning the bathroom that morning. Their eyes met when both of them were standing at the beginning of the second prayer cycle, the sheikh projecting his voice, leading the handful of men who were following him, including Hassan. This time Hassan knew he had been spotted. His gaze locked with the imam's again at the end of the prayer, compelling Hassan to approach the man and say hello.

"That was beautiful. Thank you," Hassan told him.

"The word of *Allah* is a beautiful thing, yes," the imam said, twisting Hassan's words around.

"I accidentally fell asleep here last night," Hassan admitted, wagering that it was better to confess than to be accused of something. "Maybe you noticed . . ."

"I did," the imam confirmed without suggesting any hint of judgment. "It's not unusual for men of faith to seek refuge here sometimes. And then there are the homeless, but that's not an entirely separate category . . ." He let his voice trail off instead of parsing this for Hassan, who was struck to realize that he fit into both groups as a homeless man of faith.

"I used to live nearby," Hassan offered, as if this further justified his presence here.

"Oh?" the imam asked with apparent interest. "What brings you back?"

Hassan bowed his head, not sure how to answer. "It's a long story," he mumbled.

The imam smiled. "I have time."

He invited Hassan back to his office, which was a cramped, windowless room next to the prayer hall. He offered Hassan something to drink, and Hassan said he would take anything. The imam leaned down to open up a small refrigerator underneath his desk and emerged with two bottles of Fanta. As the imam popped the tops of the bottles, Hassan stared with wonder at the bright, fizzy orange liquid inside. His first sip was like a punch of flavor, aggressive in its sweetness. Hassan shook his head to get it down, like he used to do when drinking hard liquor, his eyes wide with surprise.

"I can't believe they give this to children," Hassan remarked, feeling instantly high from the sugar. "This is lethal to a man who's been cut off from civilization for as long as I have."

The imam's expression shifted from amusement to concern. "May *Allah* ease your path from here," he said.

"People always say things like that!" Hassan responded, suddenly angry. "But can *Allah* ease my path by telling me where I'm supposed to go?"

"You are lost?" the imam asked after a moment.

Hassan's voice broke as he answered: "I've been lost most of my life."

The imam invited Hassan to tell his story then, and not knowing where to begin, he started in London. "For a little while it was the best thing that ever happened to me, until they decided I wasn't worthy of staying. They banished me because I'm from Egypt," Hassan told the imam as if the wound were still fresh. "Can you believe it?"

The imam nodded. "I'm afraid I can. The world is full of ugliness and hatred."

It didn't necessarily help to hear this, but Hassan persisted, telling the imam of how he was in the midst of completing his education when he was arrested without explanation and held in custody for twenty-six years.

"I'm sorry that this was your fate," the imam responded with measured calm once Hassan finished his story. "I know so many poor men who suffered the same, many of whom are still locked away." Hassan took this as a suggestion to appreciate his freedom and bit his lips together. "But we will win in the end," the imam continued, causing Hassan to wonder when the imam thought the end would come, whether in this world or in the afterlife. Hassan also noticed that the imam spoke using an inclusive "we," which made Hassan imagine himself as part of an army and gave him a sense of protection.

"I'm actually looking for someone who can help me take care of this place," the imam mentioned then. "The fellow who used to do it just moved back to the country to take care of his sick mother. You seem like you like it here," he acknowledged, making Hassan blush. "Maybe you want this job for a while." He said this like a statement rather than a question.

Not knowing whether he should respond, Hassan just sat there.

HAVING STEELED HIMSELF to expect nothing out of life, Hassan was surprised by the good fortune that came his way. He wasn't into religion for the miracles it promised, but he was happy to be at the receiving end of this miracle, saved as if by a higher power. The job came with the responsibility of locking up the mosque at night and unlocking it in the morning, as well as a room where he could sleep. It truly felt as if he'd walked into a divinely bestowed situation, with free rein over the mosque between the hours of ten at night and five in the morning. It was amazing to have the prayer hall to himself for hours at a time. He would sit there reciting prayers on his prayer beads or pray formally, body and all.

Hassan tried to get at least three or four hours of sleep each night before he had to open the doors to the public in the morning. There was a group of early risers who always came in between five and six; these men were usually coming from home and had cleaned themselves there, so Hassan had time in the morning to spray and wipe down the mosque's one and only bathroom (unless there was a facility for women that he hadn't discovered yet). It was the ones who came in toward afternoon and later, who'd been working all over the city, from construction sites to office buildings, who really needed to use the facilities before they faced *Allah*. Following the afternoon prayer, the mosque dependably emptied out, the imam going home for the day and most of the congregation leaving to enjoy supper with their families. This was the time of the day when the mosque was most peaceful, but also when Hassan felt most lonely. He usually napped his way through the gloom for a couple of hours. Later, a few scattered men would come into the mosque to pray the *Maghrib* around sunset, and it was usually just a couple of men who attended the nighttime prayer, neither of which the imam led—no one led—and after which Hassan locked up for the night.

After years spent in prison, Hassan found that newspapers were his new favorite reading material. Even though the national press was state controlled, it still gave him access to far more information than what he'd had on the inside. He usually skipped past politics to find the human-interest stories and reviews of movies he would probably never see. Sometimes visitors left behind books or magazines in the cubby in the lobby, despite presumably remembering to retrieve their shoes from the same place. One man even left a book that was pretty pornographic—or maybe he'd left it behind on purpose to rid himself of the temptation to indulge in its scintillating descriptions of sex. For many years Hassan had assumed that his days of having sex were behind him, and now that he was free, it was hard to imagine finding his way there with a woman again. When he'd gone out the night before to find something to eat, he widened his gaze at an attractive woman who passed him, and she curled her lip in response. Since he'd moved in and taken over cleaning duties at the mosque, he'd discovered that, in fact, this mosque had no women's section. "There are other places they can go," the imam had explained when Hassan asked him about it. "We didn't have the space or the money to build out a prayer room for them, plus the separate entrance they would need."

The mosque had boxes of Qurans to give away, printed in Saudi Arabia and funded by a wealthy Saudi family who wanted to make the book accessible to everyone. Early on Hassan took a copy for himself. At first he hid it under his bed when he wasn't reading it, as he would have done if he were still incarcerated, but slowly he got used to feeling safe having his Quran out in the open. He was living in a mosque, after all. Several times a day he had to stop and recalibrate his mind to his present circumstances, his recent trajectory felt so surreal. He continued to have dreams that he was still in prison and would wake up in full-body sweats. When this happened and he couldn't fall back asleep immediately, he went down to the prayer hall to pray.

Hassan took his job seriously, grateful for the work and all that came with it. As soon as he unlocked the door in the morning for the early risers, he tackled the bathroom, which took at least an hour to clean. He quickly learned that he wasn't the only person who came into the mosque covered in filth. The drains were always filled with gunk by the end of the day, the toilet bowls streaked with shit. Next, Hassan tidied the lobby, picking up trash and consolidating abandoned items onto empty shelves, finally sweeping and mopping the floor until it shined. Every few days he pulled outdated flyers and ads off the billboard and reorganized the papers that were left. Throughout the day Hassan cleaned the prayer hall in increments, vacuuming the expansive floor in bursts when there were no visitors. The vacuum cleaner was large and cumbersome, and he left it just outside the prayer hall when he wasn't using it, like an inanimate guard standing at the entry.

In addition to the room that came with the job, the imam gave Hassan a small stipend for food every week. He also brought Hassan a home-cooked meal every day, packaged by his wife. Otherwise, Hassan subsisted on cans of *ful maddamas* from the store and fresh pita bread he bought off people in the street, occasionally indulging in a *shawarma* sandwich or other takeout meals whose scents tempted him when he was particularly hungry.

He'd started to venture out at night after locking up the mosque, building up his courage to reengage with the world. The streets of Cairo were particularly lively at night, Hassan rediscovered during these late-night strolls. Especially during the summer months when no one wanted to be out in the excruciating heat of the day, it felt like the entire population turned into night owls. In addition to that, Ramadan took place in July that year, a month when everyone who had the luxury of controlling his schedule stayed up all night and slept during the day, thus avoiding long stretches of hunger. Fewer men came to the mosque early in the morning, so Hassan himself started sleeping in, sometimes not waking until nine or ten. It was an obvious cheat, one that Hassan was certain *Allah* was wise to, but it was a cheat that their entire society enacted collectively, shrinking the fasting window by simply sleeping through a bunch of daylight hours.

Abstaining from water during the heat of the day was the hardest part for Hassan. He didn't have much trouble giving up food for long stretches, after having had it withheld for days at a time in prison. It was being deprived of water when he was thirsty that he found most challenging.

To distract himself from needs he couldn't fulfill, Hassan adopted a more rigorous cleaning regimen. He finally took to cleaning the giant chandelier in the prayer hall. It had been bothering him for months that he could see dead bugs and dust collected in the bellies of the round glass sconces, but there were thirty-four of them—he'd counted while lying on his back in the empty prayer hall one night—and getting to each one would require the use of a ladder.

There was no ladder on the premises, so Hassan had to start by posting a notice on the billboard, asking if someone could loan a ladder to the mosque for a couple of days. The next day three ladders appeared in the lobby, and Hassan took the sign down.

He decided to begin with the inner ring of lights, which had only eight sconces. Centering the tallest borrowed ladder beneath the first lamp, Hassan looked up through the dome at the moonlit sky. There was no one praying at the moment, but there were a couple of men sleeping at the edges of the room. Hassan climbed the ladder with one hand while holding a bucket of soapy water in the other and a rag over one shoulder. He could reach the sconce from the penultimate rung, so he set the bucket down carefully on top of the ladder. The entire inner ring of the chandelier started swaying when Hassan reached inside the glass pendant to wipe it down with soapy water. This set off a delayed chain reaction in the outer rings, and soon the whole chandelier was moving.

Hassan steadied himself against the ladder as he worked. Each time he swabbed at the inside of the sconce with his wet rag, it came away covered with dead insects and dirt. He got into a rhythm of wiping down the inside of the pendant and then wringing out the rag in the bucket while the chandelier bounced lightly and came back to rest. And then he wiped it again. It took several thorough wipes to get all of the grime out of the lamp. When he was done, he slowly climbed down the ladder with the bucket in his right hand, and then moved the ladder a few feet over, underneath the next lamp.

Feeling overheated, Hassan went to prop open the front doors of the mosque to let in a breeze. There were no windows in the prayer hall, only the fixed glass dome above, so opening the doors to the outside was the only way to ventilate the space. There wasn't exactly a breeze outside, more like still, hot air, but the inside of the mosque felt hotter and even more suffocating.

Getting back to work, Hassan efficiently cleaned out the bellies of the next four lamps, and then as he was starting on the next one, he heard a loud squawk coming from near the door. He turned his head and saw a large white bird soar into the prayer hall, almost causing him to lose his balance. He braced the ladder with both hands, and it went steady beneath him. The bird came to land on the inner ring of the chandelier, very near to the lamp that Hassan was about to start cleaning. Up close, Hassan was even more impressed by its size. This was not a city bird, compact and mangy, but an elegant bird with a broad wingspan, like one you might see flying by the Mediterranean. The bird seemed to be staring at him with its black marble eyes, freezing Hassan in place.

After a moment, Hassan managed to pull his gaze away from the bird to see if either of the men sleeping in the prayer hall had noticed what was going on. They both appeared oblivious to their new visitor, still as logs in their respective corners. Hassan returned his attention to the bird, half afraid, half mesmerized. It was truly a beautiful creature and was obviously displaced. It could also easily knock him off the ladder if it came at him.

The bird expanded its wings as if to take flight, and Hassan scrambled halfway down the ladder. The bird's broad white wings were black at the tips, and the underside of its S-curved neck was also peppered with dark spots. Folding its wings back at its sides, the bird stayed where it was, turned its long neck, and looked off into the distance, still and calm. And then it opened its long, sharp beak and let out a plaintive croak.

Hassan looked down again at the other humans in the room, but they were still sleeping. For a moment he thought that he might be imagining all of this, but then the bird hopped on the ring of the chandelier, making the whole thing shake and knock against the ladder, and Hassan felt this in his body. Proof. His body was his barometer for what was real and what wasn't. In dreams it was almost as if he didn't have a body, even in the nightmares in which he was getting tortured, where he was more of a consciousness observing terrible things happening to him, rather than a body actually feeling them.

There was something unnerving about how the bird looked at him, about its very presence here. He knew men in prison who were shaped by supernatural experiences they'd had with animals. One lost his daughter to pneumonia, and the next morning he woke up to find a gecko on his chest. When another man pointed out that lizards were a dime a dozen in Egypt, the first man argued, "But they always run away from humans, right? This one didn't." Then there was his former cellmate, who said that butterflies landed on him whenever he thought of his dead mother. "You must not think of her very often," another man in their cell teased. "I think of her all the time," the man rejoined.

"Why are you here?" Hassan asked the bird quietly, continuing to grip the ladder with both hands.

The bird tilted its head but kept its hard gaze fixed on him, as if considering his question. When the bird didn't move or answer, Hassan climbed back up to the top of the ladder. His heart pounded with a theory he was afraid to voice, something about the bird's gaze. As he climbed, the bird extended its neck to its fullest degree, so that its small head perched like a lighthouse above its large body. It struck Hassan that it made a creature vulnerable to have such a long, thin neck, one that looked as if it could be snapped like a twig, but then for all of its drawbacks, a neck like that greatly extended an animal's reach.

"This isn't any place for a bird," Hassan tried, picturing the bird smashing into the glass dome overhead as it tried to make a hasty exit. Growing up, he'd watched several birds smash into the windows of his apartment with such force that it was hard to imagine they hadn't killed themselves. And theirs was just one of millions of apartments in the city.

The bird parted its beak and croaked again, this time aiming its communication in Hassan's direction.

"What?" Hassan asked, wishing they could understand each other.

The bird opened its beak again, but this time no sound came out. Then the two pointy halves came back together, the sharp end pointed toward him.

"Halah?" Hassan ventured. He hadn't said her name aloud in years, and it shook his whole body to say it now.

The bird's neck collapsed back into an *S*, which made it look sheepish and meek compared to its towering posture moments before. Hassan shook his head, believing and disbelieving at the same time. He had never stopped thinking about her, had never stopped loving her, and yet their affair was the biggest regret of his life. Even worse than the many years he'd lost in prison was what had happened between them and whatever that had triggered in Halah. He knew that even though she was the one who'd disappeared, it was likely his fault she was gone.

"I'm so sorry," he said to the bird. "I pray for you every day."

The bird stared at him for another moment, and then it spread its wings and took off, sending the chandelier into spasms. The bird circled in the air for a few seconds, coming precariously close to the edge of the dome, and then, in one smooth motion, it sailed out the door.

ONCE THE DAYS WERE COOLER and it was pleasant to be outside, Hassan made a trip to the City of the Dead. His grandparents on both sides were buried there, and he suspected that his parents might be too. Traffic crawled as they moved across the city, Hassan squeezed into the back of an overcrowded bus. He'd told the imam that he would be gone for the day, and the imam had wished him a blessed journey. Hassan didn't expect to find his family members' actual gravesites, not only because he hadn't been there for nearly forty years, but also because the necropolis stretched for miles and he didn't remember what part of the cemetery his people were buried in. It had felt like walking through a giant, dense maze of tombstones and crowded mausoleums when he'd visited as a kid. He was always amazed when his parents located their parents' graves at the ends of those long, twisting journeys.

When the Citadel came into view, rising above the city, Hassan knew they were almost there. The City of the Dead sprawled out beneath the medieval fortress, capped with the commanding Muhammad Ali Mosque, which overlooked Cairo on one side and the necropolis on two, a large shadow extending to the north and south. As the bus rounded the base of the Citadel, Hassan prepared to exit.

The majority of passengers had gotten off before this point, making it easy to reach the door now. The necropolis came into view, and then everything to his right was the necropolis. To the left, the base of the hill that led up to the Citadel. The bus pulled to the side of the road, where the traffic moved fast enough to feel like a highway, and Hassan stepped off into the street, the rush of passing cars creating a wind at his back. A low wall separated the road from the necropolis. Hassan followed the wall until he found a break, and then he entered the City of the Dead.

There were people everywhere, as if the necropolis were an active neighborhood. Kids running in the narrow aisles between the tombstones and mausoleums. Peddlers selling jasmine wreaths and boxes of Kleenex. A group of men in galabeyas walked by while chanting verses from the Quran in unison. Hassan followed them with his eyes, echoing their words in his head.

He walked without direction through the cemetery, marveling at the accumulating sights. Scores of people had clearly moved into the necropolis while he was away, Cairo's rapidly expanding population pushing beyond the boundaries of the city. There had always been the occasional guard to be found sitting in front of the larger funerary complexes belonging to the old Mamluk sultans or Islamic saints or scholars, or beggars paid by families to clean their loved ones' resting places, but now the necropolis looked like a crowded village inhabited by squatters. Hassan peeked into mausoleums without doors and saw people inside or other signs or habitation—blankets, plates, trash. His grandparents' plots were similarly structured, enclosed by four brick walls with no roof, tiny walled cities meant to hold entire families. These nearly identical, simple *hawsh* were ubiquitous throughout the cemetery. Hassan studied the names hanging over the doors of the tombs, hoping to find his family's, though he knew it wasn't likely.

He emptied his pockets for the children who asked him for money, recognizing that he needed it less than they did. Since being released, he made *zakat* every chance he could, giving to the less fortunate. He thought of what Lotfy told him once, that all people should be equal, like the teeth of a comb, and that was why giving charity was a tenet of Islam. More than ever, Hassan recognized his blessings, the great fortune of being a free man who was alive in the world when survival itself was a luxury not afforded to everyone.

AMENA, 1984

THEIR ANT FARM HAD GROWN IMMENSE, twenty feet from edge to edge, well beyond their initial conceptions. The notion was to mirror the complex infrastructure that pulsed beneath the ground, invisible to the human eye. They were working in the mountains of Colorado, on a large plot of land Adam had pieced together through accumulating cheap mining claims from the US Bureau of Land Management since the late seventies, and eventually converting a bunch of them into contiguous acreage. There were no other properties around, only an abandoned old mining town in the distance. They had to drive down the mountain to get groceries, gas, and other provisions.

Amena found herself reinvented once again. Following her brief trip to Egypt, she returned to New York and Adam. She left her grad school program behind and followed him around for a couple of years. Early on, he told her that he wanted to collaborate, but she thought this was only a ploy to pull her out of her funk, so she didn't take him seriously for a long time. He kept pestering her until one day she asked, "What could you possibly want from me?" feeling inferior to him in every way. "Your brain," he responded, as if this were obvious.

Then one night they were sitting around their apartment in Los Angeles, where Adam had his latest residency, and he said, "I want to make something that becomes something else entirely once I'm done," and Amena said the first thing that came into her mind: "You should do something with ants or termites, then. They build entire cities while we're not paying attention." Adam got the look of someone who'd just heard a remarkable idea, and from that moment on, their direction was set.

Amena resisted becoming involved with his artmaking at first. But then she found herself picking up what he was reading for research—E. O. Wilson's *Sociobiology* and *The Insect Societies*, as well as a bunch of art history books. And whenever Adam talked about the project, it was always in the plural—*what kind of materials should we use? How big should we make it?* His residency in Los Angeles was coming to an end, and they had to decide where to go next. Amena felt like it was his choice, since he was the one with a career.

That summer they moved to his land in the mountains of Colorado. The first few nights they slept in a hundred-year-old hotel in the nearby town of Estes Park while Adam combed through the classifieds looking for a mobile home they could buy and move onto his property. One day they drove down to Golden, and another, several hours to Fort Collins, both times to see RVs that looked as if they could have been the sites of murders. The next day they drove over a harrowing overpass to get to a tiny town called Gould, where an old man had an Airstream trailer from the fifties for sale. The trailer was stored in a garage and seemed to have been kept in perfect condition. Its rounded mirrored surface gleamed, and the interior looked as pristine as a museum display. Amena and Adam looked at each other and, without a word, decided to buy it. Adam had optimistically brought enough cash to purchase the trailer on the spot. They had it towed out to their land the next day.

It had been two months now that they'd been living out of a trailer and building a giant ant farm in a remote valley in the Rocky Mountains. Amena had since accepted her role as cocreator of the farm and was happily enjoying the process of making art. It felt good to be working again, fueled by a sense of purpose. It felt as if her knowledge really mattered, Adam constantly asking her questions about ant behavior, most of which she knew the answers to without having to consult textbooks. Adam hadn't taken a biology class since high school; compared with him, she was an expert in the field. She also had a strong baseline understanding of superorganisms and how colonies functioned as a communal unit made up of many parts. Amena enjoyed it when Adam sought her expertise. She spent hours each day observing the ants, sitting in a camping chair next to the ant farm. It was like being back in lab again, only this time there was no pressure to find answers.

The farm had started as a double-walled Plexiglas frame filled with sand and soil and plant nutrition, six feet tall by ten feet wide, but Adam said the flatness of it reminded him too much of a work you might find in a gallery or museum, so they added other walls at different angles, connecting the panels at the corners so the ants could move freely between them. Each pair of plexiglas panes stood one inch apart, and they were planted several inches into the dirt, inviting the ants to forage into the foreign interventions. Within a day, Amena and Adam began to see activity at the base of each clear frame. It amazed Amena how efficiently the ants worked together to expand into new territory. She watched as they carved lines through the earthen canvases Amena and Adam had installed and as their tunnels grew. She used to marvel over butterflies like this, but ants had since replaced them as her favorite subject.

"I could watch them for hours," Amena told Adam as he pulled up a camping chair to sit beside her. "It's kind of like being high, the way I just tune in and lose track of everything else around."

"I can try to find you some pot if you like," Adam offered in a deadpan voice.

Amena shook her head, smiling. "I think I can get by without it."

She hadn't told him yet that she thought she could be pregnant. She'd missed a few birth control pills while they were distracted by packing and moving, but they'd also had less sex during that time, which she hoped made it a wash. It wasn't until they'd been in Colorado for a couple of weeks that Amena realized it had been well over a month since her last period. To procure a test, she'd have to drive twenty miles to the nearest town, and she wasn't worried enough to do that yet.

She also hadn't told Adam that she'd stopped taking her medication, just in case she was pregnant. She knew she owed him honesty, at the very least, and this gave her even more cause to feel undeserving of his love. Despite how much Adam seemed to want her around, Amena felt like an impostor in his life. She hadn't exactly been an easy girlfriend, and she worried that he stayed with her only out of a sense of obligation or over fears of her instability. It embarrassed her how volatile she'd been during the brief trajectory of their relationship, surely a burden to him, though he'd never said as much.

He had been waiting for her outside the gate when she returned to JFK from Cairo, and they'd been together ever since, two and a half years now. They made love that night, as soon as they got back to Adam's studio, and then again, a few hours later, Amena climbing on top of him to wake him up. Emerging from the passionate fog of their reunion, Adam started to question Amena's behavior.

"Maybe you should get some rest. You're starting to worry me," he said

Annoyed by his reaction to her attempted seduction, Amena left in a huff and went on a six-hour walk across the city, during which she started to see the logic in his point of view.

He made an appointment for her to see the psychiatrist who'd treated him when he lived in New York in his twenties. Before the end of their ninety-minute intake session, the doctor pulled a bright green manual from her shelf, the DSM-III, and opened up to a chapter titled "Affective Disorders" that she thought might explain Amena's depressive episode during college and her recent, impulsive trip to Egypt. Amena also talked about her mother's disappearance but didn't mention the hypothesis her father once shared concerning her mother and mental illness, not wanting to bias the doctor toward a conclusion she ended up drawing in any case.

Amena's mood declined on a steep curve after that doctor's visit, too coincidental to be unrelated, from Amena's perspective. When she returned to the doctor a month later, the doctor expressed surprise at the vast change in her demeanor. "Isn't this what you expected?" Amena challenged, leading the doctor to nod sadly and admit that it was.

"We didn't talk about medication last time," the doctor said. "Maybe this time we should."

Thus began Amena's introduction to lithium. For the first few weeks, as they slowly upped her dosage, she felt nothing, which was to say that she still felt depressed. Then gradually she began to feel lighter, vaguely uplifted, like the sun peeking out from behind clouds, but at the same time she began experiencing low-grade nausea, which soon turned into bouts of vomiting. Deciding that she was better and didn't need the medicine anymore, Amena stopped taking her pills. A few weeks later, she was full-blown manic, calling up friends she hadn't talked to in years and having mostly one-sided conversations; alarming Adam with her energy, who, after just a couple of days of this behavior, asked if she'd stopped taking her medication. Amena let him know the good news: "I don't need it anymore."

"I think you might," he said, and made an emergency appointment with the psychiatrist.

Back on her pills, coupled with other antipsychotics to bring her down quickly, Amena came to the realization that she'd been more manic than she realized. What she'd felt had been so charged and exhilarating that she thought it had to be the very definition of wellness, not its opposite. She'd felt *good*, better than she'd ever felt, making it difficult to accept that she wasn't supposed to feel this amazing. Life felt flat on lithium: monotonous, repetitive, without passion or drive. Adam went through a flourishing creative period meanwhile, as if they sat at opposite ends of a seesaw, securing two grants and a solo exhibition while Amena's career faded into the distance. She felt down most of the time, despite the medication, so her psychiatrist kept tweaking her dosage until Amena started to feel some air under her wings again. With the air, the nausea returned. There was no telling when it would hit. She would feel fine for hours, days, and then sick, sick, sick, as if there were poison her body wanted to expel. Her psychiatrist prescribed an antiemetic, and once her insides stopped revolting, Amena decided to stay the course with the medicine, at least for a while. Feeling better, she turned to her old favorite pastime and found that she couldn't concentrate on the words on the page and therefore couldn't read. Without work and without books, she didn't know what to do with herself.

The second time Amena quit lithium, she felt fine in spirit but mentally dull. She wanted to prove to herself that she didn't need drugs. She'd lived twenty-five years and lost two parents; she'd survived worse without drugs and would be fine now, she rationalized. This time it was depression that dragged her into its depths once she'd metabolized all of the lithium in her system. Like stepping off a cliff, she fell into despair, and again Adam suspected she'd dropped her meds. For more than a year after that, Amena was compliant with the medication regime, tolerating the side effects and focusing on the sense of calm it gave her. But then she missed a period and had a dream about giving birth to a deformed baby. She quit her pills the next day, intending to call her most recent psychiatrist, the one she'd seen in Los Angeles before she came to Colorado, to ask advice but never getting around to placing the call. Each day that she woke up feeling fine was proof that maybe she didn't need the drugs, which sat untouched in a bottle in her medicine bag. During one of their early sessions, Amena's psychiatrist in Los Angeles had said she could have a full and successful life if she stayed on medication and kept seeing doctors, and though Amena knew she was meant to feel encouraged by this, it felt as if she were getting a life sentence.

AMENA WAS OF TWO MINDS about the pregnancy. On the one hand, it felt like a way to stay connected to her parents, to see their traits passed down through her and keep their lineage alive. On the other, *now* didn't feel like the right time to have a baby. As she considered her options, Amena thought back to when she was eight and first learned of the existence of abortions.

"I can't believe that woman would get rid of her baby," her mother complained about the mother of one of Amena's friends. Amena imagined an infant stuffed into a trash can and joined her mother in horror. "She'll regret it come Judgment Day. *Allah* does not take kindly to those who offend the course of nature, killing a child before it even has a chance to be born," her mother went on angrily, shaking her head. The grim picture in Amena's mind shifted to a pregnant woman sticking a knife into her womb. Amena pushed aside her after-school snack of pita bread and soft white cheese and burst into tears.

Amena thought of this moment now while considering ending her potential pregnancy, a decision her mother certainly wouldn't approve of. Amena still hated to think about disappointing her mother; the intervening fifteen years hadn't dulled the desire to make her mother proud.

Amena walked into the trailer to find Adam cooking bacon in a greasy pan on the stove. The smell made her instantly hungry, when moments before she hadn't been thinking about food. She came up behind Adam and hugged him around the waist. "You take such good care of me," she whispered, nuzzling the fuzzy back of his neck.

"I love you," he told her as he flipped the bacon.

Amena got choked up whenever he said these words. Swallowing down the stone in her throat, she repeated them back to him. He'd said before that he didn't want to have kids because kids got in the way of making art. At the time, Amena felt no need to share her desire to procreate, not wanting to presume that she and Adam would be together in the long term.

Squeezing around Adam, Amena went to sit down on the couch behind the stove that lined the back of the trailer. There was a table they could fold out if they were feeling formal, but usually they ate on the couch with their plates on their laps. Amena watched as Adam laid the finished bacon down on a baking sheet lined with paper towels. She hadn't experienced the culinary delight that was bacon until college, when Angela encouraged her to try some in the dining hall for breakfast one morning. As she chewed through the delicious slab of fat and salt, Amena wondered what other delights she'd missed on account of her mother's prohibitions. Amena's descent into the world of pork products was precipitous after that.

After lunch, Amena and Adam began adding another wall onto their structure. It took weeks for packages to reach them in their remote location in the mountains, and the new materials they'd been waiting on had just arrived that morning. They'd also ordered another fifty cubic feet of enriched dirt, which sat in a row of giant plastic bags against the trailer. Very few species of ants could survive at this altitude, and almost none lived above the tree line, just another thousand feet uphill from where they were. Pines and aspens and cottonwoods carpeted their plot of land, like a last gasp of nature just shy of the timber line. When they first arrived, Amena and Adam hired a crew to clear-cut half an acre for their ant farm and the trailer, which barely made a dent in the forest. They were still enveloped by it, subject to the howling of coyotes at night, the wind screeching through the trees. Amena had never experienced such isolation before, and for the first few weeks it really spooked her. The few times she'd gone camping with friends in college, there were always other people in tents nearby, but here there was no one else around.

She and Adam were adding a fourth wall onto their structure. One had felt too sparse, and two looked unfinished, so they added a third, making an open U shape. Then Adam suggested they enclose it, make it into a room, leaving a slight opening at one corner. Amena liked the idea of making it more architectural, more immersive, which felt truer to the spirit of the ants.

She and Adam had become an adept installation team by this point. They dug out narrow trenches where they intended the new panels to go and attached the panes to ones that were already standing with plastic joints. Then they covered the open side with a silky mesh fabric to keep the dirt from tumbling out when they poured it in between the panes. When they were done, both of them were covered in dirt and sweat. Adam was always a gentleman when it came to the shower, inviting Amena to go first. She loved the melting shock of hot water but kept her showers short to preserve some supply in the water heater for Adam.

She was sitting in her robe on the edge of the bed when he emerged from the bathroom with a towel around his waist. "My period is late," she mentioned spontaneously.

Adam stood motionless a few feet away from the bed. "How late?" he asked quietly, gripping the edge of his towel with one hand.

Amena paused for a moment as if she needed to think, though she had an answer at the ready: "Almost three weeks now."

"Should we go and see a doctor?" Adam responded, still holding the same pose.

"I think we should get a test first," suggested Amena, and as soon as they were both dressed, Adam had them on the road. He drove more recklessly than usual on their way into town, speeding down the switchbacks and taking turns quickly without making sure there was no oncoming traffic around the bend. "Slow down," Amena chided. "If I'm pregnant, then I'm pregnant. Getting to the drugstore faster isn't going to make a difference."

Adam turned and laughed, dissipating Amena's fleeting worry that she'd broken their relationship by bringing the possibility of a baby into the picture.

In town they went to the drugstore attached to the lone gas station and picked up a box of pregnancy tests, two bottles of Dr Pepper—Adams's favorite sweet indulgence—and a bag of Cheetos, Amena's choice. When they got back to the trailer, thirty minutes later, Amena rushed inside with a full bladder and peed on one of the tests from the box. The instructions said to wait five minutes for the results to show, but a plus sign appeared in the window immediately.

"Any news in there?" Adam asked after a moment, knocking on the door.

"Yes," Amena said, staring at the stick laying at the bottom of the sink, affirming all his questions with a single word. She opened the door. Her face must have expressed some fear, because Adam rushed in and put his arm around her.

"It'll be okay," he said, squeezing her shoulder. "We can do whatever you want."

Amena inhaled a stuttering breath, relieved to the point of tears. "I know you don't want this," she acknowledged, embracing him.

"I want you," he said, rubbing her back, "and I want you to be happy."

THE NEXT MORNING AMENA NOTICED that one of the fungus gardens in the ant farm had turned a moldy shade of green, signaling that the ants must have fed it some kind of poisonous plant. Another sign of the ants' brilliance: testing out new food sources by feeding bits of them to the fungus they cultivated inside their nests—if the fungus turned moldy or died, they knew not to consume the plant themselves.

It was odd for Amena to imagine strangers making a pilgrimage to this mountainous no-man's-land to see their ant farm, but at the same time she recognized she was making something worthy of fascination. Since they'd installed the new panes the day before, the ants had burrowed out a pattern of perpendicular lines near the base, like carvings on an Aztec tablet. Amena knelt down to admire their work. Beautiful and purposeful. She acknowledged that eventually she and Adam would have to leave, but she didn't feel ready to go yet.

Their next destination was still a question. They didn't have another project in mind, consumed as they were with the present one. Amena was advocating to go back west, while Adam wanted a cold climate for a change. Amena felt a desire to be anchored after moving somewhere new every few months for years. The tenants renting her family's old apartment in Manhattan were moving out that summer, so returning to her childhood home was an option, though not one Amena considered seriously. The idea was to keep going forward, not to languish in the past.

As she watched the ants, Amena found herself unconsciously resting her hand on her belly. She knew rationally that the embryo was miniscule, and yet she felt it there, an indiscernible spark beneath her skin. Whatever it was, already coded into its rapidly multiplying cells. Amena thought about the baby growing inside of her, wondering what it had taken from her and what from Adam. Would it be brown or white or some creamy mix of their skin tones? And what of the tendency toward mental illness that seemed to run through her family; had she passed those genes on to her child?

"I quit taking my medication," Amena told Adam that evening

as they sat holding hands in their camping chairs and listening to the crickets chirp as the sky grew dark.

"But this one was working," Adam said, loosening his grip on her hand.

"Ingesting those drugs is probably like dropping a bowling ball on that tiny bean," Amena said, coming up with the analogy on the spot.

"That's vivid," Adam answered dryly. "I'm sure you're right, but maybe we should have talked about this."

Amena felt a wave of emotion coming on, but she didn't want to let it out and prove his point. Turning her head away, she blinked back tears and said, "Sorry, I guess I just thought, since it's my body . . ."

Adam held her close that night, spooning Amena from behind. His breathing got deeper, his breaths slow and even. Meanwhile, Amena couldn't let go of the day's worries. Compounding this were memories of her manic episodes, which also started with insomnia. She got up in the middle of the night, disentangling herself from Adam, and went outside, quietly opening and closing the door. The air felt thick and humid, as if a storm were coming. Amena pulled out the toolbox they kept stored beneath the trailer and got out a flashlight. Clouds obscured the moon and stars, making the night unusually dark.

Under the beam of her flashlight, the ants moved with a frenzy inside their tunnels. She'd never noticed them being more active at night than during the day; was something unusual afoot? Amena thought about waking Adam but reconsidered in light of his concerns about her.

Instead she traced the narrow strobe of her flashlight over the walls of the ant farm, moving inside the newly enclosed outdoor room they'd created. The ants everywhere moved with the same frenetic speed, some moving up the tunnels carrying out dirt, marching over and past ants moving in the opposite direction bringing food into the colony. Her mind sparking with activity, Amena felt in sync with the tiny creatures.

The sky started to rumble, and within minutes it began to pour. Amena stood there, feeling exhilarated. She had no desire to seek shelter. She bounced around inside the room without a ceiling, her movement something like dancing, the flashlight now off and tucked into the waistband of her underwear. She wore only that and a T-shirt, which was growing quickly drenched. The sky lit up purple every time a bolt of lightning flashed.

All at once it occurred to Amena what was happening: the queens were getting ready to fly.

She rushed back to the trailer and climbed on top of Adam in bed. He rolled onto his back and lifted his hands to touch her chest. "Why are you wet?" he asked groggily.

Amena covered his mouth with hers to silence his questions. He was extremely dependable in his tendency to respond when she touched him, now slipping his tongue between her lips. Their love still felt magical, making every molecule in her body vibrate. The storm shook the trailer as they rocked it from the inside.

Amena wouldn't let Adam fall asleep afterward, compelling him instead to get dressed and come out to see the ants with her. It was a few degrees brighter now, making Amena feel like she had super-powers—an ability to see the ants without the aid of a flashlight. She took Adam's hand and led him closer.

"They look like they're on speed," Adam observed after a few seconds.

Amena chuckled. "I think they're clearing the pathways for their queens to emerge."

"The nuptial flight?" Adam asked, like an uncertain student suggesting an answer to a teacher.

Amena kissed him, delighted by his knowledge.

Adam got their camping chairs and set them up inside the ant farm. They sat together in the liminal light, listening to the faint, collective buzzing of the colony, like the sound of distant chain-saws. Despite the future being uncertain in almost every way, Amena felt a sense of confidence welling up.

Just as dawn broke, winged drones began to emerge from the top of the ant farm. They hovered together a few feet above the structure, a dark, moving cloud. Amena pressed her hands to her forehead and looked up. Soon, larger winged ants emerged from the nest—the queens. This was their chance to mate with as many males as possible to maximize the diversity of sperm they would carry in their abdomens for the rest of their lives. The drones would soon die off, but the queens could live for up to twenty-five years. A successful queen would go on to spawn a colony of thousands of workers, but the odds weren't in her favor.

The spectacle of the ants caught the attention of nearby birds and other insects. Amena watched with a stab of sadness as blue jays and purple martins and dragonflies ripped through the swarm of ants, devouring a number of them in the process. This was the way of nature. Most queens got picked off or downed by other queens during the nuptial flight; only one in a thousand would go on to successfully establish a new colony—but that one was all it took to ensure the survival of the species.

Amena turned to look at Adam, thinking what an amazing and unusual companion she'd found for herself.

"What?" he asked, noticing her attention.

"Everything," she said.

ACKNOWLEDGMENTS

My editor, Jill Meyers, made my dreams come true. I've admired her press, A Strange Object, since its launch, and I was so honored when she asked to publish this novel as ASO's first foray into the genre. Jill is a brilliant reader and razor-sharp editor, and her insights and encouragement over the years have kept me going. The team at Deep Vellum has been incredible to work with every step of the way. Will Evans is a powerhouse and admirable literary activist; Sara Balabanlilar and Walker Rutter-Bowman are passionate advocates and marketing geniuses, as is dynamo independent publicist Katie Freeman, whose infectious enthusiasm and kindness helped expand the reach of this book.

In full disclosure, my editor and I are in a writing workshop together, a group that casually calls itself the best writing group ever (well, it certainly has been for me). Jennifer duBois, Hillery Hugg,

Jill Meyers, Maya Perez, Mary Helen Specht, and Deb Olin Unferth have buoyed my creative spirit throughout the last few years and shaped this book in profound ways. I am deeply grateful for all of the wildly talented women in my life, but especially these six.

Other dear writers and friends, Margo Rabb, S. Kirk Walsh, Tyler Stoddard Smith, Amanda Eyre Ward, Lise Ragbir, Carrie Fountain, Kirk Lynn, and Chaitali Sen, are also core to my community and my heart. I also owe much love and thanks to: Kari Ørvik, Sharmila Rudrappa, Suzanne McFayden, Maya Smart, Lennlee Keep, Zahie El Kouri, Sarah Bird, Stacey Swann, Greg Durham, Tori Marlan, Crystal Mandler, and Siobhan Fagan.

My village also includes: Miwa Messer, Clay Smith, Becka Oliver, Julie Leadbetter, Nathan Thornburgh, Stephanie Prussin, Caroline Burghardt, Christina Clugston, Steve Bell, Molly Smith, Damon van Deusen, Luke Dunlap, Kirk Yoshida, Danielle Iemola-Devereux, Vero Majano, Alyssa Cannedy, Cherríe Moraga, Frish Brandt, Susan Kismaric, Annette Carlozzi, Beverly Adams, Ray Williams, Veronica Roberts, Claire Howard, Simone Wicha, Carlotta Stankiewicz, Anna Berns, Kimberly Theel, Madelyn Burgess, Adeena Reitberger, and Rebecca McInroy.

It is difficult to capture all the love and gratitude I feel for my parents, Said and Sanaa Azim, in this brief form. Immigrants from Egypt, they taught me through their example that it was essential to follow my dreams, and they have inspired me in countless other ways, including through the many stories they've shared about Egypt over the years. Since childhood I've had a best friend in my brother, Eiman Azim, who is an inspiring and trailblazing human.

My extended Egyptian family, including many beloved grandparents, aunts, uncles, and cousins, some of whom are no longer with us, have always kept me connected to the wider world, and for that I'm forever grateful. Thank you as well to my wonderful in-laws, who have believed in this book and rooted for me: Louann and Edward Sledge, Shay Cannedy, Noah Zisman, Sharona Ben-Haim, and Dennis and Sherry Cannedy.

My two amazing children, Maya and Jasper, enrich my life so deeply, and I've loved every minute of being their mama. My husband, Dale, has been at my side for twenty years and is still every bit the passionate artist I met in my youth, and a very loving and supportive partner in addition. Thank you for this great adventure . . .

ABOUT THE AUTHOR

Dalia Azim was born in Canada and raised in the United States. Her work has appeared in *American Short Fiction, Aperture, Columbia: A Journal of Literature and Art, Glimmer Train* (where she received their Short Story Award for New Writers), *Other Voices,* the *Alcalde, Sightlines,* and the *Washington Post,* among other places. *Country of Origin* is her first book.

Azim is currently the manager of special projects at the Blanton Museum of Art in Austin, Texas; she previously worked as a researcher at the Dedalus Foundation and as a curatorial assistant at the Museum of Modern Art, both in New York City. She graduated with a dual degree in art and literature from Stanford University and grew up in Colorado.

ABOUT A STRANGE OBJECT

Founded in 2012 in Austin, Texas, A Strange Object champions debuts, daring writing, and striking design across all platforms. The press became part of Deep Vellum in 2019, where it carries on its editorial vision via its eponymous imprint. A Strange Object's titles are distributed by Consortium.

Thank you all
for your support.
We do this for you,
and could not do
it without you.

Support for this publication has been provided in part by
grants from the National Endowment for the Arts,
the Texas Commission on the Arts, the City of Dallas
Office of Arts and Culture's ArtsActivate program,
and the Moody Fund for the Arts:

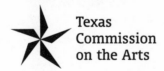

MOODY FUND FOR
THE ARTS

PARTNERS

FIRST EDITION MEMBERSHIP
Anonymous (9)
Donna Wilhelm

TRANSLATOR'S CIRCLE
Ben & Sharon Fountain
Meriwether Evans

PRINTER'S PRESS MEMBERSHIP
Allred Capital Management
Charles Dee Mitchell
Cullen Schaar
David Tomlinson & Kathryn Berry
Jeff Leuschel
Judy Pollock
Loretta Siciliano
Lori Feathers
Mary Ann Thompson-Frenk & Joshua Frenk
Matthew Rittmayer
Nick Storch
Pixel and Texel
Robert Appel
Social Venture Partners Dallas
Stephen Bullock

AUTHOR'S LEAGUE
Christie Tull
Farley Houston
Jacob Seifring
Lissa Dunlay
Steven Kornajcik
Thomas DiPiero

PUBLISHER'S LEAGUE
Adam Rekerdres
Justin Childress
Kay Cattarulla
KMGMT
Olga Kislova

EDITOR'S LEAGUE
Amrit Dhir
Brandon Kennedy
Dallas Sonnier
Garth Hallberg
Greg McConeghy
Linda Nell Evans
Mary Moore Grimaldi
Mike Kaminsky
Patricia Storace
Ryan Todd
Steven Harding
Suejean Kim
Symphonic Source
Wendy Belcher

READER'S LEAGUE
Caitlin Baker
Caroline Casey
Carolyn Mulligan
Chilton Thomson
Cody Cosmic & Jeremy Hays
Jeff Waxman
Joseph Milazzo
Kayla Finstein
Kelly Britson
Kelly & Corby Baxter
Marian Schwartz & Reid Minot

Marlo D. Cruz Pagan
Maryam Baig
Peggy Carr
Susan Ernst

ADDITIONAL DONORS
Alan Shockley
Amanda & Bjorn Beer
Andrew Yorke
Anonymous (10)
Ashley Milne Shadoin
Bob & Katherine Penn
Brandon Childress
Charley Mitcherson
Charley Rejsek
Cheryl Thompson
Chloe Pak
Cone Johnson
CS Maynard
Daniel J. Hale
Daniela Hurezanu
Danielle Dubrow
Denae Richards
Dori Boone-Costantino
Ed Nawotka
Elizabeth Gillette
Elizabeth Van Vleck
Erin Kubatzky
Ester & Matt Harrison
Grace Kenney
Hillary Richards
JJ Italiano
Jeremy Hughes
John Darnielle
Jonathan Legg
Julie Janicke Muhsmann

AVAILABLE NOW FROM DEEP VELLUM

MARIA GABRIELA LLANSOL · *The Geography of Rebels Trilogy: The Book of Communities* · *The Remaining Life* · *In the House of July & August* · translated by Audrey Young · PORTUGAL

PABLO MARTÍN SÁNCHEZ · *The Anarchist Who Shared My Name* · translated by Jeff Diteman · SPAIN

DOROTA MASŁOWSKA · *Honey, I Killed the Cats* · translated by Benjamin Paloff · POLAND

BRICE MATTHIEUSSENT· *Revenge of the Translator* · translated by Emma Ramadan · FRANCE

LINA MERUANE · *Seeing Red* · translated by Megan McDowell · CHILE

VALÉRIE MRÉJEN · *Black Forest* · translated by Katie Shireen Assef · FRANCE

FISTON MWANZA MUJILA · *Tram 83* · *The River in the Belly: Selected Poems* · translated by Bret Maney DEMOCRATIC REPUBLIC OF CONGO

GORAN PETROVIĆ · *At the Lucky Hand, aka The Sixty-Nine Drawers* · translated by Peter Agnone · SERBIA

LUDMILLA PETRUSHEVSKAYA · *The New Adventures of Helen: Magical Tales* · translated by Jane Bugaeva · RUSSIA

ILJA LEONARD PFEIJFFER · *La Superba* · translated by Michele Hutchison · NETHERLANDS

RICARDO PIGLIA · *Target in the Night* · translated by Sergio Waisman · ARGENTINA

SERGIO PITOL · *The Art of Flight* · *The Journey* · *The Magician of Vienna* · *Mephisto's Waltz: Selected Short Stories* · *The Love Parade* · translated by George Henson · MEXICO

JULIE POOLE · *Bright Specimen: Poems from the Texas Herbarium* · USA

EDUARDO RABASA · *A Zero-Sum Game* · translated by Christina MacSweeney · MEXICO

ZAHIA RAHMANI · *"Muslim": A Novel* · translated by Matthew Reeck · FRANCE/ALGERIA

MANON STEFAN ROS · *The Blue Book of Nebo* · WALES

JUAN RULFO · *The Golden Cockerel & Other Writings* · translated by Douglas J. Weatherford · MEXICO

ETHAN RUTHERFORD · *Farthest South & Other Stories* · USA

TATIANA RYCKMAN · *Ancestry of Objects* · USA

JIM SCHUTZE · *The Accommodation* · USA

OLEG SENTSOV · *Life Went On Anyway* · translated by Uilleam Blacker · UKRAINE

MIKHAIL SHISHKIN · *Calligraphy Lesson: The Collected Stories* · translated by Marian Schwartz, Leo Shtutin, Mariya Bashkatova, Sylvia Maizell · RUSSIA

ÓFEIGUR SIGURÐSSON · *Öræfi: The Wasteland* · translated by Lytton Smith · ICELAND

DANIEL SIMON, ED. · *Dispatches from the Republic of Letters* · USA

MUSTAFA STITOU · *Two Half Faces* · translated by David Colmer · NETHERLANDS

SOPHIA TERAZAWA · *Winter Phoenix: Testimonies in Verse* · POLAND

MÄRTA TIKKANEN · *The Love Story of the Century* · translated by Stina Katchadourian · SWEDEN

BOB TRAMMELL · *Jack Ruby & the Origins of the Avant-Garde in Dallas & Other Stories* · USA

BENJAMIN VILLEGAS · *ELPASO: A Punk Story* · translated by Jay Noden · MEXICO

SERHIY ZHADAN · *Voroshilovgrad* · translated by Reilly Costigan-Humes & Isaac Wheeler · UKRAINE

FORTHCOMING FROM DEEP VELLUM

MARIO BELLATIN · *Etchapare* · translated by Shook · MEXICO

CAYLIN CARPA-THOMAS · *Iguana Iguana* · USA

MIRCEA CĂRTĂRESCU · *Solenoid* · translated by Sean Cotter · ROMANIA

TIM COURSEY · *Driving Lessons* · USA

ANANDA DEVI · *When the Night Agrees to Speak to Me* · translated by Kazim Ali · MAURITIUS

DHUMKETU · *The Shehnai Virtuoso* · translated by Jenny Bhatt · INDIA

LEYLÂ ERBIL · *A Strange Woman* ·
translated by Nermin Menemencioğlu & Amy Marie Spangler· TURKEY

ALLA GORBUNOVA · *It's the End of the World, My Love* · translated by Elina Alter · RUSSIA

NIVEN GOVINDEN · *Diary of a Film* · GREAT BRITAIN

GYULA JENEI · *Always Different* · translated by Diana Senechal · HUNGARY

DIA JUBAILI · *No Windmills in Basra* · translated by Chip Rosetti · IRAQ

ELENI KEFALA · *Time Stitches* · translated by Peter Constantine · CYPRUS

UZMA ASLAM KHAN · *The Miraculous True History of Nomi Ali* · PAKISTAN

ANDREY KURKOV · *Grey Bees* · translated by Boris Dralyuk · UKRAINE

JORGE ENRIQUE LAGE · *Freeway La Movie* · translated by Lourdes Molina · CUBA

TEDI LÓPEZ MILLS · *The Book of Explanations* · translated by Robin Myers · MEXICO

ANTONIO MORESCO · *Clandestinity* · translated by Richard Dixon · ITALY

FISTON MWANZA MUJILA · *The Villain's Dance* ·
translated by Roland Glasser · DEMOCRATIC REPUBLIC OF CONGO

N. PRABHAKARAN · *Diary of a Malayali Madman* · translated by Jayasree Kalathil · INDIA

THOMAS ROSS · *Miss Abracadabra* · USA

IGNACIO RUIZ-PÉREZ · *Isles of Firm Ground* · translated by Mike Soto · MEXICO

LUDMILLA PETRUSHEVSKAYA · *Kidnapped: A Crime Story*, translated by Marian Schwartz · RUSSIA

NOAH SIMBLIST, ed. · *Tania Bruguera: The Francis Effect* · CUBA

S. YARBERRY · *A Boy in the City* · USA